WØLVES
AND
DAGGERS

STEAMPUNK RED RIDING HOOD
MELANIE KARSAK

for Jen

THIS BOOK BELONGS TO:

_____

WOLVES
AND
DAGGERS

1
RUBY RED

PERCHED ON THE ROOFTOP, I WATCHED THE EXIT OF Guildhall through my spyglass. The meeting adjourned, the members of London's most prominent guilds filed out to waiting carriages or steam- and coal-powered autos. Noisy contraptions. Clouds of soot surrounded the infernal machines. Why anyone would ever want to ride in such a contraption was beyond me.

"See anything?" Quinn, my partner, whispered.

He'd pulled out his rifle and was watching through the magnification scope.

"Not yet. Though—and just an observation—from this vantage point, they look like a flock of inebriated penguins," I said, motioning to the guild members gathered below. With their top hats and walking sticks, smoking pipes and cigars, the assembled crowd looked like a bunch of waddling lushes. Were these really the most learned inventors in London?

Quinn chuckled lightly. "It's a *waddle* of penguins, not a flock. On land, they're called a waddle. In the water, they're called a raft."

"How do you know that?"

"Told you, I'm brilliant."

I rolled my eyes then grinned at him. Quinn's face was shadowed by his red hood, but I could make out his square jaw and Roman nose. I knew that the hood hid his ice-blue eyes, which seemed unkind to the average observer, but Quinn had the patience of a saint. After all, he'd managed to mentor me and serve as my partner in the Red Cape Society these last four years. Everything I knew was because of the man hiding in shadow. Which now included the fact that a group of penguins on land was called waddle, not a flock.

I smirked. "When was the last time you shaved?"

Quinn rubbed his chin. "You don't like it? I was thinking of growing a beard."

"And what does Jessica have to say on that matter?" I asked, referring to his wife.

"Well, there was some question as to whether or not I'd been bitten."

I chuckled. "You'd have a lot more hair than just on your face."

Quinn chuckled. "So I told her."

I turned my attention back to the crowd. "Better shave it off anyway. If your lady doesn't like it, what's the point?"

"It's bloody cold out here at night. Thought it might keep me warm."

"You don't see me complaining."

"Your hair is all the way down to your... Well, you know. Hardly fair. Now, mind the job and leave me alone, or I'll grow it out to look like Merlin just to vex you both."

I snickered. "All right. I'm just making suggestions."

"You're always making suggestions, Clem. In fact, you're starting to sound like your grand-mère," he said with a grin.

"Pardon me?"

He grinned.

I winked at him—pleased to see an amused smile on his

rugged *and hairy* face—then looked below once more. "Here come the clockmakers."

The members of the Clockmaker's Guild chatted noisily as they exited Guildhall. Each wore their best pocket watch on their lapel, a telltale sign of their trade. The Motor Car Association members convened in another corner of the yard. Plumes of tobacco smoke, rough voices, and the distinct smell of brandy rose into the air.

I pressed the cold metal of my spyglass to my eye and scanned the building. Another group of guild members wearing distinctive plum-colored cravats started flowing out of the building.

"The League of Alchemists is coming now," I whispered.

"I'll keep my eyes on the ground. You watch the rooftops," Quinn said.

I nodded then stepped back into the shadows. Quinn and I had hidden in the darkness beside a tall chimney on one of the buildings that sided Guildhall Square. The view was good, the opportunity for subterfuge better.

Quinn stayed crouched, his eyes on the assembled men and women in the courtyard. Pulling up my hood, I drew my pistol from my belt and scanned the rooftops.

An early spring breeze blew across the roof, sending a chill down my spine. Quinn was right. It was unusually cold. I eyed every dark corner, every shadow. Nothing was moving. The tip we'd received had come from a trusted source. Something was supposed to go down here tonight. But what?

"There's Professor Delaney. Professor Andrews. I think... Yes, there she is. Professor Jamison," Quinn said. "She stopped by the door, talking to that naturalist."

Frowning, I scanned the rooftops.

Everything was so still.

Too still.

The nearly-full moon had given everything a hazy blue

glow. I inhaled deeply then exhaled slowly. The palms of my hands and the bottom of my feet started to get a tingly feeling. I scanned the roofs as I squeezed my hand into a fist, fighting off the terrible tingling sensation.

"Quinn," I whispered.

"What's wrong, Clem?"

"I don't know. Something is about to——" My words were cut short by the sound of a loud explosion below. I looked back. One of the autos had exploded, orange flames shooting up to the sky. Burning pieces of coal shot out of the machine.

The assembled crowd below screamed.

I looked at Quinn, both of us thinking the same thing: that was no accident.

A moment later, another auto burst into flame.

And then, from the direction of the Thames, I heard a howl.

Below, the guild members ran from the fiery explosions. Some hurried out of the courtyard and back toward the city. Others raced back inside.

I watched as dark shapes began moving across the rooftops toward us. The shadowed forms silhouetted by the light of the moon were unmistakable. And if one couldn't decide just by the shape, it was the eyes that told the tale. Red as rubies, the werewolves' eyes glimmered in the moonlight.

"Hells bells," I whispered.

Quinn's informant had told him a wolf would be at Guild-hall tonight and that Professor Jamison was the target.

"Not a wolf. A pack," I said.

"Complications. Always complications," Quinn said with a huff then set aside his rifle. "Professor Jamison went back inside."

"Well, let's go get her before someone murders her," I said.

Quinn sighed. "And here I thought it was going to be an easy job."

"When is it ever easy?"

He shook his head, pulled out his pistol, then we turned and raced across the rooftop.

One of the wolves closest to Guildhall howled loudly, hurrying the rest of the pack along.

"Dammit," I cursed then pumped my legs hard, racing across the tiles to the ladder at the side of the building, Quinn right behind me.

I descended quickly then raced across the square toward the entrance of Guildhall. Behind me, people screamed, calling for the constables, for a surgeon. I looked back over my shoulder. At least two people lay injured on the ground. The distinguished guild members fled in panic.

Quinn and I raced to the door of Guildhall. The entire place was in a tizzy. From somewhere on an upper floor, I heard the sound of breaking glass.

"Where did she go?" I asked, looking around.

Quinn grabbed a guild member wearing a purple ascot. "Professor Jamison?"

"What? What's happening?"

"Where is Professor Jamison?" Quinn asked again, giving the man a shake.

"I...I don't know. I lost her in the crowd. Maybe in the Alchemist's Hall?"

"Where?"

"Fifth door. Right."

Turning, Quinn and I pushed through the crowd, searching for the alchemist as we went.

From outside, we heard another explosion followed by a series of howls.

And then, the first scream.

"Bloody bold," Quinn said. "All this for one mark? What in the hell are they up to?"

"Good question." He was right. The packs *were* getting

more intrepid. This was the fourth attack in the last two months. The packs were snagging some of London's most learned scholars, and even our most reliable informants were being tight-lipped. Only because of Quinn's good connections with the Lolita pack had we known about tonight.

But we had never expected this.

A single wolf? Yes. A full force assault? No.

I pushed open the door to the Alchemist's Hall. Inside, four members—including Professor Jamison—turned to stare, their eyes wide with fear.

"Professor Jamison, come with us. You're in danger here —" The window exploded in a shower of glass.

"Clemeny, get her out of here," Quinn yelled then pulled his pistols and took aim.

I grabbed the befuddled alchemist by the arm as Quinn fired.

"What's happening?" the woman shrieked.

A werewolf bashed through the window. The monster, not fully man, not entirely wolf, stood on two feet. He had a maw full of long teeth. His body, a mass of muscle, covered in large patches of silvery fur, was a terrifying sight to behold.

Professor Jamison screamed. The other alchemists hid in one corner.

The wolf looked from me to Quinn then laughed.

"Red Capes," he snarled then dropped down on his front legs. Tensing his muscles, he leaped at Quinn.

My partner firmed his stance then took his shot.

The wolf yelped loudly then crashed to the ground.

Wolves. Strong, but not very bright. Especially not the newly minted pack members. For some reason, they thought the lupine infection made them invincible. It extended their lives, but no matter how old a werewolf was, silver was their enemy. Silver could end them.

From somewhere else in the building, I heard another

window break. There was a commotion in the hallway outside. I heard the telltale sound of screams and the gruff sounds of wolves. I frowned at the door. No getting out in that direction.

"Professor Jamison, we need to go," I said then pulled her toward the broken window.

The other guild members, blind to the danger, opened the door and fled in terror. Smoke billowed into the room.

"Quinn, they've set the bloody place on fire."

"Dammit."

My boots crunching on the glass, I guided the professor out of the broken window, and we headed into the alleyway behind Guildhall.

Quinn, both pistols at the ready, leaped from the window, his red cape billowing around him. He raced to catch up with us.

"What's happening?" the professor asked.

"Do lower your voice. They have excellent hearing," I warned.

"We had a tip someone might be coming for you tonight. It appears the informant was right," Quinn added.

"Informant? What are you talking about? What was that creature?"

"You don't want to know," Quinn answered.

As we turned the corner, we head a series of howls coming from Guildhall. Apparently, they'd figured out we had gotten away with their quarry. We needed to get somewhere safe. Fast.

"Threadneedle?" I said, referring to the Red Cape Society meeting place below The Bank of England.

"No. They'll expect us to go there. Saint Paul's. Let's get the professor on holy ground. We'll take the tram from there."

I nodded, and we turned and rushed in the direction of Saint Paul's Cathedral.

"I don't understand what's happening," Professor Jamison

said as she hurried along with us as we raced down the street. "Why would anyone be after me? I'm just an alchemist."

"I think you answered your own question," Quinn said.

A series of barks and howls rose from behind us.

Again, the palms of my hands began to itch.

"They're close," I said.

Quinn and I stopped.

I turned and looked behind me. Two wolves, their eyes blazing red, loped down the street in our direction.

I pulled my pistol and took a shot. The beast leaped sideways, bouncing off the wall of a building then back onto the street again. I closed my right eye and took aim once more, aiming with the left eye which was always sharper.

I pulled the trigger.

This time, my shot hit home.

The wolf yelped then fell.

The other werewolf grabbed onto a lamppost and swung himself overhead, landing behind us.

Quinn turned and shot.

The shot went wide as the werewolf jumped down.

Pulling out my dagger, I grabbed the professor, pushing her behind me.

I lunged at the werewolf. My silver blade connected with the wolf's shoulder.

The monster shrieked and pulled away, grabbing his shoulder in pain. He glared at me. "Little Red," he growled.

Little Red. I almost liked that the packs had a nickname for me. Given my petite size, they'd initially underestimated me, taunting me as "Little Red." But they soon learned that my petite size only made me a faster, smaller target. Now, four years later and with more than one pelt under my belt, the once-comical moniker was now one that evoked fear.

With the beast distracted, Quinn took his shot.

The monster yelped in agony when the silver bullet slammed into his chest.

He dropped.

"Lupercal pack," Quinn said with a frown. "Now, what's got them all riled up?"

"I don't know, but we need to go."

Quinn nodded, and we hurried on our way.

"Last week it was Whitechapel," Quinn said as we raced toward the cathedral.

"Whitechapel and Lupercal working together? *That* is a problem."

"*That* is an understatement."

We ran down the streets until the dome on Saint Paul's was in sight. Moving through the shadows, we headed toward the back of the church until we reached the garden gate. I unlatched the gate and motioned for the professor to head inside.

But once more, a familiar tingle made the palms of my hands itch.

"Quinn," I cautioned.

A moment later, a massive werewolf dropped off a rooftop and landed in front of us.

I suppressed a gasp. This was no pack grunt. Fenton was a beta, leader of the Lupercal pack, one of the oldest packs in London. There were few older or stronger werewolves in the realm.

"Fenton," Quinn said good-naturedly, training his pistols on the beast. "What can the Red Cape Society do for you this fine evening?"

"Give me the professor," the wolf said with a snarl.

Quinn looked over his shoulder at me. "Get her inside."

Werewolves could not cross onto holy ground, at least not while shifted into werewolf form, or even partially shifted as Fenton was tonight. As men, they could enter a sacred space, but it pained them greatly. I eyed the cathedral then the were-wolf. Taking the professor by the arm, I moved us both toward the open garden gate.

Fenton took a step toward us, glaring at me.

Quinn clicked his tongue at the beast. "Not so fast. The guns are loaded, after all."

"Give her here, Little Red," Fenton growled at me.

"Now, why would I do that?"

"'Cause you're going to pay if you don't."

My dagger in front of me, the professor behind me, I moved us slowly toward the gate. Fenton's ruby red eyes watched each step.

Each of us sized up the other.

Each of us calculated.

Almost there.

The wolf might be able to pull it off if he jumped now—

"Clem, watch out," Quinn yelled as the beast leaped toward me.

I pushed the professor hard. She stumbled forward into the garden.

I crouched, waiting. As the beast jumped over me, I rose and heaved him sideways, my dagger connecting with his arm.

Fenton turned and righted himself. More angry than hurt, he lunged at me once more.

Quinn shot.

A door at the back of the cathedral squeaked as it opened. The professor was safely inside. Holy ground. Out of the wolf's reach.

Howling in frustration, Fenton turned back to Quinn and me.

"You'll pay for this," he said through a mouth full of razor-sharp teeth. He held his forearm. Dark blood oozed from between his fingers. Turning, he leaped onto a nearby roof, the moonlight casting a glow on him as he disappeared back into the city.

While I was used to werewolf macho posturing, as it seemed almost a prerequisite for the lupine infliction, his words chilled me to the bone.

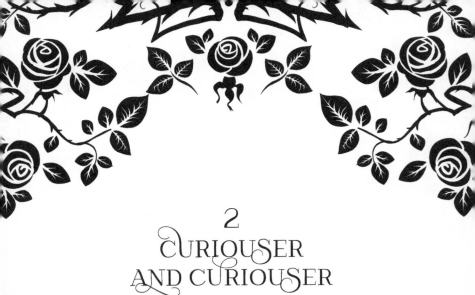

2
CURIOUSER
AND CURIOUSER

AGENT GREYSTOCK PACED THE MEETING ROOM. SHE TAPPED
her fingers together as she walked, her lips pulled into two tight
lines, her silver hair combed back into a tight bun. She wore a
suit that was the same scarlet color as our capes. I eyed her
hair, wondering if her tightly coifed locks made her head ache.

Quinn and I waited patiently as Agent Greystock
considered.

She turned back to the board at the front of the meeting
room. On it were photographs or sketches of the guild
members who had gone missing thus far. Initially, the abduc-
tions had gone unnoticed by the Society. It was only at the last
kidnapping that one of the wolves had been spotted by the
Bow Street boys. When the London authorities noticed the
preternatural, we were called in. As usual, Quinn and I had
been landed with a problem. We already knew the wolves were
up to something. They'd been raiding and robbing for weeks.
But we'd thought they'd been prepping for a big heist or
preparing to run guns. Now, we weren't so sure.

"Casualties from the incident at Guildhall last night?"
Agent Greystock asked, turning to junior Agent Harper, who'd

been part of the clean-up crew after the incident the night before.

"Two," Agent Harper said. "A driver killed in the explosion of a coal-powered auto and a valet who took a head injury."

"Anyone reported missing?"

"No, ma'am, but Guildhall's Secretary of Records reported that his office had been looted. A number of new patent requests, some schematics, and the registry of Guildhall members are among the documents missing," Agent Harper said.

Agent Greystock stared at the faces on the board.

"Oliver Dart, tinker," she said, tapping the photo. "Mavis Porter, naturalist. Toby Winston, alchemist. Neville McKee, alchemist. Byrony Paxton, professor from King's College."

Agent Greystock turned to us. "Theories?"

Quinn shook his head. "This isn't the packs' usual modus operandi. Brawling? Whoring? Sure. But not this."

"Wolves have no reason to lift these people," Agent Harper said. "And documents? I mean, I didn't know the wolves could read."

I grinned at Agent Harper. "Templar pack can read, but they're the only ones," I said then turned back to the board. "Whitehall pack and Lupercal pack can't stand each other. If they're working together, they're about to pull off something big."

Agent Greystock nodded then looked back at the board. "Why these guild members—and Professor Jamison—in particular? Why them and the patents?"

We all stared at the board.

"Ransom?" Agent Harper offered. "Or to sell the schematics on the black market."

Neither idea seemed bad enough.

"Weapons," Quinn suggested. "Maybe...maybe they're pulling minds together to build weapons."

"A good a theory as any, for the moment," Agent Greystock said with a nod. "Quinn, I want you to go back to your contact with the Lolitas. Backtrack and see what you can find out."

Quinn nodded, but I could see he wasn't pleased to be assigned the task. No doubt Jessica didn't care much for her husband hanging around with a bunch of tarty she-bitches at a brothel. But many years ago, before I'd joined the Society, something had happened to Alodie, the beta she-bitch of the Lolitas, and Quinn had been the one to get her out of trouble. Ever since, she was partial to him.

"Agent Harper, I want you to go interview Professor Jamison. She was moved to the safehouse on the Isle of Dogs. See what she knows about the missing guild members, and find out what she's been working on."

"Yes, ma'am."

"Very good. Off with you both. Agent Louvel, please come with me."

I nodded then turned to Quinn. "Ales and Ass, three o'clock," I said, referring to our favorite pub.

He inclined his head to me then headed out.

"Come along," Agent Greystock said, motioning for me to follow her from the meeting room. The halls of the Red Cape Society headquarters were busy. Other agents wearing the distinctive red cloak and silver badge passed me by, giving me a congenial nod as they went on their way. Unbeknownst to most of those living in the city of London, there were many things in our realm that did more than go bump in the night. It was the duty of the Red Cape Society, part of Her Majesty's Secret Intelligence Service, to deal with the preternatural.

Agent Greystock led me to the lift. Motioning for me to follow her inside, she pulled a lever, and we descended below the city.

"You are right that Whitechapel and Lupercal are not inclined to get along. If someone is uniting the packs for a singular purpose, then we must learn what it is," Agent Greystock said.

"You think Quinn is right? That they're building arms?"

Agent Greystock tapped her fingers together. "The guild members they are gathering are great minds, but they are not the best weapons designers in the realm. Thus far, I see no connection between them."

"Alchemists. Tinkers. Naturalists. At best, they are constructing a heinous alternative to opium. At worst, alchemical concoctions can be weaponized," I suggested.

"Do you really think the wolves capable of such ingenuity?"

I shook my head. She was right. The packs were strong, but with the exception of the Templars, not that bright. This was well beyond their capacity for creativity. The only thing they were ever good at was brute mayhem.

"Cyril is not the most peaceful alpha this realm has ever known, but he's no worse than the human gangs. This... smacks of something else. We need to find out what," Agent Greystock said.

"Cyril is old. Very old. Do you suppose nature has begun her call for a rival? If the balance of power is tipping, we have a very big problem on our hands. If the packs are about to compete for alpha, gaming and petty theft would become the least of our problems."

Agent Greystock sighed heavily. "For all their machismo, the wolves are secretive, particularly in these matters. We need someone to talk, and not just Lolitas. They only talk to Quinn because of Alodie, and the she-wolves never have a say in pack matters. You need to talk to Lionheart."

I groaned.

Agent Greystock laughed. "Yes, I know, but Sir Richard Spencer—Lionheart—and the Templars will be the pack least interested in dealing with a new alpha or getting involved in any trouble that disturbs Her Majesty. They are royalist to a fault, and they are content with things the way they are. And, I think, that werewolf likes you."

"You say that like it's a compliment."

"Clemeny, I have advised dozens of agents on your beat over the years. Sir Richard has never talked to anyone but you."

Lionheart, as they commonly called Sir Richard Spencer, the beta of the Templar pack, was a scholarly and reclusive werewolf, as was his pack. Their origins in the realm were ancient, but they had never made a grab for power. The Templars kept to themselves and their own business, which made them both easy to ignore and entirely dangerous. Secrets and werewolves never blended well. But there was good cause to go see him.

"Byrony Paxton was a professor from King's College," I said, referring to one of the names on the board. The Templar pack had made the halls of the ivory tower of King's College their home. I often wondered how the students might feel if they learned half a dozen of their professors were werewolves.

"Perhaps that will be enough of an opening to get Lionheart to talk."

The lift came to a stop. Agent Greystock slid open the metal gate and led me down the narrow, cavernous hallway, pushing open the door to the armory.

Inside, a team of smiths was working busily on new devices and machines intended for the defense of Her Majesty's realm.

"Why abduct tinkers? If the wolves are looking for brilliant minds to make monstrous devices, all they really need to do is to raid us," I said.

"Let's not pose the idea to them, shall we?" Agent Greystock said with a smirk then led me to the back of a large workshop where a little man wearing goggles that seemed to magnify his eyes times ten was working hard on a clockwork device.

I chuckled. "What big eyes you have, sir."

The old man paused his work and looked up at me. He blinked twice then grinned. "All the better to see you with, my dear."

"Speaking of. Master Hart, this is Agent Louvel. Do you have the device I commissioned for her?"

"Indeed I do," the tinker said, pulling off his goggles. He rose and went to a line of shelves at the side of the room. He pulled out a wooden box and handed it to me. "Here you are. Try this."

I opened the lid to find an eyepatch inside. The eyepatch, quite like what a misfortunate airship pirate might wear, was rigged with a number of clockwork devices and an unusual optic piece.

"What is it?" I asked.

"Come this way," the tinker, Master Hart, said then led Agent Greystock and me to an adjoining room.

Once we were inside, the man closed the door.

"Slip it on, Agent. Over the left eye."

I slid on the device, surprised when I could see through the optic. "Everything is shaded green," I said.

"Right," Master Hart said then went to the wall and turned off the gaslamp. "Agent Louvel, there is a lever located right around your temple. Please switch it on."

I felt along the edge of the eyepatch until I felt a small metal lever, which I shifted in place. I heard a click as something in the eyepatch activated, and a moment later, a strange hue lit up the optic. Suddenly, even though the room was entirely dark, I could clearly make out Agent Greystock's and Master Hart's silhouettes.

"Hell's bells," I said, astonished.

Agent Greystock chuckled.

"I call it a night array optic. There is a small aether core with a crystal device used to amplify vision on multiple waves, including enhancing night vision. All in all, it works well in perfect darkness. Still a few ghosts in the machine. Just ignore any stray undefinables you might see. It will enhance your vision in the dark. As you requested, Agent Greystock."

"Thank you," she said. "How is it, Clemeny?"

"Perfect, madame. At least now, I'll see them coming. Thank you."

"You're welcome. Very good. Lights, Master Hart."

I turned off then removed the device just as Master Hart sparked the lamp back to life. I set the optic back into the box and put it in my bag.

"Thank you, sir," I said to the tinker.

"Agent," he said with a nod, looking pleased with himself.

Agent Greystock inclined her head to the man then waved for me to follow her. We headed down the hall away from the armory and workshop to the underground rail.

"How is your grandmother, Clemeny?" Agent Greystock asked.

"Very well, madame. Thank you for asking. She inquires after you every time I see her."

"Dear Felice. Please send her my greetings."

"I will. You should come by and see her."

Agent Greystock smiled. "Are you sure about that? Every time I drop in, she insists I find you a husband. She has set out a rather specific list of requirements. She's quite convinced that if I just hire the right person into the agency, all her problems —or are they yours?—will be solved."

I laughed. "Oh, yes. There is no limit to Grand-mère's enthusiasm for that topic."

"Well, I shall assure her that I am doing my best. We'll let the blame fall on my shortcomings. Now, off to Lionheart.

Clemeny, I don't think I need to impress upon you the trouble that might be brewing if Cyril's reign has come to an end."

"No, madame. I understand."

She nodded.

We came to the end of the hall where a small subterranean train waited. While the first such public rail systems were still being planned, the Society had been using such devices in subterfuge since their invention by Archibald Boatswain in the later 1700s. Unbeknownst to most, the Society had a complete rail network under London.

I hated riding in the damned thing. All that lurching and rocking made me sick to my stomach. But I could hardly complain when my superior herself was loading me onto the train.

I slipped into the small compartment and adjusted the knobs on the dashboard. In theory, the machine would automatically adjust the switches along the rail and get me where I wanted to go. But I wondered what would happen if a rat or a rock got in the way. I had a terrible vision of myself hurtling out of the tunnel like a metal rocket, catapulting into the Thames.

Sitting down in the passenger seat, I harnessed the straps across my body. With a farewell wave to Agent Greystock, I pulled the lever. The door closed, a series of gears locking the door in place. The train began to vibrate, and I heard a loud whine. A moment later, the train compartment shot down the rail line. I closed my eyes and said a silent prayer in the hope that I wouldn't end up in the Thames today.

3
LIONHEART

I STOOD OUTSIDE SIR RICHARD SPENCER'S OFFICE DOOR IN A narrow hall of the King's College classroom buildings for a solid three minutes, raising then lowering my hand. Killing werewolves? Easy. Trying to make nice? Not so much. Trying to make nice with a werewolf who was far too handsome for either of our good? Impossible.

I had finally decided it was time to get it over with when the door opened.

On the other side, dressed in a fine tweed suit and smoking a pipe, stood Sir Richard Spencer, or as he was called on the street, Lionheart. Our best records indicated he was approximately seven hundred years old. King Richard, from whom he'd earned his moniker, had knighted him. While he was a mere child compared to many of the vamps roaming about the realm, his age and wealth of knowledge—what he had seen, what he had lived through, and survived—always astonished me. There was a reason the pack in this part of town was named Templar. These wolves had once been men. They had become afflicted during the crusades, which they truly believed was a blessing from God to complete their divine work. And, *thank God*, their philosophy on the subject left with them with a sense of honor and nationalism that often proved helpful.

Lionheart removed his pipe and looked at me over his reading spectacles.

"I was getting tired of waiting to see what you were going to do," he said. "How can I help you, Agent Louvel?"

"I'm here to talk."

"This is not the best time."

"I know it's a bit early, but—"

"You misunderstand me. This is not the best time to be seen with you."

"Then why don't you let me in before someone sees me? I did bring Scotch," I said, lifting the parcel.

Lionheart smirked, and not for the first time, I felt the dangerous charm in that grin. Given I was always partial to men with honor, a sharp mind, and yellow hair, Sir Richard Spencer was a problem. He was far too good-looking to be so very much off-limits.

"I thought you said it was early," he replied.

"I have been awake since yesterday, so it's actually night for me."

The wolf looked at the bottle then back at me. "Very well," he said then stepped aside so I could come inside, taking the bottle from my hand as I entered.

The office was lined from floor to ceiling with books, scrolls, artifacts, and maps. Everywhere I looked, I saw evidence that Lionheart was busy researching.

He pulled two glasses out of a cabinet and poured us both a drink. He handed a glass to me.

"God save the Queen," he said, clinking his glass to mine.

"God save the Queen," I said then took a swig.

"So, Agent Louvel, I assume you are here to talk about that mess at Guildhall," he said, slipping into his chair behind his desk. He pulled off his spectacles and set them on the desk.

One thing about werewolves was that when they were in human form, they gave off a dangerous masculine air that was highly intoxicating. I was told that the she-wolves, especially when they were in season, were almost impossible to resist. Like most other wolves, Lionheart was all muscle under that scholarly attire. His form was very…intriguing.

I drove away the lusty thoughts that kept cropping up.

I really needed to find myself a gentleman. Soon.

"You assume correctly. Perhaps you can illuminate me on why Lupercal and Whitechapel are working together, or maybe why they've been lifting Guildhall members."

"Lupercal and Whitechapel are not working together."

"Sorry?"

"You're behind the news, *Little Red*."

I frowned at him.

He chuckled. "I rather like the nickname. It suits you."

"Suits me? Why? Because I'm petite or because I wear a red cape?"

"Neither."

"Then why?"

"Because of how you smell."

Okay. "And how do I smell?"

"Like red roses."

I stared at him. The wolf smirked again then leaned forward and refilled both our cups.

I grinned. "I'm sure you say that to all the ladies. Well, that aside, tell me what I'm behind on."

"*All* the London packs are working together, not just those two. Templar is uninterested. I had a rather difficult conversation with Cyril on the matter. But as I reminded him, we have our own project," he said, tapping a very ragged book sitting on the desk in front of him. I noted the emblem of the Templars on the cover. "But the others… Well, it seems they've found a common interest."

"That's impossible. The packs never unite."

"Untrue," Lionheart said, lifting his glass. "We were united at least three times in the last seven hundred years."

"Okay then, why?"

He sipped his drink once more, set the cup down, and then tapped his finger lightly on the rim. "I tell you what. You have dinner with me tonight, and I'll tell you what I know."

"That seems like an incredibly bad idea."

"Why?"

"Because I smell like roses, and you have so much musk coming off you that I'm likely to do something I'll regret in the morning."

Lionheart chuckled. "Don't tell me you're afraid of the big bad wolf."

"Not at all. I have silver bullets enough for that. But I don't like complications. Thus far, I've managed to stay aboveboard. It's better if it stays that way."

Lionheart leaned back in his chair and sighed. "From your point of view, I suppose that makes sense."

"Indeed it does. Is Cyril fading? Is that why the packs are rallying?"

Richard laughed. "No," he said with a shake of the head. "If that was happening, it would be London 1666 all over again."

"London 1666? The great fire?"

He nodded.

"Then what is happening? Why are they working together?"

"Since we were disinclined to get involved, I was left out on the particulars—though I was warned that I would be interested in due time. Shows how little they know of me. Pack nonsense. God has blessed us with the lupine affliction to fulfill our holy mission. I have no interest in Cyril's agendas."

"All the more reason to lend me a hand, no?" I said with a grin.

Lionheart chuckled lightly. "I'd rather stay out of the matter entirely, but I'm vexed with Cyril at the moment. I have a colleague here at King's College who is my squash partner. Lupercal lifted her two nights back."

"Byrony Paxton?"

"Correct. No one asked my permission to remove Professor Paxton, and I'd prefer to have her back. Perhaps we can come to some arrangement?"

I raised an eyebrow at him. "I'm listening."

"Indeed. What big ears you have, so to speak."

I smirked. "All the better to hear you with, of course."

"But you hear more than common senses permit, don't you?"

I narrowed my eyes at him. "All agents have uncommonly strong instincts."

"Do they?"

"Yes."

"But they don't all smell like red roses."

"I wouldn't know."

Lionheart grinned. "All right, Agent. We'll come back to that another time. Now, if you go to this address at this hour, you will find some answers. I do recommend subterfuge. Perhaps take Agent Briarwood along," he said, referring to Quinn. Lionheart scribbled down the address and slid the paper across the desk toward me. "I would consider it a favor if Professor Paxton was found and relocated somewhere safe until the Red Capes have this mess sorted out."

"I'll see what I can do," I said then polished off the drink. I snatched up the note then rose. "Thank you for your help," I said then went to the door.

"Agent Louvel, are you sure about dinner? Would it be so bad to stray from the path just a little?"

I reached for the handle then smiled over my shoulder at him. "I'm not so easily fooled, tempting as the offer may be. Goodbye, Sir Richard."

"*Little Red,*" he said with a wink, lifting his glass in a toast to me.

My heart beating hard in my chest, I left, closing his office door behind me. I hurried down the hall and out of the building.

I really, really needed to find myself a man.

4
TO GRANDMOTHER'S HOUSE

Leaving King's College, I turned and headed toward Saint Clement Danes. My grand-mère, who was the organist at the church, lived in a flat nearby. I called her my grand-mère, but we were not really related. I had been abandoned as a baby at the church, and the widow Louvel had taken me in. She'd named me after Saint Clement, the merciful. God knows I was always grateful for her mercy. I owed everything to my grand-mère who'd raised me.

I worked my way back up the Strand, passing the church, then headed to my grand-mère's flat. I gave the door a sharp rap. There was a rattle inside and a flurry of activity.

"Grand-mère?" I called. "It's me."

The ruckus stopped, and a moment later, the door opened.

"Clemeny? Oh my girl, come in, come in. Clemeny? What's wrong? Why are you here? I smell Scotch on you. Have you been drinking? It's not even lunchtime yet! Oh, oranges and lemons, Clemeny. Let me give you a kiss," she said, pulling me into an embrace, slathering wet, but well-meaning, kisses on my cheek.

"I'm well, Grand-mère. Please, don't worry yourself."

"Worry? Who? Me? What do I have to worry about? My girl out running around the city at all hours of the night chasing after monsters. I should never have let Eliza Greystock talk me into letting you join up with her band of miscreants. And how is dear Eliza?"

I grinned. Agent Greystock was the first friend my grand-mère had made when she'd moved from France to England. Eliza Greystock had seen potential in me, and much to my grand-mère's purported dismay, had recruited me for the Society. Of course, I was eternally grateful to Agent Greystock. Well, as thankful as anyone could be when they learned that England was actually full of vampires, werewolves, faerie people, and all other manner of oddities. But still. The job suited me. It was dangerous, but I liked the satisfaction of helping people, of keeping the city safe from monsters.

"She's well, and she sends her greetings."

"Come sit down. I already had a pot of tea on, but the kitchen—oh, oranges and lemons, the cupboards are ripped apart. Spring cleaning! What a mess. But no matter. Are you hungry?"

"No. Thank you."

"Okay, I'll get you some bread and cheese."

I chuckled but said nothing. Grand-mère's effusive attention was to be expected.

"And where is Quinn?" she asked, leading me into the small kitchen where we had a breakfast table. She was right. The kitchen was a disaster. Everything had been removed from the cupboards. The entire place smelled like soap.

"We're working a case. He's…elsewhere."

"And why are you here?"

"I was at King's College."

My grandmother crossed herself. "May God protect us. You said those creatures are there teaching children! How is it permitted? Oranges and lemons, God save us all."

I grinned. Lionheart, a true Templar, was one of the most religious creatures in the realm—despite him knowing I smelled like red roses—but explaining that to Grand-mère would be incredibly complicated, so I said nothing.

Grand-mère dug through the stacks of dishes on the counter until she found a cup and saucer. She poured me tea then found a tiny corner of the breakfast table that was not heaped with the contents of the pantry, and set down the drink, moving the jar of honey closer to me. She dug into her goods once more and returned with some lemon.

"Drink, drink," she said then went back to fix me a plate. "How is Quinn? Jessica?"

"They are both well," I said, stirring in some honey. I sipped the tea, relishing the taste. Nothing ever tasted like food and drink from Grand-mère's hand. I sighed contentedly.

"And Quinn's brother, Robert?"

Hell's bells. On with this again? Robert, Quinn's younger brother, worked on an airship crew. He was a good-looking man, albeit dark-haired. He was very kind, but he lacked a certain something I needed in a man. That, however, did not dissuade Grand-mère from suggesting him—repeatedly.

"Very busy. I believe his crew has been running merchant shipments to Calais and back."

Grand-mère returned with a plate of bread, fruit spread, and cheese. She shifted pans aside, clearing a space for the food. "Oh, well, he must watch for airship pirates then. Such a brave man, just like his brother. And a good, sturdy man too. If Quinn's brother is anything like him, you're missing out. Clemeny, you must tell Quinn to arrange something for you and Robert. Quinn is such a good man. I've never seen Quinn bat an eye at another lady or curse or drink Scotch at ten o'clock in the morning," she said then gave me a look.

"Grand-mère, I told you, I am on a case. Sometimes you do what you must to get a source to talk, thus the Scotch." I realized then that if I told Grand-mère that Quinn was currently at a brothel, I might shatter her entire worldview. Sipping my tea, I chuckled when I thought about it, but said nothing.

Clicking her tongue disapprovingly, Grand-mère shook her head and looked away. "If I had ever known how many bad things were in this country, I would have told your grandfather we needed to stay in France!"

I laughed. "You think London is bad? Paris is a hundred times worse."

"Is that true?" Grand-mère asked, her eyes wide.

I nodded. "Yes. Very." Paris was a sewer. Three agents who'd gone to work cases there last year had come home in caskets. We had our own challenges in England, but Her Majesty had a strong grip on the preternatural. Between the force that was our Queen and the ancient Society of the Rude Mechanicals, a mysterious body of people who lorded over the Red Cape Society, England kept a lid on its magical issues. Well, until recently. Something told me Her Majesty would not be happy to hear about the incident at Guildhall last night.

"Humph," Grand-mère said then began stirring her cup of tea vigorously. "Well. No matter. Oh, I must tell you, Pastor Clark inquired after you yesterday. Such a sweet, charming man. You know, I think one day he will take a living in the countryside. Can you imagine a nice, peaceful life as a minister's wife? Then you can set all this danger aside before you get yourself killed. Oh, Eliza. That silver-tongued devil. Why I ever agreed to let her take you away from me, I'll never know. Yes, I'll tell Pastor Clark you were here and that you asked about him. He will be so pleased!"

"Grand-mère!"

"Oh, Clemeny, oranges and lemons, I worry about you so."

I chuckled softly and set my hand on hers. "I love you, Grand-mère."

"I love you too, my girl. Please be careful out there."

"Of course."

"And come see me more often."

"I will."

"And find a husband."

"Grand-mère!"

"Well, you were being so agreeable, I thought I would try."

I laughed then leaned forward and kissed her on the cheek. "I'll try...for you." But up to that point, Lionheart was just about my best option. Something told me Grand-mère would not approve.

5
ALES

I left Grand-mère and headed across town to Ales and Ass to meet Quinn. The pub was located not far from headquarters at Marylebone and was frequented by agents. As I approached the old building, I eyed the sign. On it was depicted a donkey wearing a top hat while drinking ale. But above that, discreetly carved, were the initials R. M., the letters encapsulated by a circle: the Rude Mechanicals. Her Majesty's secret investigative services covered a lot of ground, but our division, the Red Cape Society, were the only ones to keep the preternatural in check. But who kept us in check? Somewhere in the echelons above me were the Rude Mechanicals, a secret society whose name was whispered, identity secret, and activities even more elusive. Not for the first time, I wondered about my organization's mysterious benefactors.

"Clemeny," Allen, the tapster, called when I entered. He started pouring me a bitter. "Here for breakfast?"

I chuckled. It wasn't uncommon for me to stop by the pub on my way to an afternoon meeting—usually after I'd just woken up.

"I wish. Up still, in fact. Seen Quinn?"

"Not today."

I pulled out the small ladies' pocket watch I had tucked into a pocket on my bodice. It was already after three. I frowned.

I took the mug. "Thanks," I said, setting come coins on the bar.

Taking a seat at the corner of the bar, the angle that had the best view of the door and out the window, I pulled out the address Lionheart had given me. The address was in the factory row downriver. Such a location was out of the way of the general eye and gave the packs ample space for whatever misdeeds they had underway. I pulled my dossier out of my satchel and set it on the bar. I flipped through the profiles of the guild members and others who'd been abducted. There wasn't much to go on. The marks were talented tinkers and alchemists. Professor Paxton, it seemed, was an expert in diseases. But they'd missed Professor Jamison who, according to my notes, was the leading scholar in search of an alkahest, a universal solvent capable of breaking all matter down into its constituent parts.

I sat back and tapped my finger on the paper as I sipped my drink. What were Cyril and the other wolves after? What were they doing?

Polishing off the first mug, I ordered a second bitter and read a bit more as I waited. When I rechecked the time, it was 4:15. No Quinn. Where was he? The bottoms of my feet tingled as I thought about it. Not a good sign.

I set some coins on the bar then rose to go.

"Leavin', Clem?" Allen asked.

I nodded. "If Quinn shows up, tell him to meet me at the circus?" I said, using the codename for headquarters.

Allen nodded. "Of course."

I headed back out onto the street. I looked both directions as I thought it over.

Quinn could be at home.

Or he could be following a lead.

Or he could be in trouble.

I didn't like the nagging feeling in my gut and the way the bottom of my feet kept prickling. What was it the witches in Shakespeare's play had said? "By the pricking of my thumb, something wicked this way comes."

I turned and headed back across town toward Fleet Street, home of the Lolita pack's well-noted and highly popular brothel.

Something told me wickedness was afoot.

6
ASS

I GROANED AS I STARED UP AT THE FACE OF THE BROTHEL. IT wasn't even dark out yet, and already the place was in full swing. Music, rowdy laughter, and the smells of tobacco smoke and heady perfume filled the air. And then there was that other scent, the musky, unmistakable odor of werewolves. I rolled my eyes. This was the last place I wanted to be.

The Lolita girls and I never got along well. I suspected they already knew that unlike Quinn, who seemed to be a bit soft toward them and their plight as second-class citizens in the wolf pecking order, I had no such illusions. Human women could be some of the nastiest bitches on the planet. Female werewolves? Literally bitches.

As I climbed up the steps, I noticed a vagrant sitting in the shadowed entryway of the building next door. The small man was dressed in rags, his face shadowed. I slowed as I looked him over. A moment later, he cast a glance at me. I caught the glint of yellow in his eyes before he turned and looked away.

I frowned. What was a goblin doing hanging around a werewolf brothel?

"Careful, Little Red," he said with a wheezing laugh.

Wonderful.

A footman, eyeing my red cape skeptically, opened the door but motioned to someone inside before letting me in. I bit the inside of my cheek then entered.

The place was overly warm, overly loud, and very…ripe. A young woman—well, werewolf, really—dressed in a flowy toga of some sort, both of her breasts peeking out, laughed loudly as two mostly-naked men chased her up the stairs. From somewhere above, I heard another tart articulating her pleasure loudly, her bed creaking. The place was swarming with half-naked werewolves and men. Werewolf women were lusty lovers with a lot of stamina. The brothel turned a good business, as was evident by the number of bouncing cocks and jiggling tits I saw everywhere I turned. I tried to avert my eyes but found nowhere to look. Even the ceiling depicted an Olympian orgy scene.

Hell's bells.

"Agent Louvel," a voice purred. While the sound was all pleasantry, I hadn't missed a sharp undertone.

I turned to find Alodie, the madame of the house and pack leader, walking toward me. She had flowing yellow hair so pale that it was almost white. Her eyes were gold-colored. Her face was undeniably beautiful. And, given the sheer gown she was wearing, it was evident that her form was stunning as well. Stupidly, for a moment I felt a bit awkward. Under my leather bodice, pants, and steel vambraces, I was muscle and bone. My sinewy form kept me alive, which was all I really ever thought about. My curves were nothing compared to those of the whore. Was that part of the reason I couldn't find a gentleman? Was I too…hard?

Focus, Clemeny.

"Alodie. I apologize for coming. I'm looking for Quinn."

"Quinn?" she said then turned to the footman who shrugged.

"We haven't seen Quinn today."

"You haven't seen Quinn today? Are you sure?"

"Oh, yes," she said with a wolf-like smile. "I never miss my chance to try to convert that Red Cape."

I frowned at her. Alodie's affection for Quinn was partially why he was so successful in getting information out of her. Given his devotion to his wife, I never questioned his methods. But many times, I questioned Alodie's. How far would she go to win Quinn? You couldn't trust a bitch. Ever. Which is why I found trusting her word right now particularly difficult. The she-wolf had no reason to be honest with me.

One of Alodie's customers wandered into the foyer, stopping when he saw me. "Well, well, well, have a look at this! Alodie, why didn't you tell me you had a new girl? And she's so *fit*," a lusty man wearing only a pair of knickers said as he stumbled toward me.

"Sir, you are mistaken," I began in protest.

The man hiccupped. "Are those handcuffs on your belt? That looks fun. Oh, Alodie. Let me have her," the man said. He stumbled forward, reached out, and gave my bottom a squeeze.

It took only a second for me to pull the silver dagger from my belt and hold it to the man's neck.

"Sir, if you want to keep your fingers, remove your hand," I said.

The others around me stilled and quieted. I cast a glance around. There was a glint in the eyes of the brothel girls, a menacing red fire provoked by the sudden appearance of the silver blade.

"What? Oh. All right," the man said then stepped back. "My mistake."

"My apologies, Percy. She's not one of my girls," Alodie said then waved to another harlot. "Jewell, take Percy upstairs and give him a taste of what he's after. Agent Louvel was just leaving."

Taking me gently by the arm, Alodie walked me back to the door.

"If I ever see you in my establishment again, Agent Louvel, I will have my girls rip your throat out," she said, her voice sounding sweet.

"You can try. But I'll probably shoot you all first," I said, keeping my voice equally pleasant. "Again, my apologies. I was only looking for Quinn," I said then stepped outside.

"As I said, he was not here today. Goodbye, Agent Louvel," she said then turned and went back inside, slamming the door behind her.

Dammit, Quinn. Where did you go?

"She lies," a voice hissed.

I turned back to the entryway where the goblin was still sitting. I cast an eye up at the face of the brothel building. No one was looking. I turned and headed down the street toward the next building where the beast sat. Even from this distance, I could smell the scent of spirits wafting off him.

"Indeed?" I asked, leaning against the wall.

The goblin chuckled. "Indeed," he said in a mocking tone.

"I don't suppose you'd tell me what you saw?"

"Not for nothin'."

"Of course not. What do you want?"

"A kiss."

I sighed. Goblin men. Always on about kissing and fornication. No wonder he was poised outside the brothel. He was probably enjoying the view through the windows.

"I think not."

"Too bad," he hissed then laughed. "Prudey agent won't give a single kiss to save her partner's life."

"My partner's life? What are you talking about?"

"Oh, now you're interested, aren't you? Pucker up."

"Can we discuss an alternative?"

"All right. Show me your tits."

Oh, hell no. I pulled out my pistol and trained it on the little rat. "Try again."

"What? I'm just trying to be helpful. You're the one who's being difficult."

I pulled out my coin pouch and tossed it to him. "That will have to do. Go buy yourself a kiss."

The goblin sighed. "Fine. Fine. I saw your red-caped partner. Big man. Grey hair. They took him out about five minutes after he got here, threw him into an auto and drove off."

"Who took him out?"

"Cyril's dogs."

"Which way did they go?"

The goblin pointed. "Downriver. Strange things happening. It's not just your people they've been picking up. Two of my kind are missing too. And rumor has it, they picked up a sanguinarian."

"The wolves picked up a vampire?"

"You didn't hear it from me," the creature said then shifted back into the shadows and out of sight. I heard an odd screeching sound. "You didn't hear it from any of my kind," he said, this time his voice sounded further away.

I stepped forward and looked into the dark entryway. There was a small grate just under the front window that was slightly ajar. The goblin was gone.

I stared downriver.

Quinn.

7
MAGNUM OPUS

It was already after dark when I arrived at the manufacturing district. Spotting a ladder up on the side of the building that housed *The Daedalus Company*, I scampered to the top of the tall building then began working my way toward the address Lionheart had given me. Given it was already dark, I stopped a moment in a shadowed spot and pulled out the optic Master Hart had made. It took a little adjusting to get it to sit right, but when I turned it on, I was surprised to see how well it made out shapes in the dark.

With my sight enhanced, I headed quickly and quietly across the rooftops toward the building. Thus far, I spotted no guards on the roof. Staying hidden, I leaped onto the roof of the building then went to the levered windows which looked down into the factory below.

Directly below me was a balcony on which I spotted three guards. They were looking out the windows toward the street, all of their guns drawn. All of them were from Paddington pack.

Moving carefully, I shifted so I could see below more clearly when suddenly someone grabbed my arm.

I pulled my dagger and, turning in a flash, spun on the unknown assailant.

"Agent Rose?" I whispered as I gazed down the barrel of another Red Cape Society agent's weapon. Casting a glance behind her, I saw Agent Reid.

Agent Rose put her finger to her lips to silence me then gave me a hand, helping me to my feet. Motioning for me to follow her, I joined her and Agent Reid behind a chimney stack where I found, much to my surprise, two werewolves knocked out cold, bound and gagged.

"What are you doing here?" I whispered.

"Tracking Constantine," Agent Rose replied in a whisper.

"Constantine?" Constantine needed no last name. The vampire was well known to the Society. He was dangerous in every way imaginable and had only managed to keep from getting slain due to an edict from the crown. Apparently, he'd provided some assistance during the Napoleonic Wars. Since then, he'd been keeping to himself, holing up in some castle somewhere in Scotland. What in the hell were the wolves doing with him?

"Cyril's pack picked him up. Any idea why?" Agent Reid asked me.

I shook my head. "No. But I do know they picked up some goblins as well. And I believe they have Agent Briarwood," I said, referring to Quinn. I tried to keep my voice steady but failed. The telltale crack at the end betrayed my anxiety. Where was Quinn? What in the hell was going on?

The agents looked at one another, both of them looking distressed. Quinn was one of the senior agents. If I remembered right, he'd trained Agent Rose when she'd been recruited.

"When did they nab Quinn?" Agent Rose asked.

"Goblin saw the wolves lift him this afternoon from Alodie's brothel."

Agent Reid frowned. "There's at least two dozen wolves down there."

"Any sign of your fang?"

Agent Rose shook her head.

"Let's see what they're up to," I said then motioned toward the windows.

We approached slowly, looking inside. Below, I saw wolves —still in human form—from Whitehall, Paddington, Lupercal, and even Romulus packs. That left out only Templars, Lolitas, and Conklins. It was notable that Conklins were not there. That nasty group of buggers was always brawling.

But even more interesting was the flurry of activity at a series of workbenches below. I pushed up my night optic and pulled out my spyglass for a better look. A series of stations had been erected, and at them, I spotted my missing guild members. It did not escape my notice that each was chained by the ankle to the floor.

My eyes drifted over each person there, noting the face of Lionheart's squash partner—Professor Paxton.

"Bring him here," Fenton, Cyril's beta, said, his gravelly voice pouring from one of the side rooms.

Agent Rose barely suppressed a gasp when they wheeled out the vampire Constantine, who had been staked crucifixion-style to a modified dolly.

"What the hell?" Agent Reid swore.

A sick feeling rocked my stomach. Whatever was happening here, it was not good. I scanned the space for Quinn.

"Well, professor. Could you do it or not?" Fenton asked with a growl.

"I...I hardly know. The notes here are vague, and the prima materia from this *gentleman* is unlike anything I have ever seen," Professor Paxton said, looking back through her scope at a sample. "What is this man infected with?" she asked, looking back toward Constantine.

Fenton laughed. "You don't need to worry about that. You just do what the boss asked, beautiful," he said then reached out and stroked her hair.

Something deep within me hardened.

"What your *boss* asked is impossible," said another guild member. I recognized him from his photo as the missing alchemist Neville McKee.

Frustrated, Fenton growled then turned and punched the man in the stomach. "Shut your mouth, and get the work done."

"I have had some success here," Toby Winston, an alchemist, said. "The sample provided by your boss is reacting...based on Jamison's notes, I was able to use the alkahest she has been working with to some effect."

"Someone tell Doctor Marlowe that Master Winston has made a discovery," Fenton said.

There was a clamor of noise from the back and a moment later, a bent old man in a heavy robe, walking with a cane, along with two Romulous pack members, appeared. The man stopped by Professor Paxton's table. He looked at her work, nodded, then turned to Master Winston, motioning for the man to move aside so he could investigate.

Doctor Marlowe tapped his cane. "We are making progress here. Bring in the others."

There was a commotion, and a moment later, three were-wolves came in, dragging along two goblin men. The goblins fought the wolves, cursing them in a language I didn't understand.

My heart stopped when I saw the wolves push Quinn forward. His hands were bound behind his back.

The old man chuckled when he saw Quinn. "Ah, now we have the complete set. *Nigredo*," he said, pointing to Constantine. "*Citrinitas*," he added, pointing to the goblins. "*Rubedo*," he said, pointing to Quinn. "And..." he said then looked back toward Byrony Paxton. "*Albedo*, I believe. How does she smell to you?" the old man asked, turning to Fenton.

"Yeah, she's pure."

The old man nodded. "My nose isn't what it once was, but so I thought."

"What...what are you talking about?" Professor Paxton stammered.

"Let's get a sample from all of them. We'll use what Master Winston discovered from good Professor Jamison's notes and see what we can uncover. And when should we expect Professor Jamison? Her work is key."

"Conklin went to round her up."

"From where?"

"Red Capes had her stashed on the Isle of Dogs. We found her. They'll have her soon."

"Let's hope you have more success than you did last time."

Fenton laughed. "Well, he's *here* tonight," he said, pointing at Quinn. "So much for the fierce werewolf hunter."

Doctor Marlowe shook his head, apparently unimpressed with Fenton's bravado, then went back to Master Winston's workbench once more.

"Sample? How much?" one of the wolves asked, grabbing one of the goblins by the arm.

Doctor Marlowe signed heavily. "Use the device Master Dart made, you idiot."

"Oh. Right," the wolf said then went to Master Dart's table and picked up a syringe which had a long tube connected to it that led to a glass container wrapped with steel.

The werewolf grabbed the thing clumsily.

"You fool. You'll break it. You. Master Dart. You take the samples," the old man said. "Unchain him."

The werewolf set the device down and unchained the tinker. "Go on," he told the man.

Oliver Dart, a slim man who looked like he might faint at any moment, picked up the device and approached the goblin.

Doctor Marlowe looked over his shoulder at Master Dart. "A sample from each of those wretched beasts," he said, pointing toward the goblins. "And the Red Cape. Get what you can from our illustrious guest," he added, looking at Constantine. "We'll burn him after. He'll draw too much heat from the Red Capes. And do be gentle with Professor Paxton. We need her alive...and *albedo*," he said, giving Fenton a sharp look.

Gasping, I rose and pulled my pistols.

"Do you know that ancient werewolf?" Agent Reid asked.

I shook my head as I quickly dug into my satchel. I handed slim boxes of bullets to Agents Rose and Reid who stared at me. "Silver bullets. Right between the eyes. I'll grab Quinn."

"I need to get to Constantine," Agent Rose said. The look of distress on her face puzzled me.

Agent Reid pulled a small, hand-held bomb from his pack. "Shall we start with a distraction?"

8
BOOM GOES THE DYNAMITE

THE LOUD EXPLOSION SHOOK THE BUILDING. WINDOWPANES burst sending showers of glass onto the floor. The guards on the platform rushed downstairs while the others went to the doors.

Stupid wolves.

There was a second explosion as Agent Reid tossed another bomb toward the door where guards were standing. The device exploded, causing the whole building to rock.

I rushed down the platform, Agent Rose right behind me. Pulling out my pistol, I took aim and fired.

"Red Capes," someone yelled.

There was another explosion as Agent Reid tossed another bomb.

Growling, the wolves began to shift form.

"Get Doctor Marlowe and the tinkers out of here," Fenton called then turned. The massive beast craned his fat neck then stretched as he shifted into werewolf form.

Blasting, I shot through the crowd as I tried to get to Quinn.

One after the other, the wolves lunged at me, but in the

confusion of the gunfire and smoke, they were unsteady. In their haste to unchain the guild members, I was able to get off a few shots before the werewolves even saw me coming.

I eyed the door to see Doctor Marlowe being ushered out of the building by two of Fenton's regular henchmen.

The man glared at me, his eyes flaming ruby red.

I lifted my pistol and aimed at him.

I got off a shot, but the old man waved his hand in front of him, and the bullet went wide, hitting the wolf guard beside him in the shoulder instead. The three of them turned quickly and headed out the door.

There was another explosion.

Fenton howled.

The sound sent a shiver down my spine. I looked back in time to see the beta lunge toward Agent Reid.

"Reid," I screamed.

He looked up in time to see Fenton charging him.

Agent Rose turned and fired in an effort to protect her partner.

I raced over to Quinn, who lay forgotten on the floor.

"Quinn," I said, bending over to help him up.

"Clemeny," he said, his voice sounding ragged. "Get the guildsmen out of here."

"Let's get you up and out of here first," I told him as I quickly cut his binds.

"No, Clem. Leave me. You…you don't understand," he said.

Agent Rose screamed.

I looked back to see Agent Reid on the ground, Fenton chewing out his throat.

Agent Rose shot wildly, but at least half a dozen wolves were between her and Agent Reid.

"Quinn," I said, attempting to help him up. "Come on. We need to go."

"He's gone, Agent. They cut him open. Leave him," the vampire said.

"What are you talking about?" I asked the vampire.

"Get me down. Get me down, and I'll kill them all." With a turn of the neck, his mouth shifted, a row of jagged teeth gleaming menacingly. "Get me down, and he might still have a chance."

"Quinn?" I said, shaking Quinn's shoulder. He didn't respond. His face had turned horribly pale.

"Let me down, Agent Louvel," the vampire said.

I shook Quinn again. "Quinn?"

Agent Rose's piercing scream grabbed my attention. I looked back to see her pull herself up onto the platform. She had a long cut on her leg. Red blood marred her trousers. She pulled a sword, swinging it in front of her, and started retreating. But she was quickly running out of space.

"Let me down," the vampire screamed at me. This time, his words shook me to my core.

Leaping to my feet, I went to the vampire. "Your word you'll leave the rest of us in peace. The other agents, the guild members, and me. Your word, fang."

"Don't you know who I am?" he said through jagged teeth. "You have my word."

Dammit. There was no way I should trust him.

"You have my word. Now let me down," he yelled at me, his face full of fury.

I looked back at Agent Rose as she climbed back up the steps, skillfully brandishing her weapon in front of her as six wolves cornered her. Skilled or not, she was going to die.

The wolves had nearly unbound all the scientists, including Professor Paxton. I needed to do something. Fast.

"Hell's bells," I swore then one by one, I pulled the stakes from the hands and feet of the vampire.

The vampire's eyes glinted brightly, shimmering with silver light.

"Thank you," he said, and with speed I could not even phantom, the vampire shot around the room.

Howls of pain and anguish filled the air. The wolves called to one another, tried to warn one another, but it was too late.

In a blur of blood and body parts, the vampire exacted his terrible vengeance.

Grabbing whomever they could—including Oliver Dart, Mavis Porter, and Toby Winston—the rest of the wolves rushed to the waiting autos outside. The goblins had already disappeared.

The last of the wolves tugged Professor Paxton along behind him. Lionheart's friend fought back with all her might.

Leaving Quinn, I pulled my dagger from my belt and rushed across the room. Slicing with as much strength as I could muster, I slashed at the wolf's arm.

He let go of the Professor.

Growling, he looked from me then back into the room where Constantine devastated the remaining wolves.

"Leave her. Come on," one of the other pack members yelled.

The wolf glared at me then turned and fled.

I turned and rushed back to Quinn.

"Quinn," I called, shaking his shoulder. "Quinn?" I turned and looked at Professor Paxton who had followed me. "What happened to him?"

"They removed part of his liver. We need to get him to a proper surgeon."

"His liver? How do you…" I began but watched as Professor Paxton motioned toward one of the workbenches. In a glass tray, I spotted a piece of purplish meat.

My stomach turned. "Oh my God."

"He can survive, but we need to get him to a proper

surgeon. Doctor….Doctor Murray. Yes. He has a place in Mayfair. He could help. But we must get there quickly."

Quickly was a problem. The wolves and their autos were gone, and there was no underground transit here.

I stood and looked around the room.

There were bits of werewolf everywhere, and in the center of the space, a very bloody vampire stood, his hands shaking, blood dripping from his fingers.

Limping, Agent Rose approached him.

She whispered something to him. Her words were soft and gentle.

He shook his head.

I eyed Agent Reid who lay on the floor. His neck was a bloody mess. His bright blue eyes were glassy, frozen in a gaze fixed on the ceiling. He was gone.

"Constantine," I called. "Agent Briarwood is gravely injured. He must get to Doctor Murray in Mayfair, or he will die. I…I need your help."

The vampire looked at Agent Rose then back over his shoulder at me.

He whispered something to the agent that I could not quite hear.

She nodded.

He turned then suddenly appeared at my side.

The vampire met my eyes. "This will make us even."

"Agreed."

He picked up Quinn then in a blur of black, he disappeared back into the night.

"What was he?" Professor Paxton whispered.

"You don't want to know," I said then crossed the room to Agent Rose who stood over the remains of her partner.

Tears streamed down her cheeks.

"I will hunt that man down and kill him," she said, her voice shaking with rage.

"Doctor Marlowe. He was a werewolf…and a mage."

"A mage?"

I nodded.

Agent Rose stared. "No spell will save him. I will find him and finish him."

"Not alone," I said then set my hand on her shoulder.

9

0-0-RED

With the help of the local constables, we were able to get word to the Society of the tragedy that had unfolded. Not long after, a Society airship, boasting its signature scarlet-colored balloon, arrived to help secure the crime scene, gather evidence, and take Agent Reid's body back to headquarters.

"I'll go with him," Agent Rose said as they prepared his body for transport.

As the first team worked the crime scene, a small, second aircraft arrived. A crewman rushed down the rope ladder and over to me.

"Agent Louvel?" he asked. I eyed him over, noting the R. M. pendant on his lapel. He was one of us, an agent of the Rude Mechanicals.

"Yes?"

"I am instructed to transport you and Professor Paxton. Please come with me."

"Come with you where?"

"Classified. I'm sure you understand. Come along."

I nodded to Professor Paxton, who looked like she was thrilled to go anywhere as long as it was away from here.

Following the agent, we climbed up the rope ladder to the small airship. As soon as we were aboard, the ship turned and headed back toward the city.

Reaching onto my belt, I pulled off my silver flask and handed it to Professor Paxton.

She sighed heavily, twisted off the cap, and then took a swig as she stared out at the city. "All my life I was taught to stay away from anyone wearing a red cape. To avoid you if I saw you on the street. To look away. But you... You're a force of good, aren't you?"

"Yes. We work under the auspices of Her Majesty on cases such as the one in which you find yourself the unfortunate victim."

She took another swig. "Those *creatures*... There are more of them, aren't there?"

"Yes."

"And they walk amongst us? Look like ordinary people?"

I smiled softly, wondering how she would feel if she knew that it was her squash partner—a werewolf—who'd asked me to find her. "Yes. But they aren't all bad."

"No?" she asked with a huff as if she didn't believe me.

"Well. I mean, most of them *are* bad, but not *all* of them."

She laughed lightly.

To my surprise, the airship turned away from headquarters and began to fly in the direction of Buckingham. Only when an agent had made a horrible mistake did the Queen summon them. This shift in course did not bode well. As the ship neared the palace, I braced myself. Clearly, I was in for a lecture.

The airship docked on the platform on the roof of the palace. A fleet of attendants arrived from the palace to steady the ladder.

"Agent. Your attendance is requested," the agent of the Rude Mechanicals told me and the professor.

"Guess I'm out of a job," I said lightly.

"Hope it's not as bad as that," he said then extended a hand to help the professor down. I followed along behind her.

I dropped onto the roof of the palace and looked around. The small crowd assembled was mostly comprised of palace servants. But amongst them were also two armed guards and a Society agent.

"This way, Agent Louvel, professor," the agent of the Rude Mechanicals agent said then led us into the palace.

We walked down the narrow servants' halls to a flight of stairs. Winding down one flight of stairs after another, after another, and after another. I soon realized that we were, in fact, underground. The air was crisp and had the distinctive perfume of earth.

At the end of the stairs, the footman opened a door.

I was surprised to find Agent Greystock waiting in the hallway on the other side.

"Clemeny. At last. Are you all right?" she asked.

I nodded. "Yes. I'm fine. This is Professor Paxton."

"Good evening, professor. My name is Agent Greystock. Are you well? Do you require any medical treatment?"

"No, madame. I'm just... I'm just in a state of shock, I believe."

"That is to be expected. Please, come along," she said then motioned for us to follow her.

"Is there any word on Agent Briarwood? I sent a message back to headquarters. He was taken to a Doctor Murray in Mayfair."

Agent Greystock nodded. "I've had couriers there and back. He arrived in time to receive emergency medical attention. Doctor Murray, though retired, did what he could. Quinn is alive. In pain, but alive. Clemeny, how did you know about Doctor Murray?"

"I didn't. Professor Paxton did."

"I've studied some of his treatments, his essays on disease, his work with the late Master Hawking. He is well known in the medical community as the brightest surgeon in the realm."

"Agent Briarwood is lucky for your quick thinking and his quick delivery to the doctor's address," Agent Greystock said then raised an eyebrow at me.

"I believe Agent Rose will be following up on that...complication."

"Indeed. I was saddened to learn about Agent Reid. He was a good man and a good agent."

"Fenton's handiwork."

Agent Greystock frowned.

"Has anyone sent word to Jessica?" I asked. "She will be worried about Quinn."

Agent Greystock nodded. "She is already with him. I understand the Murrays were very obliging," she said then opened a door. "If you please," she said then motioned for us to enter.

Professor Paxton and I entered the room to find Agent Harper, Agent White, and Agent Fox. And Her Majesty.

Professor Paxton let out a small gasp.

Both of us stopped and dropped into a curtsey.

"Yes, yes. Dispense with formalities, please. Agent Louvel and Professor Paxton, correct?"

"Yes, Your Majesty," Professor Paxton and I said in unison.

Victoria smirked then looked back down at the papers she was holding in her hand. "Agent Louvel, Agent Greystock has apprised me of the events leading up to the ruckus at Guildhall the other night. I've also heard the report on the events that took place tonight. All a bit murky, I'm afraid. Can you please tell me what's happening in my realm?"

"Your Majesty, I can only tell you what I have observed. There is a werewolf amongst the packs I have never seen before. He is old—even for a wolf. The others call him Doctor Marlowe. He appears to have some skill with mage work in addition to the lupine affliction. He is the one behind this mess."

"Him. Not Cyril?"

"Is Cyril—pardon my interruption, Your Majesty—a huge man with red hair?" Professor Paxton asked.

"Indeed he is," Victoria replied.

"He was there at the factory. He was working with Doctor Marlowe, but the doctor was the one organizing our research. Cyril, I believe, was the person who captured the gentleman you called Constantine."

"So this Doctor Marlowe is using the packs for muscle. Any sign of Constantine after all this mess?" Victoria asked Agent Greystock.

"Not since he delivered Agent Briarwood."

"Make sure Agent Rose follows up. The wolves lifted Constantine from his castle in Scotland. We are to make sure all our other assets in that division are secure."

"Yes, Your Majesty," Agent Greystock said.

"I know Agent Rose will be keen to join Agent Louvel and murder every wolf in the city—

not that I blame her—but let's make sure she stays focused on looking after her own charges."

"Of course, Your Majesty," Agent Greystock said with a nod.

I chewed the inside of my cheek as I watched Her Majesty flip through the papers. I was shocked to see that she knew all our names, our assignments. I had always assumed that working as part of Her Majesty's Secret Intelligence Service was really just a title. In this case, it seemed the Queen did know who we were and what work we were doing.

"Professor Paxton, perhaps you can enlighten us on what, exactly, Doctor Marlowe had you working."

"Alchemy, Your Majesty. He had us studying the interactions between various metals and flesh and blood."

The Queen's forehead furrowed. "Whatever for? A philosopher's stone?"

The professor shook her head. "He's not after gold or even the transmutation of metals. He had us studying silver," she said then frowned. "I didn't understand why at the time. But I think... I think he was looking for a way to use an alchemical formula to fortify the blood—*their blood*—against silver. But it was no use. I was able to make some headway in determining the weakness in their humours, those peculiarities that make them particularly susceptible to silver, but without Doctor Jamison's work on the alkahest, we were able to do little."

"That's unfortunate then," Her Majesty said.

"Unfortunate? Why?" I asked.

"Because Professor Jamison was abducted from the safehouse on the Isle of Dogs earlier this evening," Her Majesty said.

"Werewolves' longevity is only cut short by two things, a natural death many hundreds of years in the making and silver. If the wolves can find a way to become immune to the effects of silver..." I said.

The Queen nodded. "Then we have a very big bad wolf problem," she said then turned to the professor once more. "Can it be done?"

"Perhaps. Like an inoculation. Our research in the course of disease is insufficient, Your Majesty. Based on Doctor Jenner's research in smallpox, we have applied the theory of inoculation to many forms of disease control. But it still quite far beyond our understanding. And yet..."

Her Majesty raised an eyebrow at the professor.

"And yet, Doctor Jamison's study from an alchemical point of view, using the theories of the Magnum Opus and the four pillars of alchemy is something I have not explored, but it does offer possibilities."

"Your Majesty," Agent Harper said, rising. The stack of

books before her was so tall that I had nearly forgotten she was even there.

"Yes?"

"This Doctor Marlowe. Clem—Agent Louvel said she had not seen him before. We have record of a practicing mage, Kit Marlowe, who was sentenced to banishment by the Rude Mechanicals in 1593. Our records indicate he went into exile in Italy and hasn't been seen in England since."

"Kit Marlowe... Christopher Marlowe, the playwright?" Agent Greystock asked.

"The same," Agent Harper answered.

"Marlowe," the Queen said with a sigh. "Seems his characters weren't the only ones looking for a Faustian bargain. Well, Agent Louvel, the werewolves are seeking to enhance their immortality by dodging your silver bullets. And this time, they have a mage pulling strings. Whatever shall we do?"

"Whatever Your Majesty commands," I said.

Queen Victoria smirked. "I like this girl," she said then turned and pulled out two sheets of paper. Snatching a quill, she jotted down notes on both then melted wax on the parchment and embossed each letter with her seal. She turned back to us once more.

"Agent White will take Professor Paxton to our secure location in Nottingham for the time being," she said then looked at the agent, who nodded. She handed one of the notes to me. "And that, Agent Louvel, is your license to use lethal force. The Britannia Accord is hereby suspended. Find that mage and kill him. I've had enough of Cyril and Fenton as well. Agent Greystock will send agents to keep a lid on the Lolitas and arrest every other werewolf we can find. And you, Agent Louvel, will deliver this letter on my behalf."

I took the sealed letter from her hand. "To whom, Your Majesty?"

"Lionheart. Go tell Sir Richard he needs to set aside his

research for the moment. After all, God has waited this long for him to finish his quest. He can wait another fortnight," Her Majesty said. "Tell him I call my Templars. They *will* help you. That is an order from his Queen," she said then tapped the letter in my hand, giving me a knowing look.

I nodded. "Yes, Your Majesty."

"Sir Richard? Do you mean Richard Spencer is..." Professor Paxton began, looking from Her Majesty to me.

"Please, professor. Come with me," Agent White said, motioning for the professor to follow her.

"I... Okay," she said then turned and followed Agent White from the room.

"If you don't mind me saying so, Your Majesty, Sir Richard has no interest in becoming alpha, nor does he have the temperament."

"Indeed, he does not, but we shall leave it to him to find a peaceful solution to that problem."

Clever Queen. "Yes, Your Majesty."

I curtseyed to her once more then turned to Agent Greystock.

"With your permission, I shall accompany Agent Louvel out," Agent Greystock said to the Queen, who nodded then turned back to the papers on her desk. Agent Greystock motioned for me to follow her outside.

"If you see Quinn, please tell him...I said to rest and not to worry," I told Agent Greystock.

"You know your partner well. I understand he was inquiring after you," Agent Greystock said.

"What's there to worry about? I'm off to go work with a werewolf to take down a different werewolf. What could possibly go wrong?"

Agent Greystock looked at me, the answer evident in both of our eyes.

Everything.

10
THE KNIGHTS TEMPLAR

ONCE AGAIN, I TOOK THE TRAM BACK ACROSS TOWN TO Fleet Street. This time, however, I made a turn off the main thoroughfare through a small arch along the street, barely noticeable under the façade of a Tudor townhouse next to a bookshop. Given it was dawn, the shopkeep had just opened the curtains on the window of the little bookshop when I slipped through the arch.

I emerged on the other side in Temple Square, the home—hidden in plain sight—of the Knights Templar.

Of course, everyone knew the Kights Templar were long gone. The gardens, church, hall, and buildings of Temple Square were just remnants of a past history, of knights of both good and bad repute, the knights of the crusades. Such men, for good or bad, were long gone. Right?

But the thing was, of course, that was about as far from the truth as one could possibly get. Some of the Templars had returned from the crusades, but not as they once were. Something had happened during their quest, and the Templars had changed, become afflicted with the lupine infection. The Templars still lived, but they were no longer just men.

Taking a deep breath, I crossed into Temple Square. I eyed the grounds warily. Her Majesty might be right that the Templars would be inclined to follow any edict she set down, but such an edict delivered via a Red Cape might not be welcomed. As I passed through the square, I spotted one man headed toward Templar Hall, no doubt for his morning meal. He stopped mid-step and eyed me warily.

Wolf.

Another man who had just started work in the flowerbeds also gave me a sidelong glance.

Another wolf.

I felt eyes on me from above, looking down on me from the windows.

The palms of my hands itched. I had literally walked into the wolves' den.

Well, I'd made the first move. We'd see what would happen next.

Just off the square was the Templar church, a small building distinctive for its rotunda. While the church was nothing to boast about in comparison to the grandeur of Saint Paul's, it must have been considered an awe-inspiring structure in the twelfth century when it was built. I opened the wooden door of the church and entered. The place was completely still. Slants of light shone in from the windows high above. It did not escape my notice that the church appeared to have had some newly refurbished architectural pieces. I passed the massive pillars and went under the dome in the round part of the cathedral. Here, the tombs of Templar Knights lay on the floor. I paused to look down at the regal figures immortalized in stone. The Templars had gone off to fight at the behest of their monarch. They were from a different time and under a different set of circumstances. But were they really any different from myself? They were the crown's warriors. And so was I.

A door at the back of the chapel opened.

I inhaled deeply and waited as the sound of footsteps approached me.

"You do know it's very uncomfortable for me to come in here," Lionheart said.

I looked up at him.

He was visibly clenching his jaw.

"Yes. I do know that. That's why I'm here. I figured it would be the safest place in the square."

"If you wanted to be safe, Agent Louvel, then coming into pack territory was probably not a wise idea."

I pulled the paper the Queen had given me and handed it to Lionheart. He looked from the paper to me then frowned and opened the missive. I watched his face as he read it over, his features darkening.

When he was done, he looked up at me.

"Her Majesty formally requests the assistance of the Templar pack. She has asked that you set aside your research and aid me in ending Cyril's reign, tracking down and murdering Fenton, and destroying a wolf mage by the name of Kit Marlowe who, apparently, is attempting to use alchemy to develop a tolerance to silver. Her Majesty has revoked the Britannia Accord and threatens to expel all werewolves from London. Unless, of course, you can assist me in getting this situation under control."

Lionheart grunted in a very wolf-like manner, a sound I had never heard from him before. The veneer of the college thrown off, I was starting to see that Sir Richard Spencer was far more wolf than he let on. He shook the paper in his hand as he considered my words, and those of Her Majesty.

"Byrony Paxton is safe. She has been taken to a secure location. *Your brothers* had her chained up, forced her to carve up goblins, my partner, and a fang named Constantine. Ever heard of him?"

"You must be joking."

"And, I believe, that mage also had some designs on her person. I was able to recover her from *your brothers*, but not without losing Agent Reid. And Agent Briarwood has been seriously wounded. Did *your brothers* tell you the scope of the activities they were planning under their new mage?"

"They are *not* my brothers," Lionheart said, temper flaring. "*These* are my brothers," he said, motioning to the men entombed before us.

My ruse had worked.

"The Templars did the bidding of King Richard. You were agents of the crown. I do the bidding of Queen Victoria as an agent of the crown. I know you to be royalists, but do you still consider yourselves Her Majesty's agents?"

"Of course we do," he said hotly.

"Very well. I guess that makes *us* brothers then. So, no more research for now. Now, we work together."

"She has called her knights. We cannot say no. So, Agent Louvel, how do you suggest we begin?"

"We need to find Cyril, Fenton, and Marlowe. The Red Capes will be arresting everyone else they can get their hands on today, and Lolitas will be locked down."

"In that case, you need to give me a couple of hours. I need to meet with my pack."

"Very well."

"You mentioned the vampire Constantine. I have had some dealings with him in the past. I cannot believe Cyril would be foolish enough to move against him."

"Foolish or not, that's exactly what he did. Many Lupercal pack members paid the price for that mistake. But, I believe, the vampire has retreated."

Lionheart shook his head. "I doubt that very much."

"We shall see. Very well, Sir Richard. You talk to your pack, and I'll meet you at one o'clock at The Mushroom."

"The Mushroom? Why there, of all places?"

"Because if you want to buy information, you need to know the best place to shop."

Lionheart raised an eyebrow at me.

I looked once more at the tombs of the fallen Templars. "I *am* sorry for your many losses," I said then inclined my head toward the knights.

Lionheart was still for a moment. "And I am sorry to hear about Agents Reid and Briarwood," he said then looked at me. "You are an unusual woman, Agent Louvel."

"Hmmm," I said then smiled. "I thought I just smelled odd."

"I never said you smelled odd. In fact, I said you smell like—"

"Roses. Yes, I know."

"Indeed. Who is your family, Agent?"

I smirked at him then turned and headed to the chapel door. "One o'clock, Lionheart. You're buying," I said then pushed open the door and left.

It unnerved me more than I wanted to show that Lionheart sensed something about me I didn't know, didn't understand.

Who is your family?

That was a very good question.

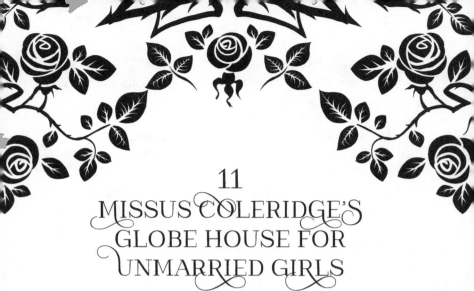

11
MISSUS COLERIDGE'S GLOBE HOUSE FOR UNMARRIED GIRLS

WITH JUST A FEW HOURS REMAINING BEFORE I NEEDED TO meet Lionheart, I waved down a passing auto, much to my annoyance—but need out-weighed disdain—and caught a ride across the Thames to South Bank. Wolves had notoriously good noses. Most agents lived outside the city or across the Thames. Passing the river, even by way of a boat or bridge, threw off our scents. Werewolves had been known to trail us from time to time. Thus far, they had not discovered—at least as far as I knew—my tiny flat at Missus Coleridge's Globe Home for Unmarried Girls, so named because the building was located not far from where Master Shakespeare's famous theatre once stood.

Checking to make sure I had not been followed, I entered the small, three-story house and headed upstairs. I moved quickly and quietly. Missus Coleridge had, no doubt, heard some delicious gossip and would want to share—for hours. I, on the other hand, wanted to sleep.

Pulling out my key slowly and quietly, I opened the door and stepped inside my tiny flat. As I entered, the board below my foot squeaked.

The door to Missus Coleridge's first floor flat opened.

"Clemeny, is that you?"

I cringed. Feeling terribly guilty, I pulled the door shut behind me, pulling the handle into the lock, wincing at the barely audible click. Missus Coleridge was a truly kind woman. I'd have to make a point of stopping by her flat and letting her gossip to me for at least an hour to make up for the nagging guilt I felt. That, and I needed to canvass the roof to see if I could get inside via the window rather than the front door.

Closing and locking the door behind me, I turned and leaned against the doorframe.

My small flat had none of the charm and feel of family that exuded from every inch of Grand-mère's home. But visiting Grand-mère opened her up to discovery, a risk I hoped to minimize at every turn. An unmarried woman, I *should* live with my relative. I *should* have a respectable flat in the city. I wanted to live with my Grand-mère. But it wasn't safe. My flat was small, dank, dark, and all around miserable. But it was better this way.

For now.

I scanned the room. You could see the entire place in one glance. Not even bothering to remove my cape, I crossed the room and lay down on my slim bed.

Two hours. I just needed two hours. Two hours after being awake for the last thirty wasn't too much to ask, was it?

Before my brain could even bubble up with a reply, I fell asleep.

12
WHAT CATERPILLAR KNEW

WHILE I WAS USUALLY LESS THAN GRATEFUL FOR THE whistle at the factory beside Missus Coleridge's Globe House for Unmarried Girls, the infernal device blasting every hour, today it kept me in check. I was awake—miserably—and back on the job before the fog had cleared from my mind. It wasn't until I was standing outside The Mushroom that my wits began to sharpen.

At precisely one o'clock, Lionheart arrived. Much to my surprise, he was driving a two-wheeled cycle. The strange device clicked and let off a hiss of steam when he turned it off. He parked the vehicle alongside the other autos outside the tavern then pulled off the leather skullcap and goggles he'd been wearing.

His yellow hair, tousled in the effort, gave him a boyish charm entirely at odds with who he really was. Or did it? Who was he, really? Before the lupine affliction, who had Richard Spencer actually been? A knight loyal to his king. Thinking of him in that regard made me see him in an entirely new light. He might have been a wolf, but he was also a warrior and deserving of my respect. He smoothed down his locks and straightened his jacket then eyed me over.

"Are you going to wear that inside?" he asked.

Or maybe not. I glanced down at my leather pants, corset, and top. My clothing was not much different from that of an airship jockey.

"The cape," he said, clarifying. "The rest looks very good indeed," he said with a smirk.

I rolled my eyes. "There are some places where it pays to be what you are. This is one of those places. For me, at least."

Lionheart raised a brow. "Really, Little Red?"

"Yes. Really. Let's go," I said then turned and headed inside.

The place was dark and smelled of alcohol, opium, and danger. There were small tables spread all around the room, the place dimly lit by colorful glass lamps, which sent blobs of jewel-colored light around the room. I motioned to Lionheart, and we took a seat in the corner.

At the bar, I saw the henchman they called the Knave. He whispered something into the ear of a little albino boy who nodded then rushed off to the back of the room. There, silk curtains were closed around a meeting space. When the boy entered, I saw at least three other people inside, including, I assumed, the boss.

"Drinks?" a pretty tart asked, leaning in such a manner that we had a clear view of her jiggly breasts.

Lionheart sneered then averted his eyes.

The tart hadn't missed the expression. She leaned back then turned to me, a steely expression on her face.

"MacCutcheon. Two glasses."

The girl nodded then went back to the bar. She stood close to the Knave, who lifted his drink. He spoke in a low tone to the girl. She eyed us over her shoulder then answered him. So far so good. I scanned the room. I saw gunrunners, opium dealers, airship pirates, and thieves. And they spied me. They eyed my red cape warily.

"They're talking about us in the back," Lionheart said, easing back into his seat.

"Good. Keep listening. How did your meeting with your pack go?"

"I can hardly concentrate on them and talk to you at the same time. Let it suffice to say that we will do as Her Majesty asks."

"Good."

"We'll see."

"Here you are," the tart said, returning once more. She set down glasses in front of Lionheart and me. "Compliments of the house, Agent."

"Thank you. If Caterpillar is available, a word?"

The girl nodded but said nothing else.

She returned to the bar where she spoke to the Knave, who polished off his drink then turned and went to the back. He gave Lionheart and me a passing glance. Devilishly handsome scoundrel. Why were all the rogues so desperately attractive?

I sighed. I really needed to find myself a man.

I lifted my drink. "God save the Queen."

"God save the Queen," Lionheart replied, clicking his glass against mine. He took a long drink.

I could sense Lionheart's discomfort. I had, on many occasions, felt the same air coming off Quinn. It was as if Lionheart was reluctant to be bothered with this problem. Quinn had never meant any disrespect to me or the job, but of late, I had sensed a weariness in him. But Lionheart was more than seven hundred years old. He had a right to be weary. Yet, still, I could tell he'd rather be anywhere else, doing anything else, than sitting here.

"Professor Paxton," Lionheart said as he set down his

drink. "I don't suppose you'd tell me where she is. Since we are, as you said, brothers in arms."

"I'm afraid not. North. More than that, I cannot say."

"And she is safe where she is?" he asked, his voice cracking very slightly at the end.

Did the werewolf have some genuine affection for the professor? I turned and looked at him, my eyes narrowing. There was something there, but I wasn't sure what. Whatever it was, he'd hidden it quickly.

Lionheart lifted his drink and sipped once more.

"I swear that she is safe. Once the matter is in hand, I am sure she'll be able to return to London."

He nodded. "And how is Agent Briarwood?"

"Recovering."

"At our meeting today... My pack didn't know about Doctor Marlowe. We didn't know the nature of their research. In fact, there was some debate amongst the knights as to whether or not we should stop the work. Immunity to silver would help us continue our quest."

I raised an eyebrow at him. "But you're here."

"In the end, we decided that God gave us this particular vulnerability for a reason. We shall not seek to meddle in his work." Lionheart flicked his eyes toward the back. "He's coming."

The Knave crossed the room. "All right. Come along," he said, motioning for us to follow.

Lionheart and I rose and followed the Knave to the back. Passing through the curtains, we found Caterpillar, one of London's biggest crime bosses, waiting. He was sitting with his feet up reading over some papers. Behind him stood two guards. He picked up a glass of absinthe and took a sip, and eyed Lionheart and me.

"Rather a bad day to show up here, Agent," he said then tapped the papers he was holding. "Thanks to the Red Capes, seems I'm out quite a lot of money and some business partners to boot."

I smiled at him. He might be a wily criminal, but it was unlikely he had any idea his business partners were werewolves. We'd probably done him a favor, in the long run.

"My apologies."

Caterpillar smirked in the most charming of fashions. "Agent Louvel, I'm told."

"Indeed."

"But you are unknown," he said, looking at Lionheart. He lifted his drink and sipped once more.

"An associate," I said.

Caterpillar shook his head and set his drink aside. "I don't deal with unknowns, Agent. And, as I said, the Society has disrupted things around here today. Perhaps it's best if we part ways before we even begin."

"But I'm here to buy, and you're here to sell. I'm looking for someone who has gone to ground. You sell. I'll buy. Don't worry about my associate. He's a silent partner."

Caterpillar eyed Lionheart. "Who are you looking for?" he asked, turning to me.

"Cyril."

Caterpillar's eyes narrowed. Cyril ran one of the biggest crime syndicates in London and often butted heads with other operators, including Caterpillar. From what I could tell, the two of them kept an uneasy peace. Yet if I were Caterpillar, I'd most certainly want Cyril out of the way.

Caterpillar looked over his shoulder and waved for the little albino child to come to him. He whispered in the boy's ear.

I cast a glance up at Lionheart.

His eyes flicked toward me, but he said nothing.

The pair exchanged a few more whispered words then Caterpillar turned to me once more. "I apologize, Agent. We heard that there was some trouble downriver last night, but we don't know where Cyril has gone. I wish I could be more help."

"And that's your final answer?"

"I'm afraid so."

I frowned. "Very well. Thank you for your time."

"And for the drink," Lionheart said, inclining his head to Caterpillar.

The crime boss nodded to Lionheart then motioned for one of his henchmen to show us out.

Lionheart and I headed outside and walked over to his cycle.

"Did you know he wouldn't talk?" Lionheart asked.

"Maybe."

Lionheart chuckled. "But you guessed he would know where Cyril had gone."

"Of course."

"And you assumed with my good hearing, I would be able to pick up the information?"

"Well, did you get the location?" I asked.

He nodded. "A hangar in the yard near the airship towers," he said then pulled on his cap, goggles, and gloves. "Well, are you going to climb on?" he said, motioning to the back.

I stared at the infernal machine then groaned.

Lionheart chuckled and handed me a pair of goggles. I pulled the goggles on, then, much against my will, I climbed on the back.

"Hold on to me," he said.

I wrapped my arms around the werewolf. He was muscularly built. The feel of his body, the closeness of our embrace, felt entirely too familiar and stirred up a longing in me that made me blush.

Lionheart laughed. "Careful, Little Red, or you might agree to that dinner yet," he said then turned on the engine. The machine let out a hiss of steam.

"I'm not sure Professor Paxton would appreciate me accepting that invitation."

Lionheart looked back over his shoulder at me. "Are you always so observant, Little Red?"

"I try."

Lionheart grunted then turned the cycle onto the city street.

13
THE ENEMY OF MY ENEMY

THE AIRSHIP TOWERS ALONG THE THAMES WERE HOME TO A busy international port. The towers loomed over the London skyline. The fabulous balloons and gondolas floated in and out of port headed to Ireland, Scotland, and back across the Channel to the European port of Calais and beyond. From here, other ships rigged for longer travel would make the treacherous trip from London to Ireland then to the Azores in a cross-sea voyage to the Americas.

Seeking to blend in with the other travelers, Lionheart parked his cycle outside Rose's Hopper, the popular pub located near the towers. I pulled off my red cape and stashed it in my satchel. Wordlessly, Lionheart motioned to me, and we headed through the crowd, around the back of the towers to the hangars and garages in the shipyard where tinkers and mechanics built new ships, made repairs, or showcased the latest in airship designs. The place was busy enough that no one paid any attention to us.

As we walked, we noticed a crowd had gathered around to see a master tinker unveil a new airship about to come up for auction.

Taking me gently by the arm, Lionheart guided me into the crowd.

"The others will mask my scent," he whispered. "There," he said motioning with his chin to the next hangar down.

I followed his gaze. Sitting outside the hangar were two autos that I recognized from the warehouse night before.

"Ladies and gentleman, you have never seen an airship quite like this one before. Faster than the *Stargazer*, lighter weight than any ship of Spanish design, and equipped with the latest engineering designed in Bavaria, meet the newest creation in our fleet," the man at the front of the crowd said.

The crowd *oohed* and *ahhed* as the doors to the hangar opened to reveal an impressive airship. The crowd moved forward, taking Lionheart and me along with it.

As we entered the hangar, Lionheart steered me to the left. He deftly lifted two mechanics' overcoats from the wall. Pulling one on, he handed the other to me. We slipped on the coats then moved out a side door. Blending in with the busy crowd, we made our way toward the second hangar.

"Guards in the windows," I said. "Two guards on the door."

Lionheart inhaled then exhaled deeply. "Fenton. But no Cyril. And no mage. But I—" He paused. He turned and looked all around him. "This way," he said, motioning for me to follow him to the airship repair tower not far away. Here, airships were anchored aloft as they were being re-outfitted with new gear pieces, getting repairs on broken propellers, or making other changes.

Keeping our heads down, Lionheart and I headed up the steps of the tower.

I could tell from his movements that Lionheart was tracking someone.

We walked up the stairs to the second level then down a row that led to an empty berth.

"Cyril, the mage, and two others recently came this way," he said then looked toward the skyline.

"Are the others still inside the hangar? The tinkers? Fenton?"

Lionheart nodded.

I looked around. No one seemed to be on the airship docked nearby. Moving quickly, I slipped onto the ship and went to the prow. Settling in, I pulled out my spyglass. Lionheart moved in behind me.

I scanned the hangar. From this vantage point, I could just see through the windows. Inside, I spotted a few new workbenches.

"Professor Jamison," I said. "And Master Winston. Looks like…Whitechapel and Paddington."

"A runner came this morning. Noah was arrested, and most of his pack along with him."

Noah was the beta of Conklin pack. I was very, very glad to hear he'd been taken off the streets. "Good."

Lionheart said nothing.

I looked back at him.

"And just what does Her Majesty plan to do with the packs once she's taken them into custody? She can hardly keep them chained forever."

Something told me Her Majesty could and would keep them chained forever, if the mood struck her to do so. "I don't know."

Lionheart cleared his throat.

"What is it?"

"Templar will face ramifications for helping the crown."

"Ramifications, meaning revenge?"

"Yes."

"Then I guess you'd better just become alpha."

"There is nothing I could want less, Little Red."

"I'm sure another solution will come to you."

"Let's hope."

I sat back. "I'll send word to the Red Capes. We'll round them up now and get the alchemists out of there."

Lionheart shook his head. "If Her Majesty wants this threat eliminated, then it must be eliminated. Her knights will return tonight. We'll wait until Cyril and the mage return and take the situation in hand."

"Good. Where should I meet you?"

"I was referring to the Templars and only the Templars."

"Last night I found my partner half dead because of Cyril, Fenton, and that mage. Not to mention what happened to Agent Reid. I'm coming, whether you want me there or not."

"I won't be able to protect you."

"I don't need you to protect me."

Lionheart frowned at me. "I need to go and ready my brothers. Do you want a ride back to your headquarters?"

"No, thank you."

"It's really not an inconven—"

"I've had enough of that infernal machine," I said with a smirk.

Lionheart nodded. "Very well," he said then rose. "Tonight… Be careful, Agent Louvel."

"You too, Sir Richard."

He grinned, bowed in the most courtly of manners, then turned and debarked the airship.

I leaned back once more and gazed through my spyglass. Rather than spying the building, I turned and watched Lionheart as he made his way through the crowd.

So, he and Byrony Paxton had…something.

I sighed.

That something was a whole lot more than the nothing I had. I loved my job, but it would be nice to have someone. I rose and closed my spyglass. Maybe I didn't have someone I loved like that, but I did care about the people in my life. I pulled out my pocket watch.

I had enough time.

14
MEANWHILE, IN TWICKENHAM

AFTER LIONHEART HAD GONE, I HEADED BACK INTO THE city. My first stop was at one of the oldest millineries in London, The Palatine Crown. The hat shop, which boasted an excellent array of gentlemen's top hats and petite ladies' top hats, sat along a quiet street. When I entered, I found the milliner sizing an aged gentleman for a new hat.

The hatter cast a glance up at me. I tapped the tiny badge on my waist.

The man nodded then turned back to his customer.

Going to the back room, I went to the side wall where a stack of crates rose to the ceiling. The wooden crates, marked as silk, leather, manikins, or cloth, took up most of the wall. I slid my fingers along the edge of the tallest crate marked *red velvet*. There, I found a tiny lever. I switched it to the side. A door built into the crate swung open. I slipped inside, closing the crate door behind me, then headed to the hidden door along the rear wall. On the other side, I found a flight of stairs that led downward.

I followed the stairs down under the city to a tunnel. Two

metal trams sat waiting. I slipped inside. This time I set my controls to take me to the outskirts of London. Strapping in once more, I activated the lever, waited for the clicks, then held on with all my might.

THE TUNNEL LET out southwest of London in a nondescript building under Twickenham station. I exited the building, mindful to cover my tracks, and headed toward the small village square. I passed through the quaint town to a small cottage on the outskirts. The little Tudor-style home with its charming garden exuded all the sweetness one might expect of a sedate country family. I doubted any of Quinn's neighbors realized he was one of the most skilled killers in all the realm.

As always, I scanned around me for signs of, well, anything. But there was no one nearby.

I went to the door and knocked.

Quinn's footman cast a suspicious gaze out the window.

I waved to him.

A moment later, the door opened.

"Agent Louvel," he said, motioning for me to enter.

"I'm here to see Quinn."

He motioned for me to follow as he headed upstairs. I had been inside Quinn's house on a number of occasions, but never in the family areas of the home. The house, as I understood it, had once belonged to a relative of Jessica's and had been passed down to her. Quinn had grown up in the city, a wild creature like myself. But he'd always seemed content, at peace, at home with his wife.

The footman motioned for me to wait as he went into one of the rooms.

Inside, I could hear Jessica and Quinn.

A moment later, the footman reappeared, Jessica along with him. Jessica's curly black hair was a tangled mess. The dark rings under her eyes told me she hadn't slept.

"Clemeny," she said, pulling me into an embrace. "Thank God."

"How is he?"

"Recovering. The Society brought him home by airship this morning. Doctor Murray, such a kindly gentleman, accompanied him. He said... Quinn had been injured but would recover. Quinn isn't saying much about what happened. The doctor gave him laudanum. He's in pain. Thank God, he's mostly been sleeping. What happened?"

I exhaled deeply. Quinn never liked Jessica to worry. If she really knew everything we saw, everything we did...well, Quinn kept that from her. It was not my place to change that. "Bad men, doing bad things."

She frowned but nodded. "Why don't you go inside? I'm sure you have a lot to talk about. Let me go downstairs and have Mary make you something to eat."

"Thank you," I said, squeezing her arm.

I went inside. Quinn lay on a large bed, half dozing as he looked out the window. There were several amber-colored bottles at his bedside.

"Quinn," I said softly then went and sat down in the chair by his bed.

"Sorry, partner. I messed up," he said then frowned.

"Messed up? Hardly."

"Well, I'm here, and you're there. And now you've got no one backing you up."

"On the contrary, Her Majesty has seen fit to force me into a new, albeit temporary, alliance."

"With whom?"

"Lionheart."

Quinn tried to laugh, but I could see it pained him. "Clemeny, I'm sorry. Cyril's pack jumped me. I woke up on a table with someone cutting me open. I don't even remember what happened after that."

"Well, it seems the wolves are in league with a mage who's been living in exile. I believe Elizabeth banished him, if that gives you an indication of how long he's been plotting revenge. Apparently, he's been trying to develop an immunity to silver."

"A mage?"

"Indeed, a werewolf mage. Doubling down on annoying, aren't they?"

Quinn smiled, but his grin was not as bright as usual. "How did I end up at the doctor's flat? I don't remember anything."

"Constantine."

Quinn stared at me then narrowed his gaze. "I think... I do remember him being there. I remember the wolves cutting him. Constantine," he said, his voice full of disbelief. "The wolves must have lost their minds. But why did he help me?"

"I think it was a combination of my setting him free, his desire for revenge, and something *odd* between him and Agent Rose."

"Agent Rose? That's surprising."

"Isn't it? But you don't need to worry about that. By the time me and my *temporary* partner are done, we'll have most of the wolves rounded up and jailed. If Lionheart becomes alpha, maybe things will quiet down by the time you return. Hell, maybe it will become so quiet we can switch to magical artifacts. Or should we join the Pellinores?"

"The Pellinores? And hunt dragons?"

"Why not?"

"Lionheart will never want to become alpha."

"Makes him the best man for the job then, doesn't it?"

"Maybe."

"Well, you can ask him yourself when you're feeling better."

"No. No, Clem. I don't think so."

"What? I don't think Lionheart minds you too much. He's really not that bad. I think he—"

"No," he said then shook his head. "Not that. I...talked to Jessica. I'm tired, Clem. This was the end of the line me."

My breath caught in my throat. "What?"

"I'm going to turn in my cape."

"But Quinn…"

Quinn sighed. "The doctor said it will take time to recover —months. I don't want to waste my life worrying about wolves. When I am well enough, Jessica and I want to have a family of our own. There's still time for us, but not if I keep working like this. I'm tired of being cold, in danger, always hunting some monster."

"But that's the life."

"Yes, it is. And I'm done with it."

A million emotions tried to bubble to the surface. I wanted to tell him no. I wanted to tell him he couldn't leave me like that. But I had no right. He was my partner, and he'd been a damned good one. And the truth was, I understood. I reached out and took his hand. "I'll miss you."

"No. You'll come to dinner every night. And one day, when you're settled down, our children will play together. We'll impress them with true stories of things they won't believe and think we made up. Werewolves, vampires, and goblins living in London? Who could ever believe such nonsense? They'll think we're senile, but we'll know better."

I smiled. "That's a nice vision." Nice, but far from the future I saw for myself.

Quinn squeezed my hand. "I know you," he said. "You

want to go down in a blaze of gun smoke. One day, you'll change your mind."

"Maybe you're right."

"Have I ever been wrong before?"

"Remember the time you were going to shake down that vagrant, but he turned out to be a ghoul? You nearly lost your hand."

"Yeah, okay, but just that once."

"What about when you forced me to drink that Chinese absinthe so we wouldn't offend our informant? You said we would we be fine. We both retched for three days straight."

Quinn laughed. "Yeah. Sorry about that one. Okay, okay. Maybe I have been wrong once or twice."

I smiled at him. "Have you told Greystock?"

"Not yet."

I nodded.

"At least now I'll be able to grow out my beard in peace."

"Retiring is no excuse for growing out a beard," Jessica said as she entered the room carrying a tray. She set it on a table near the window. "Eat," she told me. "I know you're going to give me some excuse about needing to leave or being busy, but eat first. Grandmother Louvel would never forgive me if I didn't feed you."

I smiled at her then rose and went to the table. My mouth watered to see the freshly baked scones, clotted cream, and jam. I tore into the food at once.

"Just like Quinn. Your stomach is upside down. You don't know if it's night or day."

"At least my stomach isn't literally upside down," I said through a mouthful of scone. I winked at Quinn.

"Very funny," he said then shook his head.

"Agent humor," Jessica said with a roll of her eyes. She turned her attention back to her husband. Sitting on the bed beside him, she slipped his hand into hers. Quinn gave her a long, loving look. She leaned in and set a kiss on his forehead. The power of their love was tangible.

My cheeks full of scone, I sighed enviously.

I really needed to find a man.

"Hey, Quinn, how is your brother, Robert?"

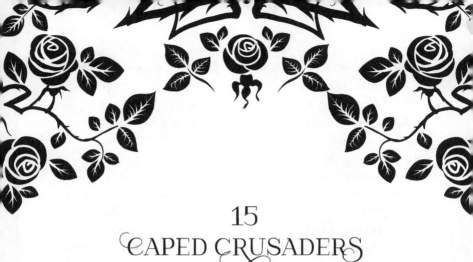

15
CAPED CRUSADERS

I LEFT QUINN'S HOUSE JUST AS DUSK APPROACHED. Apparently, I'd nodded off at some point because I'd awoken at the table with scone crumbles on my shirt listening to Quinn snore as Jessica sat quietly in the corner sewing. In a hurry, I made my way back to the tram and to the city.

The worst thing about my beat was the fact that I hardly ever got any sleep.

Well, that and the werewolves.

And the fact that my partner, who I relied upon to keep me alive, had decided to call it quits.

That meant I'd either get landed with someone I didn't particularly like or have to train someone new. Neither option sounded appealing. Quinn was like an overbearing older brother. I was going to miss him terribly, but I could hardly blame him. Not everyone could do what we did. You'd have to be half mad to want to.

Barking mad, in fact.

I laughed at my own joke. Yeah, it was going to be hard to find a partner who was a good match for me.

As soon as I returned to the heart of the city, I headed to

the airship towers and took the lift up. The towers were divided into multiple platforms; the third platform at the top of the towers housed the big airships that traveled abroad. On the platforms below were the smaller transports and the occasional pleasure cruiser. A floating brothel, such vessels had been widely popular twenty years before. Since Victoria came to reign, however, they'd come under tighter restrictions and were far less common. Nothing, however, stopped the scoundrel airship pirates from docking in London. They always had some excuse, permit, or reason to be there—none of them lawful. That happened to work out very well for me this particular evening.

I headed down the platform on the second level on the airship tower. Spotting a vessel that looked like it was about ready to debark, I went to the side of the ship and whistled to the captain.

I cast a quick glance at the name of the vessel: *Elven Rue.* Odd name.

"*Oui, mademoiselle?*" one of the crew members said.

Having been raised by a French grandmother, I was suddenly very glad that I was fluent in both French and English.

"Mind making a small detour? I need a lift," I said in French.

The man frowned then relayed my question to the captain.

"*Non,*" the captain said. "We're in a hurry. I won't be stopping at any other ports. I want to get across the Channel before dawn."

"I don't need a port. I need a quick drop-off. Just a pause in your departure. That's all," I said then produced a bag of coin. I needed to remember to put in for some reimbursements. Between buying off goblins and airship pirates, it was beginning to be an expensive week.

The man sighed. "Dropped off where?"

"The shipyard," I said, motioning over my shoulder.

The man furrowed his brow. "Just walk."

I smirked. "Not quite what I had in mind," I said.

The captain eyed me suspiciously then waved for me to come aboard, his hand outstretched.

"A rope down to a roof. I'll be off your ship before you know it," I said, handing him my bag of coin.

"A roof?"

"Yes."

He shook his head then went back to the wheelstand. I lingered behind him. The airship lifted up and out of port.

"There," I said, pointing to the hangar where I'd seen the pack earlier that day.

The airship turned as if it was merely preparing to round the towers and set out on its course.

The captain locked the wheelstand and motioned for me to follow him to the side of the ship. He yanked on a rope, ensuring it was safely secured to the deck, then handed the line to me.

"Your getaway, *mademoiselle*," he said with a grin.

I nodded and went to the side of the ship.

From this angle, I could see inside the hangar but would remain unseen. I tossed the rope over and looked down, ensuring that it fell close to an area with solid footing. The captain had marked the location well, putting me just at the corner and out of sight from anyone who happened to gaze up.

I climbed up on the rail of the ship and grabbed the rope. I nodded to the captain and holding on tight, slipped down the rope to the building below, landing as softly as possible on the roof.

Quinn would have loved this.

Well, the old Quinn would have loved this. Now my partner was cut up and lying in bed looking ashen. And Agent

Reid, who'd been a good colleague and fearsome vampire slayer, was dead. Who in the hell was this werewolf, Marlowe?

Overhead, the propeller on the airship *Elven Rue* clicked on, and the ship turned south. The rope disappeared back onto the deck. As the ship turned, I eyed the captain who removed his cap, lifted it in farewell, then guided his airship back into the night.

Moving quickly, I worked my way toward one of the windows that looked below. Lying on my stomach, I pulled out my spyglass and looked inside.

Cyril and Fenton were standing just inside the hangar door having an argument. Cyril, who was at least two hands taller than Fenton, shoved his beta. Fenton lowered his head in submission and stepped back.

Bloody wolves.

I eyed Cyril closely. Ginger nightmare. His neck was as big around as my waist. He was much larger than Fenton or Lionheart. His raw force and tendency to use violence for any solution were what had kept him in power for many years.

But it had also cost him.

Rumor had it that Cyril's last mate had run off with their son, fled to the Americas after Cyril had shown signs that he would be no easier on his own blood than he was on anyone else. It had been twenty years now. Despite his power, no she-wolf ever went willingly to him, including Alodie. More than once, Quinn and I had turned his pack away from human brothels for fear of what might happen to the human girls when the wolves were done with them. It was sick business. I admired Lionheart's ability to curb his urges, even if he did pick up on the scent of roses every now and then.

I heard the sound of an auto pull up in front of the hangar. A moment later, another wolf opened a side door. It was Damien, a wolf from Conklin pack. He rushed across the room to Fenton. Once again, a sharp conversation erupted.

I looked away from the pair and scanned the place for Marlowe. I found him in a corner with Professor Jamison. The professor's long, silver hair trailed down her back. She looked disheveled and exhausted. Marlowe slid his finger across some lines on a scroll then directed the professor's attention to the text.

I sat back.

The wolves already had long lives. If they became immune to silver, there would be no stopping them.

We had to end this work before it was too late.

I kept up my surveillance, waiting for Templar pack to arrive.

The materials Professor Jamison and Master Winston had been working with were being boxed up, while Marlowe nagged Cyril to the point of irritation. I watched as the lesser pack members headed back and forth across the yard toward the airship towers, pushing pallets of crates with them. Using my spyglass, I watched the wolves take the boxes to a ship and load them aboard. The wolves were planning to leave.

I had already started to strategize how I might take on the entire pack—and probably die in the process, a prospect that was not too appealing—when the palms of my hands got that strange tingly feeling. Aside from the werewolves below, the yard was fairly well deserted. Only the occasional drunken airship crewman passed by. Regardless, something was coming. Standing, I looked back across the skyline toward Tinker's Tower. It was nearly midnight. The moonlight shimmered down on the rooftops, giving everything a sheen of blue.

In the far-off distance, I heard a howl.

And then another.

I cast a glance inside. The wolves below stilled, then Fenton started rounding up the humans.

"Put out the lamps," Cyril called. "Get the alchemists on the airship."

"Red Capes?" Damien called.

Cyril craned his neck to breath in the air. "No," he said with a low and mean growl.

I looked back across the yard. Shadows shifted, yet I could see nothing, not even the telltale red eyes of werewolves.

Working quickly, I dug into my bag and grabbed the night optic array. Pulling it on, I looked below. I closed my right eye, looking through the optic with my left. Cyril's wolves moved to guard the doors. I saw them shift and change into werewolf form. But in the back, Marlowe, Fenton, and the humans were preparing to make an escape.

From the darkness somewhere around the yard, I heard a low, dark howl.

The sound chilled me to the bone. While the sound was not human, I knew it was Lionheart.

A series of howls answered in reply.

"Christ, boss. What's happening?" I heard Damien ask.

"Templars," Cyril said. I could hear the sneer in his voice.

The murmuring voices of the wolves below became silent.

"We should retreat," Damien said.

The sound of the smack was audible. "Say that again, and I'll kill you myself."

"Cyril," someone called.

The boss moved toward the front of the hangar.

"Christ," Damien said again.

I moved to the front of the building to see what had caught the wolves' attention then gasped when I saw. I pushed up my night optic for just a moment.

There, in the yard before the hangar, stood the Knights Templar. Not a pack of werewolves or a gang of men. Something in between. Two dozen armed soldiers wearing the white capes with the red cross of the Templars stood ready for battle, their leader at the front. All of them armed, not just with long claws, fangs, and muscle, but with helmets, swords, and shields.

Their gold-colored armor had been smelted to fit their physique in shifted form. The moonlight glinted off their armor. They were a magnificent sight to behold.

"Screw them. Open fire," Cyril called.

The front door slid open so Cyril's werewolves could attack.

Lionheart, who'd been standing at the front of his men, motioned to the knights and in a blur of swirling white and red capes, the Knights Templar swarmed the hangar.

I slipped on my night array lens once more then turned and ran back to the open window. I grabbed a chain attached to a lever and slipped inside.

Fenton and Marlow rushed the alchemists out the back door.

I cast a glance back at Lionheart and the Templars. I didn't want to leave the werewolf. Everything depended on him defeating Cyril. Everything. But if I didn't go after Marlowe now, and the werewolf got away, I'd end up chasing him all across the realm.

Looking back one more time, I spied Lionheart amongst the fray.

He paused, nodded to me, and then turned once more, his blade glimmering in the moonlight.

I turned and raced to the back of the hangar. I knew where Fenton and Marlowe were headed. I just needed to get there in time and figure out how I was going to kill a werewolf mage and a beta all at once.

16
ALPHA
AND OMEGA

PUMPING MY LEGS HARD, I RACED BACK TO THE AIRSHIP towers. In the distance, I heard that someone had raised the alarm and was calling for the Bow Street boys. I shook my head. Complications. Always, complications.

When I got to the towers, I saw that Marlowe and the others had already boarded the lift to take them up to the second level. I turned and raced up the steps, eyeing the airship the wolves had been packing up.

Dammit. They were already pulling up the anchor. The balloon of the airship filled with hot air, making the balloon glow with orange light. The ship made ready for departure. Fenton and the others hurried down the ramp. When Professor Jamison struggled, Fenton clocked her on the back of her head with his pistol then threw her over his shoulder.

Marlowe cursed loudly at him.

I arrived at the last step, turning the corner just in time to see the crew pull up the last lead rope.

Hell's bells. I was too late.

If I shot out the balloon, the ship would crash, killing the very people I was trying to rescue. I eyed the platform.

Jumping onto the ship that had been docked just behind the werewolves' craft, I raced to the bow of that airship. I pulled out my silver dagger, sliced a supporting rope, and then swung from that airship to the werewolves' craft.

My stomach rocked as I swung haphazardly through the air between the ships. There was far too much space between me and the earth below. Pushed by the force of my acceleration, I swung over the back of the airship, dropping onto the deck before the rope lost its forward velocity.

But my landing was not subtle. I hit the deck hard.

"Little Red," one of the werewolves yelled then turned toward me.

Taking aim, I shot.

Having taken them by surprise, the werewolves, who were still in human form—so not to alert the airship guards, I supposed—were slow to react. All the better for me. I was able to get off three shots before I heard the door to the captain's cabin open.

Fenton and Marlowe emerged.

Fenton moved to lunge at me, but Marlowe raised his hand, making him pause.

"Kit Marlowe," I said. "Her Majesty asked me to remind you that you were sent into exile. Your sentence has not been commuted nor revoked. If you would kindly re-exile yourself— and I can assist you if you will not—then all this drama can come to an end."

The old werewolf laughed. "Tell Her Majesty I am disinclined to agree. As for you," he said, then whispered something softly, making a strange arcane figure in the air, "I think I'm quite done with bravado."

A strange feeling washed over me, and quite against my will, I felt myself moving toward the side of the ship as if pushed by a gust. I gasped. The mage had cast a spell on me. Pulling away with all my might, I sought to resist the spell.

The mage frowned then whispered again, once more drawing the invisible arcane symbol.

I tried to lift my arm, trying to get my weapon on the monster so I could get off a shot, but my arm felt so heavy. It seemed as if it was being pressed down a thousand men. Yet slowly, inch by inch, I lifted my gun.

"What is this?" Marlowe said through gritted teeth. "What are you doing?" This time, he spoke aloud, shouting his spell in Latin.

I resisted once more, but could not break out of the spell as I felt myself slowly sliding toward the open plank. If I didn't break free, I would be thrown to my death.

Fenton laughed, "Goodbye, Little Red."

"No," I whispered. "No!" I resisted with all my might. I closed my eyes. *No.* In that single moment, I felt something powerful flutter alive inside me. The power was something larger than me, greater than me, but soft, gentle, no lighter than a butterfly. But this deep power, delicate as it might have been, was made of sturdy silver.

I stopped cold.

"No," Marlowe said, glaring at me. "It cannot be."

A split second later, a strange sound distracted me. I heard wings and the squeaking sound of bats. Gasping, I looked back to see a massive black swarm of bats cover the deck of the airship. In that single moment, two of the remaining wolves screamed and fell over the side of the vessel. A moment later, moving in a torrent, the bats swirled then disappeared, leaving behind Agent Rose and Constantine.

Fenton growled. Seeing the hopelessness of the situation, the coward grabbed a rope on the deck of the ship, then swung off, leaving Marlowe alone.

Marlowe glared at Constantine then started casting another incantation.

"Constantine," Agent Rose warned, but she didn't need to

say anything. With strength that impressed and frightened me, the vampire flew across the deck of the ship, picked up the mage, then sank his fangs deep into the werewolf's neck.

There werewolf's spell died in his throat. To my horror, I watched as the vampire sucked the wolf's blood, the werewolf's body shrinking in his hands like he'd been left to dry in the sun.

Pulling myself away from the terrible sight, I raced to the side of the ship and watched as Fenton disappeared back into the night.

"Hell's bells," I swore then turned and looked around for another rope.

At that same moment, I realized the ship was descending. Quickly.

I scanned around. No captain. No balloonman.

"Clemeny, the ship," Agent Rose said.

"The tinkers are inside," I said, pointing to the captain's cabin.

Understanding, she nodded. "Go. Go. We've got this."

Grabbing the rope, I turned and jumped off the airship. I slipped down the rope and landed on the rooftop below. Slipping on my night optic, I caught sight of Fenton as the werewolf turned and ran away from the airship towers back into the city in the direction of Tinker's Tower and Trafalgar Square.

Gritting my teeth, I turned and raced behind him.

He wouldn't get away that easy.

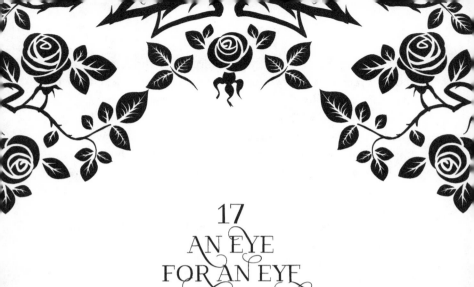

17
AN EYE FOR AN EYE

I COULD HEAR THE SOUND OF MY BOOTS HITTING THE cobblestone, the beating of my heart, and the telltale grunt of the werewolf racing ahead of me. If I let Fenton get away, I was failing everyone. I was failing to avenge Quinn and Agent Reid, endangering Lionheart, and putting the Society at risk. There was no way Marlowe could have survived Constantine's terrible revenge. But letting Fenton get away meant war between the packs. As vexing as Lionheart was, I now understood his true nature. He was a knight. That had never changed. He had acted because his monarch had told him to.

Fenton howled loudly then scurried up the side of a building. I raced behind him, scampering up a ladder and onto a rooftop.

Now we were on familiar ground.

He hung from a church steeple and glared back at me, his eyes fiery red.

I pulled my pistol, steadied my breath, and forced my heart to be silent as I trained my weapon on the figure silhouetted against the moonlight.

Inhale.

Exhale.

Taking aim, I pulled the trigger.

Too late.

He turned and raced off across the rooftops.

"Hell's bells," I swore through gritted teeth then took off after him. My heart pounded in my chest as I leaped from the rooftop across the alley. When I landed, the tiles under my footfall broke and went crashing down to the cobblestones below.

Ahead of me, the wolf barked, a sound that almost sounded like a laugh. The beast looked back over his shoulder at me, his eyes glimmering red as rubies in the moonlight.

I gritted my teeth, realizing then that the werewolf was moving with purpose. But to where? We raced past Tinker's Tower then into the city and up the Strand.

Fenton jumped to the street below.

A horse whinnied loudly, and a moment later, a woman screamed.

I rushed across the roof, balancing on a loading beam above the door of the tannery, then grabbed a rope and dropped onto the street.

And then, because apparently, I was some kind of idiot, I raced in the direction of the monster and the screams rather than away from them.

Grand-mère would have called me a fool.

Grand-mère.

The wolf looked back at me, his teeth bared but a wickedly gleeful expression on his face.

Oh no. No, no, no.

Wolves had keen hearing and a sense of smell that was without compare. Had Fenton trailed me? Did the packs know where my grand-mère lived?

Of course, they did.

Of course.

We raced down the Strand, past the theatres, St Mary-le-Strand, and then toward Saint Clement Danes.

There was no doubt in my mind where he was headed. There was only one person in this world I truly cared about save Quinn, only one bargaining chip a werewolf could hold over my head, and the werewolf was headed on a straight course toward her.

But this was my neighborhood.

I turned, slipping down a side alley. I turned right then left, rushing down a narrow passageway, through a stable, and into a side alley that would exit onto the street between me and the building in which my grandmother lived.

I burst out of the alley and onto the street just as Fenton turned the corner.

Pulling both my pistols, I took aim at the monster.

"Stop," I said commandingly.

The wolf slid to a stop then eyed the windows of the building. He could make the jump, crash through the window, and grab my grand-mère if he wanted. I flicked an eye upward and caught sight of her silhouette through the curtain. He could do that, but not before I shot him first. It was dark, but the optic I wore outlined the monster perfectly.

I could feel him watching me. I could feel him waiting to see what I was going to do.

"Come on now, Fenton. No need to make it personal. Let's go back to headquarters and have a chat."

"Not going to happen, Little Red," he said, his voice was raspy. "You let me go. Now. Or I'll rip out dear granny's throat."

I frowned. "Now, we both know that's not an option. Cyril is, no doubt, dead by now. Marlowe as well, or did you miss Constantine making a snack out of that crusty old bugger?

Speaking of, even if I don't end you now, the vampire will likely hunt you down and kill you. I have some nice silver cuffs here. Let me go ahead and slip them on. Show Her Majesty you're willing to talk. Maybe she'll let you rot away somewhere, spare your miserable life."

"Or, you holster those pistols, and I walk."

"I can't do that."

"You aren't leaving me with options, Little Red," he said then looked up at the window once more.

I pulled the hammers back on my pistols.

The werewolf growled, his anger boiling. "You must be either be really brave or really stupid."

"Probably a bit of both, I confess," I said. I closed my right eye, looking through the optic on the left. I could see him even more clearly this way. There was no way that werewolf would get past me.

"Shame to kill you. You're too pretty. Wonder if you taste as good as you smell."

Again with the smell. His odd comment threw me off guard.

The beast crouched then lunged at me.

Dammit.

Taking aim, I shot at the monster.

The beast yelped but came at me again. I shot once more, but he kept coming. I felt my breath go out of me as the were-wolf slammed me to the ground. My pistols bounced out of my hands as I hit the cobblestone hard.

A slathering face, half-man half-wolf, looked down at me as he pinned me to the ground. He was bleeding profusely from both his stomach and his left shoulder. He barred his teeth, slobber dripping onto me as he glared down at me. He eyed the optic I wore.

Sneering, he slashed the device off my face.

I screamed as his claws raked my face.

But at that same moment, my instincts kicked in. I reached into my belt and grabbed the silver dagger that I always wore. Squeezing my hand around the blade tightly, feeling the silver sing in response to my touch, I heaved it with all my might and slammed it into the werewolf's chest.

Fenton let out a strange howl that quickly faded into a gurgle then tipped over, falling off me.

Gasping, I sat up.

I couldn't see out of my left eye. Blood was dripping down my face. I quickly grabbed a scarf from my pocket and held it against my eye. Fenton lay on the street. He had transformed fully into wolf form as they all did when they were dead.

Sneering, I knelt beside him.

"This is for Quinn," I said then sinking my silver blade into his flesh, I skinned off a massive piece of silver fur from his hide.

I rose then, my knees shaking, and looked up at the window.

Grand-mère was pressed against the glass. When she saw it was me, she screamed.

Black spots swam before my eyes, and I tumbled to my knees. I stared down at the silver blade in my hand. Strange. Through the hazy vision of my bloody eye, the blade shimmered blue.

The front door opened. "Clemeny," Grand-mère screamed, rushing into the street. She scooped me up in her arms. "Clemeny, oh my God."

"Send word to Greystock," I whispered.

"Clemeny? Clemeny! Missus Rossiter, send for a surgeon," Grand-mère called to a neighbor who must have come outside to see what all the commotion was about.

"Is that a wolf? A wolf? In the streets of London?" the woman replied, astonished.

"Stupid woman, send for a surgeon!" Grand-mère demanded then turned her attention back to me. "You're all right now, my girl. Don't you worry. You got that old sinner. Don't worry, I'm here," she said.

And then I fainted in her arms.

18
WHO'S AFRAID OF THE BIG, BAD WOLF?

I WOKE IN A TOO-BRIGHT ROOM WITH AN AWFUL HEADACHE. I opened my eyes slowly, but a sharp pain rocked my left eye so terribly that I let out a little whine.

"Agent, don't try to open your left eye. Let me go fetch the doctor. Just lie back and rest."

"Where am I?" I eyed the woman carefully, noting the pin on her lapel, the initials R.M. encapsulated in a circle. She worked for the Rude Mechanicals.

"Newstead Abbey," she said then turned and left.

Newstead Abbey? What in the world was I doing in Nottingham?

My whole body ached. I reached up and touched my face. There were bandages on my cheek and forehead, and my entire eye was covered.

I closed my good eye and lay back.

I heard footsteps and voices in the hallway. A moment later, the door to my room opened. Someone sat down at the side of my bed and took my hand. I opened my eye a crack to see Agent Greystock sitting there.

"Clemeny," she said softly.

"Agent Greystock. How is Grand-mère Louvel? Is she all right?"

"Fine, fine," Agent Greystock said. "Angry with me, but fine."

"What happened?"

"Fenton. You were gravely injured. The surgeon informed us you may have lost use of your eye permanently. And... you have a scratch on your face, from your hairline to your cheek."

I paused a moment. "I... I meant with Lionheart and the others. Is everyone all right?" While my chief concern had not been about my own injuries—it was plain to me that I was banged up—I considered her words. The wounds she described were both severe and disfiguring.

Agent Greystock nodded. "Agent Rose reported in," she said then shook her head. "Willful girl. Bold, brave, but reckless. Cyril is dead. Marlowe is dead. Lupercal pack... They're either dead or arrested, as are Whitechapel, Conklin, and Paddington."

"Arresting werewolves won't do much to ease their seething anger."

"No, but deporting them to Australia will. They will either accept the new alpha, or they will take a long ride bound in silver to the colony of thieves."

"The new alpha... Lionheart?"

Agent Greystock nodded, but she looked pensive. "For now, at least. He is adamant that he doesn't want to retain the role. He met with Her Majesty. I was there. It was a *difficult* conversation. But he inquired about you and sent his wishes for your speedy recovery."

"He's not half bad, for a werewolf."

Agent Greystock smiled lightly, but I could see her mind was still troubled.

"What is it?" I asked.

"Clemeny... I can't forgive myself for what has happened to you, Quinn, and Agent Reid. I underestimated the packs—"

"We all did."

"No. I should have seen a larger problem was brewing. I missed it. I, well, I have asked for a transfer to archives."

"No."

"It's time for someone with more experience in the field, someone who will understand your work and the danger, to take charge. Her Majesty took my suggestions for a replacement into consideration. She has selected an agent based out of Scotland who comes highly recommended and is well known for hunting demons. By the time you recover, he'll be on the job."

"But Agent Greystock... First Quinn and now you? The job won't be the same."

"No. But Lionheart will need you. Her Majesty will need you. A smooth exchange of power must take place, or there will be chaos. The Red Cape Society must take a prominent role, and word on the street is that *Little Red* is the most feared werewolf hunter in London. I need you back to work. Agent Hunter will be expecting you to report in as soon as you are fully recovered."

"Agent Hunter?"

"Your new commanding officer."

I frowned. "Sounds like a prat."

Agent Greystock chuckled. "Well, I guess you'll have to see for yourself. There is a lot of work ahead of you. Whichever wolves Her Majesty doesn't send off to enjoy the wilds of Australia will be turned loose back on the street with nothing more than a promise that they will behave and follow the leadership of the new alpha."

"Highly unlikely, you know."

"Of course. That's why you need to recover soon. London has always had a werewolf problem. It will be up to you to keep them in check. Get some rest, Clemeny. Her Majesty needs you," she said with a smile then turned and headed back out of the room.

I lay back on my pillow and closed my good eye.

It would be all right.

Lionheart would get the packs in check, and I would get any outliers in hand. I'd recover and be back on the street in no time. Fenton was gone. And despite whatever ugly mess was under my bandages, nothing would stop me from keeping the streets of London safe.

I had never been afraid of a big bad wolf.

And I wouldn't start now.

ACKNOWLEDGMENTS

Many thanks to Becky Stephens and Jessica Nelson for their help shaping this book.

A special thanks to all my Steampunk Fairy Tales ARC readers!

Thank you to Karri Klawiter for designing such a beautiful cover.

Thanks to Mark Fisher and my friends at Electromagnetic Press for hauling my books all over the country!

As always, thank you to the BIC group, Carrie Wells, Erin Hayes, Margo Bond Collins, and my beloved family for all of your support.

ABOUT THE AUTHOR

Melanie Karsak is the author of *The Airship Racing Chronicles*, *The Harvesting Series, The Burnt Earth Series, The Celtic Blood Series*, and the *Steampunk Fairy Tales Series*. A steampunk connoisseur, zombie whisperer, and heir to the iron throne, the author currently lives in Florida with her husband and two children. She is an Instructor of English at Eastern Florida State College.

KEEP IN TOUCH WITH MELANIE ONLINE

MelanieKarsak.com
Facebook.com/AuthorMelanieKarsak
Twitter.com/MelanieKarsak
Pinterest.com/MelanieKarsak

Check out all of Melanie's *Steampunk Fairy Tales*
Beauty and Beastly: Steampunk Beauty and the Beast
Ice and Embers: Steampunk Snow Queen
Curiouser and Curiouser: Steampunk Alice in Wonderland

Ready to go airship racing? Meet Lily and her crew in *The Airship Racing Chronicles* (this series contains mature content)
Chasing the Star Garden
Chasing the Green Fairy

JOIN MELANIE'S NEWSLETTER

http://eepurl.com/cM53pv

Tango
A History of Obsession

Virginia Gift

Also by Virginia Gift
How the U.S. Fought and Lost the Vietnam War
Hanoi: Vietnam After the War

ISBN: 1-4392-1462-X
ISBN-13: 9781439214626

Visit www.amazon.com to order additional copies.

REVIEWS AND COMMENTS FOR
Tango – A History of Obsession

I recently read your new book and had to write you to tell you what a fantastic piece of work it is…you have really encapsulated the history of this dance and by doing so from the perspective of the "obsession," it is simply brilliant! The book gives a nice clear view into our world of Argentine Tango today as only a true tanguera could project…I feel it is a good educational tool for my students. You have done a great service to the community of Argentine Tango worldwide. *CRISTY COTE – San Francisco Performer/Choreographer/Instructor*

I love it and I'm impressed with the amount of research that went into it. It amazes me that anyone has time to assemble all of this information. I sent the following promotional blurb to 3,200 people on my email list: "Tango Enthusiasts, I'd like to call your attention to a new book by Virginia Gift called "Tango, A History of Obsession". This book (almost 500 pages) is the most complete and detailed account of tango's history that I've ever read. The author discusses tango from all aspects: musical, political, historical and philosophical but with an emphasis on the dance – as she is a tanguera herself. You'll find it well researched with many quotes and references from historical documents as well as from current dancers from all over the world." *CLAY NELSON – Portland, Oregon – Teacher/Organizer of Tango Festivals & Events*

This book is an informative, interesting and provocative discourse proving that the tango could never be simply an obsession. *GUSTAVO NAVEIRA – Buenos Aires – Teacher/ Performer/Choreographer/Creator of Tango Nuevo*

There are many tango books but *'Tango – A History of Obsession'* is a very special one. It kept me up reading even though I was tired from a great milonga night! A must for all dancers. *BRIGITTA WINKLER – Berlin and New York – Teacher/ Performer/Member of Tango Mujer*

This book is a serious, dedicated and precise analysis that encompasses the culture of tango. Read this book to know the enduring history of tango. *RODOLPHO DINZEL – Buenos Aires - Teacher/ Performer/Author/Member of original cast of 'Tango Argentino'*

I am impressed with the quality of the writing. It is a terrific book and I will do a bang-up job telling everyone who pauses in my path on or off the dance floor. *Lucille Krasne – New York City – Organizer of 'Esmeralda's Milonga'/ Organizer of Tango Festivals & Events in NYC/Creator of 'Hit & Run Tango'*

Virginia, I am reading your book now and I find it very interesting and entertaining. I hope you sell a lot of them at my Tangoweek. *NORA DINZELBACKER – San Francisco – Nora's Tangoweek*

The section on the contemporary tango scene is the best that has been written; the only one that is truly up-to-date. It's fabulous! An easy read with a serious academic approach. *BOB MACKENZIE – San Francisco – Tanguero/ TV Journalist*

*"Any day that passes in which you
have not danced at least once
should be considered a lost day."*

(Friedrich Nietzsche, 1844-1900)

*"The tango is a dance of indescribable beauty, with the
finesse of ballet and the fire of flamenco."*

(Michael Baryshnikov, 1985)

DEDICATION

*To my three favorite tango partners: Frederic Barez
in France, Miguel Bejarano in Mexico and to the
memory of Anna Maya Theys of Finland. We started
out sharing joys and miseries on the dance floor and
ended up fast friends.*

*I'll be forever grateful to tango luminaries Rodolpho
Dinzel and Gustavo Naveira for the many hours they
spent with me sharing their experiences and thoughtful
analyses of the intricacies of the tango world.*

Tango.

PREFACE
'GOTTA' DANCE

"Tango is nothing if not transformative."
(Chiori Santiago, Writer, The Smithsonian,
"The Tango is More Than a Dance")

While researching this book, I came across an article titled "Born to Dance" that reported on experiments and observations by scientists who were examining the genetics of professional dancers, trying to determine why some people seem to need to dance while others don't. I felt it gave me an excuse for my new found passion and it explained why I found myself living part-time in Northern Mexico, retired after more than a forty years as a history teacher, happily ensconced in a new endeavor. I had morphed into a part-time professional Argentine Tango performer and teacher. How did I get so lucky?

I cannot remember not loving to dance. When I was five years old, living in a small town in rural Pennsylvania, there was great excitement when we learned that we were to have a visiting tap dance teacher. I don't know where the teacher came from; it was in the middle of the Depression, so perhaps he was an out-of work dancer from New York City. My father's salary could not have been good working for the WPA but I, the only child, begged to take lessons, so somehow the money appeared for this luxury. We purchased the necessary metal taps, installed them on a pair of my shoes, and I joined the tap class. I loved it, and drove my parents and Aunt Arlene, who boarded with us, quite mad with my constant, morning to night, tapping around the house. I am not sure how long the visiting teacher stayed around, but no one replaced him when he left, and that was the end of my tap dancing. In high school and college, I danced regularly during lunch hours, after school, and on weekends. (There really wasn't anything else to do in this small town.) During my teaching years, I kept up my interest in dance by choreographing school musicals and chaperoning high school dances.

Once, when visiting New York City, trying to decide what to do with a free evening, I noticed that *Forever Tango* was playing in a downtown theater. I remembered reading rave reviews when it played in Paris, where I lived at the time, but when I considered watching people dance only one style of dance for several hours, I thought it might be a tad boring. (Of course I knew nothing about tango and I did not realize that tango is actually many different types of dances and music.) However, I decided that because the reviews had all been so highly favorable, I should attend. Five minutes after the lights went out and the Sexteto Mayor began playing its amazing music, and although the dancing had not even begun, I was hooked on tango. Once the dancers appeared on stage, I told myself that as soon as I returned home to Paris, I would take tango lessons.

Once back in Paris, I located a dance studio that taught all types of dance, including Latin dances. I signed up and stuck it out through the Cha-Cha, Mambo, and Rumba, waiting to get to the tango. I was very disappointed because it was nothing like the dance I had seen on the stage. When I mentioned this to the teacher, she and several of the students said, "Oh, you want the ARGENTINE Tango."

I eventually found some Argentine tango teachers and to my surprise, tango was not as easy to learn as it was to watch. So I became a 'tango junkie.' Some days I took two classes back to back and when I could afford it, I would squeeze in private lessons. With other students from my classes, we would frequently finish a class, change our shoes and then run to the metro to go to another lesson in another part of town. My days became oriented around tango, and before long I was neglecting my research project for a book on 17th century Vietnam, which was my area of teaching speciality, but now my primary interest was to become proficient in the tango. I attended numerous workshops and tango festivals and then felt the next logical step was Buenos Aires, where I worked every day with one of tango's greatest names, Rodolfo Dinzel. Since then, I have been spending six to eight weeks a year in Buenos Aires.

At first I stayed in tango guesthouses or shared rental apartments with one or two American friends I had met at international festivals. When visiting Buenos Aires, invariably I run into Argentine, Parisian or American friends, so there is never a shortage of company to attend milongas, practicas or lessons.

How, in my late seventies, did I become a tango teacher and performer? Pure serendipity.

I bought a small adobe house in an isolated, famous pottery village in northern Mexico thinking it would be a good place to write my history books. When American tourist groups came through, I frequently inquired if anyone danced Argentine Tango, and on a few occasions, I hit it lucky. At such times, the visiting dancer and I would nearly always perform a demonstration in the local Posada, local restaurant, or in my house.

One day an American friend living in my village brought me a flyer he had taken from a store window in the nearest large town, Nuevo Casas Grandes; it was an advertisement for the commencement of a tango class. I telephoned the teacher, Miguel Bejarano, and asked if it was the Argentine Tango. When his answer was vague, I was sure it was the Ballroom version. He said he was an experienced folk dance teacher who taught at the nearby university, at various public schools, and at the cultural center of Nuevo Casas Grandes, and had taken social dance lessons including tango, in Chihuahua City. I told him I was only interested in 'Argentine' tango, and we agreed to meet. When we tried dancing together, it was clear he was a good dancer with excellent rhythm, and since I was desperate to have a dancing partner in Mexico, I offered to teach him Argentine Tango. He immediately fell in love with the tango and all its possibilities and we soon were experimenting with sophisticated movements, laughed at our mistakes, while enjoying ourselves immensely.

Because of Miguel's widespread reputation as a teacher and performer of Mexican folk dances, we were invited to perform at a dance festival in Nuevo Casas Grandes in an enormous nightclub filled with several hundred spectators. The audience was only familiar with Mexican country music and dance so we were an exotic success. I got my first taste of show business and applause. I loved it.

After that, we were in demand to give performances at festivals and celebrations of all sorts. I have turned into a terrible ham, with elongated leg extensions and elaborate firuletes (small foot movements). It is not quite Broadway, but the Mexican audiences are very enthusiastic and enjoy the music and dance; applause is always loud and long.

Talk about "fifteen minutes of fame." People now recognize me in the streets or restaurants and often ask me for my autograph. Once, after a free outdoor local festival performance in Nuevo Casas Grandes, I was touched when a very old toothless man dressed in ragged clothes came up to me with tears in his eyes, and took both my hands in his and told me he had never seen anything so beautiful.

In retrospect, I consider myself lucky to be where I am, with new friends, a new passion, and most likely an addiction which is not physically harmful, and is probably even good for me. I decided to write about my experiences in the hope that readers might find the history and obsession of the Argentine Tango as interesting as the dance itself and perhaps be encouraged to try it.

INTRODUCTION

How a Dance Brought Social, Political, and Economical Change to Argentina

"Anything that makes its mark in the world,
anything that turns people on in the way
tango has in the 20th century,
is worth looking at and worth asking how it
does that and why it does that."
(Simon Collier, Historian, Vanderbilt University)

Few people outside Argentina are aware that the tango, long recognized as the most sophisticated and elegant of partnered social dances, had its origins over 150 years ago in the slums of Buenos Aires as a partnered dance between men. There is a split in tango communities that sharply divides dancers obsessed with dance and others, primarily academics, musicians, singers and assorted intellectuals, who obsess over the music and lyrics, but care little for the dance.

The tango was originally a dance forbidden outside the slums of Buenos Aires, invented by poverty-stricken male, European immigrants who went to Argentina at the end of the nineteenth century to escape religious and political persecution. They worked in the slaughterhouses by the Rio de la Plata, living next to equally poor gauchos (Argentine cowboys) who had been displaced from their rural pampas, freed Black slaves, and destitute Spaniards who hadn't made it in Argentine society. They mixed with sailors on leave and the soldiers from a nearby Army barracks, crammed together in dark tenements seeking company and fresh air in the courtyards and sidewalks. Some had brought part of their cultural heritage from their homelands in the form of musical instruments: violins, guitars, flutes, and the bandoneon. Outside on the sidewalks and courtyards, they communicated with each other through music they improvised and because of the shortage of women, the men amused themselves by dancing with each other to the emerging new form of music. The dance they invented was the tango.

In spite of its humble origins, the tango went on to become an "icon" for an entire, huge nation. What other country has named its presidential plane after a dance? Or has annual holidays to celebrate it and various tango artists? What other social dance is officially taught for credit at its National Naval Academy? Or has built an enormous metal statue of the dance's signature musical instrument, the bandoneon, in mid-city?

Social dancing has been around since people began walking and has served as a means of communication without words to celebrate communal events, such as a successful hunting or warrior expedition, or joyful or sad emotions. There are folk or national dances that have been alive for centuries, some of which have captured international attention such as the polka, the flamenco, the Irish and Scottish dances, and the belly dancing of the Middle East. Most of these dances have remained provincial; they are exotic to watch, but outside their own countries they are normally restricted to national celebrations and theatrical performances, and have not attracted enormous numbers of foreigners to become interested enough to learn the dance and practice it in their own country. But tango touches something in people to make them want to learn to dance it, whether or not they have had previous dance experience.

Because men vastly outnumbered women in early Buenos Aires, men dancing together had no sexual connotation. After a while, they began to take dancing seriously, inventing new movements and trying to steal steps from competitors. Far from being effete, the dance became a more and more popular form of entertainment and was very much a macho activity: to dance tango better than anyone else was considered an admirable manly achievement. It still is.

In the first years of the 20th century, tango moved from the seedy barrios of Buenos Aires across the Atlantic into the highest levels of aristocratic Paris society. It took on a new image with men in tuxedos and women in elegant gowns. For three decades tango reigned as the most popular social dance in the major cities and resorts of Europe and North America. It became an unprecedented dance obsession referred to as "tangomania" and "tango fever," a fad in society salons, theaters, balls, cabarets and grand hotels. But social, political, and economic events worldwide overshadowed interest the tango.

Tango then went into a decline for the next 30 years only to be reborn in the mid-1980s with a new generation of passionate dancers. This new generation of tango came to be known as Argentine Tango. The 'old tango' of international fame, which is now called the Ballroom Tango, is still danced in many countries, except Argentina.

Ballroom Tango - Argentine Tango

A common saying among Argentine Tango dancers is: "The only thing that Ballroom Tango and Argentine Tango have in common is that two dancers face each other."

I am frequently asked by people not familiar with the tango about how to tell the difference between the Ballroom Tango and Argentine Tango. My response is always: 'If no one is smiling and the dancers look as if they are in pain, then it's the Argentine Tango."

What is called Ballroom Tango, originated when Great Britain was emerging from the Victorian Era. Many felt that the tango steps, with bodies rubbing up against each other, were not fit for polite society, and that the steps should be modified. To curb the fear by some that the cleaned-up tango might slip back to using unacceptable moves, British dance teachers codified the tango into mandatory patterns of six-eight steps (figuras) that had to be memorized and never, ever changed. In English-speaking countries, the British Tango was also called the International, American, or most commonly, the Ballroom Tango which became the obligatory style for national and international Ballroom Tango contests to this day.

Ballroom Tango rules are so exacting that they dictate the *degree* of each step, the positions of the arms and hands, the head snaps and tilt of the head, and the broad smile. Anything different is not acceptable. Ballroom Tango dancers are normally oriented towards competition, dancing only in schools, while Argentine Tango dancers go dancing in public or private dance halls. Argentine Tango dancers rarely have contests because it is too difficult to judge improvised dancing.

Jean Juillot, thirteen-time champion of French Ballroom Tango dancing wrote: "Ballroom dance has been codified since 1914 and has only about twenty-five basic movements used in each dance." Accredited Ballroom Tango instructors all teach by the same book, printed in over seventy languages, and there is little or no conflict about what is correct or acceptable. The standards of Ballroom Tango are unquestioned, as is the terminology. There is no discussion about what to call a movement, and any innovative changes must be approved by The World Dance & Dance Sport Council in London, England. In contrast, Rodolfo Dinzel, master teacher and performer of Argentine Tango, once decided to codify basic Argentine Tango figuras but wrote, "I stopped when I passed 3,000." In his book, *Tango and the Quest for Freedom*, he calls tango "a dance of options" because Argentine Tango dancers can invent new steps at any time and use any steps in any sequence.

Unlike Ballroom Tango dancers, Argentine Tango dancers never stop arguing about the dance, and many tango communities are in constant turmoil, quarreling either among themselves or on the internet. Ballroom Tango dancers are constantly concerned about making a wrong move, but Argentine Tango dancers don't have that worry about because as long as a step or movement is graceful and elegant, mistakes are not acknowledged. Some dancers have commented that if you make the same mistake twice, you've invented a new step.

Ballroom Tango is easier to learn because to become proficient, all you have to do is follow the rules. For example, Ballroom dancers must step to each beat, while Argentine Tango dancers have three choices: to step either to the beat, the melody, or mood of the music. Ballroom Tango partners mirror each other's steps, but Argentine Tango partners frequently dance very different, complicated steps at the same time. There are no written rules for Argentine Tango and no central organization to enforce them; no one oversees the quality of teaching. There is no central accreditation, so teachers are able to teach whatever they want, which is sometimes good news, sometimes bad news, which has resulted in the axiom "All you need to become an Argentine Tango teacher is a pair of dance shoes."

Argentine Tango dancers travel to other cities and countries for workshops and festivals in search of something new to see and try, but Ballroom Tango dancers have no incentive to travel because they are not permitted to stray from their choreographed movements. An internet contributor, Mr. Goldberg, lamented, "You can begin learning Ballroom Tango in England, take lessons in Tokyo, travel to Copenhagen or Australia and return to England and never receive anything but similar instruction by licensed instructors who teach by the same book."

Adherents of the Argentine Tango consider Ballroom Tango's inflexibility to be boring, or as one dancer said "All motion and no soul." Some Ballroom Tango dancers switch to Argentine Tango for fear of losing their freedom, but it is unheard of for Argentine Tango dancers to switch to Ballroom Tango.

Tango has again burst out of Argentina to the rest of the world but this time there is not the same awareness among the general public, and little of the frenetic activities of the previous "tangomania," perhaps because there are now so many other events competing for media attention. Today's tango phenomenon is more subtle, although in many ways it surpasses the earlier dance fad because globalization makes it easier to reach more people. New tango schools and venues for dancing are sprouting up all over the world; this time they are not restricted to important cities, but have invaded small towns and unlikely places such as Mongolia,

Nepal, Albania, South Africa, and China. Recently, Nora Dinzelbacher, a well-known Argentine teacher touring Japan for the first time, was amazed to find over 600 students in her class which was held in a gymnasium.

Today's Argentine Tango dancer learns not only from Argentine teachers who constantly circle the globe, but many travel to dance at regional, national, and international tango festivals that draw large numbers from all over the world. In Istanbul, there is a weekly weekend tango marathon, and in the Netherlands a popular once a month weekend marathon is attended by dancers from all over Europe; a small town in Finland, north of Helsinki, hosts an annual five-day tango festival with paying participants numbering over 120,000!

ACKNOWLEDGEMENTS

The very fact that this book exists is due to the support of a great number of people. I would like to thank:

My three sons. Although at times some questioned my sanity, and in spite of their perplexity, they have been helpful with suggestions and criticisms. I spent many years trying to persuade them to learn tango but with little success. ("We've seen what it's done to your life.") Christopher finally succumbed and took tango lessons several years ago when he came to visit me in Buenos Aires. As I expected, he became enchanted with it immediately and even bought tango shoes. (I'm still waiting for the other two sons to 'see the light.')

Daughters-in-law Karine and Sarah have been wonderfully encouraging and my young granddaughter Ada has already exhibited proof that she's going to be an excellent tango dancer. Barbara Kamm, a colleague from my teaching days in Paris, courageously spent countless hours in my living room attacking endless gaffes, misspellings, structural and grammatical errors. My former daughter-in-law, Mary Rabe, vastly improved the quality of the text with her creativity and panache. Lenny Porges valiantly corrected one of the later drafts and made excellent suggestions, as did Rob Young, University of Arizona, Tucson. Paul Sonnenburg helped with early drafts. Kathy Doyle was endlessly enthusiastic and helpful in her efforts for the drafting of this second edition and Ted Graham housed me while doing research in the Library of Congress.

Many dancers who become seriously involved in tango make some strong, long-lasting friendships. In the United States, Linda Lucas, of Washington, D.C., was a perfect partner at international workshops and was helpful in researching facts on her computer. Mary Jane Finley, of Phoenix, Arizona, and I meet occasionally to dance in Buenos Aires and other cities; she once traveled to my village in Mexico to perform and give tango lessons to appreciative locals. Berette Salazar, of St. Louis, Missouri, and I first met as roommates at a tango festival in Montreal. (Later we shared housing in Buenos Aires where, one day in July of 2001, we looked out our windows and saw the streets filled thousands of noisy people demonstrating by banging large spoons energetically against metal pots and pans, while piles of tires burned in the streets and police hurled smoking tear gas canisters. This turned out to be a general strike which brought much of the country to a standstill in protest against proposed government spending cuts).

In France, my lessons with the renown Imed Cheman, (argumentively the best tango teacher in Paris,) were pleasurable, sometimes painful, but always first rate, while Gilles Cuena helped improve dancing. In Paris, France's expert and author on tango lyrics, Fabrice Hatem, made useful suggestions. Chita Wilcox has been a welcome companion at milongas, and Jacqueline Friedrich, internationally recognized wine and food expert, practices dancing with me and has spent hour after hour listening to my complaints of writing about tango. Equally as patient with me: Ron Bowen, Danny Zarifian, Angelica Seppala, Elizabeth Landwerlin, Renee and Bill Bowen, Hal Halvorsen, Barbara Roush and David Graham.

ACKNOWLEDGEMENTS

In Mata Ortiz, Mexico, Steve Rose provided transportation and compiled music CD's (that were used in performances by my partner Miguel Bejarano and me,) and aided with my ongoing battles with the computer. Blanca Chinolla learned more than she wanted to know about tango as did Emi and Spencer MacCallum, all of whom frequently lent us practice space in their lovely adobe homes. Neighbors Anna and Ralph Malanga, Susan and John Pifer, and Barbara and Gordon Pierce asked about the book's progress and tried hard not to let their eyes glaze over when I answered them.

In Buenos Aires, tango-author and expert dancer, Julie Taylor, read parts of the manuscript and made useful suggestions; Luis Lencioni helped turn me into a passable dancer. I thoroughly enjoyed the company of dancers Silvia and Roberto Helguera throughout my many visits. I'm greatly indebted to dancer Dolores "Bimba" Juareguialzo, and her dancing pals; who took me with them to milongas and other festivities.

I want to thank all the acknowledged and unacknowledged contributors. Over the past eight years I circulated an informal questionnaire at tango events in the U.S., Europe and Buenos Aires; names were optional, although I did ask for gender, age, nationality, occupation and asked them to share their tango-related experiences. I have included a large number of quotations in the hope that dancers' own words would bring more immediacy to the content. There are also quotes from the Tango-L internet site of Massachusetts Institute of Technology and other internet sources. Other quotes are from my notes made at milongas, classes, workshops and tango festivals, where I shamelessly listened in on so many interesting and fascinating conversations.

TABLE OF CONTENTS

❦

CHAPTER ONE

The Obsession

"Tango is not a fashion but an addiction, a drug and as such the more you are exposed to it the more you become an addict."
(Miguel Angel Zotto, Tango Performer, Teacher)

One leading American dictionary defines "obsession" as a "compulsive preoccupation with a fixed idea"; another adds, "Obsession is a valid term to be applied when life styles and values alter drastically." By such criteria, around the world there are a great many obsessed Argentine Tango dancers, but some prefer the label "impassioned." Although other social dances certainly attract enthusiasts, few find their lives drastically changed because of the dance. With the tango, however, the dancer's passion, dedication, and devotion to his/her dance has become legendary.

One tango devotee reports, "I started dancing tango because I was trying out different dance modes. I tried swing, then Salsa...and when I hit tango there was no reason to move on." A telling instance is the story of the popular San Francisco television journalist Bob MacKenzie, "I decided to do a program on the tango fad in San Francisco. When interviewing dancers, I could see that the tango was so important to them that it filled their lives, and I thought that nothing like that could ever happen to me. Then one night after the program aired I ran into one of the dancers, who invited me to join him at a milonga (a tango dance). He persuaded me to try some basic steps and here I am a year later at a tango festival in Buenos Aires with my world turned upside down as I plan to sell my vacation home in California to buy an apartment in Buenos Aires."

Few dancers object to their passion being characterized as an addiction, and many speak of being "hooked" on tango as a positive development in their lives. Several years ago Portugal's ambassador to Argentina was informed that a group of thirty prominent Portuguese were coming to visit Buenos Aires expressly to dance the tango. Feeling that he ought to know something about the dance, he arranged to take tango lessons. Enchanted, the ambassador admits to having quickly become "thoroughly addicted."

Another San Franciscan, mechanical engineer Homer Ladas, saw a flyer for tango classes when he was twenty-seven, and signed up for lessons. "I was soon dancing ten hours a week, then fifteen, then twenty. At a tango festival in Amsterdam I danced twenty-six hours non-stop." After September 11, 2001, he took a leave of absence from his work to teach tango and never returned. Ten years after his first encounter with tango, he was running a popular milonga in San Francisco.

Engineer Marc Pianko was walking in downtown Paris and passed in front of the Argentine night club, *Trottoirs de Buenos Aires* (the sidewalks of Buenos Aires) and heard tango music coming from inside. He went inside to watch the dancing, was intrigued, and then sought out a place to take lessons. Eventually he and his wife founded the non-profit organization, *Te Temps du Tango,* which produces the prestigious bi-monthly tango magazine and promotes tango in France with weekly classes, frequent workshops, and large festivals at various sites in France throughout the year.

Echoing Mr. Pianko's experience, British film-maker Sally Potter first encountered tango while walking down the same Paris street and heard tango music coming from the same Argentine night club. Ms. Potter relates the experience of entering the club, watching the dancers awhile, speaking with the teacher, and signing up for private lessons on the spot. Before long, she dropped the film project on which she was working, went to Buenos Aires, and produced the award-winning film, *The Tango Lesson.*

When working on films, actor Robert Duvall frequently brings tango teachers onto his sets so that he, the cast, and the crew have something interesting to do during the long, boring intervals between takes. The star calls the tango his "hobby" and has taught tango classes at the Argentine Embassy in Washington, D.C. He also notes tango's ability to reduce stress, quipping, "It keeps you off the dope."

Canadian Pierre Lang of Montreal said, "My first encounter with tango came when a friend twisted my arm to go to a tango hall. When I put my feet on the dance floor, it was finished. I was condemned to dance the tango for the rest of my days." Today Mr. Lang owns a tango dance studio, edits a tango magazine, hosts a weekly milonga, frequents tango festivals, and is a leader of Montreal's thriving tango scene.

Marc Celaya of Los Angeles, wrote, "Twelve years ago my life was a mess; my wife split and I had no job. I decided to take swing lessons, but a friend talked me into going to a tango class. I was immediately hooked; a light went on in my head. Now tango fills my life. I teach and work as a professional tango DJ at milongas in California, and I produced the first tango show at the Hollywood Bowl."

Argentine actor Carlos Stazi began taking tango lessons in his forties, "I heard that producer Carlos Saura was going to cast Buenos Aires dancers for his film "Tango!" and I decided to try out. Under the impression that a few sessions would make me eligible to be cast as a dancer, I immediately began taking lessons. Obviously, I didn't get the job, but I got hooked on tango. I started going to the *Confiteria Ideal* every day during lunch and danced in the evenings. Now I teach tango and have a popular milonga in central Buenos Aires."

Beyond Mere Connection

Seldom, say dancers, do they begin tango lessons with the idea of meeting members of the opposite sex. For those who might do so, such notions are quickly dispelled as the newcomer encounters the seriousness of the dancers and begins to glimpse something of the immense complexity of the tango, its allure, and its rich culture.

There is the appeal of the learning rituals, a shared process at once satisfying and pleasingly serious, which leaves little room for socializing or flirting. Dancers arrive at class, dancing shoes in hand, greet other students and the teacher, put on their shoes, and begin warm-up exercises. Once class begins, there is no talking, and dancing and communication in between dances tends to focus on steps and techniques. When class is finished, dancers slip back into their street shoes and head home.

Such seriousness holds strong appeal for some dancers. One Japanese student in a Paris tango class told a new acquaintance that he had quit Salsa lessons "because the women were more interested in talking and flirting than in dancing."

While tango's obvious physicality may initially attract people interested in connecting, the dance itself almost always becomes central. And for some dancers, the subtly complex demands of tango serve as an effective social screening mechanism: the sophistication of the dance and its contexts seems to draw accomplished men and women who practice and value social grace and good grooming. Novice tango dancers are usually surprised at how swiftly they become entangled. It is seldom that "with time" the tango simply "grows" on dancers. Tango commonly ensnares its happy prey with disarmingly immediate ferocity. Thousands of dancers have found themselves, like Mr. MacKenzie, with their "worlds turned upside down." Although some recent initiates may complain about the changes in their lives, for the most part the experience is viewed as immensely positive. Because of its many facets and its appealing ambience, tango attracts a wide diversity of persons and for diverse reasons.

Tango's First Embrace

One questionnaire respondent told of going to a dance studio where he had signed up for Salsa lessons: "On walking towards the classroom to take my first Salsa class, I passed a room where Argentine Tango was being taught. I walked in, joined the class, and never got to Salsa." Another wrote: "I went to sign up for Salsa lessons and discovered there was no class to suit my schedule. Instead, I signed up for Argentine Tango and permanently forgot Salsa."

Berette Salazar, a St. Louis psychiatrist, was on her way to a swing class at a dance studio when she was called into an adjacent studio and persuaded to serve as a partner in an Argentine Tango class. "I was hooked immediately. Since then I've made ten trips to Buenos Aires and am already planning my next visit."

Inspired to Dance

Some people come to the tango from serious involvement in other dance disciplines – ballet, modern, ballroom, folklore and others. Having seen or heard about tango and seeking to expand their dance repertoire, such newcomers approach the tango anticipating that their prior dance experience will ensure early proficiency. Such expectations are quickly and mercilessly dashed. While some students are so disappointed that they soon quit, most end up abandoning their other dances. Gilles Cuna, now a popular tango teacher in Paris writes, "I was a modern dance performer and ten years ago took my first tango lesson as a lark. The tango arrived in my life and vice versa. In order to live well, all I need is the tango."

The experience of one Buenos Aires tango instructor evokes aspects of tango's late-twentieth century turning point: "I used to be a folklore and modern dancer, and for me, like many young people in my country, I was not the least bit interested in tango. But in 1984, when *Tango Argentino* became a success, there were no professional tango dancers in Argentina – they were all on Broadway. So when foreigners began to come to Argentina to learn tango, we got 'invented.' Folklore and modern dancers were told to 'go on the stage and dance tango.' At that time, I hated tango, which I felt was for old people, but in order to earn money I decided to try it. My Father said: 'Your life is going to change. You will not be able to stop dancing tango because the tango will capture you.' I said, 'Yeah, yeah, yeah!' But it was true; my life changed. Today I only dance tango. I need to dance tango."

Nearly fifty percent of the informal questionnaire respondents indicated that they first became interested in tango when they saw one of the tango shows that began traveling the world in 1984: *Tango Argentino, Forever Tango, Tango Passion, Tango x2* and others. What audiences had known of tango at the time was exclusively Ballroom Tango, the choreographed dance known outside Argentina. But *Tango Argentino* presented a totally different dance, which had evolved in Argentina but was essentially unknown beyond its borders.

The New York Times reported that audiences "were stunned by the music and the verve and passion of the dancers." Even before each performance ended, more than a few enthralled show-goers were thinking about finding somewhere to take tango lessons. Jim Maes of San Francisco related his response to *Forever Tango,* which was originally booked for one week but ran for ninety-two weeks: "I went to see *Forever Tango* three times; it brought tears to my eyes. I fell in love with the beauty of the dance, the passion and the power and was soon taking lessons six times a week."

Those who elected to take tango lessons were in for a surprise. The performers they had seen were so graceful that they made the dance look 'do-able' to those in the audience and the fact that many of the performers were middle-aged and overweight heightened the impression that "anyone could do it." Said Bob MacKenzie, "When we went to see tango stage productions, we came out of the theater convinced we could learn to tango. It seemed tantalizingly within reach. What on earth led us to believe such a thing? Do we go to an opera and decide to take voice lessons? Do we go to the ballet and decide to take ballet lessons? No. But after watching two hours of incredibly complicated footwork danced to highly sophisticated rhythms, we left the theater thinking, 'I can do that!' and immediately determined to look for a place to take lessons. What incredible arrogance. What ignorance!"

Another internet contributor commented on those who decided to learn tango after seeing the shows: "We didn't have the slightest inkling of the infinite subtleties of what we'd seen, nor of the lifetime of work involved in achieving the grace exhibited while legs were flashing in and out of partners' spaces or elegantly gliding in walking steps across the stage in perfect timing with the extraordinary music; we all imagined ourselves doing the same thing with just a bit of practice. But we all paid for that arrogance - and continue to pay - by living with constant humility, with which we are all only too familiar."

They Can't NOT Dance

"Why do I dance? It's good for me," responded more than one dancer. Some explain that the physical contact is important to all humans. "Why do I dance? I love the music and I do it for the hug; to me it's hugging to music." Capturing a particularly salient facet of the dance in the 21st century, Bob Mackenzie writes, "One of the appeals of tango is that it is unashamedly romantic and sentimental in a time when it's considered cool to be kind of passionless and distant and to be an amused observer. You can't be half-hearted about doing the tango."

On first seeing the Argentine Tango danced, some people say "That's nice," or "That's interesting," and get on with their lives, while others say "Wow! I've got to do that!" and promptly find out where they can take lessons. Some scientists think that serious dancers may possess an innate proclivity for movement to music. Argentine psychiatrist

8

Christina Guez wrote: "My take on it is that many tango dancers have something in their psychological make-up that draws them to it." Recent scientific studies of the genes of professional dancers suggest there may be a physiological, gene-based reason that compels some people to make dance a serious part of their lives.

While most dancers don't spend much time analyzing why they love to dance, all agree that dancing makes them feel good. And although addictions are generally unhealthy and otherwise harmful, that is not always so. For example, people can become addicted to exercise, which is generally accepted as beneficial. Not uncommonly, when someone accustomed to regular exercise misses a workout, they are in a bad mood for the day: they have missed their "fix." So too with tango: its exercise stimulates the production of endorphins in the brain and induces a natural high that a dancer comes to crave – which is a "healthy addiction."

Indeed, some dancers claim that when they begin to feel a bit depressed, they can often "ward it off" by taking a tango lesson. One dancer commented that when dancing and concentrating on the intricate music and movement, the sorrows and preoccupations of daily life are left outside. For some, change is more substantial and leads to altered lifestyles and to development new feelings, ideas, values, perceptions, and attitudes.

The First Steps

Popular dances are commonly linked to a social activity, and few dances are sufficiently complicated that lessons are needed before venturing onto a public dance floor - not so for tango. Because tango simply cannot be 'faked,' no self-respecting novice will dance in public until they have weeks or months of lessons and practice. Even then most beginners experience some apprehension; few men or women feel comfortable dancing in public until they have danced for a year or more.

Most people begin their lessons without fully realizing the difficulty of the dance. Before long (teachers concur that the average is several months), students commonly reach a decision point: to quit or to make a serious commitment to tango. In short order, dancers realize that there are no shortcuts to proficiency and that perfection will always lie just beyond reach. Like ballet dancers, tango dancers soon accept that they will take lessons for as long as they continue to dance. The goal is improvement, however modest.

The types of people willing and able to commit the requisite time, effort, and money to dance tango are varied. Beginners, particularly professional dancers from other dance disciplines, are astonished at the difficulty of tango. Although some appreciate the subtlety of movements, they commonly say to themselves, "How hard can it be?" The first lesson dispels such presumption. Even for experienced social and professional dancers, initial forays into tango leave them frustrated, humbled and even angry. Every tango dancer has a sad tale to tell. Charles Roques says, "I had a strong background in partner dances, including Ballroom Tango, and was used to becoming reasonably proficient in a new dance very quickly. Instead, I felt as if I had to throw out everything I knew and start over again from nothing. It was *very* frustrating. I nearly burst into tears at my first lesson."

Linda Lucas, of Washington, D.C. speaks of her first lesson: "I'd studied ballet, modern dance and tap dance for more than twenty years and I expected to do well. My attempts to execute the simple steps of the teacher were pathetic. Again and again I asked the teacher to repeat instructions, but I could not emulate his movements with any degree of satisfaction. When the lesson was over I felt devastated, but I had an unrelenting, focused thought: 'I will learn to dance tango and dance it well." Six years later, Ms. Lucas gave her first professional tango performance in Washington, D.C.

While going through my files for this book, I came upon a plaintive letter I wrote to one of my sons. "Dear Tim, I took another private class yesterday from Imed. (Arguably the best tango teacher in Paris.) I seem to be doing O.K. (after four years of dancing and countless group and private lessons), except that: my *tour* (a circling turn around my partner) is not up to snuff, my foot placement is no good (the feet should be pointed slightly outward), my boleo is a disaster with my hips not swiveling enough, my head is in the wrong place, I'm not stepping close enough to my partner; when I turn or do backward ochos, my right hand is pulling too hard on my partner's hand (throwing him off balance). I am too far away from my partner, I'm rushing the molinette; the ball of my foot sometimes touches the floor after the heel; I tried to sneak a forbidden look at my feet; my posture is not straight enough. The teacher keeps repeating, 'Don't forget to relax!' Yikes! Relax? How is that possible? Why do we do this dance?"

However much dancers may complain about the difficulty of tango, none wants to simplify it. Having persevered through years of lessons, they are proud of their accomplishment and pleased to associate with others who have "made the grade."

Divided Passions: The Intellectual Divide

There are those on the intellectual side of the tango 'divide' who revere themselves as the guardians of

11

tango culture and regularly take part in the plethora of conferences and debates - both written and oral - on various aspects of tango culture and history. This camp includes professors, journalists and writers, as well as interested laymen who attend the many regular meetings, social affairs and conferences organized for the general public and also arrange tango concerts. In Buenos Aires there is the esteemed and prestigious Academy of Tango and Academy of Lunfardo (a tango language), and in the world's major cities there are formal and informal organizations whose members publish books, write papers, translate lyrics, and publish journals and newsletters. (Reading through the Buenos Aires publications one might not even be aware of the tango as a dance; there never seem to be photographs of dancers with the same faces appearing with predictable regularity.) These organizations also propagate the "culture of tango" by sponsoring competitions and exhibitions of art, photography, sculpture, painting, and short literary works with tango as the theme.

The French, with their love of the written word and their long, special relationship with Argentina and the tango (tango's first venture outside Argentina was to France), probably more than any other people, have a particular fascination for tango lyrics and music. There are literary cafés in Paris that feature regular debates or 'conferences,' where hours are spent analyzing some aspect of tango poetry, Lunfardo, music, or Argentine Tango history and its influence on Argentine culture.

Much intellectualizing of tango unfolds on the internet with intense and often lengthy debates on such topics as technique and floor-craft, the effects of tango on Argentine history and culture, and the tango's influence on other cultures where it is danced. Teaching methods are analyzed and compared to those within and beyond Argentina. The very nature of tango seems to invite debate. It is difficult to imagine other social dancers sitting about analyzing their dance as a "reflection of culture" or asking one another to ponder the Salsa's "basic generic/universal insights of relationships between men and women." And who might be found probing the "meaning" of the meringue? One of the favorite topics on the internet is the serious discussion of 'the meaning of tango' although many dancers reply, "who cares"?

And They Don't Even Dance!

Not many dancers are aware of the sharp divisions in tango communities from early times to the present. Tango is the only social dance to embrace an entire artistic and literary culture that includes popular and classical music, dance, serious poetry, and the unique Lunfardo language. Not all tango enthusiasts are passionate about all aspects of tango culture, so cliques developed of those drawn to one or another aspect of tango; the cliques hardened into two factions, whose members are separated by education, money, and class.

One side of the chasm is dominated mainly by academics and assorted intellectuals, professional musicians, and writers and poets. Vocalists are included in this group because they interpret the lyrics which are considered serious poetry reflecting historical and contemporary Argentine society. Most people on this side of The Divide don't even dance! They may attend milongas (tango dances) to listen to the music and lyrics and to meet with like-minded friends with whom they exchange CDs, tapes, and sheet music; to plan meetings or singing practices; or to discuss upcoming concerts and conferences or tango related debates.

On the other side are the dancers; they only want to dance. Dancers have little or no interest in intellectualizing tango; very few attend symposiums and lectures analyzing the music and lyrics, or Lunfardo. They just want to move to the music. The dancers are a world apart from the 'intellectuals,' tending to be from the working class: taxi drivers, plumbers, butchers, hair stylists, office workers, etc. Professionally and socially the two groups don't mix. Some don't even talk to each other. Behavioral psychologist, Dave Witter, added, "'Doers are not always 'thinkers.' Some of the finest tango maestros I know don't have anything profound to say about the dance: their explanation of it is that it is simply their dance."

Although the two groups are separate, they sometimes meet to organize tango festivals designed appeal to both dancers and non-dancers. Depending on who does the organizing, the events can be lop-sided towards one side or the other. Tango workshops and regional or international festivals are usually oriented more towards dancers, although most international festivals include lip service to the non-dancing components of tango with a few conferences or symposiums on some aspect of tango culture.

However, if the events are organized by non-dancers, the programs place much less emphasis on dance than on the cerebral aspects of tango. For example, a recent two-month long "Sixth Annual Paris and Suburban Tango Festival" featured a combination of dance classes, cinema, theater, art expositions, *'soirees gastronomiques'* (lots of empanadas), and *'bals'* (what milongas are called in France). Ordinarily, at international or national festivals, ninety to ninety-five percent of activities are dance oriented, with lessons and workshops featured, but this Paris festival included only nine practical dance workshops and seventy non-dancing events, including debates, conferences, concerts, and exhibits. On inquiry, it was divulged that there were few, or no, dancers on the planning committee.

Tango Concerts

Tango concerts attract far more non-dancers than dancers, particularly outside the U.S.A. If dancers go out to hear tango music, they want to dance to it, not sit down to listen to it. Although there are a number of excellent small American tango orchestras, there is not nearly the enthusiasm for tango concerts in the U.S. as there is in Europe, Japan, and other parts of the world.

In the classical musical world, tango is respected for its complexity, originality, variety, and sophistication, and tango concerts are usually filled to capacity. They feature classical tango dance music from the late 1800s through the 1940s, as well as the modern music of Astor Piazzolla; the 20th century Argentine composer who invented a fusion of tango, jazz and classical music. The new electronic tango music appeals particularly to contemporary youth, including those who don't dance. Germany, Holland, Italy, U.S., and Japan all have excellent tango orchestras that tour the world playing all types of tango music; some are so good that they are repeatedly welcomed in Argentina.

Dance Therapy: Science and the Dance

While most dancers appreciate that dance is good physical exercise, modern research confirms that it offers significant mental benefits as well, including the slowing of age-related decline in mental acuity. At the 2005 annual

15

meeting of the Society for Neuroscience Studies, Patricia McKinley, of Montreal's McGill University, reported results of a study involving the tango. "The hot moves of the Argentine Tango not only keep the aging body in shape, they also may help sharpen the aging brain. According to the study, a growing body of evidence indicates that challenging leisure activities... may offer a boost in brain power that could offset the declines that can come with old age."

Previous studies had suggested that a sweat-breaking workout may help keep brain cells in top form, but Prof. McKinley also knew that the activity had to be something that seniors would enjoy. She picked the tango, a dance that's both fun to do and involves a series of complex movements that can improve balance. Her team recruited thirty seniors ages sixty-eight to ninety-one, mostly women, but men came, too. Half the group received tango lessons, and the other half were assigned to a walking group.

Dancers felt a boost in self-esteem almost immediately. "They would start in with sweat pants and sneakers, but after the third or fourth class, the women had on make-up and jewelry. Both walkers and tango dancers had better scores on memory tests, but only the dancers showed improvement in balance and motor coordination. That finding suggests they'd be at less risk of falling, a significant gain for older, frail people who can break a hip and never fully recover."

The French magazine, La Salida, reported: "In 2008, the city of Rosario, Argentina, hosted the First Congresso de Tango-Therapie, attended by international doctors who have studied the benefits of dance on health, particularly cardio-vascular problems, depression and anxiety. Psychiatrist

Federico Trossero, author of the book *Tango-Therapie*, underlined the interest in tango because of the benefits of communication it introduces in social relations.

Born to Dance

Although many dancers know they like to dance because it makes them feel good, scientists are examining whether or not certain people dance because they feel *compelled* to do so. They need to dance. Contemporary research is verifying the genetic and neurobiological contexts of the dance and establishing that "intelligence, athletic ability, and musical talent are linked to our genes and brain 'hard-wiring.'"

Dr. Richard Ebstein, a psychology professor at Hebrew University's Scheinfeld Center for Genetic Studies, writes, "Animals have courtship dances and I think that human dancing represents the further development of a very ancient animal trait.... Also, the fact that dancing is universal and has existed in all human societies, even those communities of man separated geographically by tens of thousands of years (Native Australians, Native Americans, Africans, Eurasians) attests to the very early origin of dance in our evolution as a species."

Dr. Ebstein and his team examined the DNA of currently performing dancers and their parents and discovered that dancers tend to possess variants of two genes involved in the transmission of information between nerve cells, one of which is a transporter of serotonin. The second is a receptor of the hormone vasopressin which modulates social communication and human bonding. "People are born to dance," Dr. Ebstein told *Discovery News*. "The genes we studied are related to the emotional side of dancing — the need and ability to communicate with other people and a spiritual side to their natures that not only enable them to feel the music, but to communicate that feeling to others via dance." Socioeconomic considerations, however, can also influence who dances. "Those of us without a twinkle-toes predisposition," added Dr. Ebstein, "can still become good dancers, since it's not only a question of having the right genes, but also training and motivation, that make professional dancers."

Transformative Tango

"My life has changed since being involved in tango. I concentrate more on enjoying people and less on material things." (Joan Radley, retired bank executive.)

"I kicked a thirty year, four pack-a-day smoking habit on the first try. I don't think I could give up tango." (Nancy Ingle,) Washington, D.C.

Comments from dancers who have fallen under tango's spell reveal diverse consequences from their immersion — wide-ranging, substantive, and occasionally life altering. Dancers who succumb to the tango may find their lives transformed. Most are pleased with such changes, and many attempt to persuade friends to try the tango as a means of improving their lives. They cite changes physical and non-physical, spiritual and mental — altered outlooks on life, attitudes towards others and the world around them, and even changes in their self-perception.

Many dancers orient their lives around tango; it affects the way they live their lives, with whom they socialize, and how they allocate their free time or arrange business and leisure travel to accommodate tango. Their wardrobes and posture visibly change, and budgets sometimes groan from the expense of group and private lessons and travel to regional, national, or international workshops and festivals. Such devotees carry dance shoes in their cars and joke about needing a "tango fix," or how their hands tremble if they don't know when they will dance next.

Reports a Paris florist, Jules Mussuto: "If on a Sunday night I do not know when and where I will dance during the next week, I feel close to panic." Says Ernest Pile, a research chemist in Nashville, "Tango reaches inside of me to a place I never knew existed. I was always a wallflower and a nerd growing up, and I only developed confidence after I started dancing tango. My life has changed in that I gear many activities around tango or places where I can go to tango. It simply took me over. Mondays I fly from Nashville to Atlanta to dance tango because there is no tango in Nashville."

Another Paris resident, Chita Wilcox, spends four to five months dancing each year in Buenos Aires. She said: "In my teenage years I used to watch my mother dance tango with her friends, and I decided that one day I would learn how to dance tango and be good at it. So, in memory of my mother, I decided to learn it and look lessons in Paris from Pablo Vernon. After seeing the show *Tango Passion,* I decided I had to go to Buenos Aires. I am a devout Christian, and in Buenos Aires I have met Christian friends and even a former pastor with whom I dance. I realize the tango has a sexual and sensual connotation because of its early association with the brothels of Buenos Aires, but I dance to dance; I enjoy the violins, piano and bandoneon and I think of my mother. In Buenos Aires I am known as the *missionera y millionaria.*"

Bob MacKenzie jokingly lamented, "My life has become a mess. My laundry is never done, my house is never clean, and show me someone who hasn't moved furniture around, or out, in order to practice. I'm going broke paying for tango lessons. I just completed the one-week CITA (Congresso International de Tango Argentina) tango festival in Buenos Aires in 1999, with a week of six hours of lessons daily, watching tango shows at night, and going out dancing after that – sometimes until five a.m. I can't remember when my feet didn't hurt." Mr. MacKenzie stayed on in Buenos Aires after the weeklong festival and took two more weeks of private lessons daily, after which he headed off to a weeklong tango festival in Miami.

Most dancers express pleasure with changes in their lives, and some even find them therapeutic. One dancer, prone to temporary depression, says that she "can usually ward it off by making an appointment for a private tango class." A newspaper article reported that a Scandinavian ambassador to Argentina was overheard at a Buenos Aires reception to declare, "Since doing tango, I've given up my therapist."

Besides transforming their wardrobes and lifestyles, some dancers alter their homes to accommodate tango, such as the woman in Washington, D.C., who built a dance studio onto her home where she hosts regular dance lessons and workshops with visiting Argentine teachers. In Seattle, Mary Jane Finley emptied her large dining room and holds weekly Thursday night tango open houses, to which dancers bring snacks and soft drinks. Peter Esser of Eugene, Oregon, built a dance studio in his house, complete with floor to ceiling mirrors and a dance barre for practicing technique. Ms. Kelly of New York said: "At first I danced one day a week but eventually it became six days a week. I moved out furniture and put in mirrors and a barre."

Actor Robert Duvall's life was transformed when he first became interested in tango after seeing *Tango Argentino* in New York. He began tango lessons when he later made his first trip to Buenos Aires. On his farm in Virginia, near Washington, D. C., he has converted the second floor of his large barn into a dance studio where he regularly hosts milongas and lessons and workshops given by visiting Argentines. In 2002 Mr. Duvall directed and starred in the film *Assassination Tango,* about a New York hit man sent to Buenos Aires who becomes fascinated with the tango.

Because they know their dancing will be closely watched by other dancers at milongas, many dancers take more than ordinary care with their appearance, posture, and wardrobe. For some, their new interest in looking good is viable both on the dance floor and off. The phenomenon is recounted by Dick Witter of Washington, D.C.: "I have much more social confidence, I am more outgoing, I'm more 'daring' about life in general; I'm more confident in my physical abilities, better dressed, and better groomed; there's a major shift in priorities, time in particular, but also money; I think I have a more interesting image to others (including non-tango people), and my self-image is more interesting. I have more friends and acquaintances from all over the world."

New York tango entrepreneur, Lucille Krasne, told a friend about visiting Berkeley, CA, to teach a summer course, usually staying with friends who were "genuine 60s people": they wore Birkenstocks and love beads, the husband with long hair and an unkempt beard, his wife with similarly long locks and tie-dyed clothes. One summer, returning to visit her friends, she was amazed to find her hosts transformed, he with a neatly trimmed beard, she elegantly coiffed, and both quite stylishly dressed. She asked about the dramatic transformation and they responded: "We took up Argentine Tango."

Some dancers feel that tango has made them more sensitive to others' passions. Luisa Zini, from Italy writes: "When talking with tango friends, the usual talk is about the obsession with the dance. Now I can better understand all my male Italian friends obsessing over soccer. I used to think they were completely nuts. However, in the past three years since dancing tango, I find I cannot refrain myself from talking about this amazing dance. When I am on the phone I end up talking about tango; it is impossible to avoid the subject."

Not everyone appreciates being considered obsessive about tango. On a tango cruise in the Caribbean, I hosted a round table discussion with dancers, titled 'Tango Obsession.' When I told one of my sons about it he said, "How are you organizing it? Will they start off with 'My name is...and I'm a tango dancer?'"

One of the participants was an attractive actress from New York. She listened attentively to participants tell of their addictions, how and when they began tango, and how it affected their lives. When it was her turn to speak, she pointedly asserted that while the others might be obsessed with tango, she definitely was not, and cited some of the many other interests in her life. When asked how frequently she danced, she answered: "I have been taking lessons and dancing five or six times a week for the past year and a half." She was taken aback at the outbreak of hearty laughter.

While few life changes rival that of the German physician who gave up his gynecology practice to become a tango teacher, tales of change of occupation are not all that unusual. Tango star Fabian Salas trained as a lawyer but now works full time as a tango performer and teacher, and organizes the annual Congresso International de Tango Argentino festival in Buenos Aires. Sally Potter, the filmmaker wrote: "When

I first started taking tango lessons it was a break from the intensely cerebral, sedentary process of script writing – the 'serious' work I was doing at the time. But what began as something on the sidelines of my life—something done for pleasure, for fun – became an obsession. Then the obsession became a fire fueling a new film. I abandoned the script I was writing and made my film, *The Tango Lesson*."

One-time professional boxer Diego Riemer (*El Pajaro, The Bird*) left the sport to work full-time at tango. Metin Yazir was a house painter in Turkey and became a popular tango teacher on the international circuit. Daniel Carpi, an Argentine who moved to New York City to earn a Ph.D. in neuroscience, abandoned his thesis to become a tango teacher and entrepreneur with a weekly milonga, *La Belle Époque*, and a tango website. Tioma Maloratsky, a native of Moscow, gave up a career in physics to perform and teach tango; Hanif Butt, a Boston orthodontist, reduced his dental practice in order to devote more time to teaching tango and running a tango association that he founded through which he organizes dance events - classes, workshops, festivals, weekend brunches, and tango travel. Mariano "Chicho" Frúmboli, one of today's leading tango performers, was a classical theatrical actor before turning full time to tango.

A Korean martial arts seventh-degree black belt teacher of Taekwondo went to Buenos Aires to teach Taekwondo and Kung-Fu and soon grasped the tango live wire. "People were reluctant to teach serious tango to a foreigner," he writes, "and it was very hard for me to find a partner. I even stopped eating kimchee to avoid the smell." He studied with ten different teachers and danced occasionally on the stage. After five years he decided to teach tango to "his people" and moved back to Korea to a village close to

Seoul, where he opened a small dance studio and tango café, with tango music and typical Argentine fare.

Travel to Dance - Buenos Aires to the Ends of the Earth

Another change in tango dancer's lives is that many begin to travel to experience dancing in a different environment, either on their own or in the many workshops and international tango festivals that take place year round, all over the world. Some of the "tango junkies" (called *les possedees* in France) become compulsive about attending workshops and festivals that are ongoing.

The tango is the only dance with its focus on only one city, Buenos Aires. Tango dancers think nothing of traveling thousands of miles and spending thousands of dollars to dance tango in Buenos Aires. It seems perfectly natural since the goal of Argentine Tango dancers all over the world is to 'dance like an Argentine.' In any discussion of tango - style, technique, floor-craft, dance hall etiquette, music, etc. - the point of reference is always, "How is it done in Buenos Aires?" Thus, those who are able to do so, plan to visit Buenos Aires - the tango *Mecca* - at least once, for a total immersion experience. Many dancers are not satisfied with one visit but return again and again.

Dancers travel to exchange their ideas in an increasingly universal context but with local adaptations. To dance in Amsterdam, Lille, Boulogne, Montreal is to have different experiences.

At the beginning of the current wave of interest, students of tango learned to dance from traveling Argentine teachers or from local teachers who trained with Argentines. But today, although Argentine teachers constantly circle the globe giving lessons, dancers increasingly, want to go to Buenos Aires where they can enjoy total immersion in tango with a multitude of dance opportunities nearly around the clock. Buenos Aires draws dancers of all ages from all parts of the world. Some go on short, one-week or two-week vacations, and others take extended sabbaticals of six months to a year. Many stay in tango guesthouses that cater to dancers (and their strange schedules) because they enjoy the multilingual atmosphere and presence of enthusiastic companions for practice, taking lessons, or going to dance halls. Some dancers rent apartments on a yearly basis or buy an apartment at Argentina's low real estate prices and go to Buenos Aires as often as they can. It's also possible to rent a room with a 'tango associated family' or in one of the inexpensive hotels.

Tango tourists normally concentrate only on tango while in Buenos Aires. They have difficulty squeezing in time for laundry or food shopping as they rush from group classes to 'practicas' to private classes, then dance at milongas that start at midnight and last until five or six in the morning. One day a dancer from Milwaukee, in Buenos Aires on business, showed up in the lounge of his tango guesthouse around noon looking dazed and complaining about noisy, early morning street traffic. "You know what? I've just discovered that most of Buenos Aires is not on tango time." Many dancers take extended periods of time in Buenos Aires on sabbaticals from work, and there are those who simply quit their jobs to live the life of "tango bums" for six months to a year or two. Others feel compelled to spend even more time there.

For some of the more seriously obsessed, the lure of tango in Buenos Aires is so strong that they can't bear not to be there. Americans, Europeans, and Asians have pulled up roots to join the expatriate community of tango dancers. Some find work in their professions, and others teach English. Sarah La Rocca, a young art teacher in Washington,

D.C., quit her job to move to Buenos Aires. "She lived the nocturnal life of an expatriate American tango bum," reported the New York Times. "Like others, she would rise in the mid-afternoon to practice the tango, take a class in the evening and go out for coffee and then to a tango club. She would arrive after midnight and stay until six a.m., eat breakfast, and go home to bed. When her money ran short, she taught English to bank executives." Janis Kenyon, who moved to Buenos Aires ten years ago after visiting there five times, reported, "I could no longer live with just one night a week of tango in Chicago. I am obsessed with tango." New York playwright and actor Jef Anderson went to Buenos Aires to perfect his Spanish. He became involved in tango and stayed thirteen years, working as an English teacher and then as a tango teacher and performer.

While the Argentine people are famously friendly and welcoming to foreigners, most are genuinely nonplused about the foreign tango dancers. They find it difficult to believe that anyone would travel so far to dance tango, something they take for granted and which is not particularly fashionable today in Argentina. Taxi drivers, shopkeepers, clerks, waiters - anyone who encounters foreigners - usually ask why a foreigner is visiting Buenos Aires. The days when tango was the obsession in Argentina may have faded in memory, but with the worldwide revival of interest in the dance, that is changing. However, not many outside Argentina know that not only do dancers become obsessed with dancing tango but that many musicians and singers obsess over music and lyrics.

CHAPTER TWO

The Attraction

"The Argentine Tango holds a unique place in couple dancing. The bodies are closer, more intimate than in any other dance form, and the legs move faster and with more deadly accuracy ... Add to this the music – melancholy, ecstatic, growling, predatory, soaring, seeking, heartbreakingly beautiful – and you have the ingredients for something more than a craze. You have a genuine participatory art form."
(Sally Potter, filmmaker, "The Tango Lesson")

"Argentine Tango is ...
A snowflake experience.
Unique.
Beautiful.
Evanescent.
Melted into memory."
(Robert Fulghum, author, "All I Need to Know I Learned in Kindergarten")

Unlike other social dances whose principal purpose is amusement, tango has a specific goal; each dance is supposed to be a new work of art, at once creative, elegant, and graceful, an adventure never to be exactly repeated. Tango dancers do not consider having fun sufficient reason to be on a dance floor for they approach each dance as a new opportunity to 'do it right,' even though perfection is acknowledged to be out of reach. An improvised, well-executed step or adornment of five seconds is good for a week of self-satisfied reflection, even though no one else may have

29

noticed it and the dancer may not be able to repeat it. The memory of it lingers, much like the memory of a golfer's hole-in-one, and for many soon becomes an obsession.

Tango as an Art Form

Artists and non-artists alike are drawn to tango because of its creative essence. Dancers compare tango experiences to poetry and painting, while people from the sciences also recognize tango's creative appeal. Software engineer Larry Carroll observes, "An improvised dance is an artwork, rather like an extemporaneous poem in free verse. Improvisation of tango steps is essential because the sophisticated structures that tango musicians play isn't suitable for the dancing of rigid, memorized complex figures."

Tango resembles jazz in that both originated in society's lower strata and rose to lofty heights favored by intellectuals in prestigious theaters and concert halls.

Improvisation: Tango is to Buenos Aires as Jazz is to New Orleans

Both tango and jazz, emerged at the end of the 19th century but on different continents, both in riverside urban ghetto environments – Buenos Aires and Montevideo flanking the Rio de la Plata for tango and New Orleans on the Mississippi for jazz – Each began with improvised music. The musical cultural background of Buenos Aires had an influx of musically literate European immigrants with their folklore, opera and popular music. The Italians dominated tango music whose compositions were copied out and arranged.

Without an equivalent European tradition during its early development, jazz, which originated in American black community of New Orleans, thrived on spontaneity and improvisation of material from diverse sources, particularly African musical traditions.

One difference between them is that although early improvised tango music began to be composed and written down, the dance continued to be improvised. Jazz in contrast to tango originated as improvised music and that continues to be its hallmark. The relationship between the dance and the music in tango and jazz differ in the primacy of the dance itself. In the world of jazz, the music is central, with dance playing a decidedly subsidiary role. Unlike the tango, no specific jazz dance form developed with its music.

Throughout their distinct evolutions, however, improvisation distinguishes both jazz music and tango dance disciplines. Whether in an after-hours jam sessions in a Greenwich Village basement club or on the floor of a Buenos Aires milonga at sunrise, the jazz musician and the tango dancer contrive their intricate complexities essentially newly minted in each moment. None of the early jazz musicians or tango dancers could have imagined that their improvised efforts would ever become the darlings of intellectuals - so far from their own societies.

Both tango dancers and jazz musicians create their music by assembling new and pre-learned phrases into varied patterns, and sub-patterns, or figuras. Tango and jazz are sometimes compared to chess, a highly intellectual activity, because both require the capacity to think several moves ahead. Ideally, a dancer moves without needing to think about steps or technique, inspiration arcing directly from the music, but the leader must stay constantly alert to dancers all around him both for the purpose of how to forge ahead on the dance floor and how to avoid colliding with dancers coming at him from all angles. At this level of sustained improvisation, the accomplished dancer enjoys immense intellectual and emotional satisfaction, heightened by the ever-present risk of failure. As do jazz musicians striving for their art's ultimate experiences, dancers pursuing tango's loftiest peaks must be willing to take genuine risks. Says one tango devotee, "This similarity between jazz and tango is the only reason I am dancing."

The Thinkers' Embrace

"You know what?" exclaimed a student at a Buenos Aires workshop, "This is a thinking man's dance!"

Mingo Pugliese, a distinguished tango performer and teacher from the Golden Era, tells of a conversation early in his career with a man so knowledgeable about tango that he was called "*Marquituito La Biblia*" – Marquituito the Bible. "I asked him if he would teach me to dance the tango. Marquituito told me, 'No, I'm not going to teach you how to dance. I'm going to teach you how to think.'" It is precisely such focus that many dancers especially savor.

If, in Argentina, the tango has historically been the "dance of the people," the self-taught working classes, then in the world beyond Buenos Aires it was destined to become the province of prosperous people who enjoy the means and leisure to attend lessons, workshops, milongas, and festivals. The contemporary international tango community attracts an eclectic array of successful men and women from middle and professional classes – scientists, engineers, lawyers, doctors, and academics. There are fewer people from the working classes, however, although the numbers appear to be increasing, most notably among young people.

Dancers claim that one of the attractions of tango is that it requires substantial thought and concentration in order to dance even moderately well. As a consequence, unlike other social dances where little or no thought is necessary, both partners must constantly pay close attention to their body movements or risk embarrassing stumbles, falls, or collisions. Because its powerful demands on the mind leave little room for unrelated thought or emotion, tango offers a refreshing escape from the worrisome world beyond the dance floor. "I connect with the dolorous spirit of a lot of tango music," writes a dancer, "It affords me the opportunity to take some of the energy I have relating to certain unfortunate events in my life and transform them into something positive and joyous. It is also social, so I go out and have fun instead of languishing at home."

New Orleans tango teacher and performer Alberto Paz wrote in the newsletter "El Firulete," that tango particularly appeals to scientists and engineers because "they are locked in a mental embrace, with numbers, theories, and codes, and have traded sensual experience for platonic flirtation with a machine. Tango can help fix that... The first thing you do is embrace a total stranger, keep your mouth shut, and listen to the music...you learn what your partner is feeling. It is a shocking and devastating experience. In an increasingly alienated world, these moments of sheer connection are important."

Some tango-smitten scientists analyze tango in the language of academe, reflected, for example, in a long paper on tango technique titled, "Improvisation: An Algorithm for Converting Music to Movement." One internet observer wrote, "The movement in each tango is in the moment, how the partners feel 'right now' – and it will never be precisely the same again. This was invented for a universe of relativity and quantum mechanics. Dynamic. Uncertain and slightly scary."

Because the dance is so intensely immediate and complex, it requires a high level of concentrated communication between partners. One view holds that tango is only tango that is "danced as one" and must involve the "death of the ego.

The tango leader must choreograph his dance on the fly, directing the movements of his partner while circling the dance floor counter-clockwise, being careful not to interfere with dancers in front, behind, and alongside. While protecting his partner from collision with other dancers, he must anticipate where he wants to go and where and how he will place his feet. The leader must be fully aware of the music and how he intends to interpret it with the patterns he is creating in this moment and those he will create in the next. Simultaneously he must always be aware of his partner's foot placement and on which foot her weight is bearing, for to direct a step in the wrong direction could easily result in disaster.

The follower must also be fully attentive. With no advance cues, at each step she must be poised to move in any direction, and while following the leader's guidance, she must be instantly and constantly prepared to alert him to any potentially dangerous movements of dancers behind him. The dance partnership remains equilaterally dynamic. A skilled follower imaginatively creates opportunities to draw a leader into executing figures for her own amusement or as a challenge to the leader, thus capturing the lead from him. A well-practiced follower enjoys wide creative latitude in that she can essentially do whatever she chooses so long as she does not miss a beat. Capturing that tense equipoise of freedom in restraint, anthropologist Julie Taylor in her book, *Paper Tangos,* reminds her readers, "He can tell me where to put my foot, but he can't tell me how to put it there."

For a beginning dancer, such freedom may seem a long way off. A tourist from Wisconsin attending group lessons in Buenos Aires expressed a common frustration. Closely observing the teachers' demonstration of a figura and confident that he understood the explanations for each movement, he tried them himself but simply could not capture the pattern: "The trouble with me," he murmured, "is that my feet are too far from my head."

Lunfardo: The Language of Tango

Seemingly unique in the culture of popular music and dance, tango alone came to be identified with a language, or at least a dialect – Lunfardo – that today is a lively vernacular endemic to Argentine Spanish and not unlike dialects characteristic of urban ghettos such as London's Cockney or Dublin's rhyming slang. Many dancers feel that a tango cannot be fully appreciated without an understanding of the lyrics, while others don't think it's a good idea to become overly concerned about tango lyrics and the many Lunfardo words they contain. Intellectualizing too much, they argue, takes the fun out of the dance and lyrics. One internet contributor invoked physicist Werner Heisenberg's Uncertainty Principle and the related observer effect, which suggests that the very act of measuring something changes its nature, and continued, "I think the same is true for tango. When we discuss, we risk making the discussion more important than the actual phenomenon."

Most dancers outside Argentina show little interest in tango lyrics and instead focus on the music as it applies to their dancing. Some tango lyrics are so heavily laced with Lunfardo even native Argentines have difficulty understanding them. Most non-Argentine dancers happily dance to tango songs without the foggiest notion of what the songs are about. Periodically internet tango sites sizzle at length with debates about whether or not ultimate satisfaction can be had in dancing to words not understood. Because Argentine Tango demands that dancers interpret the music, some advocates insist that dancers should learn Spanish. Others urge that Lunfardo should be studied as well so that dancers may "dance to the songs more meaningfully," and that interpretation can only be "poignant and enjoyable" if dancers understand what the songs are about.

"How sad it is for some folks who really enjoy tango but miss out on the wonderful words," one observer wrote. "True, I had to learn a lot of Lunfardo to understand some of those tangos." A contrasting view comes from Melinda Bates of Washington, D.C.: "Frankly, I can't see how my dance could be more enjoyable if I understood that the protagonist is singing about how miserable he was about losing his partner's love and how he felt the only recourse for him was to put a knife in her back and then one in himself so they could die together." (A detailed explanation of Lunfardo will be found in a later chapter.)

Tango: The Silent Language of Dance

Learning the language of tango is similar to conventional learning to speak a foreign language. First the words are learned, then phrases, then sentences, then paragraphs. In tango, technique and simple steps are usually learned first, and then steps are linked to form a phrase or pattern, the *figura*. Dancers strive to put the dance phrases together with grace and elegance, according to the music and flow of dancers on the floor. As in spoken languages, users are encouraged to vary words (steps) and phrases (figuras) in order to avoid boredom and add interest to the conversation (dance). One mark of a successful tango is not to dance a pattern more than once in a piece of music. This is not easy, particularly for beginners.

Although all partnered dance requires some communication between leader and follower, social dances other than tango draw upon a comparatively few fixed steps and patterns; the leader's role in directing the dance is straightforward enough. Should the follower lose her way, she need only glance at her partner's feet and mirror his steps, which is impossible in tango since much of the time the partners will be executing different steps and patterns or dancing to different rhythms or beats of the complex music.

Thus, leading and following skills are more important in tango than in any other social dance. The leader must communicate his intentions through subtle, non-verbal actions with definite and clear leading. In tango's silent conversation, the leader suggests movements to the follower, and the follower wordlessly accepts or rejects the suggestions.

Not Erotic, but Intimate; Sensual but Not Sexual

Because of the embrace and closeness of body movements, the intimate speechless conversation in tango is often perceived by spectators as being erotic, an impression far from reality. When dancing, serious tango dancers are primarily interested in dancing well while creating an interesting and enjoyable work of art. They are well aware that dancers sitting at tables are closely watching dancers on the floor, looking for good or unusual moves, and noting lapses of elegance. Dancers know they are "on stage" and appreciate that it is not the place for seduction and romance.

To eavesdrop on a few moments of shoptalk among tango dancers, one quickly dispels a common outsiders' misconception about tango's sexuality in that the tango is amazingly sensual without being sexual. In fact, it is almost as if bringing in overt sexual energy would be an intrusion, a dilution, or diminishment of what is available. In tango, partners are happy to connect with their partner to create a time and space where they engage at a molecular level and as such it is intimate. And when the dance is over, it's over – everything becomes a part of the past; they can acknowledge what they shared and move on to the next moment.

An important aspect of the dance that sets tango apart is that although the intimacy of the embrace and foot and leg movements appear to suggest sexual interest or seductive intent, dancers rarely think of their movements as erotic. Far from eroticism or emotion in the minds of the dancers, their focus is on the highly controlled movements of their feet. Uninformed spectators who see foot movements that force a partner's legs apart and into 'sandwiches' where the woman's foot is embraced by the man's feet, or the woman brushing her foot against the man's calf, for example, may erroneously infer signals of erotic intentions.

The early tangos danced between men represented a sort of duel between male dancers, a model recaptured by the gang in *West Side Story*. Tango aficionado Robert Duval contends that the dance is not sexual: "The tango is a war between legs."

Tango is sensual in that it is essential for couples to touch one another to connect regarding the couple's feelings about the music in order to interpret the music. The more intense are the feelings of the music, the better the dance. But rather than romance, partners' thoughts must be on mechanics and technique. Each dancer has to be totally absorbed in the partner on a communicative rather than a sexual level.

However, some dancers allow that they occasionally feel an exaggerated intimacy, a sexual pull, during a dance. But everyone is aware that it "just isn't done" to make romantic advances. The more intense the feelings of the music, the better the dance, and although bodies touch, sometimes very closely, there is no choice but to concentrate on mechanics and technique. As a result, the tango dance floor is considered to be a socially controlled and secure environment for both partners. Charles Roques wrote on the internet, "Tango is very romantic for me, but I don't use it as a means to pick up women... I try to be very cautious about crossing that line. After all, we dance close and make physical contact in a way that off the dance floor would be considered very forward."

The Tango Trance

Few social dances are so intense that they are able to generate such strong feelings during a dance – "when everything clicks" – that create a trance-like state of affects in one or both partners. Although there is no intimation of expected sexuality, dancers sometimes experience what has come to be called the "tango trance," or "a three minute love affair." One dancer explained the feeling: "The best tango is when after it's over I feel as though I should have a cigarette."

Generally experienced by more accomplished dancers, the tango trance doesn't occur often, sometimes never. It can happen between two people who are friendly, with two who have never met before, or even with a partner not particularly liked. Because the tango trance is so elusive, subjective, and personal, dancers themselves best convey its essence. A dance student at a Pablo Veron workshop in Paris declared: "When this dance works, the feeling is fabulous and exhilarating. It is the closest thing I ever expect to come to flying.... It is poetry in motion."

"It is possible for the trance to be experienced by only one partner at a time, since in tango it is difficult for two people to agree on anything, much less a 'feeling'. The late Martha Graham's famous comment captures such moments, 'when one feels at one with the universe'."

Others have said: "It doesn't happen every night. But when it does happen, it's very powerful and it keeps you looking for it. It's almost like a meditative state where two people can transmit feeling to each other without speaking; although the tango trance might be experienced once, there is no knowing when or if it will ever occur again. I've never met anyone who could explain it." And yet another respondent wrote: "The sensation is that the boundary between you and your partner melts away and you in effect become one with your partner."

Once someone has experienced that searing connection, that momentary union and intimacy, they want more of it. So they pay tons of money, suffer painful shoes, invest time and sweat in classes and practicas.

Few Casual Tango Dancers

Because the dance conveys an obligation to create something original and beautiful, dancers take the responsibility seriously; this is usually reflected in the lack of smiles of dancers' faces. The tension of creation or fear of failure is evident in the "tango frown" or "tango grimace" but may lead uninitiated spectators to worry that the dancers are truly miserable - while the truth is that they are having a wonderful time.

Tango is Hard on Relationships

"Romantic couples can very rarely be good dance partners. The tango often tears couples apart, and it is better to be dance partners with someone with whom you have no romantic interest." (Richard Powers, Dance historian, Stanford University)

In part because of its broad freedom of movement, the complexity of its music, strict adherence to technique, and the familiarity of its dance floor codes, tango can engender extraordinary emotional intensity for couples. Each dancer's performance is so inexorably linked to the partner's that is essential they communicate with total concentration, wholly immersed in wordless dialogue of leaders' requests and followers' acceptance. Breakdowns in dance communication can arise from many causes, among them inexperience, lack of skill, and behavior perceived by one partner to be problematic, even unacceptable.

Intensely focused dancers may sometimes lose their sense of humor and flexibility. Leaders, responsible for the choreography and tone of each dance, may sometimes assume a brusque tone with their followers. If his partner fails to respond appropriately to what he perceives to have been his clear lead, afterwards he might ask her why, when he had led a move correctly, did she do something else? One woman reported that when dancing in Paris and executing a *gancho* (a swift kick between her partner's legs) that was not indicated by the leader, she was reprimanded by her French partner: "Je ne fait pas le tango du cirque!" (I don't do circus tango!) Another hissed menacingly at his partner, "Move only when I tell you to! Don't anticipate!"

If dancers disappointed with their partners are strangers, it's not difficult to solve such problems. But friends or long-term partners not uncommonly find that tango puts a strain on relationships: "I feel that tango magnifies relationships and shows everything that is hidden and brings it to light. It's like putting a relationship under a magnifying glass. It's a dangerous dance!"

With other partnered dances there is little to disagree about, so the emotional level stays low; people dance for amusement, for diversion. With tango, however, the implicit obligation to honor the music and create a new and beautiful dance each time generates pressures, both self-induced and external, to dance well, but only in true partnership.

Because so many elements of tango are open to interpretation, differences of opinion about movement or technique sometimes produce scowls and spoken criticism both on and off the dance floor. Lacking the diagramed structure common to ballroom dance, interpretive differences and expectations can easily lead to sometimes heated discussion.

It is one thing to be annoyed by a partner's lack of attention or skill during one dance, but differences can continue at home and sometimes linger for days, and arguments between partners sometimes end in vitriolic public disagreements. Parallels between tango, outside Argentina, and the card game bridge are sometimes seen because similar personality types are drawn to both activities: bright, intellectual, often upper-middle-class people who enjoy challenge with their amusement. Bridge partners know well the importance of such cooperation, depending wholly upon one another for success: inept bidding or careless play can quickly result in serious discord and worse.

Barbara, an internet contributor, writes, "My husband and I took up tango in the 27th year of our marriage. Before tango we had almost never had a fight. Tango practice engendered major disagreements.... I think tango brings out basic issues of domination, submission, equality, not to mention more esoteric opinions of style, technique, etc. If a relationship is not strong enough, if the commitment is not there, tango can be dangerous." Another internet contributor wrote: "An important thing to keep in mind if you mix tango and romance is that you don't let tango become more important than the relationship."

At a weeklong workshop in Umbria, Italy, several couples displayed daily disputes, their agitated criticisms punctuated with scowls and deep frowns that were embarrassing to watch. At the end of the week, teachers Gustavo Naveira and Giselle Anne were asked, "How many divorces do you think have resulted from your workshops?"

At the extreme, "Try as you might to escape it, tango is war."
— Robert Duval

A Sense of Community

An inveterate conversation opener at any tango event is, "How long have you been dancing tango?" Answers may convey clues to the skill level of a potential partner or the respondent's degree of seriousness, matters seldom of interest to non-tango dancers. The tango's deep sense of community is particularly evident when dancers travel to workshops in locales where they know no one but easily fit in: "If you dance tango, you are greeted by strangers as if they had known you for years." Conversations are easily begun, friendships quickly formed.

Many dancers are attracted to the tango's sense of community. Accepting that the dance itself provides the principal dynamic force that binds contemporary dance communities together, it may be confidently asserted that no other dance generates such diverse and compelling attraction as does tango.

In a reality that may at first glance seem improbable, tango's appeal spans widely diverse personality types, occupations, and social strata. Despite the dance's somewhat elitist image, tango communities may, in fact, be the most democratic of any in popular dance. (In Argentina this is not always the case because tango dances are often social affairs.)

Normally, regardless of physical or mental challenge, age, gender, or sexual preference, the only criteria for acceptance into the tango community is a person's ability to move around the dance floor in an elegant manner and a strong desire to dance often and well. Further, a chronic shortage of male dancers ensures that any good male dancer, regardless of age, appearance, or social standing may be confident he can dance pretty much every dance with any woman he chooses, even the most sought-after partners – the youngest, most beautiful, and most talented dancers.

Ageless Eclecticism

By the opening decades of the 21st century, the tango universe emerged as a thriving, all-encompassing transnational coterie whose members were essentially unconcerned with one another's age, appearance, educational and professional achievements, social standing, wealth, or other conventional criteria of social acceptance. All they care about is the quality of the dancing.

Although there is undisputed appeal of youth in tango communities, there is a refreshing absence of ageism. One

San Francisco dancer effused, "Among the things I like most about tango is that without problems or insinuations, I get to embrace other people's husbands/lovers, not to mention uncommitted single men of all ages. Some could be my father, some could be my grandchildren, and of course all the delightful gentlemen in between." Others appreciate friendships that are sometimes formed with people who might have no contact were it not for tango.

Tango exerts a strong appeal to those who recognize an activity with no age bounds, something they will be able to enjoy for a lifetime. It attracts those with an openness of spirit who are not locked into dancing only within their own age or social group; at any milonga it is not unusual to see partners with age differences of twenty to fifty years. At most other public dances, the average age tends to be in the twenties to thirties, whereas a tango dance will almost always have a majority of dancers aged forty, with many ten to twenty years older. Dancers say that they enjoy the give and take of partners who are not in their age group.

Robert Fulghum, author of *All I really Need to Know I Learned in Kindergarten,* described himself as a beginning tango student who was welcomed into the tango community even though he was: "a white-haired, seventy-year old man whose pot-belly shows no matter how hard he tries to suck it in." He discovered that although all were welcome to join the community, he found that regardless of age: "Tango is not for wimps. Tango training requires stamina, fitness, and the ability to make quick, graceful moves without falling down." He wrote about going to Buenos Aires to study tango. "To spend three months in a foreign city learning a dance may seem, on the face of it, a frivolous enterprise. Self-indulgent play. But there is more to it than that. The adventure was meant to be a gift to myself in honor of my 70th birthday. Affirmative exile to keep the fires burning in my belly—the ones that are stoked by being provoked and stretched and disturbed by a new environment that requires a high alert of all my senses. A plunge into a culture not my own. To go consciously naïve about what I would find and experience. To go to the well of tango armed mostly with the tools of enthusiasm and an open mind. The fear of the unknown matched by the excitement of the possible."

On each of my own dozen or so visits to Buenos Aires, also initiated at seventy, I remember dancing with an Argentine gentleman, very small and slight in stature, who said his age was in the mid-nineties, and he certainly looked it. He danced every day, sometimes at both matinee and evening milongas, and although his skills had diminished, he enjoyed his pick of the most attractive and skilled women. He obviously enjoyed every minute of his time in the milonga. He frequently asked me to dance, but he looked so frail and was sometimes so unsteady on his feet that each time I danced with him, I worried that he might expire right there and then. (In 2007, I was saddened to read in one of the tango magazines of his passing.)

Traveling Tango

Another aspect that makes tango unique is that few non-tango dancers travel so widely and frequently as do tango enthusiasts. Since the phenomenal successes of the theatrical tango shows in the mid-1980s, the dance has flourished dramatically all around the globe, particularly in the prosperous nations of the West. Eager to incorporate new ideas into their own dancing, they are beckoned by ceaseless rounds of workshops and festivals where dancers may observe and learn new steps, styles, and techniques, with the added attraction of travel to destinations they might not otherwise visit.

Unique within popular dance, Argentine Tango continuously fields troupes of professional dancers that tour the world offering performances and lessons. Since Fred Astaire and Arthur Murray fox-trotted off the scene, no grand household names have come to illuminate social dancing, but there is a distinguished informal cadre of Argentine Tango stars who travel extensively to regional, national, and international festivals. When dancers live in places where Argentine performers and teachers do not regularly visit, they will travel great distances to see these performers. Complementing the opportunities to study with famous teachers and attend theatrical performances, followers of the international circuit relish meeting old acquaintances and making new ones from diverse cultures. The heady atmosphere of "total immersion" at tango events especially favors swift, intense friendships and camaraderie reminiscent of the magic of children's summer camps.

Particularly for dancers not sharing a common language, such relationships might be fleeting but nevertheless valuable. At a monthly tango marathon in Nijmegen in The Netherlands that attracts dancers from all over Europe and beyond, I was asked to dance by a man of obvious Middle East origins, and before the music began I attempted to make small talk in a common language by asking him if he spoke English, to which he replied 'No'; then I asked about French or Spanish. With a quick smile, he ventured, "I speak tango," and off we danced. He was a good dancer, so after a few turns; I tried my trick of stealing the lead. Both of us laughed heartily while he struggled to regain the lead – which he did with elegance and grace. After our dance, we separated with warm feelings about people from distant lands.

Although dancers may not keep in touch with those they've met at a workshop or festival, they frequently run into one another at subsequent events. On the first day of any international festival, eager dancers greet one another with broad smiles of recognition, kissing, and welcoming hugs. From diverse countries, many have formed fond, enduring friendships and arrange to meet at particular tango events or to visit Buenos Aires at the same time, sometimes sharing an apartment or staying in the same tango guesthouse.

Mingle With the Best

Among the attractions of tango-related travel is interaction between students and the "stars." Many famous tango performers and teachers travel widely, so that a non-trivial incentive for dancers to travel is the opportunity to mingle with such luminaries without needing to fly all the way to Buenos Aires. Participants observe performances close-up and enjoy private and group lessons with top dancers, a learning privilege seldom enjoyed in other disciplines. In between lessons and at meals, ample informal opportunities arise to meet and become acquainted with celebrities. Occasionally, stars will dance with students. For many tango dancers, to study and converse with Maria Nieves or Rodolfo Dinzel would compare to an aspiring ballet student joining Mikhail Baryshnikov at the barre.

Spiritual Call

In common with true cults, tango newcomers are warmly welcomed and quickly accepted, made to feel desired and comfortable by both beginners and advanced dancers. Experienced dancers well remember their first awkward attempts on the dance floor and do their best to encourage novices whom they commonly invite to coffee breaks or meals. They make time during and after class to answer questions and to illustrate steps or movements. Traditionally, new dancers are made to feel welcome by being addressed in tango's familiar honorifics, 'tanguera' or 'tanguero' – a gesture of inclusion even though the titles indicate nothing about skills, merely that the person is seriously interested in tango.

Although the cult label in its religious sense is surely hyperbole, occasional observers see in tango elements commonly associated with religious experience and spirituality in general, and in conversation within the tango fraternity, references to the metaphysical and the spiritual often recur. Internet contributors explain: "Tango for me is a soul thing, very spiritual. Argentine Tango dancers are totally free to express their inner spirit of the dance. After a tango dance lesson, workshop or whatever, I have a feeling of peace. It is great. My soul is at rest." " You incorporate tango into your life. In many cases, it's like a religion."

A questionnaire respondent wrote: "In Argentine Tango people are totally free to express their inner spirit of the dance…After a tango dance, lesson, workshop or whatever, I have such a feeling of peace, and it is great. My soul is at rest." Another said, "Tango for me is a soul thing, very spiritual." Yet another observed, "The more one experiences the inner contact with the self through the practice of tango, the more agreeable it gets. The process is comparable to the spiritual quest that allows a gradual and increasingly enjoyable connection with the inner self, the inner being with the soul. Tango is another mystical ritual for the human soul."

A Western scholar visiting Japan approached a Shinto priest in a small temple and said, "I've been to a good many ceremonies and have seen quite a number of shrines, but I don't understand the ideology. I don't understand your theology." The priest slowly shook his head, "I think we don't have ideology. We don't have theology. We dance."

As with other groups of fervent devotees, tango dancers are inveterate proselytizers. Convinced that theirs is the most beautiful and interesting of dances, they want their friends to experience the same pleasure they do. Most dancers admit to having tried at one time or another to convert a friend to tango, seldom with success. Wrote one dancer on the internet, "I believe my non-tango friends think they understand my enthusiasm, but I doubt they really do. I just let them think what they will about why I enjoy it so." Said another, "A few tango dancers become so devoted to their particular brand of tango that it becomes a religion, and they display some of the more reprehensible aspects of fanaticism and claim their style to be the only 'authentic' style. Or they assert that everyone in Buenos Aires dances their way.... Real tango is much more than any one person's image of it.... It's a rich fountain of possibility, a complex palette of colors, a sophisticated language of expression."

Perhaps unsurprisingly in the context of tango's parallels with order, discipline, and spiritual devotion, conversation among devotees sometimes includes the word "guru," defined by the American Heritage Dictionary as "a personal spiritual teacher; a teacher and guide in spiritual and philosophical matters; a trusted counselor and adviser; a mentor." Just as movements and cults often rely upon gurus to guide them, in some cities where there are many tango practitioners, a guru-like aura may surround certain teachers reputed to be especially fine – and charismatic.

Guru status often increases in proportion to the number of student followers.

Sometimes students will only attend milongas frequented by their teacher, and word circulates among student followers in advance about when and where he or she is going to dance. Although students don't actually sit at the guru-teacher's feet, among women a certain amount of vying for attention occurs, and many sit as close as possible in the hope of being chosen to dance by the guru, who may appear as if he is surrounded by adoring disciples. Some teachers encourage such adulation, while others seem a bit embarrassed by it. A few make it a practice never to dance with students at a public dance, some do it rarely, and fewer do it frequently. Because each teacher imparts a particular style, savvy observers are able to discern a dancer's teacher by watching dancers at a milonga.

When dancers come to feel that tango is consuming too much of their lives, they may decide to stop dancing, for a while or permanently. Some talk of quitting "cold turkey" or of getting "deprogrammed." At one Buenos Aires festival, a dancer from New York announced, "When I get home I'm going to a shrink to see about getting deprogrammed from tango." Sitting at the same table was a St. Louis psychiatrist, Barette Salazar, who responded: "Gee, I can visualize a whole new area of specialization for me. With my dancing experience, I should be able to make a bundle deprogramming tango dancers."

Gilles, a Paris financial journalist announced, "I've stopped dancing tango because it was keeping me from looking for and finding romance." He has been sighted among the spectators at the outdoor dancing by the Seine River and at occasional concerts, but he has not resumed dancing. Most dancers dismiss the notion of deprogramming because they feel their lives are so enriched by tango that the thought of stopping never enters their minds.

Elitism, Empathy, Factions

As with other human enterprises that attract fervent adherents, from religions to political parties, the lively tango community exhibits spirited controversy and considerable factionalism. Among substantive issues and ideas sparking debate are the respective places of traditional and modern music on the dance floor, open or closed embrace techniques, and many more. But while matters relating to the dance itself present endless possibilities for contrasting views and feelings, the fundamental currents of all human psychology and sociology are what most profoundly influence the dynamics within the tango community.

However vibrant and resilient their core harmony, dynamic communities based on a common interest frequently give rise to rival cliques within, and the globally diverse and energetic world of tango is no exception. Tango's most divisive issue may be the choice of dance styles, and since the early 1900s dancers have argued about which is the "real tango." Some clique members appoint themselves arbiters of correctness, delivering such derisive dicta as, "That's cute, but they don't do it that way in Buenos Aires." Such folks are tagged as "The Tango Police," or "Tango Nazis." Accompanying such unappealing behavior is the more general tendency within social groups – from teenage girls to country clubs – for the emergence of in-groups and snobbery. When such polarization develops, those who are not part of established in-groups may be left with no illusions: no matter how hard they practice or persist, they will never earn a place at the "in" table. "Non-in" women should not expect an invitation to the dance from an "in" man; and only the most audacious "non-in" fellow would ask an "in" woman to dance. Exceptions are sometimes made for exceedingly attractive young women with knockout figures, better yet if clothed in exotic dress, or handsome men of any age.

Inevitably some dancers are drawn to the aura of elitism and exclusivity associated with dancing tango, an allure seldom evident in other social dances. In part because of the difficulty of the dance and admiration for achieved mastery, a certain hierarchy almost inevitably evolves within subsets of the larger community, a sort of social Darwinism. Moreover, and not without irony, since its introduction to Paris at the beginning of the 20th century, the tango has often been perceived simultaneously as a dance of the aristocracy and the wealthy, and as a meritocracy, a "dance of the people," with laurels bestowed on the best dancers, no matter their origins or social standing.

Tango friends and acquaintances enjoy the additional bond of appreciating the effort and accomplishment of those who have persevered to learn something extremely difficult. Besides the mutual recognition of their achievement, they appreciate that for many dancers tango has become a central part of their lives.

Fashion and the Dance

Many religious communities decree dress codes only when adherents attend religious events and others extend them to everyday life. In tango, the opposite is true; dancers can wear anything they please to milongas, so long they are neat, clean, and allow full leg motion. At lessons or practicas, women often wear trousers and any of various top styles, while men wear trousers and a sports shirt or sweater;

jeans are rarely worn; scruffiness of any sort is definitely out. For milongas, many women dress elaborately in cocktail dresses of sequins, fringes, and shiny materials. In order to ensure free leg movement, narrow skirts must be split at least to the knee, and sometimes to the thigh. Although not mandated, black is by far the most popular color for both men and women; bright red is second. Both have become "tango colors."

However, there are always exceptions to the norm. At the Balago, a Paris nightclub dating from the 1930s, Argentine tango is danced on Sundays until midnight, and then Salsa takes over. One night Salsa dancers arrived early and invaded the dance floor and tried to dance to the tango music. Two tango dancers, one in his twenties, the other in his sixties, stood at the edge of the floor, watching the goslings in undisguised contempt. The young man said to his colleague, "I think tango dancers are obligated to dress correctly to denote respect for such an elegant dance."

Among the first professionals to break the dress code was the Argentine performer and teacher, Mariano "Chicho" Frúmboli, one member of the quartet of performers and teachers called *New Tango*. He lives in Paris, and when he began appearing at milongas sporting pink hair, earrings, large baggy pants and shirt, and pink sneakers, people were at first amazed, and many laughed dismissively. But when they saw him dance, their laughter died.

Because spectators' eyes are on dancers' feet and because comfort is essential, shoes acquire great importance. Indeed, at a tango dance it is possible to look around the hall and distinguish the better dancers even before anyone steps onto the dance floor: only excellent dancers wear flashy shoes. Some women wear shoes of bright colors with trim of silver or gold, sometimes with rhinestones and sequins. Many accomplished male dancers also obsess about shoes, with black patent leather being the favorite, but bright or even two-tone colors are sometimes seen. While Argentines commonly dance in their street shoes, in other countries street shoes are never worn on the dance floor, where rough soles and the grit they hold will damage the floor's fine finish. Smooth, thin-soled leather or suede soles that enable dancers to glide and pivot easily are much preferred, and dancers are always looking for the "perfect shoe" that is practical and attractive.

Tango dancers outside Argentina do not dance in street shoes, but bring dance shoes and change into them when they arrive at the dance event, to the amusement of the Argentines. The few Argentines who do bring special dance shoes would never consider changing them at the tables as do the foreigners, but retire discreetly to the rest rooms for shoe changing.

With men and women alike, suitable shoes are essential for comfort and for precise footwork. Women generally prefer high or medium-high heels with some sort of strap across the instep to keep the shoe from moving on the foot; closed toes help protect feet from clumsy partners. Thin suede or fine leather soles enable dancers to pivot and turn more easily and permit a better grip of the floor. Rather than slip-on styles, men favor laced shoes for instep protection and to prevent slipping inside the shoe. Some young dancers buy tennis or other sport shoes and have the soles replaced with suede.

When, How, and Where Will We Dance?

Social tango dancing is not found in conventional dance clubs because the proportion of people dancing tango remains small, and there are comparatively few places to dance. Outside large cities milongas are usually held several nights a week, frequently in such offbeat venues as old warehouses and the back rooms of cafés, bars, or restaurants after regular clients have left. They also dance in church halls, cultural centers, gymnasiums or charmless dance studios with no place to sit. In New York City, tango is danced in a former slaughterhouse on the river docks. The fact that tango must be sought out adds to its mystique. In many cities dance venues change frequently, not unlike American speakeasies of the 1920s but without the password. Lucille Krasne explained the principal obstacle to the operation of tango dance venues is that: "Restaurants, bars, and cafés don't want us," she notes, "because we don't drink. All we do is dance."

JOHN GILBERT & MAE MURRAY
(La Veuve Joyeuse)

383

CHAPTER THREE

The Dance: Styles – Music - Technique

"The tango is two bodies, four legs, and one heart."
(Juan Carlos Copes, Argentina,
Choreographer, Performer, Teacher)

In Argentina, tango is primarily a social event, with dancers sitting at the same tables each   week to converse and do some dancing. Although rigorous data is not easily available in other parts of the world, organizers of tango events do not necessarily expect to make a profit and consider themselves lucky if they manage to break even. Their main interest is in popularizing tango and to make sure they and their friends have a place to dance.

The accepted goal of Argentine Tango dancers is aesthetic – to create a unique, beautiful, graceful, and elegant dance, a deeply collaborative objective that motivates couples to dance well for themselves and one another. When accomplished well, the tango is a dance of extraordinary complexity, intricacy and subtlety. Its sweeping flow is characterized by swift, dramatic changes in direction and position punctuated with smoothly staccato movements. Basically the tango is a walking dance involving straight lines and pivots to music which utilizes three time signatures: 4/4 for the "tango" tango, 2/4 for the milonga, and 3/4 for the tango waltz. The footwork in any signature, however, can be exquisitely intricate, depending on the partners' fancies.

Part of tango's appeal to dancers is its difficulty, and many dancers are drawn to the Argentine Tango for the challenge. Except for some staged performances, all tango's

59

steps and movement are "choreographed" in the moment – couples are free to move how and where they wish, within limits of space and courtesy to other dancers. Interpretation of the music, depending on the feelings generated by the music, is left to the leader, who improvises steps and body movements "on the spot" so that no two tangos are ever the same.

However, the freedom of movement around the dance floor does not exclude accepted techniques which make lessons and dedication essential. Once a threshold of technique skill levels are reached, dancers soon begin to savor the tango's elemental interactivity, its characteristic dynamic interplay between partners that gives the dance so much of its powerful appeal. Suddenly beyond the early work, practice, and frustration, there emerges a sense of the profound freedom, frequently followed by obsession. In the book, *Tango: An Anxious Quest for Freedom*, Rodolpho Dinzel analyzes the dynamics of the tango couple, their allotted space on the dance floor, and the role of aesthetics.

Tango Music Rhythms

Tango music has three distinct and easily identifiable rhythms: the classic tango, the milonga (also the name for tango dance halls), and the tango waltz, but instead of dancing only to the beat, dancers can also move to the melody or mood. This frequently results in partners doing very different steps at the same time, with the leader dancing to a slow beat while leading his partner to take faster steps following the melody or partners dance the same steps on the same beat. Within a single tango, frequent changes in tempo may signal dramatic changes in mood and rhythm that dancers should acknowledge. It is a tango maxim that "dancers who simply do steps without responding to the music are not dancing the tango." Most of the music played at today's tango dances is from the thirties, forties and early fifties, making it easier to dance to the music because it is familiar.

Classical Tango

Classical tangos (in contrast to the milonga and the tango waltz) generally share a strong, uncomplicated beat and are easily danced to, but much of the music includes tempo changes within one song. A piece begun as a slow rhythm may switch to a faster one or even to double time and back again. Also, there is the pause (which does not occur in the milonga or waltz) when nothing seems to be happening, but which many dancers regard as an important element of the dance. The tango is almost always slower than either the waltz or the milonga, which gives dancers the freedom to dance off beat, on the beat, or to the melody or the music's mood. There is also the freedom not to move at all, the all-important pause.

A peculiar aspect of the tango is the musical and non-musical pauses between phrases, when the leader stops movement on the floor. The pause may be the most overlooked element of dancing musically and navigating well. A pause can be a great strategy for adjusting to crowded floor conditions and to refine one's timing. Upon pausing, other little, subtle, and stationary movements can also be found. They can provide among the most rewarding moments in a shared tango.

Pauses can actually be initiated in many places, not necessarily only when the music stops, although they are not used when the music is rapid. Movement on the floor ceases during a pause, but the bodies may unobtrusively mark time with several shifts of weight so that intention is shared internally between the partners but hidden from others. Some claim that pauses make the next beat "that much stronger," Dan Boccia wrote: "One of the hidden powers of tango is the ability to pause but still retain the feeling and motion of dancing and connection with your partner and the music. It may look like the man stops dancing to allow the woman to express herself with adornments, but we know that the man is still dancing, still interpreting the music, still navigating. To me, during these moments, the partnership connection is often intensified dramatically. Tension can be built up, allowing the opportunity for explosive releases."

Milonga

The milonga rhythm originated in rural Argentina, played and sung by itinerant *payadores* (usually black gauchos) who roamed the countryside in the early 1900s and later became popular in the cities. Between 1910 and 1920, the predominant milonga rhythm was lilting and march-like, but during the 1930s it accelerated, drawing upon the African slave's *candombe* drum rhythms. Although some milonga songs of gypsy origin are mournful, slow, and heartrendingly beautiful, most milongas played today are light-hearted and lively. The milonga is considered by some dancers to be the most difficult of the three types of tango because its phrasing leaves no time to mend mistakes. It was not until 1950 that the raising of the foot off the floor by either partner was first seen in center city milongas. As with all tango, there are no rules of movement; some leaders prefer to walk smartly to the rhythm with short or long bouncy steps; but most dancers favor short steps, their lightness sometimes bordering on the comic. Many intricate steps uniquely suited to milonga music have been devised, offering a diversity that is not without complication. Michel Ditkoff observed, "Part of the difficulty of dancing milonga is that dancers have to realize the difference between notes and beats. If you try to step on every note, you will be exhausted half way through a song. If you stay on the beat, you don't have to rush."

Waltz

The tango waltz is faster than the conventional Viennese model although it is based upon the three-beat rhythm and, as with all tango, movement is improvised with no obligatory steps; everything is valid as long as dancers observe the beat. Some steps have evolved that are particularly appropriate to the waltz rhythm, and they are commonly used. Thus, although ordinary tango steps can be used for the milonga and waltz, many dancers like a change from the classic tango and prefer to add variety to their dance – one reason for the frequency of workshops devoted to the milonga or waltz.

The Nuevo Tango Music of Astor Piazzolla

During the 1960s, Argentine composer Astor Piazzolla (1921-1992), a classically trained pianist, bandoneon player, and orchestra leader, played and arranged tango dance music with enormous success. He and his family spent their early years in New York City, where he became fascinated with jazz, and began to experiment with a fusion of classical music, jazz, and tango – music he insisted was meant not for dancing, "only for listening." The term *Nuevo Tango* soon became attached to his exquisitely refined work, which hardcore traditionalists maintained was "not tango music at all" and which the composer himself referred to not as "tango," but as "modern Argentine music."

Despite his wishes, Piazzolla's compositions became inseparably associated with stage tango. Outside Argentina, a set of Piazzolla music is often incorporated into an evening of dance, customarily at the end, but in Argentina it is heard mostly in milongas frequented by young dancers; older dancers don't consider any music composed after the 1950s to be "danceable."

Contemporary Music: Gotan Project and Technotango

"The trio treats tango with love and respect, but also with a little irreverence." (Philippe Cohen Solal)

The entirely new technotango music was started by the band, *Gotan Project,* a European trio consisting of Argentine Eduardo Makaroff, Parisian Philippe Cohen Solal, and Swiss-born Christoph H. Müller. After they began playing their unique versions of the tango at the start of the new millennium, electronic tango music – soon dubbed "technotango" – emerged. The fusion of tango and electronic music has enjoyed wide popularity among young tango dancers as well as with audiences who do not dance tango: their CD, *La Revancha del Tango,* sold more than a million copies and it has recently been showing up as background music for the prestigious BBC television commercials that have nothing to do with tango. *Gotan Project* concerts in Europe are consistently sold out; their CDs fly off the shelves, and in classes and milongas outside Argentina, a tanda of electronic tango music is often played.

Other techno-tango groups have since appeared but they are largely confined to milongas catering to younger dancers. Many seasoned tango enthusiasts are delighted that such music is drawing the next generation to the tango, providing hope that the dance will not suffer the strangling neglect of the 1960s and 1970s.

Contemporary Orchestras: Old Music

Of the many tango contemporary groups from countries outside Argentina performing around the world, some compose their own music, but most play original dance music from the 1940s and 50s. Some specialize in music for listening; a few earn invitations to Buenos Aires. Peculiar to tango, today there are modern orchestras that play only the music of the Golden Age and in the very same style. In Buenos Aires, Beba Pugliese plays piano and conducts an orchestra that exactly replicates the style of her famous father, Osvaldo Pugliese. (Outside Argentina, alternative tango is danced to swing music of the 40s and 50s and is revered by swing dancers, but there are no orchestras that play only the historically accurate duplications of orchestras from that period.)

Dance Styles

"Tango is so rich and flexible that it acts like a Rorschach test. Everyone sees themselves in it; this is why we go nuts about whatever style we adopt, because we have fallen in love with ourselves." (Larry Carroll, dancer, engineer)

When talking about the enormous choice of movements in tango, performer and teacher Carlos Gavito – *star of Forever Tango* – insists, "The more you know, the less you need." Perhaps not surprisingly, there appear to be as many ways to dance tango as there are dancers, confirmed by the familiar saying, "Five dancers discussing Argentine Tango will have fifteen opinions."

There is no definitive style of Argentine Tango, nor has any authority been recognized as arbiter of how it should be danced. Each dancer is expected to create an individual style. Some believe that many steps and "figuras" should be complicated and showy, but experienced dancers recognize that elegant tangos can be achieved with a minimum of movement.

Some dancers prefer to dance a single style consistently, but most moderate their style according to each piece of music. It isn't even unusual for a leader to switch styles during a single piece. Beginning dancers who first learn a particular style with one teacher may not realize that there are other styles from which to choose. Eventually in workshops, festivals, or demonstrations, they will be exposed to other styles. Good teachers know that one style is not necessarily best for everyone and encourage their students to work with other local teachers and to attend festivals and workshops given by visiting Argentine Tango teachers. Commented Larry Carroll, "As beginners become more experienced, they can build their own style, taking what they like from others, perhaps adding their own unique contribution, which others can use. So, tango continues to become richer, like an artwork that is never finished but is always complete and beautiful."

Disputes about style are as old as the dance itself. In the 1920s, a prominent French magazine, *Caritas y Carinos,* featured a long article illustrated with drawings of couples dancing the salon tango and fantasy styles. The amusing narrative discussed the proponents' views of which could be considered "the real tango." Debate has increased with the emergence of additional variations during tango's history. Some dancers believe there is one "true tango" – the style that evolved only in Buenos Aires and that any change is anathema and debases a great art form. Others consider change positive, as a source of growth and renewal. Maria Nieves, one of the most prominent and revered of contemporary milongueras, spoke of changing styles and her long partnership with famed choreographer, teacher, and performer, Juan Carlos Copes: "We changed and revolutionized tango and gave it respectability, and young people must do the same. We invented a lot of our own steps. They must invent theirs. We found our own personality and style, and the young have the responsibility to do the same. Tango must change or it will die."

The Salida: 8-Count Basic

Improvisation cannot be taught, so asking a beginning tango student to improvise in a first lesson is akin to giving a blank canvas and box of paints to a beginning art student and telling him to create a work of art, without being taught the basics of painting. During the 1940s when so many people were beginning to learn tango, some teachers taught an opening back step pattern (salida means to leave). This method, still in use by many teachers today, is only meant to be a framework or suggestion of a way to begin a dance, with the possibility of alteration at any time. Many teachers use a basic pattern for beginning students as a way to get them moving around the dance floor to the music and to help them adjust to tango rhythms.

Differences in dance styles are patently visible in the salida, which can be improvised in many ways: with long, sweeping steps, shorter steps, or a combination of the two; long or short pauses can be introduced as well as simple or intricate decorations inserted between the steps. (My all-time favorite is called the "40s salida," when the leader does a weight change on the third step followed by a pause before joining his partner at the end of the salida. Very elegant.)

Milonguero Style

"*The milonguero style tango begins with a hug.*" (Carlos Gavito)

Of all the tango styles, the milonguero style engenders the most controversy because its adherents insist that it is the "true tango" of Buenos Aires. The milonguero style is based on a close embrace in which the partners' torsos meet at an angle or touch directly head on, with relatively short, tight, subtle steps. Some say the milonguero style developed during the 1940s when there was little space on crowded center city dance floors.

The term milonguero is applied to skilled dancers without formal training, who have been dancing in Buenos Aires since the 1940s and 1950s. A myth holds that milongueros never took formal tango lessons but learned with friends on the sidewalks and practiced in the academias until they became good enough to be welcomed in the milongas. Girls and women largely learned at home with family and close friends.

Outside Argentina today, where most dance floors are usually more spacious with little worry about crashes, the milonguero style has been danced by a relatively small proportion of dancers, but it is currently becoming more and more popular. The Argentine Tango introduced to the world after the mid-1980s production of "Tango Argentino" had an open embrace, but in the 1990s, after visiting Buenos Aires milongas, American tango teachers Daniel Trenner and Rebecca Schulman introduced the milonguero style to the U.S. and other countries, which at the time had known only the open-embraced Ballroom Tango. However, today many dancers outside Argentina have adopted the style, although it does not have the popularity that it does in Argentina.

This close embrace, also referred to as "club style," "apilado," or "confiteria" style, is danced chest to chest, with torsos touching and with tight turns with some leaders opening up the embrace a few inches on the man's left side. Each partner leans forward, keeping their own balance, and form a shared axis, called "the bridge" or "A-frame." (Carlos Gavito, star of *Forever Tango*, was famous for his exaggerated lean of nearly forty-five percent.) Their feet are only far enough away from one another to permit steps, in a rather awkward-looking position favored only by milonguero-style enthusiasts. Wrote American teacher Tom Stermitz, "Carlos Gavito looks very good when he does the *calesita* (turn) in a huge lean with a tall, skinny ballerina, but I'm pretty short and when I try to do that, it looks more like the Marines hoisting the flag at Iwo Jima."

Many non-Argentines find dancing smack-up against a total stranger to be unnerving and prefer the looser, salon style of open embrace. Also, many dancers find milonguero style more difficult to dance because the restrictions on movements become so subtle that they frequently are not visible to spectators. Milonguero style dancers make no attempt to cover much floor space. Judy Margolis remarked, "Carlos Gavito rarely passes anyone on the dance floor, and is happy to progress only fifteen or twenty feet during the course of a three-minute tune, if that is all that space allows."

Many dancers do not appreciate those who insist that the milonguero style is "the" only one worth dancing. Michael Parine wrote: "There is nothing specially magical or better about dancing in a very close embrace. One can have a perfectly lousy dance in a close embrace as in a more open salon style. It is a big mistake to criticize and devalue someone's dancing because of some preconceived or arbitrary ideas about what is "real" tango and what is not."

Today's Salon Style (combination of early Orillero & early Salon)

Today's salon style is a mélange of the walking tango early styles of salon and *orillero* (Spanish for suburb,) and today is the most popular style outside Argentina. It was originally danced as a simple, unadorned walk to tango rhythm and at one time was the only style permitted in center city dance halls.

Dance floors in the 1940s became so crowded in central Buenos Aires that dancers had to shorten their steps; feet were kept on the floor, with no elaborate embellishments. Under the influence of the dancers Cachafaz and Petroleo, posture became straighter and the embrace tighter. A few danced an A-frame, still in use by some dancers, in which couple's upper bodies are in a close embrace, but the feet are apart to permit the woman to do ochos and small, close to the floor embellishments.

In most places today, the salon style has meshed with *orillero* and depending on whether or not the dance floor is crowded, couples switch styles within one dance — from salon to *orillero* style. Unlike the "glued together" milonguero style, the complete or partial separation of torsos provides for a wide range of movement, giving dancers more opportunities for expression.

Orillero

The *orillero* style of the 1940's was originally danced in the outlying barrios of Buenos Aires where the dance halls were not so crowded. It was danced slower than in previous decades, using sometimes extremely elaborate steps that took less space. Carlos Gavito advised, "Use no more than 4 × 5 meters." *Orillero* can be danced in a closed or open embrace but when it's danced in a tight embrace the couple must adjust their arms frequently to accommodate the turns and leg movements. Some embellishments need considerable space so if a couple wanted to do fancy figures that would hinder the line of dance they had to move to the space in the middle of the line of dance. The style can be playful and amusing to dance and to watch. It was not until 1950 that the raising of the foot off the floor by either partner was first seen in center city milongas.

Fantasy − Stage Tango

Fantasy tango or stage tango is not danced in regular milongas because it is danced with an open embrace, using exaggerated steps and figures that sometimes resemble classical ballet movements and thus it needs lots of space. Fantasy tango is seen primarily in tango shows, but sometimes it is danced by a few couples on uncrowded floors at the beginning or end of a milonga. Because many of the elaborate movements hold up traffic, dancers of the fantasy style usually do not move in the line of dance, but stay in the center of the floor. Carlos Gavito, master of the subtle tango, and no fan of fantasy tango became annoyed with some of his students when they flung their arms and legs out from their bodies. "Remember, you are not so many washing machines. Instead, think of yourselves as swans gliding in the water."

Whether for the stage or for themselves, partners who dance fantasy style, usually create and choreograph their steps, but not all fantasy or stage tango is choreographed. There are some stage performers who refuse to dance choreographed steps and movements - ever. Today, those who want to dance fantasy style in a milonga either go very early or stay on very late when their dancing does not interrupt the normal line of dance.

With exceptions, such as Gloria and Rodolfo Dinzel, Maria and Rodolfo Cieri (recently deceased), and a few others who pride themselves in dancing on the stage exactly as they do in a milonga, tango shows are choreographed. In such shows, steps set to a particular piece of music use familiar dance patterns generally laced with personal innovations that are memorized and rehearsed until the piece is ready to be presented. Fantasy tango is characterized by leaps, lifts, splits, high kicks, and long leg extensions. Many tango dancers thoroughly dislike fantasy style, as does Silvia Gisell, Argentine dance critic, who wrote in Buenos Aires' daily newspaper, *La Nacion*, "The dreadful tango-fantasia where women's legs are profusely displayed; where they are tossed around like marionettes, ending with their heads upside down becomes the "Spasmodic Tango" when a woman forfeits her grace for the grotesque display of kicks, and dance loses its meaning."

American and British or International Styles

American style vaguely resembles Argentine Tango in that it follows the line of dance, but it is danced with basic figuras generally phrased to fit standard Ballroom Tango music in counts of eight. The International (also known as British Style) style is highly codified and structured, with no place for innovation. Each rhythmic pattern must be memorized and not varied, making it easier to compare contestants' performances. This is the style used today in competitions.

New Tango

Argentine teacher and performer Gustavo Naveira considered the inventor of New Tango, is credited with adding new dimensions to the classical form of teaching tango – analysis of the movement itself – and began dancing a combination of improvised steps and figuras with a more extensive variety of combinations of step patterns.

Naveira's analysis explains the locus of rotation for each step: the front and back cross and turns form the structure of the dance and other choreographic elements. This approach to teaching tango explores all the possibilities of a certain movement, and some dancers who tend to be analytical and perfectionist find such teaching particularly satisfying. His innovative ideas attracted younger dancers and performers, including Fabian Salas and Mariano Fromboli, who have worked devotedly to research and practice the elements of the dance. Their results have been labeled "New Tango," not to be confused with Piazzolla's New Tango music.

Mike Hamilton comments, "What Fabian and Gustavo and Chicho have done is 'think' about the dance a lot. They've asked why does one step work and another not? What are the fundamental elements involved in the movement? It's all quite intellectual.... They have taken the tools they developed by thinking about the dance and pushed its limits. In my opinion, the results are often beautiful. Obviously some people don't think so. I get the impression many people don't want to think about tango: they just want tango to be a purely physical and emotional experience."

Inevitably, a schism arose between those who resist change and those who advocate the "New Tango" and argue that its adaptation of steps and figuras from the past honors tango's defining tradition of improvisation. The New Tango has become so prominently misunderstood that Gustavo Naveira offered to present his thoughts in his own words on the subject, written especially for this book.

Gustavo Naveira and Giselle Anne
Photo by Hartmut Schug

NEW TANGO

By Gustavo Naveira

Social Class

It is clearly valid, today, to speak of a new tango.

Historically, the tango has struck observers by its effects within the social classes. It has been said, for example, that in Buenos Aires the tango came from the lowest classes, later making an ascent to the upper or aristocratic classes. To many people, this fact has signified something essential in the tango. To the contrary, it has been said that in Europe the tango first appeared in the upper classes and later descended towards the bourgeoisie, etc.

While this play of upward and downward mobility may have been the case, it is much more interesting to note that what is happening now with the tango, everywhere in the world, has nothing to do with any kind of movement between social classes.

This fact is noteworthy precisely because at this time people from all social backgrounds are dancing the tango. Better said there are people of all types. There are no restrictions. We see the rich, the poor, the intellectual, the ignorant, the prestigious, the marginal, the famous, the unknown, the crude, the fat, the thin, the beautiful, the ugly, we see executives, workers, first class, economy class, businesspeople, street vendors, government employees, the unemployed, aristocrats, and whoever. What is really important is that they dance well. So, this is one of the first important elements that demonstrate the presence of a "new tango."

Modern Life

At the same time, we should be aware that people in our present world have needs that are very different from those that existed when the tango reached its height in the 40's. And the difference is even greater in comparison to the era of the tango's birth at the beginning of the 20th century. People now live under much greater pressures, due fundamentally to the advance of technology, the bombardment of information and the unprecedented growth of communications. In this environment, the tango tends to appear as a great revelation, refreshing and renewing, capable of effectively alleviating these pressures.

As a way of summarizing this, given its complexity, and also to introduce the reader to this perspective, I will point out some attractive aspects of the tango of today, which in many cases can be solutions to the problems of modern life:

- *The possibility of direct, personal participation. One is not simply a spectator or listener.*
- *The encounter with the opposite sex. The endless game of indirection in the meeting of man and woman.*
- *The redefining of roles within the couple through the given game of the dance.*
- *The development of awareness of the other person, which is necessary and essential for dancing.*
- *An alternative to loneliness.*
- *The chance to lose oneself in the game of improvisation.*
- *The sense of infinite possibilities in the choreography (A sense which in fact is accurate).*

- *The sense of power which comes from mastering the complexity of the dance.*
- *The chance to distinguish oneself in a real way. The impossibility of lying about one's own ability.*
- *A solution for stress.*
- *Possibility of social connection and a sense of belonging which come from a specific activity practiced in groups.*
- *Possibility of a kind of diversion and entertainment which is full of substance.*
- *The pleasure of the unusual, the different, the new, the exotic.*
- *The chance to be involved in a world which is beyond the control of governments and large corporations, and the pressures that these things habitually exert on people. Milongas are always somewhat hidden from view and are held in unusual places on any given day and time.*

The 1940's

Other important elements for this analysis arise from an observation of all (or at least most) of the partner dances of the past. We see immediately that there was a worldwide movement, which was at its peak in the 40's and 50's, and ended with the 60's.

When we refer to this peak of the 40's and 50's, we are speaking of a phenomenon fundamentally related to the music. Dancing was simply a way of expressing the passion and fervor provoked by the music. It was not the primary motive. The environment of that era generated a great breeding ground that produced composers, musicians, and singers of unique brilliance, who gave us musical works of incalculable value.

Those decades saw a cultural, artistic and social explosion, which extended throughout the entire Western world, as seen in American jazz, the valse musette in France, the Cuban son, the Brazilian samba.

Today the situation is very different. Today it is a question only of dancing. This current dance phenomenon cannot be attributed to a musical event, as in the 40's, given that we dance to old music. Today there is no music capable of producing an impact of the kind the music of that era produced, which could affect people so strongly, leading to the need for expression in dance. Today the need to dance exists, but it has other motives. So, we dance to old music, simply because there is nothing better, which demonstrates that the emphasis now is exclusively on the dancing. We seek to dance the tango well-- as well as possible; therefore we use the best music. Thus, even though people may dance the same or with the same steps, the factors that motivate them to dance are different.

New Tango Style

There is great confusion on the question of the way of dancing the tango: call it technique, form, or style. The term "tango nuevo" ("new tango") is used to refer to a style of dancing, or is considered to be that, which an error is. In reality, tango nuevo is everything that has happened with the tango since the 1980's. It is not a question of a style.

It often happens that mediocre dancers, trapped in a crude and sentimentalized way of dancing, and confronted with the logical impossibility of distinguishing themselves, will call their dancing "traditional tango," in order to confer on themselves a kind of prestige.

Similarly, when they find themselves with good dancers, dedicated to the development of the dance and showing real ability, they will try to pigeonhole them with some inane term such as "tango nuevo," in order to give themselves an equal status, as in the "traditional" versus the "new". This creates an infinite confusion. Nothing could be further from reality.

The words "tango nuevo" are neither a specific term nor a title (except in the case of a musical work by Piazzolla.) The issue here is how we use our language. With this in mind, these words directly express, through their literal meaning, what is happening with tango dancing in general; namely, that it is evolving. "Tango nuevo" is not one more style; it is simply that tango dancing is growing, improving, developing, enriching itself, and in that sense we are moving toward a "new" dimension in tango dancing.

New Tango Embrace

There has been much recent discussion in the community of tango dancers on the problem of the embrace, dividing the dance into "open" or "closed" style, which is also a matter of great confusion. Open embrace or closed embrace, dancing with space or dancing close, these are all outmoded terms. This is an old way of thinking, resulting from the lack of technical knowledge in past eras. This simple and clumsy division between open and closed is often used by those who try to deny the evolution of the dance, to disguise their own lack of knowledge. Today it is perfectly clear that the distances in the dance have a much greater complexity than a simple "open" or "closed." There are multiple distances, and they interact constantly with other factors, such that the structure which underlies the dance is always determining and regulating the distances involved. That is to say, what is happening today is that we have the ability to use all and each one of these distances simply when we wish to.

This division is all right for beginners or for average dancers, who tend to have little real dedication, and therefore usually dance at a single distance because it is all they can manage. But for the really dedicated dancers, those interested in a real and true deepening of the dance, this simple division between closed embrace and open embrace is not even remotely sufficient.

This colorful and somewhat comical situation is found only in Buenos Aires, because it was here that the Argentine Tango was born, and it is here that we find these people who lived the history of the tango. But in all the large cities and in many smaller cities around the world, the tango is danced today with no relation to Argentine culture, with no knowledge of the tango's history, with no knowledge of the music, and without the presence of any of these "milonguero authorities." In all parts of the world there are groups of people who come together for practices, classes, milongas, shows, festivals, congresses, etc., of tango dancing, only because they are attracted to this special dance with its very particular characteristics. They are passionate if not fanatical for the tango, and they have none of its cultural background. They frankly do not much care if the tango they dance is the exact original, and they do not depend on the supervision of any Señor Milonguero. They look for quality in the dancing, and in some places they have reached very high levels. They are after the development of the dance, for the pleasure of dancing, given that tango dancing is interesting in itself, whether it comes from Argentina or any other place.

And this situation is totally new. Never in history has something like this happened, neither with the tango nor with anything else. This is also not a question of the diffusion of Argentine culture (the idea is idiocy); neither the politicians nor the journalists in Argentina are even aware of what is happening with the tango around the world. No one has specifically undertaken any diffusion; tango dancing is a reality, which diffuses itself in a genuine way and without any help from the media.

This is to say that the presence of the tango in the world is not connected to the history of the Argentine Tango, which took place in Buenos Aires. The tango's presence in the world is a fact completely unrelated to history. It is unique, new, powerful, and it has just begun. It is not a "revival," and it is not the "return" of the original tango.

For all of these reasons we can, today, speak of a tango that is truly new.

Folk Dances: Precursors to the Tango

In recent years, young Argentines have begun to take an interest in their country's folk dances such as the "chacarera" which is a line dance and the "candombe" and "murga," which are danced individually or in groups, as well as the early form of the tango embrace taken from the waltz, the "canyengue." A few teachers specialize in teaching and performing these dances and give regular workshops in Argentina or on international teaching tours. Others have experimented with totally new ideas, with different variations of steps associated with tango or other types of dance music, such as swing and the blues.

Canyengue

The canyengue is an early form of couple dancing in vogue from the 1890s to early 1930s; it had a tight embrace with the woman's arm around the man's neck while her hand was held on the man's hip. Both leader and follower mirror one another's steps. Today it is treated as a folk dance; a curiosity apart from regular tango, but at some milongas a "tanda" (set) of canyengue may be included in an evening's dance. A few teachers (Argentine and others) promote it with workshops and performances where they wear costumes of the late 1800s. Some have researched early illustrations and perform and teach the canyengue using old-time music, such as the Tuba Tango, which is jaunty and sometimes comical, making it a pleasing diversion from regular tango.

Like contemporary tango, the canyengue is improvised and more playful than the *orillero* style. Its distinguishing feature is the posture, with the knees bent in almost a crouching position and the torso slightly bent – which is different from tango's upright stance. Instead of contemporary tango where partners are meant to be directly in front of each other, canyengue partners are usually off center of their partner's torso. One unique aspect of the dance is that with his right hand the leader occasionally swings the follower's left hand back and forth in an exaggerated pendulum movement, synchronizing their arms in rhythm, while doing long walking steps. The leader sometimes drops one hand and leaves it dangling at his side for part of the song, or places it jauntily in his pocket, leaving his partner to place her arm at her waist or to swing at her side.

Candombe

An early form of tango was the very rhythmic, drum-oriented "Candombe" brought to Buenos Aires by slaves from Africa during the 17th and 18th centuries. During Carnival, candombe dancers formed bands (comparsas) with drummers and paraded through the streets. Today the candombe is considered a "folk dance," sometimes danced on stage for an entire evening's performance, but it is not danced socially. Many people have difficulty determining whether a piece of music is a milonga or candombe, but drums provide the clue that is candombe.

Interest in the candombe is minimal in Argentina, but across the river in Montevideo a large black community supports many candombe drum bands and clubs. The line-dance movements to drum music in carnival parades are illustrated in drawings and prints from the pre-tango period, before the 1870s. In Uruguay, candombe drum music is sometimes interestingly fused with jazz and modern music, but it doesn't seem to have caught on elsewhere in the world. The candombe is considered to be the direct forerunner to the canyengue, which was followed by the tango.

The Murga

Another product of early carnival "comparsas" influenced by Negro slaves is the Argentine murga, which is also not a social dance. It is a sort of a moving theatrical activity that mixes dance, juggling, poetry recitations, music, and short theatrical pieces performed by participants who parade around the city to the fast, vibrant murga music, stopping at various places to give improvised performances. The ambience is light-hearted and humorous, sometimes tinged with social criticism. The music is provided by drums and other percussion instruments, flutes, and contemporary saxophones. Participants dress up in colorful jester-like costumes with brightly colored high top hats and color-coordinated capes decorated with sequins and beaded work.

The dancing differs from candombe in that although arms are swinging and bodies swaying, there is lots of jumping up and down in "an explosion of limitless expression." The end of each song is accompanied by a few really big jumps – as high as the dancers can leap. The murga, with its flamboyant attire and its uninhibited movements, smacks of wildness and thus is not closely related to the controlled passion and low-key dress of the tango.

As with the candombe and canyengue, there are tango teachers today who are interested in keeping the murga alive. Luis Bruni, of Paris, says, "The murga opens a new door to creativity." In 2007, Antwerp hosted a large murga festival, and others are occasionally organized elsewhere.

Swango and Rueda

A few teachers in the United States have been promoting the idea of a sort of folk dance by dancing tango steps to jazz or swing music, calling it "Swango," and some have invented the "Rueda," which is a form of Country and Western line dancing to tango music with a leader calling out, square dance style, the names of tango steps to be executed in unison. Both have had limited success and, indeed, some believe these dances are an example of improvisation and evolution of the dance gone mad. Charles Rocques says, "There will always be attempts to integrate other forms into tango, but at the same time there will be those of us who respect the purity of the original classic tango and will preserve it. I find stuff like the Rueda and line dances a little silly but OK and harmless.... But just don't call them tango."

Some dancers worry about the Swango and question whether they should dance tango steps to non-tango music. John Trimble asked, "Is it a betrayal of the tango to dance the mechanics of it to other music? To me, boleos and blues feel closer to the Argentine Tango I love, not the brass band Ballroom Tango. If the real thing is lacking, is it better to confine oneself to recorded music, or is it permitted to stray in such circumstances? I want to be true to tango, but if I dance to non-tango music am I being unfaithful?"

Needless to say, internet conversations run the gamut from the indignant to the delighted. Ms. Cristy Cote, a tango teacher in San Francisco, wrote: "The new dances are a good thing for tango; if it weren't for new ideas we'd all still be dancing canyengue. I, too, believe in the preservation of Argentine Tango in its authentic forms but why not have a little fun with Rueda, too?"

Feeling the Music

"All the passion in the world cannot make you a great dancer if you don't have decent technique." (Anonymous)

"Great dancers are not great because of their technique; they're great because of their passion." (Martha Graham)

Beginning tango dancers face the dilemma of whether they should first concentrate on the passion of the dance, permitting the music to take you 'wherever,' or whether the dance should be controlled by the intellect – thinking carefully about steps and body movement. There are those who feel that disciplined structure has the most importance in a well-danced tango while others believe in giving priority to the creation of something unique, using the freedom of expression that tango allows.

Some teachers instruct beginning dancers to "dance to the feeling of the music" no matter where it takes them on the dance floor while others tell them it is essential to learn the basics before trying for creativity: "learn the basics and worry about the feeling later." Small wonder beginners have a difficult time trying to make sense of it all.

Tom Stermitz wrote on the internet: "The duality is in trying to preserve structure and maintain order as opposed to challenging structure to create new order. Ironically in tango and the performing arts in general, the two polar opposites are essential...dancing with a partner is akin to having a conversation. The dance is the language and dancing is the dialogue. To learn a language, one must learn grammar and vocabulary. This is "analytic." It means learning something from which everything else in the language is derived... Once dancers have mastered the grammar and vocabulary, how do they use their new language? They can repeat cliché phrases (i.e. standard figures), or they can create new phrases. Tango will accommodate either approach; one of the coolest things about it is that opposites are essential because otherwise it would not be possible for two people who have never met before to dance a tango together."

The Walking Dance: The Tango Walk

"The most important thing about the tango is its tempo. You must, before you can dance it at all, understand and appreciate the music, and the best way to learn this is to walk—with or without a partner—in time to it." (Modern Dancing, Irene and Vernon Castle, 1914)

The great Carlos Gavito used to tell his students to "Walk like a panther."

As if testing the ground before them, tango dancers are encouraged to step lightly, with the body erect and taut. In earlier days, for the first six months to a year, teachers only permitted their students to walk to the music, but this is not the case in today's era of instant gratification. Frederic Guerin, an Argentine teacher in Paris, declared: "If I didn't let my students do anything but walk; I'd be out of business within months."

Most dancers of the Salon style attempt to land on the toes most of the time but all land on their heels part of the time. It is considered elegant to walk in one straight line; this causes an equilibrium problem which can be overcome by turning the foot about thirty degrees outward.

About thirty-five years ago teachers began using a basic figura of eight steps, called the "eight count basic" to be used as an exercise for beginning students - to give them something to do with their feet while concentrating on interpreting the music. Today it is a universal teaching tool, not necessarily meant to be used in the dance, although of course anyone is perfectly free to use it or any part of it on the dance floor.

Technique

The styles of tango are a subject of endless debate, but there is negligible controversy over technique. Whether the bodies are close or far apart, the couple should seem to glide effortlessly and elegantly around the floor, in perfect harmony with each other, the music and the dancers surrounding them. There is no leaping about to avoid bumping into other dancers, no ungainly movements to stay in the line of dance, no evidence of stress.

Posture and Balance

Good balance is essential since neither partner may lean on the other for fear of putting him/her off balance, possibly leading to a stumble. If a dancer is unable to balance alone, it is certainly not possible when dancing with another.

Partners must always be aware of their posture: head erect, chin up, shoulders relaxed, and no looking at your feet or those of your partner. The fundamental body position has an inward lean of the upper body of both partners that provides room for footwork. Each partner must be aware of their own "axis," their "center" or "balance point," and be responsible for maintaining their own equilibrium without throwing their partner off balance. The axis is an imaginary line running down the middle of the body, perpendicular to the floor, connecting the middle of the head with the ball of the foot. Movement is created by weight displacement when the leader puts pressure onto a partner's equilibrium axis, forcing her to move to a new axis.

Technique for Leaders and Followers

The leader is fully responsible for the dance. He must observe the counter-clockwise line of dance and is expected to creatively interpret the melody and mood of the music, devising steps anew and providing clear leads for his partner to follow. Because it is his duty to see that his partner is always safe from contact with other dancers who enter their space, the leader must be aware of all the couples surrounding them; he must determine how fast they are moving and in which direction, all the while being conscious of his style and technique.

The only acceptable technique for directional leading is through movements indicated with the leader's chest. Both partners' torsos remain parallel, with the follower's torso always directly in front of the leader so that when the follower's upper body moves in one direction, her feet and legs will invariably follow. Because they have learned to move only in the direction of the leader's chest, followers sometimes become frustrated and resent leaders who use their arms to push and pull them. Further, contradictory instructions may lead to awkward, even dangerous moves. The follower must always be on her own axis after each step, never leaning on her partner. One woman, however, says that when finding herself dancing with an objectionable partner – a poor lead, poor hygiene, or merely obnoxious – she ensures that he won't ask her to dance again by leaning heavily on his shoulder throughout the dance.

Because not all movements necessarily involve progression from one point on the floor to another, leaders may choose to execute figuras (usually four to eight steps) in place, taking care not to impede the line of dance. Many figuras are initiated with the legs, usually after the leader's foot blocks the follower's, requiring her to pause to discover the movement he wants her to execute next. The leader sets the woman's body in motion microseconds before he begins his own movement because, if his upper body moves first, she will (and properly) move to avoid being stepped on. Carlos Gavito used to say, "I lead, but I follow."

There are also non-directional leads that cue the follower to stand still and not to take a step, as when the leader wants the follower to execute a *calesita*, a turn around the man's body, or a lean onto the leader's chest while he sweeps (drags, actually) his partner's foot across the floor for a few feet. A slight upward pressure of his right hand on her back, for instance, alerts the follower to "Stand still, please, we're about to do something special."

Although it is the follower's principal role to implement her dance companion's leadership, she is no mindless marionette. If she is an accomplished dancer, an imaginative follower can and often does initiate movements herself in response to the music or her fancy. Depending upon the music and dynamic of the dance, the leader will sometimes indicate to his partner that she may contribute to the creation of the dance by executing *firuletes* (adornments) to her heart's content. Such embellishments can be anything she may feel like doing with her feet and legs that space allows and that doesn't interfere with the beat of the music. Adornments may include drawing small or large circles on the floor with her non-weight-bearing foot; high or low *boleos* (leg swings); tapping the floor with toe or heel; and running the side of her shoe up the outside of her partner's trouser leg (to the knee only). Fanciful or simple, these improvisations are hers, and she is not to be rushed.

After each step, the follower must bring her feet (or heels) together - as does the leader - with her weight equally distributed on both feet so that she is poised to move instantly in any direction. Ideally, the follower's movements are so deftly swift that she is "like a shadow" of the leader. One dancer spoke of a pleasing game with his favorite partner when he would attempt to "lose her" on the dance floor: "Try as I might, I could not get her to make a movement that wasn't what I'd anticipated."

A skilled follower may enjoy capturing the lead from her partner, sometimes initiating a game of passing it back and forth several times. The shrewd follower undertakes such play only with good dancers, preferably those with a reliable sense of humor; however, some men do not happily surrender the lead. If the follower is particularly adept, she can artfully manipulate the leader into steps that she chooses. Emphasizing equality between partners, some teachers, particularly Rodolfo Dinzel and Daniel Trenner, encourage their students to practice the exchange of leadership roles within one dance, an exercise that allows them to appreciate the role of each partner and to more thoroughly understand the dance itself.

Groundedness

Another aspect of technique is the dancers' relationship to the dance floor in an attempt to be "grounded." If ballet dancers appear at times to dance above the floor, with light, minimal contact, the tango dancer's energy should channel down into the floor by "caressing" it with their feet. In addition to elegance of movement, it assists dancers' balance and prevents other dancers from being injured by "flying feet." There is to be no bobbing up and down of the torso.

Pivots

Both leaders and followers constantly use pivots to change direction. They are executed by joining the feet together before the pivot, making the turn, then taking the next step. The rotating foot is the pivot, with the axis over the soles of the feet. To stop a turn, the pivoting foot's heel presses against the floor to act as a brake. It is easier and more graceful looking if the knees are slightly flexed. Embellishments can be added so long as they do not interfere with the beat.

Ochos

Ocho is the Spanish word for eight and refers to a dancer's foot tracing a figure eight in front of his/her body. A complete ocho involves a step to one side, a pivot and then a sharp turn to the opposite direction which is usually repeated at least twice, sometimes more. It can be executed as a stationary or moving position.

Flexed Legs

Because neither the follower nor the leader is always aware of exactly in which direction the next step will lead, if legs are flexed it is easier for dancers to keep their balance while waiting to move from one position to another. If the muscles are locked, it is difficult to make sudden moves gracefully and quickly.

Dissociation from the Torso: Feet and Knees Together

Tango's body movements are strictly divided between the calm and relaxed upper torso, parallel to the partner and the action of the legs, which have no relation to the static torso. After each step, partners immediately return feet and knees together, as if a large rubber band controls them. If partners are on their axis, they are prepared to take a step in any direction with grace and ease. Open knees do not look neat, and tango technique and aesthetics are all about being clean and neat.

The Steps

Ganchos

Ganchos (hooks), swift kicks between a partner's open legs, are almost always a led movement although either partner can improvise them at appropriate moments. If the static partner is not to be wounded, it is essential that specific technique in that one leg performs the kick while the other leg acts as the support. When one partner hooks a leg around the other partner's leg, it is called a gancho. This is almost always a lead movement although either partner can improvise one at appropriate moments. In order to avoid the kick injuring the partner's leg, the thigh should be crossed over the partner's thigh just above the knee; the knee points towards the floor, the leg crosses in front of the partner's support foot. The kick should be made "with attitude," assertive and rapid.

Sacadas

The sacada is a movement where one partner displaces a partner's trailing leg with pressure from the foot or thigh, depending on whether a low, medium, or high sacada (soft, fluid kick). The movement is in two phases with the dancer doing the sacada making contact with the partner's foot, then pushing it away in the opposite direction. If a medium high or high sacada is desired, the movement contacts the calf or thigh. The movement must be made against the soft, muscular areas—the instep, calf or thigh, of the non-weight bearing (or trailing) leg. Otherwise nasty injuries can be sustained. (Until 1950, only low floor-sweeping sacadas were performed. Then steps that lifted one off the floor were introduced.)

Sweeps, Arrastres, Barridas

All three names apply to the movement whereby a dancer stops a partner's movement by placing a foot parallel and right next to the partner's foot. Once the feet are in contact, the one leading the sweep (usually, but not always, the leader) pushes the partner's foot with his own along the floor for several feet. This is not considered as a step because there is no change of weight or body movement, thus the term "arrastre," which means drag in Spanish, and "la barrida," from the verb "barrer," which means "to sweep," and in this case refers to the action of "sweeping" the partner's foot with the leader's foot - a one time action.

Etiquette and Floorcraft

Dance floor etiquette and floorcraft remain essentially set in stone both outside and inside Argentina. Although the improvisation aspect of tango thrives and prides itself on freedom of movement and style, the rules of behavior on the dance floor are universal and conspicuously rigid. For more than one-hundred years milonga "codes" (Spanish, *codigo)* have dictated what is acceptable in tango dance halls. Among the universal rituals are these:

1. Absolutely no talking while dancing. There may be brief conversations before, between, and after dances, but not when feet are moving. There isn't any diversion of attention from the partner while dancing: no glancing around the floor looking for friends or admirers and no idle glances at others' dance styles, new shoes, or clothing. All attention is to be focused on some portion of the partner: eyes, chest, collarbone, lifted hand, cleft of neck.

2. At the start of each dance when the music begins, the partners either wait in silence or engage in

polite conversation until both have ascertained the type of music to which they will be dancing. The leader may have the couple subtly sway to the rhythm; then, after several seconds, all the couples on the floor begin to move simultaneously.

3. Each couple's movement is dictated by the counter-clockwise line of dance. By custom, dancers choose among several "lanes" according to their skill level and by the style they are dancing. More experienced dancers try to stay in the outside lane, where the movement is usually smoother and there is room to do steps for modestly elaborate steps that need space. Dancing in the less-crowded center are the 'fantasy' and slower dancers. It is bad form to move back and forth across lanes or to cut across the room, and because the length of dancers' steps varies, leaders must take care to maintain their place in line. Failure to do so is considered not only a grave violation of etiquette but, worse, bad dancing.

Robin Thomas of New York conveys the dance floor dynamic this way: "Tango is not a race; there is no finish line. Therefore, there is no reason to overtake. You can dance as fast or slow as you want and take as big steps as you want, but all must move around the dance floor at relatively the same speed.... Patience! There's nothing wrong with covering miles and miles doing little circles behind the person in front of us, waiting for them to move on. There is the simple rock step.... Being patient gives you a chance to respond creatively to your environment rather than to show off by dancing as though you were in a vacuum."

In the early days in Buenos Aires, when dance floors held hundreds or even thousands of dancers, if the flow of the line of dance was interrupted, a "bastonero" (a big man with a long stick) forced the offending couple to dance in the middle of the floor, which was most embarrassing. Occasionally knives were drawn to emphasize a dancer's displeasure at a violation of the floorcraft code. In any case, a serious infraction was sufficient reason to be asked to leave the dance hall. Today's offenders can expect at least a storm cloud of withering looks, perhaps followed by a flash of strong language.

Even when a couple appears to be dawdling, it is impolite to "tail-gate" or to pass the couple in front of you, who should always be permitted to move at their own speed. Likewise, couples should not hold up dancers behind them with complicated figuras that take up time and space and impede traffic.

Sound floorcraft is actually no small challenge, its mechanics requiring vigilance and care, as noted by Evan Wallace: "Leaders should avoid crashes by mentally deducing, based on their current positions and velocities, whether any of the other couples could conceivably reach the same spot as he in roughly the same amount of time it takes him and his partner to get there."

The consequences of a moment's lapse of attention or indulgent discourtesy can be most unpleasant, usually for the follower, as noted by Nancy Ingle in imagined comments to a partner: "The biggest problem I have is that (if there is a collision) it is my Achilles tendon that gets kicked, not yours. It is my stocking that gets snagged, not yours. It is my red suede shoe with black polish all over it. You might glare at the guy who gets in your way, but it is my body which takes the hits.... The guy who weaves in and out of traffic to advance three car lengths thinks he is a fantastic driver – he never sees the brake lights of the drivers who must react with skill to avoid a wreck."

Ineptitude, particularly colliding with another couple, is the most egregious behavior on the dance floor. Collisions that range from annoying bumps to serious falls are not all that rare. Although women experience most dance floor injuries because they are usually in front of the leader, "like a shield," and skirts exposing their legs make them more vulnerable than men in trousers – it is the rare tango dancer who has not known a wicked bruise from a heel to the instep or a kick on the shin, sometimes drawing blood. A Finnish friend of mine suffered a broken rib on a Paris dance floor when her partner thrust her into a *boleo* too forcefully. Christopher Schmees commented on the internet: "I have seen leaders who manage to bump into non-moving targets such as tables, chairs, even columns! Or, more accurately, they let their partner do that. If I were a woman, I would not dance with a person who doesn't take care of me."

The possibility of "dance-by shootings" once became a hot internet topic, with weeks of postings about "dance floor rage" citing examples of justification for violence on the dance floor. Larry Carroll, on the other hand, decided to be philosophical about dancers who ignore the line of dance in order to do elaborate, space-consuming figures: "I've come more and more to feel that these obstacles are as much a part of dancing as the sides of the floor and pillars in the middle. These idiots are so self-centered and arrogant that they can no more change than the pillars that hold up the roof. If I let either obstacle annoy me and ruin my dancing, I'm being an idiot myself."

Close Call at the White House

Melinda Bates, who worked in the Clinton White House, wrote about a state dinner given by the Clintons for Argentine President Carlos Menem at which poor floorcraft could have caused an international incident. The after-dinner entertainment was provided by a local tango orchestra, QuinTango, with exhibitions of tango dancing.

"As the two presidents were leaving the East Room, Mr. Menem suddenly grabbed Hillary. Next thing we knew he was leading her across the floor. President Clinton then asked an Argentine lady to dance, and *they* started off across the floor. Of course, he cannot tango, but as a musician he has a wonderful sense of rhythm, and their dance was responsive to the music. Then other dancers who were part of the tango entertainment also began to dance. The most interesting part was when Pablo Veron (star of the movie *"The Tango Lesson,"* considered to be one of the best professional dancers in the world) and President Menem bumped into each other rather hard (guess whose fault?) They both stopped and looked to see who had bumped into them – after all, who would dare to bump the president and, equally, who would dare to bump into Pablo Veron? The look that passed between them was priceless. Recognizing each other, Pablo acknowledged the president, the president acknowledged the great dancer, and off they went."

TANGO
COMPADRE

DEL
SAINETE
EN UN ACTO

Música
Criolla

PARA
CANTO Y PIANO

LETRA DE
P. PICO Y C. M. PACHECO

MÚSICA DE
FRANCICSCO PAYÁ

SOCIEDAD ARG. DE COMPOSITORES
PROPIEDAD RESERVADA
FLORIDA 385-Buenos Aires

Nº 95

N 424
0·80

Coproducción CLUB DEL TANGO - Editorial Inca - Buenos Aires - Argentina - Serie Bailarines

CHAPTER FOUR

The City: Buenos Aires

Just the atmosphere of Buenos Aires milongas makes one want to dance the way Argentines do – simple, to the music, and with the heart... nowhere else can you experience the level of dance than there is there."
(Internet)

Unique among dances, tango revolves around a single geographical center - Buenos Aries - Argentina's storied capital city. And it is the rare tango dancer anywhere in the world who does not yearn to make the pilgrimage to Buenos Aires. Many have visited at least once or plan to visit in the not-so-distant future. Those fortunate enough to possess the time and money make the journey several times a year; others find that visits do not provide enough tango and simply move to Buenos Aires.

One need not actually travel all the way to the banks of the Rio de la Plata for lessons from the masters or to watch revered tango dancers perform because dozens of tango professionals regularly tour the world offering performances, lessons, and workshops. Dancers may travel far fewer miles to regional or national workshops or festivals on their own continent rather than journey to nearly the bottom of the world. Nonetheless, the flow of tango dancers to Buenos Aires swells each year, with many spending several weeks or months, some enjoying extended visits on leaves of absence from their work. Argentine government reports indicate that 400 million pesos annually are spent by tango tourists.

Why do so many tango dancers go to the trouble and expense of traveling the great distance to Buenos Aires to dance? Some, in a metaphysical mode, speak of going to "the source" of tango and venerate Buenos Aires as the only place to absorb the mystique of that magical dance. With more than 130 weekly milongas annually 2007 and seeming endless practicas and group lessons, dancers who come from small tango communities with only one or a handful of places to dance are bowled over. They talk about how special it is to go to a milonga in Buenos Aires.

Like classical ballet and modern dancers, tango enthusiasts expect to take lessons as long as they are able to dance, and visits to Buenos Aires afford access to the greatest concentration of world-class teachers and performers. Part of the attraction is the opportunity to "mingle with the best" at the evening milongas. Often dancers follow their favorite teachers to festivals and workshops around the world and some become friends off the dance floor. Most professionals are accessible because they regularly attend milongas, and getting to know highly respected and famous dancers can be the most important aspect of a dancer's journey to Buenos Aires.

Because of its distance from North America and Europe, it wasn't until recently that Buenos Aires has become a prime tourist destination. With increasing instability in the Middle East and threats of terrorist activity elsewhere in the world, Americans in particular have found Western Hemisphere destinations increasingly desirable. In 2004, some 3.5 million tourists visited the Argentine capital; in 2005, 3.9 million; and in 2006, readers of *Travel and Leisure* magazine voted Buenos Aires "the 7th best city in the world to visit," one place ahead of New York City. It was also named "one of the gay-friendliest capitals of the world," citing a growing number of gay clubs and milongas.

Besides being the Mecca for tango, Buenos Aires is a compellingly attractive and cosmopolitan city, resembling Paris and other European cities with its turn-of-the-century architecture, wide, tree-lined avenues, countless small parks, corner cafés, and *confiterias* (pastry shops offering coffee, sweet cakes, and light meals). Its three million people are scattered among forty-eight barrios, each with its distinctive personality.

Visiting North Americans and Europeans often feel more at home there because with few exceptions, citizens are of European heritage, so visitors are not automatically viewed as tourists as they may be in other parts of the world.

In addition to the increase in tango tourist activity during the last decade, Buenos Aires has become a haven for foreigners who have moved there and are transforming the sprawling metropolis into conclaves of artists, musicians, designers, writers, and filmmakers. They've been followed by trendy restaurants and boutiques, many of them up-market, a mix of "Latin élan and European polish." In 2003, there were no French restaurants in the city until Manuel Schmidt, an architect from Paris, went to Buenos Aires and opened the Brasserie Petanquer in San Telmo. Denny Lee quoted art gallery owner Daniela Luna in The New York Times (2008): "There's a clash between European and Latin American Cultures that's fascinating."

Not as much in evidence are the writers, journalists, and screenwriters who have settled in Buenos Aires, many of whom use Buenos Aires as background in their works. Marina Palmer left New York City to live in Buenos Aires, where she wrote the novel "Kiss and Tango," a story of the protagonist's romantic adventures in the tango world. Robert Duvall made a movie about an American Mafia hit man who followed his prey to Buenos Aires and became obsessed with the tango, and Francis Ford Coppola is making a movie about Italian immigrants in Argentina.

Buenos Aires may be the most nocturnal city in the world. Tango dances last through the night until past dawn, and throngs of people, including families with children in tow, frequent the streets long past midnight. Movie theaters offer 1:00 a.m. showings, and some cafés and restaurants are open all night. Ice cream enthusiasts delight in gelati parlors that not only offer their treats but will also deliver them to your home; some are open twenty-four hours a day. In this city filled with Italians, pizza is to be had on every other street corner and will be speedily delivered to your door, day or night, by a cheerful young man on a bike or motorcycle.

Getting Around

Buenos Aires is an easy city to navigate, and all manner of transport is inexpensive. The subway system (the Subte) is clean and efficient, with most of the railcars fitted with electronic signs hanging near the center displaying the name of the present and upcoming stops. In each station, smiling, attractively uniformed male and female attendants are posted near turnstile entrances to help with the *jetons* (tokens) or to provide information and directions. Buses run around the clock, tearing through the city at an alarming speed, serving broader reaches of the city and suburbs than the Subte, which does not operate all night.

Throughout the city, taxis are readily available. Drivers are invariably polite, friendly, fast, and fearless. Because tourists are comparatively rare, drivers are invariably curious as to the nationality of their passengers and often question them about their home countries and why they've come to Buenos Aires. Perhaps unique among cabbies, they always round off the fare downward and express surprised appreciation when tipped.

Buenos Aires is famous for its cafés on nearly every corner, reputedly more than any city in the world. An astonishing portion of Argentine leisure seems to occur in these lively places – the drinking of coffee, eating, reading, and writing, watching television, talking on cell phones, and chatting with friends. In the cafés outside the city center, men play cards or dominos for hours. Argentine women, it appears, frequent the cafés and confiterias (serving tea, coffee, pastries, and light meals) more than do their counterparts in other Latin countries.

Various cafés are known for particular political orientations, literary movements, or cultural enthusiasms – including, to be sure, tango, notably the Ideal and the Tortoni, about which tangos have been composed. Confiteria Tortoni and Confiteria Ideal in the center of the city are bastions of art nouveau decoration with historical connections to tango. Since the turn of the last century, the Tortoni has been home to Argentine writers, intellectuals, and tango enthusiasts, and hosts weekly evenings of tango conferences, lectures, concerts, and dance demonstrations. The Ideal has tango dancing every day from 11:00 a.m. in its turn-of-the-century upstairs dance hall and holds evening tango shows in the ground floor confiteria.

Restaurants are plentiful, their meals copious and inexpensive, and almost all of them offer take-out and delivery service for anything on their menu. Argentine beef needs no elaboration; steaks are impossibly delicious, ample, and easy on the pocketbook. Although inflation has been creeping into the economy, everything is still relatively cheap. Not only is food a bargain, so is most everything else, with reasonable prices for antiques, clothing, entertainment, and service. Large and small open-air and indoor markets dot the city, selling everything from food to socks.

Where to Stay

Hotels are in abundance, with rooms available from well under $100 per night, to luxurious hotels as the one designed by Philippe Starck, which starts at over $400 per night. Tango tourists tend to stay at one of the many small hotels catering to dancers by providing information about classes, teachers, practicas, and milongas. They also rent apartments, which are generally remarkably inexpensive, and some dancers even purchase apartments which, when they are not using them, they rent to other tango dancers through word of mouth, the internet, or advertisements in tango magazines.

In recent years, however, tango guesthouses have become popular, with many reporting nearly one-hundred percent year-round occupancy. Most are converted private apartments and commonly accommodate up to a dozen guests; some are modest, with guests sharing baths and a telephone. All offer a common kitchen and a room for dining and socializing; most provide internet access and a room with wooden floors for private lessons or practice, and some arrange for teachers to give group lessons on site.

Dancers particularly favor the tango guesthouses because they combine camaraderie with an atmosphere of "total tango immersion" available nowhere else. When tango dancers are not dancing, it is generally acknowledged that all they want to talk about is tango. Conversations unfold as dancers relax in a guesthouse patio, invariably some soaking or massaging their feet while others ice aching joints. Discussions may include pros and cons of dance styles and techniques, dance teachers, dance floors, DJs, the best milongas, practicas, private lessons, and where to buy the best dance shoes. Such gatherings provide a place to complain or enthuse about dance partners past, present, or possibly future. No one is concerned with anyone's profession or financial or social status, and no matter the time of day or night, there's always company to go dancing, to take lessons, to talk tango, or to call for deliveries of pizza or ice cream.

Another attraction of the tango guesthouses is that everyone keeps the same weird hours: up at noon, brunch, an afternoon lesson practica or milonga, sometimes a nap until supper – at ten or eleven, then shower and dress for a milonga from midnight until dawn, then to bed, up at noon, and so on.

The multinational atmosphere of the guesthouses attracts dancers who meet people from all around the globe whose consuming interest is the tango, making it easy to quickly feel at home with complete strangers. At one guesthouse's communal dinner, someone looked around the table and noted that among the dozen people at the table, there were six different languages being spoken. An amazing number of dancers make several trips to Buenos Aires annually and also attend festivals and workshops in other countries. Casual acquaintances sometimes become fast friends with bonds formed and cemented at tango events throughout the world. Some remark that the ambience at festivals and workshops is not unlike that of a kid's summer camp.

Porteños - The People of Buenos Aires

Residents of the city proudly refer to themselves as "porteños" – meaning those who live in the port city of Buenos Aires – distinguishing them from residents of other parts of Argentina – "the provinces." Porteños know themselves as attractive, suave, street-wise, fashionable, and well-educated, the designation "porteño" being a distinction reserved only for residents of Buenos Aires (with presumed European heritage) and bearing a unique connotation of pride and, for the men, machismo. For many porteños, Argentina outside Buenos Aires is populated by just so many peasants – an arrogant condescension understandably grating for Argentines beyond the capital's city limits.

Argentine Identity: Continuing Crisis

Because the Spanish were the first colonizers, the national language is Spanish, but the language is so enriched with colloquial variations of Italian and Lunfardo that Argentine Spanish differs piquantly, if not substantively, from that of the rest of Latin America. The Italians have left the greatest imprint on Argentine culture: when greeting or bidding farewell to one another, for example, the expression is always "Ciao" or "Ciao-Ciao" no matter the sex or age. Speech has the cadence of Italian and is seemingly not possible without elaborate hand motions, and the pizza parlors and gelati stands on almost every block constantly evoke the country's links to Italy. While the number of people with Spanish lineage is significantly smaller than those with an Italian one, Spanish culture endures in the importance of cafés, a reserved courtliness of manner, and perhaps most notably, the keeping of late hours.

The legacy of loyalties to European heritage is reflected in contemporary politics which is frequently riddled with factionalism based on ethnic origins. In addition to myriad descendants of Eastern and Western Europe, there has always been a large Jewish population in Buenos Aires, and Arabs have gained increased influence, greater perhaps, than their numbers might suggest. The recent Argentine president, Carlos Menem, for instance, is of Arab extraction.

For decades, Argentines have dealt with the conflict between loyalties to their European ancestry and attempts to be "one-hundred percent Argentine." The question of "true identity" bothers so many that they end up on the psychiatrist's couch, reflected in the dubious distinction of Buenos Aires in possessing the highest percentage of psychiatrists and psychologists of any city in the world. A popular local joke asks: "What is an Argentine? An Italian; who speaks Spanish, acts French, and wishes he was English."

Trying to be Argentine, while identifying strongly with European roots, has taken a toll on establishing a unified national identity. One psychiatrist told a visitor, "Argentines don't know who they really are." Some are convinced that the resurgence of interest in the tango in Argentina may have arisen because the tango is one of the few things undisputedly one-hundred percent Argentine and, as such, has become a national icon – something of which they can be proud.

Argentines attach no stigma to psychotherapy, and people on all social levels freely discuss their therapists with friends and acquaintances. There is even a Buenos

Aires neighborhood nicknamed Barrio Villa Freud because of the many psychiatrists and psychologists living there.

Tango luminary, Rodolfo Dinzel, explained, "Argentines have a sense of self worth that is not able to be achieved. Their point of reference is high but the reality is unattainable; their ideals are grander than reality. Argentines are educated to appreciate the finer things of Europe but hardly any of them will ever be able to travel abroad to see originals of the famous paintings they've seen in books. They won't get to visit the famous architectural sights, which are familiar to them only through photographs. From the end of the last century, all Argentines who could possibly afford it went to Europe at least once in their lives. But for the majority of Argentines, their sense of aesthetics and comfort is just not within reach. This inevitably leads to great frustration." Relating an experience during his first visit to Madrid, Mr. Dinzel says, "I went to the Prado and saw a Van Dyke I recognized and broke into tears."

Unlike European immigrants who came to New York during the last half of the 19th century, immigrants to Buenos Aires did not rapidly assimilate into Argentine society. Although they did not create New York style ethnic ghettos, they did cling closely to their European ties. In the United States, by contrast, second generation children sought strongly to become "American" as soon as possible, by going to public schools and insisting on speaking English at home. In the United States, parents and children adapted quickly to American customs and wholeheartedly rejected those of the old country. But in Buenos Aires it was the opposite; they clung to the idea that their home countries were superior to their new homeland. Indeed, many of the middle and upper classes, who never accepted

Argentina as their homeland, sought to isolate themselves geographically in the center of town, through education and customs.

A psychiatrist of Spanish extraction told of a recent trip, his first to Spain, with his father to visit his home village. When his father introduced him to residents, it was as "Guillermo, my Argentine son." Guillermo said that he was greatly affronted: "I had always felt I was Spanish, and I informed them that I was Spanish, not Argentine."

A vivid example of such a persistent Eurocentric identity came when I had a knee injury and became acquainted with a physical therapist of German heritage working at the British Hospital who consistently refers to herself as German, even though she is fourth generation Argentine. She attended a German school and does not dance tango; most of her friends are German, and when asked about tango in her social set, she explained, "Only the natives dance tango. I don't know anyone who does the tango except for a brother-in-law, and he's Italian." She later said that she believes her children should be better integrated outside the German community and that "next year" she plans to take her children out of the German school and send them "to a public school with the natives." When asked what she meant by "natives," she unhesitatingly answered: "The natives are the Spanish and Italians."

The English, too, have kept apart from much of Argentine society, leading to many Argentines feeling that the English are snobbish, haughty, and arrogant as result of an attitude they developed in the 1800s when they came to dominate much of Argentina's commerce and government. The Falklands War remains a sore point among many Argentines. In the nineteenth century the

English took over the Falklands, a complex of two large and many small islands in the South Atlantic Ocean east of Argentina, known to Argentines as the Maldives. In April, 1982, Argentina invaded the Falklands, launching an undeclared war claiming the islands had been part of the Spanish Empire and therefore belonged to them; the English prevailed, and the islands remain under their control. The Argentines, however, were very bitter about the whole experience and resentment is still strong.

The "keeping to themselves" of European immigrants was primarily instigated by the affluent and moderately well off middle classes who sought to preserve a unified, cultural front to the mixed bag of nationalities that was ordinary Buenos Aires society. They established their own first-class school systems and highly respected hospitals and clinics, which are still in existence. Scattered around the city are buildings with placards on their facades identifying them as clubs for people from specific European towns, regions, or countries. It was here that Europeans have kept their language, music, culture and customs alive. Contacts made there helped them settle into the new country, find jobs, put their children into schools, and feel at home in the New World. Their buildings range from the elegantly decorated and prestigious turn-of-the-century mansions such as the Club Espagnol (open today to the public as a restaurant), to modest local clubhouses with restaurants and bars and places to dance. Tango found its way into the small social halls, enabling it to survive during the decline of 1960s and 1970s. Today, in the neighborhood barrios as well as in the center of town, the clubs still function, many catering to family outings and open to the public for restaurant meals and tango events.

Looking Good

"Even the humblest Italian has a strong sense of self-esteem, as well as a fatal weakness for beauty and surface appeal, "la bella figura." (Beppe Severgnini. La Bella Figura: A Field Guide to the Italian Mind)

The concern for "looking good" is generally credited to the Italian majority, and their concern with identity is not unrelated to Argentines' interest in appearance and their pride in being identified as porteños. Besides spending time and money on psychiatrists and their inner harmony, if many Argentines can't feel good about themselves, they bolster their esteem by spending time and money on at least "looking good." Consequently, visitors to Buenos Aires comment on the unusually high number of beauty salons and cosmetic shops; Buenos Aires is recognized as "the cosmetic surgery capital of the world."

In most places, people who have cosmetic surgery are reluctant to share that information with friends and acquaintances and usually do their best to conceal it. But not the Argentines, who boast of having had their eyes "done," their face "lifted," or a tummy "tucked." Shop girls and men office workers speak openly about saving money for cosmetic surgery. Former president Carlos Menem freely talks about having had surgery for facial improvements, and it seems perfectly normal to Argentines that their ex-President has no qualms about discussing his altered hairline and cheeks. Argentine television has regular programs on cosmetic surgery, complete with rather frightening live operations.

Both men and women porteños are careful of their appearance. In the streets or at milongas most are slim, attractive, and dressed to kill. Some think that the Argentine man's preoccupation with appearances is a product of the country's machisimo Italian heritage, a society of men who notoriously place great value on appearance.

One day when having lunch with a small group of professional middle-aged Argentine women I knew from a group tango class, I remarked, "I'm glad to see that older Argentine women from the generation who did not learn to tango are now taking tango lessons. But why don't I see Argentine men of the same age in classes?" The women all laughed, and one immediately replied: "Argentine men like to look good, and there's no possible way to look good when learning the tango. Argentine men are too macho to appear in public trying to do something new. If they do try to learn the tango, but don't immediately 'get it,' they quit dancing."

Two of the women told relevant jokes: "Why do Argentine men stand outside in an electrical storm and look up at the lightning? Because they think God is taking their picture." And: "How do you make money off an Argentine man? By buying him for what he's worth and selling him for what he thinks he's worth."

Comments Rodolfo Dinzel, "Good appearance and neatness is not only a contemporary propensity. From the earliest times, no matter how poor people were in the ghettos, it didn't matter if clothes were mended or tattered but it was always a matter of pride to leave the house clean, with every hair in place."

Dr. Steve Hoffman, an American on his fourth visit to Buenos Aires, observed, "Argentine men, whether living in or outside their country, are concerned about their figures, and slimness is paramount in the milongas of Buenos Aires – except for the genuine shorter, rotund, older milongueros.

Younger men, as well as women, deny themselves food to get as slender as possible in order to look their best on the dance floor."

Piropos

Women who "look good" are frequently rewarded with *piropos,* a tradition from Spain, which is a "verbal flower" tossed to a woman of any age walking alone. And although it is a form of flirting or flattery, nothing crude is implied, as there frequently is in the North American whistles of construction workers to a passing girl (never older women). Piropos, by their nature, are brief.

In *Travel* magazine, Kaitlin Quistgaard wrote: "A piropo is the most simpatico of flirtations, a kind of street poetry that a man whispers just when he's close enough to look a woman in the eye. At most, a person walking beside you might hear the piropo but often no one does, not even the mystery man looks to see your response. The compliment arrives quietly, like an anonymous gift; it has long been a part of Argentine daily life but a piropo is never ever offensive. It is by definition a single sentenced compliment that is poetic or comical, or better still, both. Some examples: "'Blessed be the mother who gave you birth." "If beauty were a crime, you would deserve life in prison." "So many curves and here I am without a car.'"

Julie Taylor, an attractive American with long blond hair and who lives in Buenos Aires, is the target of many piropos. She told of one of the nicest piropos directed to her in a milonga by a sometime tango partner. "One day when we were dancing, he was unaware that I was about to leave the country. He invited me to some activity the following week, when I would already be gone. This was the time of the Great Eclipse of the sun, and the papers were full of

115

news about how the Europeans were preparing to observe this phenomenon, with photos of strange glasses people were going to wear and telescopes that would be used. Suddenly breaking the rule that you never talk during a tango, he asked incredulously, "So you're leaving?" When I assented, he expostulated, "But Julie! The eclipse is in *Europe!*"

The closest thing your septuagenarian author ever came to receiving a piropo was in January 2008. When purchasing a newspaper at a street side kiosk, the attendant —an attractive middle-aged man – gave me change with the comment, "Aqui tienes, mi hija." (Here you are my daughter.)

Even Dogs Look Good

Perhaps porteños look upon their dogs as an extension of their identity, a way of emphasizing their "porteño-ness." Their pets are most likely to be purebred dogs.

Tourists visiting Buenos Aires commonly remark on the number of leashed dogs in the streets – yet another way in which Buenos Aires differs from other Latin American countries, where animals are often treated badly. In Argentina, household pets are popular, particularly dogs, although cats are also to be seen sporting fancy collars. Porteños spend a lot of time in the streets with their dogs, and dog owners easily fraternize with other dog fanciers in the many small parks where dogs are welcome. There are more walkers with more dogs in Argentina than I've ever encountered.

To see seven or eight and more dogs with a single walker is not unusual; I once counted twelve dogs, and a friend claims to have seen seventeen. The groups of dogs, frequently of the same approximate size – small, medium or large – are something to watch in action. They are always calm and well disciplined, never straining at their leashes or nipping or bumping the other dogs. They walk at the same pace and all sit down at the same time when they come to the crosswalk. On command, they sit, and then stand to cross the street. One friend told of seeing a group of dogs whose leashes were not held by the walker but were grouped together within a circle of nine dogs, which moved as one, crossed streets, and sat down at only verbal commands.

Argentines want their dogs to "look good" and, like their porteño owners, many dogs in Buenos Aires are extremely chic. On chilly or rainy days, a majority of the dogs are decked out in brilliantly colored raincoats, fashionable sweaters, from turtlenecks to multi-colored cardigans and fancy capes. Jeweled collars and leashes adorn even lowly mutts. Every barrio has numerous dog-grooming salons and do-it-yourself dog washes, and there is a plethora of veterinarians located in storefront offices in almost every other block. Animal supply stores advertise home deliveries of all pet related needs such as food, supplements, medicines and vitamins.

Scattered around the city are small neighborhood parks with fenced areas where dogs are unleashed and happily run free. Whatever the reasons, Buenos Aires is awash with dogs and, alas, pedestrians are wise to step carefully as the concept of cleaning up after pets has seemingly not yet occurred to most owners.

Tango Tourists

An estimated 25,000 hardcore tango enthusiasts travel to Buenos Aires each year to attend milongas, take classes, purchase tango clothing (primarily shoes)' and consume copious quantities of Argentine beef and gelati. So many cruise ships now dock in Buenos Aires that a tango impresario is building a 1,200-seat venue to present tango shows. A novelty advertised in 2007 is a tango Yiddish tour organized in Paris by the Valiske Association of France, whose goal is "To become acquainted with the famous interpreters, dancers and researchers connected with the world of tango and Yiddish culture in Buenos Aires."

Although foreigners are amazed at the scores of places to dance every day in Buenos Aires, tango in Buenos Aires today is not nearly as important as it was in the Golden Era of the 1940s to mid-1950s. In spite of the international tango revival that began in the mid-1980s (after the fall of the last dictatorship), renewed recognition in Argentina has been slow. Even so, with more than one-hundred public milongas a week, there is more tango in Argentina than elsewhere. Tango's decline from mid-1955 to 1985 was nearly total and has not yet fully recovered from the neglect of that period.

Because they have been unaccustomed to seeing many tourists, Argentines who come into contact with foreigners in Buenos Aires invariably ask them where they are from and why they have come all the way to Argentina. When they happen upon a 'tango tourist,' their reaction is one of disbelief.

Some are so shocked that they don't know how to respond. Many laugh and say "it can't be true." Some stare in total disbelief, others throw up their hands and say,' Why?" If there is more than one Argentine present, they look at each other in puzzlement, as if they had come upon a rare tropical bird in the middle of the city. For most Argentines, tango is not important in their lives, and they have great difficulty understanding why anyone would travel thousands of miles and spend a lot of money to do something they can do every day – but don't. It makes no sense.

Tango in Buenos Aires

"Total immersion in tango" is an attraction not available in any other city because nowhere else has tango yet entered into the mainstream of social dancing. Although since the Golden Era the number of tango dance halls has diminished considerably, there are still more than enough to satisfy the most serious tango junky. Few evening milongas close their doors before five or six in the morning, and many visiting dancers fill their days with group and private lessons, practicas, and matinee milongas until there are few hours left for sleeping. Outside Argentina, time and effort are needed to discover where it's possible to dance tango.

The Upper Classes and Tango

Although the tango permeated Argentine society before its decline, there are still some upper and middle class families who disapprove of the tango for their friends and even for their grown children. My ophthalmologist told me of friends of his who hide their tango activities from their parents and family members, including spouses.

The "rich and famous" are definitely not in evidence at public milongas or group classes or practicas. Instead, those who are interested in dancing tango, but are not eager to step out of their social milieu, gather together with like-minded friends and hire a first-class tango teacher to give weekly lessons to a select group at one of the elegant upper class town houses or apartments. Some host elaborate tango dinner parties with live orchestras at their private mansions (many with swimming pools and extensive gardens) located in the elegant suburbs.

I've been delighted to be included both at private lessons and at some lovely dinner parties. Once, I overheard a conversation where a certain middle-aged man's name was mentioned in connection with the dance declaring, "Ah... but his mother doesn't know he dances tango."

Tito Palumbo, publisher and editor of the popular magazine *B.A. Tango,* in a 2005 interview explained that as far as most Argentines are concerned: "Tango doesn't sell in Buenos Aires. No one cares about tango anymore. The tango shows close here after a brief run; they're not the least bit as important as they are outside Argentina. Tango is still, for many, a 'shameful' activity, even though nearly everybody can dance it, there are not many real fans."

Tango historian and editor and publisher of the magazine *Club de Tango,* Oscar Himshoot, echoing such concerns said: "People outside Argentina are dancing more tango than those inside, especially the upper classes. There is no passion for the tango in Argentina today." Mr. Himshoot, one of Argentina's foremost tango historians, agreed with Mr. Palumbo's assessment of contemporary tango in Argentina. His tiny office and store has one of the best collections of tango CDs and just about anything else having to do with tango: sheet music, newspaper and magazine articles, posters, and photographs. He sadly told me: "I hardly get any Argentines who come here to buy CDs or tapes, or to look at my historical collection. The Europeans and Americans come in great numbers."

Milongas in Argentina

The term "milonga" not only identifies a tango dance rhythm but is also the name of a place where tango is danced – a public dance hall, a club, a private gathering, or the event itself. It is a touchstone of dancers' discourse wherever tango thrives.

Nevertheless, there are still more than enough Argentines to dance at the 'cornucopia' of milongas in Buenos Aires. Tango tourists make up only a small part of those dancing tango. Although there are some radical differences in Argentine milongas from those outside the country, most tango tourists quickly acclimate to them.

Most milongas begin with matinees during lunch hour, during mid or late afternoon, and last until midnight or later. Each milonga is a separate entity lasting from three to six hours, sometimes following another milonga in the same dance hall and sponsored by different people in the same locations each week. Live orchestras seldom begin to play until sometime between one and two in the morning.

The general atmosphere at milongas in Argentina is similar to those outside the country in that they have bright lighting so that dance steps are easily observed, and there is certain amount of propriety not found in clubs where other dances are practiced. Sometimes there can be one set of Rock and Roll, the cumbia, or chacarara, in which the lights are turned way down. This is generally not the case outside Argentina.

Milongas in Argentina are significantly more social than elsewhere. Outside Argentina dancers tend to arrive, change shoes, dance, watch other dancers, dance some more, then change shoes and depart. In Argentina it is a place to meet friends, perhaps flirt, enjoy a meal or snack, drink, and table-hop to talk with old and new acquaintances. Many reserve the same table each week, and everyone knows everyone else at tables in that section. Some few don't dance at all; for others, dancing is secondary to socializing and may only dance one or two sets. But in spite of the relaxed atmosphere, there is a certain formality in which everyone respects the rigid codes of the milonga – for the tango is treated as the highly respected force that brings them together.

At neighborhood milongas the dancing may be interrupted near midnight and the tables pushed together in long lines so that everyone may enjoy a steak dinner. Such barrio milongas almost always include children running about, occasionally dancing with one another or with family and friends.

The seating at the tables surrounding the dance floor is strictly segregated (if there is a small bar, it is for men only) with separate sections for men and women and a smaller section for mixed couples. This code is breaking down in a few milongas that cater to young people, but generally the custom remains in effect. Many milongas favored by the older generation may have a free Bingo game in the middle of the evening, some with substantial prizes.

Milongas in Argentina adhere to strict codes that have been in effect for over a century. At all milongas the line of dance is strictly observed, with dancers carefully respecting the space of others and dancing according to the available floor space. On crowded Buenos Aires dance floors, thoughtful dancers forego steps requiring lots of space to perform – boleos, ganchos, sacadas, volcadas, colgadas, and all extended leg movements. Fantasy style couples wait until the waning hours when the floor is less crowded. (Once, in Buenos Aires, my partner led me into a step that caused me to jolt a ringside table. Leaping from his seat, a man sitting alone at the table began shouting what I took to be obscenities so threateningly at my partner that he had to be restrained.)

Dance floor etiquette is rigorously followed, and there is a specific code for terminating a dance before the end of a tanda. There is no talking while dancing, only briefly before and after a tanda. Strict codes govern accepting and refusing invitations to dance. Non-observance of the codes on the dance floor may not result in a dancer being tossed out as it used to be (as was the case in earlier times) but generates withering glances and muttered criticisms. Even today, in Argentina it is not unheard of for verbal insults to result in fisticuffs.

Dress Codes

In Buenos Aires, going to a milonga means dressing up for both men and women, and if dress codes are not observed, admittance to a milonga will be denied. The Argentine concern for appearance is in evidence at milongas, whether held in the afternoon, in the evening, or at night. Argentine men have always dressed up for milongas, partly to conceal their lower class origins. Older men are impeccably groomed in freshly pressed suits, white shirts, and ties, their shoes highly polished, their hair slicked back with *gomima* (hair gel), and they smell of after-shave. Milongueros appear invitingly suave in their suits and ties and do not stand out as being from an earlier era. It is different for women. It is rare to see older women dancers of distinguished appearance because when they were young, the tango was restricted to the lower classes.

Not a few milongueras, like milongueros, are overweight, but that doesn't stop them from dressing to the hilt in styles from the Golden Era. Cocktail dresses that were the rage during the 1940s and 1950s vie for attention with provocative dresses with hip-high slits or long skirts and elaborate blouses. "Slinky" is the key word, with an abundance of satin, sequins, and shimmery fabrics and decorations. Many Argentine women uninhibitedly wear skin-tight dresses and skirts two sizes too small, some with dangerously daring décolleté, and shoes of glittery materials in an array of colors including imitation leopard skin heels with matching blouses. Most wear heavy make-up, and some dancers of advanced years wear elaborate beehive hairdos. Mixed in with those wearing dress and hair styles from the forties are slim, attractive women in designer pants and contemporary, elegant dress.

For some dancers, passion for the dance is accompanied by passion for dance shoes, so for many tourists the most interesting shopping in Buenos Aires is in the shoe stores. Some shoe manufacturers send clerks to visitors' hotels or guesthouses to measure for custom made shoes – at inexpensive prices – to be delivered several days later. The downtown Flabella store is almost always crowded with clients, some of them attracted there by the owner, Eduardo, a handsome stereotypical, hand-kissing, neck-nuzzling Argentine flirt, who acts as a partner when clients want to try dance steps while trying on potential purchases.

Tandas

Many milongas in Buenos Aires have live music on the weekends with orchestras of five to nine musicians, who don't usually start playing until well after midnight. Otherwise there are DJs, many who become famous and are in much demand for their judicious choice of music tempos and orchestras to match the varying styles of dance.

All milongas in Argentina have music structured into tandas of four or five songs of the same rhythm. Sometimes if the music is not live, records that are played are all by the same orchestra or else songs of the same rhythm by different orchestras. The music is from the 1930s to early 1950s. (This is not always the case in the rest of the world, where tandas are not always observed and occasionally there is some technotango or even music by Piazzolla.)

It is expected that partners will dance one tanda then change partners – a gracious way to avoid implying anything negative about the partner's dancing as well as a confirmation of the tango's commitment to variety and improvisation with styles and dancers. It has been estimated that the division of tango songs in a typical evening is seventy percent tango, twenty percent milonga, ten percent waltz. The end of a tanda is marked with a *cortina* (Spanish for curtain), which is a minute or two of non-dance music that cues dancers to leave the floor and couples separate and return to their tables to await a change of partners for the next tanda.

A structured tanda gives the couple ample time to accommodate to one another's styles. The first dance is customarily tentative, with the man leading a simple dance. In the second, the man assays progressively complex movements to see whether or not the partner can easily follow him and to discover if she anticipates or waits for the lead – all knowledge needed before undertaking more elaborate steps. If the second set is satisfactory, the man will break out his repertoire of favorite steps, so that by the fourth set, apprehension erased, both partners may relax and thoroughly enjoy themselves. Before a tanda ends, if one partner is not happy with the other, a simple "thank you" indicates the end of the partnership, and both return to their tables. It is a huge putdown and not used often.

Some men say that tandas allow them to be chivalrous to a woman they've noticed who hasn't had many (or any) invitations, or to be gracious to a friend or to someone with whom they feel obliged to dance. He waits until the third or fourth song of a tanda before asking the woman to dance, thereby needing only to finish the tanda. He can feel gallant without committing himself to an entire tanda.

In order for women to be invited to dance by other men, some couples routinely arrive at a milonga and sit at separate tables reserved for those of their gender. They do not dance with each other, and at evening's end meet up and depart together.

Changing Partners: The *Cabeceo*

Foreign women visiting a Buenos Aires milonga without knowing the unique manner in which invitations are issued are initially nonplussed, but after decades of use, the *cabeceo* (in Spanish it means "a little head movement") in regular milongas is ironclad. Nearly every male dancer in Buenos Aires uses eye contact to invite a woman to dance. Indeed, should a man approach an Argentine woman's table to ask her to dance, he will almost certainly be refused or simply ignored.

The man's correct way to issue an invitation is to wait at his table or at the small bar and survey the room until he catches the eye of his prospective partner. If their eyes meet, he nods his head ever so slightly toward the dance floor. If she's amenable, the woman nods a discreet "Yes," perhaps with a smile. Once the contract is mutually affirmed, the couple, maintaining visual coordination, will meet at the edge of the dance floor nearest the woman's table. Exchanging no words beyond a quiet greeting, they embrace in preparation for the dance.

Potential embarrassment lurks when a man nods to a woman sitting behind or adjacent to another woman who mistakenly believes she is the object of the nod. She smiles, stands, walks to meet him at the edge of the dance floor, only to realize the man is not smiling at her but at a woman approaching behind her. With tables and chairs so close together, such confusion is not uncommon. When in doubt, the experienced woman may raise an eyebrow or discreetly touch a finger to her body with a querying look, or mouth the question, "me?" Alternatively, she may delay rising from her seat until the moment when the man reaches the dance floor and she can see that he is truly locking eyes with her and not her neighbor. Such clarification helps prevent loss of face for the "rejected" one. (One time I mistook an invitation to be for me when in fact it was for the woman at a table in back of me. We both stood up and started walking toward the dance floor and the rather handsome man walking in our direction. When we got close, the man indicated that it was not I he had invited, but the "other woman." However, he was very gallant and said he would come back for me for the next tanda, as indeed he did, so I saved a bit of face.)

Many foreign women (and no few Argentines) dislike invitations by eye contact because they find it humiliating to sit passively, almost as a suppliant, and wait to dance at the whim of a man. Observed Robin Gray, "The man retains the power of choice, while the potential hurt and rejection falls upon the woman. A few times I have fixed my eyes upon someone who saw me looking but did not ask me to dance. Meanwhile I am sitting and sitting, feeling foolish. My request had clearly been rejected, but in a way that absolved the man of any responsibility: he could just slink away without acknowledging me."

Some women, however, like the custom because it avoids making them look impolite, or "snooty," for refusing a dance. Julie Taylor, an excellent dancer, reported that once an American man approached her table, and she told him, "I'll dance with you this time, but please don't come to my table again. It puts too much pressure on me." American Janis Kenyon elaborated: "The *cabeceo* takes practice – precise timing and a sharp eye. One can avoid an awkward situation by learning patience. Give the man time to walk across the floor. He will make eye contact with you to confirm his sign. The cabeceo isn't foolproof, but ladies, it's the only way you can get to dance with the best of Buenos Aires." Another American expressed her opinion more forcefully: "I give no mercy dances. I dance with whom I want to the music I want. I feel in control; no man can approach my table without permission. There is none of the sitting down with you and monopolizing that often occurs in the U.S. I love it!"

One night at a popular Buenos Aires milonga frequented by excellent dancers, I was sitting at a table with three Argentine women friends. I had not danced, but my companions were consistently popping up at the beginning of each tanda, and I watched them wistfully as they joined partners at the floor's edge. A middle-aged, only moderately attractive Argentine woman at the next table (the tables are always very close together) who was dancing every dance noticed my plight and leaned over to counsel me: "Look at the dance floor until you see a man whose dancing pleases you. When he sits down, lock your eyes on him and no one else. Do not take your eyes off him even if he looks away. Watch me!" She proceeded to follow her own instructions with a formidable gaze at her selected quarry, and within minutes the man nodded an invitation. Impressive!

Some say the custom survives because of the importance Argentines place on appearances or "face," since it is possible for a man to invite someone to dance without fear of a rejection being noted by everyone in the room. Should a man cross the room and be turned down, he is perceived to be humiliated; but if he is invisibly declined with a discreet nod he can invite an alternate partner with no one the wiser for his rebuff. If a woman sees a man looking at her and chooses not to dance with him, she merely turns her head and looks the other way.

Some men refuse to take "no" for an answer, in which case they circulate the room with eyes locked onto their target, but then will never approach the table where the women are sitting. At any milonga there are men with whom, for one reason or another, women do not choose to dance. At the end of each tanda, such fellows determinedly circle the room, trying to catch someone's eye, while the women turn their heads here and there to avoid having to acknowledge the probing glances. When a searcher is unsuccessful, his circles become smaller, involving a great deal of eye shifting on the part of the women as he moves around the room, always watching. One woman reports that a man she knew walked by her table and, without looking at her, whispered, "Look at me, please." He'd been trying to catch her eye but, rather than break the code, he verbally asked for eye contact so he could "honorably" invite her to dance.

In Buenos Aires milongas, once a contract is made by "locked eyes," it is regarded as extremely rude for a woman to refuse the implicit invitation. It is possible to refuse invitations by never looking in a man's direction, by acting interested in anything other than the man, i.e., the wall paneling, another dancer's footwork, or her finger nails. Such niceties become problematic for the woman who wants to dance and must look at the men's sections to see if anyone is looking at her. Women become adroit at skimming a room for eye contact while deftly flicking their eyes away from the undesirables.

Advice to Women Tourists

Janis Kenyon, an American who moved to Buenos Aires and has studied milongueros for years, explains some of the subtleties of the invitation process. First, she notes, "Men who go to a woman's table do so because 1) she is a tourist, and 2) she will accept his invitation. What the women don't know is that these local dancers only dance with tourists because they are not good dancers themselves and cannot get good local women dancers to dance with them. They will continue to invite the same women to dance for hours. If you are willing to dance with bad dancers, the good dancers will never invite you. Ignore the men who come to your table, and they won't bother you again."

Ms. Kenyon continues, "There are some milongueros who never use the *cabeceo*. Milongueros carefully select the women with whom they want to dance and will not invite a partner whom they have not seen dance. They wait for their favorite orchestra, and they may not dance a complete tanda. Their invitation is proffered by movement of the lips, mouthing *"Vamos"* (let's go) – with no head movement."

David Derman

For decades, one of Buenos Aires' familiar faces was milonguero David Derman, who spent the greater pat of his life in milongas. He was unique in that after dancing with each new partner, he entered her name in a little black book he carried with him. In neat columns he noted a number by his partner's name, nationality, and the site and date of their dance. When I danced with him, I was registered as number 7,163. He knew by heart the numbers of the famous women with whom he had danced, including Madonna, and he used to gladly cite their names while leafing to the correct page.

After each new dance, he would take out of his jacket a piece of paper folded in half—playing card sized—on which he marked the data about their dance. Inside was printed, "You are my dancer number ___," followed by the phrase, "Thank you for dancing with me," in English French and Spanish. Below the text was a small color photo headshot next to his address and telephone number. On the back he signed his name next to a tango-related poem and a photo of a red rose.

Derman did not look the part of the stereotypically handsome Latin tango dancer; he was short, balding and roly-poly with a sweet Santa Claus face. But he was always impeccably turned out in a suit and tie, freshly ironed shirt, and highly polished shoes. In his seventies, he danced in milongas three or four times a week. He said that he learned to dance in academias, first practicing the follower's role with boys, then as he grew older, with men. (He recently passed away.)

Lessons and Practicas

In Buenos Aires it is not necessary to call friends or search the Net to find out where to dance, for the city's many newsstands carry several tango magazines (some of them free) that, among articles and other tango information, list the dozens of daily possibilities for dancing. Apart from some one-hundred-thirty listed weekly milongas, there are group lessons, practicas, and private lessons allowing a breathless dancer to stop briefly only for breakfast while dancing around the clock.

Group lessons are available from ten in the morning throughout the day until ten in the evening; a recent issue of *B.A. Tango* listed some thirty-eight group classes offered daily as well as many daily practicas. Private lessons are available from teachers who are generally less expensive than elsewhere in the world, except for the famous "stars.'

Practicas are informal dances in which dancers can practice steps and technique. There is no structured teaching, but practicas are sponsored by one or two teachers who are available for advice and are responsible for the recorded music, sometimes provided by a professional DJ. Dancers follow the codes of conduct and, by and large, couples are left to dance as they wish, although some teachers run hands-on sessions and observe, encourage, and correct dancers; others wait for dancers to approach them with problems or questions. Practicas are held in dance studios, nightclubs, or restaurants any time from mid-day on into late afternoon or early evening. Frequently teachers will host a practica directly following a class so that students may practice what they learned in class. Similarly, practicas are sometimes held several hours before a late night milonga, in order to permit students to warm up and practice.

Some practicas are so relaxed that professors encourage dancers to change partners frequently, and a very few even encourage women to ask men to dance. Unlike milongas, during practicas dancers may stop and practice or correct steps. Occasionally couples may seek advice from one another, particularly if they have shared a previous class. Couples may seek advice from other dancers on the finer points of a particular figura (generally six to eight steps), and it is not unusual to see two men dance together to illustrate steps. Generally speaking, dancers are exceedingly generous in helping one another.

Dress at practicas is casual. For Argentine women, the range of attire runs from knee-length dresses, trousers, or tight pants through short skirts and tight-fitting or see-through blouses. Visitors tend to dress down a bit, in trousers and a top. Men wear slacks and sports shirts, sometimes with ties. Many older Argentine men don't feel right dancing the tango unless they wear a suit and tie.

Separate Seating

The Confiteria Ideal, a noted Art Nouveau building in central Buenos Aires, boasts a restaurant/café/teashop on the ground floor and a dance hall on the second, and is popular with visitors because of its period architecture and decoration and its reputation for informality and warm welcome to foreigners. The women sit on the right side of the dance floor, the men in the front of the central section, and more women at small, single tables across the room. As at most milongas, couples sit apart from the men's and women's sections.

Recently I went with French tourists, (we were three men and three women) to the Pavadita matinee milonga. At the entrance we were asked if the women wished to dance. Surprised at the question, the women answered, "Si!" at which point we were informed that we had sit in the women's section while the men were directed to the men's section. Another part of the hall was reserved for milongueros who sat on a stage at occupied tables on a raised eight by ten platform from which they surveyed the dancers while commenting to their friends. From time to time, a few might deign to invite a woman to dance – invariably an Argentine milonguera or a pretty young foreigner.

At milongas and practicas there is almost always a surplus of women, meaning that being an excellent dancer provides no guarantee against sitting out an entire evening. Writing about her trip to Buenos Aires, Naomi Bennett observed, "It was difficult to get dances and I sat too much. There were fifteen to twenty single women sitting at tables in competition." Skilled male dancers do not dance with women they haven't seen dance, but the young and pretty stand the best chance of an invitation. Unattached women foreigners sometimes attend milongas in small groups with at least one man whose job it is to dance with each of them so that watching men can decide if they want to dance with a stranger.

Taxi Dancers

One solution for older women who have trouble finding partners is to hire someone to dance with them. Many of the organizers of group tours to Buenos Aires provide partners – Argentine men who are good dancers – for the extra women. Also, some male teachers are willing to provide visiting women with this service for a reasonable fee plus entrances, a drink, and taxi fares. This practice has become more popular in recent years as more and more foreigners visit Buenos Aires to dance. Some men have also begun to advertise their services as taxi dancers in various tango publications.

There are those who vociferously object to this practice and talk about dancers prostituting themselves. But many women are happy to pay for a skilled partner if it means they can avoid sitting in the milongas night after night being ignored in favor of young, pretty women who are chosen not only for their looks but also because they are excellent dancers. My own take on it has been: If I fly 10,000 miles and invest hundreds of dollars to go to Buenos Aires, I want to be sure I'm going to dance, not just watch, and I will spend whatever I can afford to enjoy the best possible dance experience in the short time I am there. If I want Spanish lessons I pay for conversation classes, so why not pay for 'tango conversations'? At an evening spent at one of the milongas featuring a free bingo game, I once had an unusual opportunity to enhance my taxi dancer's earnings when I won $200, which I shared with him.

Men in Milongas with Agendas Other Than Dance

By and large the Argentine men go to milongas to dance, but there are those who regularly attend milongas frequented by foreign women and have other agendas. Some men are looking for sexual adventures they feel sure are easily had with women on their own, so far from home. Some are there for the chance to make extra money by pretending to visitors that they are qualified tango teachers and eagerly press their calling cards into foreign hands. Still others are hoping to strike up a romantic relationship that would enable them to travel to foreign countries.

Argentine women call men looking for sexual excitement "cafécito men" because they invite women out to have a cup of coffee. These men like to spice up their dance by thrusting their legs between the woman's legs in a suggestive manner, by grabbing her so far around the back that there is a brushing of the chests, by kissing her on the cheek or even the lips, and by suggestive whisperings in the ear. The Argentine women ostracize these men, but foreign women are sometimes susceptible to their "charms."

Tango historian, Oscar Himshoot, wrote: "There are more tango teachers in Buenos Aires than there are students." Their mode of operation is simple. When dancing with a foreigner of any level of skill, they whip out a calling card that identifies them as a tango teacher, and most teach in their homes or in rented studios. Flattering words about the tourists' dancing ability pique the dancers' interest so that when a suggestion is made that his/her style could be improved with a few private lessons, deals are frequently struck. Unfortunately, tourists are not aware that no reputable teacher will ever give out a card unless it is requested.

There are enough stories of successful romantic relations to warrant the hope that the hustler will be embraced and taken to the U. S. or to Europe as a protégé dance teacher in the woman's home community. He ingratiates himself with his "mark" with words of love and adoration. At the least he receives free meals and drinks, taxi fares, and soon accepts 'loans' to pay bills or buy some needed clothing. The ultimate goal is usually for the 'teacher' to be invited to travel (all expenses paid, of course) to the woman's home on a temporary basis to give tango workshops. These arrangements don't always turn out well when some men don't want to disengage from their sponsor's hospitality.

Hustling in the milongas has become so prevalent that the April, 2000 issue of B. A. Tango had an article by Argentine Beatriz Pozzo warning women tango tourists to be careful. Cherie Magnus of Los Angeles posted on the internet her view of "the dark side of B.A. milongas": "When I got home from my fourth trip to Argentina I remembered my adventures as fascinating and fun as always but this time I saw the dark side. What I saw in the milongas was that everyone, and I mean everyone, was either buying or selling, and many were doing both. My eyes had been closed to this before...It was all so wonderful and artful and everyone just loved the tango like I do. I observed and participated in the Romance of Tango – the Real Thing. Wow. This time I saw, sure the love and skill of tango, but also the ambition, desperation, insecurity, frustration, poverty, buying and selling of favors and dancing, jealousy, backstabbing deceit, lying, people using people, self-centeredness, ego, ego, ego – and greed for both money and attention."

Cherie's experiences, however, did not prevent her from moving to Buenos Aires. She wrote: "We have a greater chance of going to Tango Heaven in a Buenos Aires milonga than anywhere else. The level of skill and experience is without equal. Anything else is beside the point."

Similarities and Differences

Obviously, milongas outside Argentina don't harbor tango hustlers, but milongas in other countries are in many ways similar to those in Argentina. In Argentine milongas the music is rigorously programmed and social conduct conforms to strict codes honored for more than a century. When dancers want to tango in Argentina, their choices are practically unlimited with more than one-hundred commercial places to choose from every week. Abroad, where tango lies outside the mainstream of popular dance culture, the logistics of setting out to dance are not trivial, for venues are seldom advertised or listed in telephone directories. Tango must be searched out on the internet or via word of mouth, giving it a hint of illicit adventure, a mystique of a shadowy underground activity.

Once tracked down, a milonga differs altogether from merely "going dancing." Dance objectives are different, each venue's ambience varies, and milongas are often held in unconventional places. Instead of an evening of varied rhythms such as Salsa, swing, or Rock and Roll, only tango music is played throughout the evening.

In contrast to the familiar image of tango dancers in a dim-lit hall, cigarettes dangling from lips, drink glasses cluttering tiny tabletops, most of today's milongas are smoke-free, and many outside Argentina are alcohol-free as well; entrance fees often include soft drinks and bottled water. If alcohol is available, it is consumed moderately, even by the French, who customarily do not consider anything worth doing without wine.

In 2001 Johanna Siegman informally queried dancers on the internet about mixing alcohol and tango. A few responses: "The dance itself is more satisfying than anything we can ingest to get satisfaction." "Lucidity, not alcohol, makes it 'easier' to do this particular dance." "Alcohol gives bad breath." "It's hard to look good when you're drunk." In Paris, tango teacher Gilles Cuena wrote on a questionnaire: "The tango itself is intoxicating enough, we don't need anything else."

The atmosphere in milongas, outside as well as within Argentina, is agreeably calm, free of loud chatter, raucous laughter, or hailing friends spied across the room. Unlike the glittery lighting effects favored in other kinds of dance halls or clubs — flashing strobes, laser beams, or spinning disco balls — the illumination for milongas is relatively high level and uniform for three good reasons. First, good light ensures that spectators can easily enjoy the detail of the dancers' movements; second, it allows dancers to safely and gracefully navigate the counter-clockwise flow of the dance around the floor; and third, it makes possible the interplay of the subtle visual cues — the *cabeceo* - essential to connecting with potential new partners for the next tanda.

Then there is the milonga's all-important music. From either a small ensemble of musicians or a well-modulated sound system comes the unique music of the tango, much of which will seem exotic indeed to listeners unfamiliar with the genre. And unlike conventional clubs where the dancers tend to be of a particular age group, at milongas it is not unusual to see dancers whose ages range from their twenties to their eighties and dance partners with age differences of decades.

Propriety and Independence

"In the early days — the 1940s and 1950s — people did not go to milongas looking for the opposite sex, but for approval. The true tango dancers went to the dance halls to dance, to shine, to be the best." (Mingo Pugliese)

Today, everyone knows that a woman who goes to a milonga alone is only interested in dancing. And what's more, if she's by herself, the odds are high that she is a very good dancer: it would be a daring novice indeed who would venture onto a milonga's dance floor. Perhaps the absence of an alcoholic ambience enhances propriety and security, but the inherent seriousness and purposefulness of the tango milieu allows unaccompanied women to maintain their dignity, confident that they will not be inappropriately approached.

Outside Argentina, women frequently wear clothes to milongas that they would not dare to wear in the street. Wrote dancer Gayle Devereaux, "I guess women feel safer wearing sexier, flashier clothing while tango dancing than with other dances because the men seem to accept it as part of the dance, and not that you are trying to get them to sleep with you." Another woman said, "It's a code. It's a culture. You can wear your spikiest heels and your highest slit skirts and still feel as safe and protected as at a church social."

The value systems of middle and upper-middle class women undergo a radical change from their usual reactions when they spot an "Argentine-looking" man coming into a local dance hall. Any Latino who might never be given a second glance in any other venue acquires instant desirability, causing females to perk up in attempts to be noticed. If such a man's appearance or comportment is seen as "possibly Argentine," as opposed to merely "Latin," women's eyes glitter with hope that he'll invite them to dance, for odds are that if he's Argentine, he's a good dancer. Many women imagine that black shirts and suits and slicked-back dark hair (better with a ponytail) would be worn only by a good dancer. Fancy shoes complete the picture; ostentatious shoes are another common indicator of accomplished dancers. So, skinny or fat, the important things to look for in putative partners are to be found at the top and bottom.

Because the tango embrace requires closeness, there is an awareness that personal hygiene is important, and everyone is expected to be neat and clean – and to smell good in the bargain. Perfume and cologne are much in evidence, and at many milongas breath mints are available at the entrance or at the bar. Dancers can be seen "popping" them discreetly and offering them freely to one another.

A few women have learned to lead; either because they want the challenge or hope to improve their skills through a better understanding of the dance – or because the dual skill increases their opportunities to dance. Although Argentina has resisted the trend, the practice has become commonplace in North America and parts of Europe.

Courage on the Dance Floor

Many beginners lack the courage to attend formal milongas and instead dance only at lessons, practicas, or at home until they have attained at least the intermediate level. Many experienced dancers choose to sit out the occasional dance not only to rest but also to observe those on the dance floor looking for something new to add to their repertoire. From the sideline, observer commentary is predictably profuse: "Did you see that adornment?" "How did he do *that?*" "Her extension is great." "How did he manage to get into that cross-step?" "What a great salida!" An internet contributor wrote: "Milongas can be intimidating to newcomers because there are people sitting at tables watching them (and often being exceedingly uncharitable). There are people who take a lot of classes but rarely, if ever, go to a dance. This is probably due to a combination of social anxiety and of people's lives being so busy. Some may, God forbid, have other interests."

We Want to Dance NOW!

A common attitude among tango dancers is that one should be able to dance whenever the opportunity arises. Even in many large cities outside Argentina, apart from the usual after - dinner hours, a place can be found to tango at lunchtime, after work, or during early evenings. In Buenos Aires "matinee" milongas begin at lunchtime and go on throughout the day; by moving around judiciously, it is possible to dance at one place or another from before lunch until five or six the next morning.

Smaller tango communities may not be large enough to support a choice of places to dance every day of the week, so organizers must scout for places to hold milongas. Dance studios are often easily available, but the appeal of their good floors is offset by the often spartan atmosphere – utilitarian chairs or benches without tables and no provision for serving refreshments. Although cultural centers, churches, clubhouses of civic organizations, school gyms, and municipal halls sometimes open their doors to dancers, somber settings prevail there too, sometimes with only the occasional lonely chair. Some restaurants and cafés let dancers come in after dinner, in the hope of making extra money during the slow hours. Such expectations frequently meet with disappointment, though, and the dancers are asked to find another place. A few dancers open their homes and move furniture around to host weekly milongas. Some have built extra rooms onto their homes in order to hold regular free milongas that are open to anyone who wants to dance. Many "open house" milongas are potluck affairs, with refreshments ranging from simple to elaborate.

Little or No Profits for Organizers

Although milongas in Argentina are commercial enterprises, outside Argentina not many milongas expect to make a profit because most of them are organized essentially to promote the local tango community and/or to ensure that the organizers and their friends will have more places to dance. An internet correspondent wrote, "To my knowledge, nobody runs a milonga as a for-profit venture. A milonga is a labor of love; admissions usually barely cover the costs (especially if food and drink are provided) and the DJ (often poorly paid). That's why many milongas don't last more than a couple of years – eventually the rents go up and rather than raise admission fees, the milonga changes venue or disappears altogether. The hosts either have a real job or are retired. I doubt you'll find many people who can say their main job is milonga organizer." At many milongas dancers are encouraged to contribute homemade snacks which are set out on a table with paper plates, plastic utensils, and cups; sometimes there is a container for contributions to help cover expenses. If not free, refreshments are provided at a modest cost.

Added interest for Argentine tango comes from dancing in unusual places, and such venues abound. In New York City there is tango in a section of a meat packing plant on the docks by the Hudson. In a cultural center in downtown Paris, dancers and spectators must sit on gym equipment, and in another arrondissement milongas are held in a sixth-floor warehouse walk-up that appears to have had no maintenance since the Revolution. Mounting the decrepit stairs is perilous and tiring, and dance hazards include gaps in the floorboards. In the summer in cities across the U.S. and Europe, dances are held in parks, on bridges, on riversides, and on wharves by the Mediterranean. Many cruise ships that regularly depart from Miami, New York, and Los Angeles for the Caribbean, Mexico, and Alaska offer tailored tango programs.

Creative Solutions

"We may not have much money but we have imagination," says Lucille Krasne. Tango dancers welcome any excuse for a special dance, as is illustrated by the following internet posting: "11 weeks to New York's tango festival where we will celebrate the 100th anniversary of the Staten Island Ferry. Last year we celebrated the 100th anniversary of the subway."

One benefit of having to search for suitable dance venues is the devising of creative solutions that allow dancers to enjoy interesting and unusual places. Dancers come from all over Europe, for instance, to dance in Paris by the Seine River every warm, non-rainy night from May through October, beginning about eight o'clock and continuing until one or two in the morning. The smooth concrete floor is set in a small amphitheater abutting the river, with five rows of concrete benches for spectators. On balmy nights, tour boats and private boats slow to a stop, allowing passengers to watch the dancing (and sometimes applaud) - the scene is magical. (It's good that tango dancers don't drink because the dance floor is so close to the water that an overly energetic movement or faulty lead could set dancers splashing about in the river, which reportedly happened not long ago.) This milonga is run by volunteers of the Temps du Tango, a not-for-profit group, with a hat passed for donations to buy CDs and sound equipment.

Other milongas-on-the-water have sprung up in recent years. Again in Paris, a monthly milonga is held on a large tourist boat docked on the Seine across from the Louvre Museum, and on the city's outskirts another is hosted in a turn-of-the-century dance hall alongside the Marne River in a setting featured in Impressionist paintings. In Shanghai, tango is danced in a park by the Pearl River; in Cambridge, Massachusetts, on a bridge over the Charles; in Marseilles, on the docks. And milongas are held waterside in Seattle, London, Geneva, Istanbul, Berlin, and elsewhere. In Buenos Aires, to be sure, the strains of tango melodies echo invitingly above the ornate bandstands in several center city parks as well as the docks of the Rio de la Plata in La Boca.

Alternative Milongas: Gay and Lesbian Milongas

Another innovation of recent years is alternative milongas dominated by young dancers. They sometimes have funky decorations and some of the dance floors are in deplorable condition. Dress codes are relaxed and body piercings are popular; many dress in punk clothing and sport shoes. Traditional codes are breaking down: there are no tandas, the line of dance is not obligatory, and the *cabeceo* is not requisite.

Sometimes the embrace is exchanged within one song, with partners keeping their place and physical contact but changing the positions of their arms when the leader turns into the follower. Others dance only as leaders or followers. Invitations may happen on the dance floor and partners can be exchanged there. According to "Tango. com," the idea of changing roles of the leader or follower in alternative milongas has been reflected in the teaching of tango classes to encourage learning both roles. The music is also different, with electronic or fusion music mixed with traditional music.

The ambience of alternative milongas is playful rather than serious, and couples of the same sex are not frowned upon as they frequently are in regular milongas. Some of the alternative milongas cater to gays or lesbians, or both, and their numbers are increasing as more young people take to the tango. The relaxed atmosphere attracts not only the young but also beginners and foreigners who are put off or intimidated by the strict codes of traditional milongas.

Most gay milongas are open to anyone, but there is one, "Entre Nosotros," organized by an institute of lesbian feminists, which is closed to men. The first gay milonga, 'La Marshall,' opened in 2003 as a place for men to practice.

Club Villa Malcolm bills its milongas as "Tango Cool" and is known for its openness to new styles and experimentation. "La Devina" opened its doors in 2004 as a practica for women; although the clientele is mixed, regular milonga codes are not enforced.

Gay Gauchos

Considering that Argentine male Gaucho culture is unabashedly macho, it is surprising that gay gauchos have come out of previously closed closets and onto tango floors. (They have been so "outed" that television spot commercials have begun appearing every day that advertise over a dozen regional gay organizations, complete with telephone numbers.) In January, 2008, there was an hour-long television program showing them dancing tango and graceful folk dances. Milongas where gay gauchos gather have also become popular among heterosexuals.

Aspects of Tango in Buenos Aires

Tango Classes

After the military coup of 1955, which was at the start of tango's decline, an entire generation of Argentines did not learn to dance tango. Subsequently, interest in tango in other parts of the world, spurred a revival of interest in the tango within Argentina. Now the middle-aged, whose generation didn't learn tango, are taking lessons. Older Argentines say they are learning the dance because they are aware of the tango's renaissance in other parts of the world, making them appreciate their cultural heritage: they are "glad to see Argentina recognized for something besides beef." A poll taken in 1966 indicated that ninety-one percent of young people between the ages of eighteen and twenty-nine believed that the tango became more popular among Argentine youth as a means of "finding a national identity in the face of galloping globalization." There are a few who said they look to the tango as a form of socializing, and recently divorced men and women believe it is a good place to meet potential partners. Others say they want to learn because they are aware of the latest tango fad in the rest of the world, which has made them appreciate their own dance, and they want to learn it.

A child psychiatrist who has been dancing for only a year said he began lessons because he frequently attends international conventions or symposiums that included dinner/dance events. When tango music was played, he used to be embarrassed when people of other nationalities got up to dance and he was forced to admit he was an Argentine who didn't dance tango.

Argentine Youth Taking Tango Lessons

The largest group of new faces in tango classes is Argentine young people. Although Argentines historically have looked outside their country for cultural influences, young people today have begun to look inward, searching for an appreciation of things Argentine. Also, the governmental tango programs for primary through university levels, directed by Rodolfo and Gloria Dinzel, have had an influence. At her studio, Olga Besio specializes in teaching special tango classes for children of all ages. She is aided by her two teen-aged children who have been dancing professionally since they were not much more than toddlers.

The worldwide interest in Argentina has influenced the young to look to tango as an "in thing" to do. Others hope to become professional performers and teachers and are learning it for the same reasons that many Third World boys play soccer. If they become good enough, it is a means of earning money and a chance of world travel. Mr. Palumbo is cautiously optimistic about tango's future in Buenos Aires and believes that this second burst of popularity for tango will continue to grow. "For one thing, it is a cheap evening's entertainment. Where else can you go out for a long evening and only have to spend $5?"

An intriguing fall-out from the interest in tango is that young people and many older dancers have begun to take an interest in Argentine folk dances, and many milongas have at least one tanda of the line dance, *chacarara*, and the partnered *canyengue*. These dances have also caught on outside Argentina, and at many milongas dancers who have taken chacarara lessons face each other with their arms gracefully swinging over their heads and dance rapid, stomping, intricate foot movements.

Government Promotion of Tango
"No one should have to pay to learn the tango. The government should give free lessons to all, including foreigners who come here."
(Oscar Himshoot)

Some government officials agree, for it is now a requirement for cadets at the Argentine Naval Academy to take tango lessons. One day at Mr. Himshoot's office, I met Olga Gil who teaches tango at the Academy, and she told me the reasons for requiring the lessons: "In recent years, naval officers and trainees on the Argentine Navy's training frigate, the "Libertad," that circles the globe on flag-waving voyages were embarrassed when they visited world ports where, at local social events, the tango was invariably played in their honor. But when locals invited them to dance the Argentines had to admit they did not know how to dance, their national dance. Someone in authority felt this situation was "barbarous," so after some controversial discussions, the tango was added to the official curriculum." Apparently the Army has not seen fit to emulate this patriotism, possibly because they don't go around the world "waving the flag."

Both the Argentine federal government and the municipality of Buenos Aires have launched programs to promote tango. There is now an annual Buenos Aires tango festival with several weeks of free lessons, concerts, and dance performances. Annual national and international tango dance championships are sponsored on several governmental levels. Recent Congressional legislation gives tax breaks to tango composers; tango performers traveling abroad receive some advantages and exceptions to certain import and export duties. Tango performers, musicians and dancers have been lacking sufficient protection for proper working conditions and social benefits; only recently have they successfully formed a union-like association that acts on behalf of its members.

The *Ley de Tango*, (the Tango Law), passed in 1977, provides that "tango be taught on all levels of schools, from primary to university." Unfortunately, the wording of the law, "to be implemented gradually" has not been conducive to rapid action, so it is not nearly universal. Some tango artists have initiated projects designed to educate and stimulate student interest in tango. Gloria and Rodolfo Dinzel have been working with the Department of Education, the Department of Cultura, and the Orquesta de Tango de Buenos Aires to produce weekly tango programs at school levels in Buenos Aires. In 1999 they produced twenty-three programs in the twenty-one school districts at primary and special education schools for the handicapped.

The programs open with the well-known author, Oscar del Priore, who talks about the history of tango music from its origins to the *'orquesta tipica'* of the golden Age of Tango. A vocalist then discusses lyrics, including some Lunfardo words and expressions, and students are encouraged to ask questions about tango poetry and music. Then students get a chance to sing a few tangos. The last part of the program is an exhibition of various tango dance styles by professional dancers from the Dinzel studio. At the end, students are invited to dance with the dancers and with each other.

The Academy of Lunfardo continues to work on a Lunfardo dictionary whose members analyze the use of Lunfardo in tango lyrics and in present day literary use, and also holds classes in Lunfardo.

There are two government subsidized concert orchestras, a national orchestra and a Buenos Aires city orchestra. The Orchestra Nacionale de Tango plays at the Teatro Nacionale Cervantes, which also has a tango museum and a library open on Mondays. The forty-piece Orquesta del Tango de Buenos Aires orchestra is supported by the city of Buenos Aires and gives free concerts at the Teatro Presidente Alvear one afternoon a week.

The government now promotes tango extensively. When Prince Charles of England visited Buenos Aires, a photograph flashed around the world showing the Prince (albeit with a pained expression) with tango professional Variana Vasile's leg wrapped seductively around his thigh. A state dinner in Washington for Argentine President Carlos Menem featured tango dancing by professionals and tango enthusiast actor Robert Duvall. In an effort to promote tango in the U. S., Mr. Duvall has been named President of the Argentine government-sponsored

Academia Nacionale de Tango in Washington, D.C. On inquiry, no one at the Embassy seems to know quite what his duties are. Let's hope he does.

In 1991 the Academia Nationale de Tango (The University of Tango) was established with a prestigious three-year program of music appreciation, tango literature, study of Lunfardo and tango dance history and practical lessons. Gloria and Rodolfo were instrumental in the creation of the University and still teach there on a regular basis.

Located above the prestigious Café Tortoni in downtown Buenos Aires, the Academia Nationale de Tango sponsors classes in tango music, poetry, and dance. The Academia Nationale de Tango recently sponsored a Carlos Gardel poster contest based on the theme, *"Gardel, Lunfa y Senor."* There were three-hundred-thirty-three entries with contributors from the US, Spain, Mexico, France, Colombia, Uruguay and Brazil – as well as Argentina.

The first public statue of Carlos Gardel was erected in downtown Buenos Aires in March, 2000, on a corner near the house in which he lived in Buenos Aires. The four-meter bronze standing statue was presented in an elaborate ceremony sponsored by the Academy of Lunfardo, with a long list of attending government officials, including President de la Rua and luminaries from the academic tango establishment. In honor of Troilo Anibal's birthday of July 11, the National Day of Bandoneon was declared by the federal government. The holiday is celebrated with concerts, radio, and television programs, making Argentina the only country in the world with a national holiday honoring a musical instrument. Troilo was the second most revered tango musician (after Carlos Gardel).

However, for many serious dancers, the academic associations and statues are not sufficient, and they believe the government should do more to promote tango. Milonguero Miguel Angel Balbi, who has been dancing in the milongas for fifty years, thinks the government should make a greater effort to preserve Argentina's tango heritage: "Tango should be subsidized. Dance halls for practicing and dancing should be available at no cost. Television should show more tango. As it is today, there is only one tango station and that is cable, which poor people can't afford. There should be some tango on all stations. The government subsidizes the study of Lunfardo, but what good is that to the average Argentine? That money should be put into tango dance, which can be enjoyed by everyone."

In 2002 the municipality of Buenos Aires initiated an annual international tango dance competition open to amateurs and professionals. As in earlier times, there are two divisions, Salon and Fantasy (also known as Show). Winners receive modest sums of money and opportunities to tour in Argentina. Recently the world competition was won by a couple in their 60s; tango must be the only dance competition where this would happen.

Radio, Television and Publications

Today in Argentina, enthusiasm for the tango doesn't come close to that of the Golden Era, nevertheless it is readily available on radio and television. Radio FM 82.7 plays tango all day every day. The cable television station, Solo Tango, broadcasts 24-hours of tango. Other stations play one to three hours of tango daily. Argentine law limits the amount of time that radio and TV are permitted to devote to foreign music, but judging by the music played in taxis and shops, either the foreign percentage is very high or the law is being ignored.

Private and government-sponsored tango magazines or journals are available free or at a minimal price at milongas, at dance studios, and at the Academia Nationale de Tango and other tango organizations. The best-known tango publication in Buenos Aires is Tito Palumbo's *"B.A. Tango,"* which began publishing in 1995 and has an estimated circulation of 40,000. It lists where and when to dance, to take lessons, to buy tango shoes, and to find lodging, and it has photographs of dance teachers, performers, and tango visitors, mostly taken in the milongas and at local tango events, with color covers of original contemporary art.

In addition, Mr. Palumbo publishes the smaller formatted BA Tango quarterly *"Trimestrial Guide"* with a circulation of 10,000 in Spanish, English, Dutch, and French, which lists places to take group tango lessons and private lessons as well as to attend practicas and milongas. It lists disc jockeys available for employment, where to rent practice rooms, cafés, and restaurants with tango shows, as well as theaters and radio and TV stations that feature tango. Mr. Palumbo says he got the idea for the small format of 'Guide" because when the listings were included in his bi-monthly BA Tango magazine, he saw so many people carrying it around folded in half to fit into their pockets that he decided, "Why not print it in a size that is convenient for carrying around?"

The *"Tanguata"* magazine lists places to dance and take lessons; it is bi-lingual, with English translations of articles on tango history as well as interviews and stories on contemporary events. It features several photographs taken in milongas, festivals, and workshops as well as of foreign tango visitors.

Tango historian Oscar Himshoot's *"Club de Tango"* magazine takes a more serious, academic tone. Each issue's cover has a color replica of a vintage tango sheet music. He usually writes an article on some aspect of Lunfardo and sometimes analyzes period tango lyrics, plus there are articles on historical tango musicians, dancers, lyricists, and events as well as interviews with noted contemporary dancers.

In 2006 three other tango magazines appeared: *'La Milonga Argentina,'* *ArgenTango*, and the pocket-sized *Diostango*. The Academia Nationale de Tango and the Academy of Lunfardo each publish free, weekly two-page newspaper-format information sheets covering activities of the organizations, articles interpreting and analyzing lyrics containing Lunfardo, and numerous photos of tango academics giving each other plaques and awards.

Dancing in the Streets of Buenos Aires

CHAPTER FIVE

Globalization

"Tango fever is sweeping the world."
(Dance Magazine, November 1997)

*"Buenos Aires will remain the principal source of tango although
I find the tango is losing some of its Argentine identity as it
becomes an international art with common denominators."*
(Esteban Moreno, professional Argentine dancer)

*"And so the tango, born of the poor streets of a distant time and
place, finds a new frontier for growth, and begins to leave its
origins behind, in speaking deeply to the larger world. Those of us
who have loved it, and whose lives have been altered by it, trust
that its emerging journey will carry this hypnotic dance, which
has now flowered in three centuries, through the new century and
beyond."* (Jef Anderson)

The tango, although unseen and virtually underground for a significant period after the 50s, has survived in an unbroken lineage over one-hundred and fifty years as a social dance in the most authentic sense. No other social dance has lasted so long nor has been as important and widespread. The waltz is older but is no longer practiced as part of a true social dancing culture; there are national or folk dances from diverse cultures that have existed as long as the tango, or longer, such as the polka, Irish and Scottish dances, flamenco, and dances of a tribal nature. But these dances have remained provincial, unaffected by foreign environments; exotic to watch, appreciated by many, but none has ever become a global or universal form of expression as a social dance. Tango seems destined to become one.

Even though today the tango might not be receiving the hype and attention it did during its first, frenzied introduction to the world at large; it is, nevertheless, being danced in more cities and countries than ever before. With the internet and globalization, cultures around the world are fusing in a myriad of ways, and tango is a part of that globalization.

Tango is More Important in Certain Countries - Some of Them Surprising

In some countries where Ballroom Tango had been important, contemporary dancers have taken up the new Argentine Tango with extraordinary enthusiasm. Elsewhere Ballroom Tango never suffered a decline in interest and is still the preferred style. Because of the number of dancers and the quality of their dancing skills, several countries today stand out as the most important tango communities outside Buenos Aires, among them Germany and The Netherlands. And then there is Finland!

FINLAND

"The Finnish tango is one of the few genuinely original things in Finnish music and popular entertainment. (1999 Tangomarkkinat Festival brochure)

"The tango has become an accepted form of Finnish culture. Even those Finns who personally have other musical preferences feel that the tango belongs to Finland just as much as skiing and the sauna." (Pekka Gronow, Finnish Music Quarterly)

Most Finns really believe the tango is a Finnish invention, and considering the extent to which it has permeated Finnish musical culture, it is not an unreasonable assumption. Doesn't the tango belong to hot-blooded Latins? The Finnish Tango, however, is not to be confused with the Argentine Tango because the dance, the music, and lyrics are distinctly Finnish. Non-Finnish Argentine Tango dancers consider the Finnish Tango to be a watered down version of the real thing that can even be considered a folk dance because in Finland tango is a rural dance, not urban as it is in the rest of the world. The Finns are obsessively attached to it.

Today, the tango is the most popular form of social dancing in Finland and it is believed there are more people dancing tango in Finland than in any other country. It certainly has the highest percentage of dancers per capita of any country with its weeklong annual festival in Seinajoki, about four-hundred miles north of Helsinki, which draws more than 130,000 paying participants! (When I first saw this figure in an *International Herald Tribune* article, I felt the number had to be a mistake.) I went to the Finnish Embassy in Paris to ask for information on the festival. They gave me the name of a French expert on Finnish tango, Robert Grelier, and also the address of the festival headquarters in Helsinki, which sent me brochures. The information confirmed attendance figures and reported that the festival was first organized in 1985 with only 18,000 participants. Other countries feel that if their tango festivals are attended by more than 1,000, they are a wild success.

A Finnish travel agency brochure for the festival says: "Finland is a veritable Mecca of tango" and boasts of "the world's largest outdoor dance floor - capacity, 20,000." The majority of the week's activities take place under huge tents, in indoor and outdoor pavilions, as well as in the open air. Even Seinajoki's main street Tango-Katu (Tango Street) is transformed into a dance floor. The 1999 brochure rather proudly exclaims, "The melancholy Finns and the fiery Argentine Tango is an experience which can leave nobody cold."

Culminating each year's festival are the tango vocal and dance contests, during which a Queen and King of Tango singers are proclaimed. Throughout the week there is much speculation and mounting interest in anticipation of who will be the winners. It is an especially important event for singers. The vocal competition is elaborate and lengthy and includes singers who have successful careers in both opera and tango in Finland.

Tango obsession permeates the country year-round. No sooner is the festival over then a local Seinajoki radio station begins to publicize next year's contests, and cities and towns across Finland hold local competitions to select the ten best tango orchestras and the ten best singers. Thousands of candidates are examined in elimination rounds, and in July the winners go to Seinajoki for the final competition before a jury composed of well-known artists from the musical world, television, the local public, and festival officials. It is a deadly serious event with the singer-contestants accompanied by a forty-piece symphonic orchestra; at the end of the week the King and Queen of Tango singers are chosen.

Recent festivals have featured all-night tango marathons, dance lessons, instrumental lessons, vocal concerts, singing contests, dance contests, children's concerts, training for singing contests, a seminar on "Women in Tango," performances by students from dance schools, and "Ladies' Choice Dances." The dance contests are open to amateurs but the competitions have come to be more and more dominated by professionals who go through rounds of elimination try-outs before the festival. Several past winners left their jobs in order to become full-time tango teachers.

Early Finnish Tango

Tango was first performed publically in Finland in 1914 by Danish dancers at 'Fennia,' a prestigious hotel in Helsinki; and in 1915 an opera singer sang a tango in a restaurant where customers got up and danced. However, aware of tango's lowly origins, the upper classes of Finland were scandalized, and it wasn't accepted by them until the1920s, after the dance became a fad in the rest of Europe and the U.S. The tango gained popularity when Russian officers danced it during the Russian occupation of Finland.

Finnish interest in tango includes not only the dance. The music and lyrics are also held in great esteem, possibly more than in any other country. Most countries keep the original Spanish lyrics for tango songs, but by the 1930s the Finns were writing their own tangos with their own music and lyrics in Finnish. According to Mr. Grelier, "more than two-hundred and fifty Finnish tangos are written each year. Tango carries so much respect and musical prestige that recently, a liberal theologian suggested that the tango 'Satumaa' - the best known tango in Finland whose lyrics talk of paradise lost set to a solemn, hymn like melody — should be included in the official psalm book of the Finnish Lutheran Church.

How the Finnish Tango is Unique

"There are few phenomena that have traveled so far and yet managed to root themselves so deeply into the Finnish soil as the

tango. Not only was the original tango welcomed and fostered in Finland, but over the years it has also developed a new identity and become part of our way of life." (1999, Tangomarkkinat Festival brochure)

With the exception of a few places in the capital of Helsinki, the Finns have not been interested in the new wave of tango, preferring their own, familiar style. The Finnish Tango is neither Ballroom Tango nor Argentine Tango. Argentine Tango aficionados tend to turn up their noses at the Finnish tango because the steps are so simple and unsophisticated and the music so uncomplex. A recent internet Argentine Tango-List dialogue illustrated this.

"A friend of mine, a non-tanguero, heard on a radio program that the highest percentage of tango of dancers per capital is in Scandinavia countries. I told him this couldn't be true; it would have to be Argentina. Does anyone know a source for such statistics?" A quick internet response was: "I don't know how accurate the statistic is but I hear that there is a lot of Argentine Tango danced in Finland." Someone else wrote: "Finnish tango maybe. Argentine Tango no." Still another commented: "A friend from Finland gave me some tango CDs. Believe me, it ain't Argentine!"

Several years ago in Paris, the Finnish Embassy put out flyers at various milongas inviting people to attend a tango dance at their Cultural Center. I had already read and researched the Finnish Tango and was eager to see it for myself, so I convinced three dancer-friends to go with me so that we would be two couples. The small dance hall was elegant, with a wonderful wood floor, and there was live music with a trio that included an accordion (but not a bandoneon) and a male singer. The bland music was hardly identifiable as tango. The vocalist was calm and did not use histrionics to accompany the lyrics as do the Argentines. My friends and I danced a few tandas; aware that we were being carefully observed by the Finns. We watched the Finnish dancers and listened to the music, then left after about an hour. It was an interesting experience but not - at the risk of appearing snooty - one to be repeated. (Later I learned that in Finland the tandas have only two numbers and there are no "cabeceos" because both men and women invite. Also, they stand rather than sit between tandas.)

Finnish tango steps are closer to the International or American ballroom tango and bears little resemblance to the Argentine tango. The few steps, generally two steps forward and one-step back, are repetitious and uncomplicated, and the partners' steps mirror each other. Body movement is with the beat, rather than the melody, and there is only one style, that of a relatively close embrace, with a certain amount of 'bounciness' to the steps. Much of the music starts as a march then gets smoother and softer in the middle. An internet contributor observed that Finnish tango music and dance resembles "a Fox Trot with a tango flavor." There are no changes of tempo and mood, which gives so much verve to Argentine Tango music.

Finnish Music and Lyrics

The most famous Finnish composer of tango music was Toivo Karki, who combined the style of German marches with the traditional melancholic melodies of traditional folk music. He was so prolific that at the beginning of the

1940s he had written half of all Finnish tangos causing the Finnish radio to limit the playing of his tangos. He then resorted to writing under pseudonyms.

The main reason that Finnish music does not sound very tango-like is that the bandoneon is replaced with an accordion, losing the hard edge that makes the bandoneon the signature instrument for tango. Many believe that "without the bandoneon, there can be no tango." Another, radical departure is the use of tropical instruments such as the marimba and maracas, which are never, ever used in Argentine Tango. Also, with two-hundred and fifty new Finnish tangos being written each year, there is a plethora of recent contemporary tango music to which the Finns like to dance, whereas the Argentine Tango dancers almost all prefer to dance to original Argentine Tangos from the 1930s, 1940s and early 1950s.

Contributing to the impression that tango is indigenous to Finland is that Spanish tango lyrics are not translated into Finnish, partly no doubt due to the fact that there are so many Finnish tangos written each year that there is no need to translate from the Spanish. Also, the subject matter of the original lyrics is not at all in line with Finnish ideas of what should be celebrated.

Some Finnish tango lyrics date from the 1930s, but composers increasingly flourished in the 1940s under Russian occupation when, according to a Festival brochure, "it was that then people were torn apart, sometimes for good and feelings of longing and loneliness were intensified." The Finns discarded the Argentine themes of unhappiness, unloving prostitutes, tales of deceit, alcoholism, poverty, defeat, desertion. The topics of their lyrics ranged from bitter to sweet. According to Barry James, writing in the *International Herald Tribune*; "During the war against the Soviet Union, tango lyrics with Nordic imagery of snow and lonely countryside, white nights, and trees fostered nostalgia and loneliness of troops at the front. Listening to the mournful tangos seemed to make the Finns ever more determined to defend their homeland."

In Finland the tango appeals primarily to middle-class, middle-aged couples and is considered an essential part of summer activities, with dancing in outside pavilions. Thus, Finnish tango is set apart from other countries in that vacationing urbanites mix freely with the rural population.

The Ambience of Tango in Finland

Another way Finnish Tango differs from the Argentine is in the atmosphere of the dance halls. There is no stricture on talking while dancing, permitting partners to carry on lively conversations or flirtations. They dance heartily, obviously enjoying themselves (no 'tango frowns'), and many take advantage of time between sets to throw down a few - or many - alcoholic drinks - which adds to the conviviality. They are obviously out for a good time, which contrasts with the Argentine Tango dancers who are so serious about the dance.

Unlike in other countries, Finnish tango has long had an appeal to the younger generation, some of whom declare that they prefer the tango to disco music because "it permits us to embrace." Robert Grelier explains that there are other, not so superficial reasons at the roots of tango popularity in Finland. "Finnish men are very introverted and talk very little. The tango lyrics speak for them." Chiori Santiago wrote in the Smithsonian "because the tango entrenches melancholy it makes it the perfect pastime for the emotionally restrained Finns." Psychologist Dave Witter wrote on the internet: "Yeah, what's with those crazy Finns? I think the tango is more popular in Northern than Southern Europe. In Southern Europe it's kind of redundant – people are on the make all the time there and are not abashed about expressing and acting it out. I think for the frozen Northerners it provides a legitimate, non-threatening means of penetrating that armor. You can get an experience of intimacy without having to actually break down a lot of personality barriers...then you jump back into your shell. So tango is a good outlet for what might otherwise stay bottled up."

The Argentine Tango now seems to be making slow inroads into the Finnish tango scene; it's been reported that several dance schools in Helsinki are teaching Argentine Tango. According to Heini-Elina Soutamo: "The tango has lately returned a little bit back towards the original Argentine one; some singers present the translated original Argentine lyrics...there are some re-translations of the lyrics - no more adjustment for the Finnish public but the original feelings, desire and passion .... Argentine Tango has recently gathered more and more enthusiastic dancers throughout the country, with the largest communities in Helsinki and Tampere, in the middle of the country. There are several Argentine Tango orchestras. The oldest one (the milonga) originated ten years ago, has been asked to perform in Buenos Aires and other international tango festivals. Some international tango groups have performed and given lessons in Finland."

JAPAN

"The tango is our symbol of national identity. Japan's acceptance and valorization of the tango legitimates our existence as a nation, a culture, and people. The tango in Japan - so far away, over there - is thrilling, flattering, our farthest flung, least likely cultural conquest." (Quoted by Marta Savigliano, Economy and Politics of Passion)

Another country where one would not ordinarily expect to find great enthusiasm for tango is Japan, where the dance has had the longest uninterrupted dedication and interaction with Argentina. Since the 1920s, there have been a steady stream of Argentine teachers and musicians touring Japan to teach and perform, and Japanese tango orchestras are held in such high esteem that they regularly tour Argentina.

In the early days of tango, Japan was considered to be the second capital of the tango although there had not been an historic interaction with Argentina as with Paris, but Japan has been the one country that has most consistently and visibly kept tango alive and well. No one is sure of the origin of the word tango, but there is a Japanese word 'tango' that is the name of a city and region of Japan, and one of Japan's five popular celebrations is named 'tango.'

Some observers believe that the Japanese and Argentine cultures have important elements in common, noting that Japanese enka (popular songs) have topics similar to Argentine lyrics of sadness, separation, forlornness, hopelessness, regrets, and other melodramatic themes, such as the tragic courageous practice of 'hara-kiri.' Also, as in Argentina, lyrics tend to be oriented towards men, are usually sung by men, and are particularly popular in 'karaoke' bars.

However, being on the other side of the globe with an Eastern popular culture so totally different from that of the West, Japan's Argentine Tango scene differs from other parts of the tango world. For starters, tango dances are not called milongas but 'tango parties,' probably because from the beginning tango was viewed as an elite dance of distinction and upper class rather than a product of public dance halls or clubs. Related to these differences is that, if taken seriously, tango in Japan is an expensive activity. A tango party entrance fee or lesson can equal the price of a month's groceries for a couple, whereas in other countries prices are minimal in order to keep the dance attractive to the popular public. In Japan, according to Astrid, who lives in Tokyo, tango dancers tend to be "businessmen, single women and men, graduate students with well-off parents and wives of well-off husbands who fill their mornings with playing tennis, their afternoons with violin lessons, flower arrangement classes, and private tango lessons." The Japanese seem to have no problem with the tango's reputation for exclusivity because, unlike its humble beginnings among nameless men in the slums of Buenos Aires, in Japan tango's beginnings are easily traced directly to a nobleman, Baron Megata, who moved in the highest aristocratic salons of Japan.

Baron Megata

In 1920 Baron Tsunayoshi Megata, a top Japanese nobleman, arrived in Paris for cosmetic surgery to remove an unsightly mark on his face. On his forays into Paris' nightlife, he fell in love with the tango, so much so that he stayed in Paris for six years and became a superb dancer. He wanted to continue living there but when his father died in 1926 he was obliged to return to Tokyo to assume responsibilities as head of his important family. At a going-away party, some of Megata's French friends gave him a present of a dozen tango records. Once in Tokyo, Megata decided he could not give up the tango, so he decided to teach it to his aristocratic friends at parties in his elegant home. It was an immediate success and the tango records began to circulate among upper class salons. Because their record labels were in French, Japanese thought that "this obsessive music was French."

The tango rapidly became so popular that Megata decided to open a free dance school for upper class Japanese, where he taught the tango, along with the waltz and Fox Trot. As a professor, Megata was very strict, insisting that his students dress correctly. He himself was always impeccably dressed in the fashion of high society. Also, he would forbid his students to eat Japanese sauces before going to a dance, and if a man perspired too much, he was not permitted at Megata's dances.

The tango caught on quickly, but the only tango records in all of Japan were those few that Megata brought with him, and dancers eventually got bored with the same songs. Megata then sent to Buenos Aires for a catalogue of Argentine Tangos ordering a huge number to be sent to Japan. The records took a very long time to arrive, and "the cost was great," so Megata convinced a Japanese record company to produce tango records.

At first the publisher was reluctant to embark on such a project but was eventually persuaded to print several hundred copies. They sold out rapidly, and production was increased. The success was so impressive that Megata and some of his enthusiastic students took it upon themselves to import an Argentine 'orquestra tipica' to tour Japan for the "fabulous sum of thirty-thousand yen." (At this time a university graduate was earning sixty yen a month).

The 1930s saw so much interest in tango that several Japanese tango orchestras were formed, one of which had a bandoneonist who had studied the instrument in Buenos Aires. Photos from the period show that following the French lead, some of the orchestras performed dressed as gauchos. In 1934, the first exclusively tango dance competition in Japan was organized by a close friend of Megata's.

It wasn't long before a social dance industry was established in Japan with "shako" (ballroom) schools established around the country. Unlike Megata's school, the lessons were a commercial undertaking, and the teachers and organizers made money not only by teaching but also by writing manuals and arranging competitions. The shako schools included the tango with other modern dances: the Fox Trot, the waltz, Rumba, Samba, etc., and it became a thriving business, as it is today.

Dancing tango reflected class consciousness. Megata and his followers of "Tango a la Francaise" represented distinction and class, while the ballroom instructors taught the sanitized International Tango primarily to the middle classes. To this day in Japanese society, shako instructors are *considered to be a cut below the Argentine Tango dancers. Ballroom Tango is preferred by the unsophisticated masses, while Japanese aristocrats and upper classes want their tango pure. (This social distinction also mirrors ballroom and Argentine Tango dancing in the rest of the world.) Japanese ballroom teachers claim they do not permit the Argentine Tango to be performed at their Odeon dance hall in Tokyo "because the intertwined legs suggest an inappropriate display of sensuality," and is considered vulgar. Dress is another distinguishing factor setting Argentine Tango apart in Japan because shako students attend dance lessons in glamorous evening gowns, while Argentine Tango dancers, as in the West, dress much more informally.*

Baron Megata was a colorful figure, recognized not only for his dance skills and unselfish propagation of tango, but also for his interest in motor sports. He was the first Japanese to import a motorcycle - a Harley Davidson from the U.S. In 1981, a tango, "A lo Megata" (In the Manner of Megata) was composed and popularized to honor his memory in popularizing the Argentine Tango.

If Megata was the pioneer of tango in Japan, his friend, Junzaburo Mori, was the most passionate propagator of the dance. In 1930 he wrote *Tango*, the first book about tango by a Japanese author, and then in 1933 he published a book of instructions on how to dance tango. For many years he wrote a monthly column, "The Voice of Buenos Aires," for a popular monthly magazine. He died in 1978.

During World War II, Japan sided with Germany and both countries banned Western music except for German and Italian classical music, and the tango. After the war many tango dance halls appeared in Tokyo, most with neon signs and Spanish names such as Milonga, Caminito, Tanguera, Felices, and Paris. In 1947 the Orquesta Tipica Tokyo was formed with vocalists singing tangos in the original Spanish.

Although U.S. and British pop music displaced the tango in Europe and Argentina, tango continued to be popular in Japan. Tango dancers and musicians continued to be invited to Japan, and the Argentine military dictatorships that suppressed the tango from 1955 to mid-1980 had no influence in Japan. Mingo Pugliese, a renowned teacher and performer, credits the Japanese with saving tango for the world:

"The resurgence of tango dancing coincided with the restoration of democracy in Argentina, freedom of association and a more stable economic climate. If anybody can really be credited with keeping the tango alive it is the Japanese because all through the darkest period of Argentine history, they continued to bring musicians and dancers to Japan. Eventually they started to travel to Buenos Aires, and the rest of the world followed."

In 1954, Juan Canaro and his orchestra became the first Argentines to play in Japan. The start of their nineteen-city tour was met with a confetti-strewn parade and welcome signs that said: "We've been waiting for this moment for twenty-five years." They were enthusiastically received across the country, playing twenty concerts in eighteen cities. In 1957 orchestra leaders Fresedo and Troilo went to Tokyo, where they gave concerts and worked with Japanese orchestras.

In 1957 there were twenty-five Japanese tango orchestras, and Tokyo had fifteen tango clubs. In 1966 the Japanese band 'Orquestra Tipica Porteño' toured Europe and South America and from the forties and fifties onwards, the tango has consistently been prominently featured on many musical programs. In 1961 Juan Canaro's more famous brother, Francisco, toured Japan with a troupe of dancers and singers and gave twelve performances in nine cities; in 1965 he did a twenty-three-day tour. In 1965 Osvaldo Pugliese's orchestra, "Tango Brillante," performed in a Tokyo theater.

In 1961, Gloria and Eduardo Arquimbau first toured Japan with Francisco Canaro's orchestra: Eduardo noted: "A trip to Japan in that epoch was almost like going to the moon today. I said farewell to my family because I didn't know if I would come back.... Today it is very common, but those days it was very difficult. While there we appeared on one of the two color television programs in the country, making us artists of the television era." (*El Firulete*, 2000.)

In 1978, the Japanese government officially endorsed its interest in tango when it issued a beautiful stamp honoring Carlos Gardel. In 1989 another stamp was issued with a picture of a couple dancing tango. The caption read, "100 years of Friendship between Argentina and Japan" - in both Spanish and Japanese. Japan later inaugurated an annual 'National Tango Day' to be celebrated on 5 May.

Today, Japan continues to be on the itinerary for important Argentine dance teachers. Recently San Francisco based Argentine Tango teacher and performer, Nora Dinzelbacher, undertook her first tour to Japan. I spoke with her shortly after her return, when she was a teacher on a tango cruise in the Caribbean in 2001; I asked her about her experiences teaching in Japan. She said that when she arrived at her first class, she was expecting a large turnout but was amazed to discover there were six-hundred and twenty students waiting for her! I asked how she ever managed to teach a class of this size; she explained "It was held in the gymnasium of the Olympic Village and there were two huge screens at the either end. I rotated circles of students in a line of dance so I was able to give individual attention to those in front of me." Ms. Dinzelbacher was very impressed by the seriousness of the students and their respect for the culture of tango. She said her experiences in Japan were "the highlight of my teaching career and I'm looking forward to returning as soon as possible."

Japan is a beacon for orchestras, dancers and tango shows. 'Tango Argentino' played there in 1986, and 'Forever Tango' has returned for numerous visits. Traffic of tango orchestras is two-way, with Japanese orchestras traveling to Argentina for concerts and dances, such as Koyi Kyotani's Tango Trio, the 'Astorico Orchestra', and 'Che Tango,' which is a group of older Japanese men under the leadership of gray-haired Suiyokai. In 1951 an orchestra directed by Masao Koga traveled to Buenos Aires and gave three sold-out concerts in a prominent theater on Avenida Corrientes.

In Japan, tango dancers are more interested in competitions than are dancers in most other countries, no doubt because of the long-time popularity of Ballroom dancing in Japan and today in Japan, dancers far surpass Argentine Tango in numbers. After the appearance of the 1997 movie *"Shall We Dance?"* which was about the joys of ballroom dancing in Tokyo, the number of ballroom schools and clubs in Tokyo tripled, bringing the number to more than one-hundred.

Today's Japanese tango differs from tango in most parts of the world in that there is not the mixture of generations normally seen on the dance floor. One obvious difference is that they are held early in the evening, with most of them beginning between five and six and lasting until nine o'clock. Ballroom dancers who go to nightclubs to dance tend to be older, while younger people dance at private parties. But, as in other countries, ballroom dance involves primarily people interested in competitions - which are held several times every month; dress is formal, with men in tuxedos and women in elaborate gowns. In order to curtail the many dancers who dance stage, or fantasy tango, some dance clubs have signs that announce "no gancho or boleo is allowed on this floor."

Currently, Argentine Tango in Japan has pretty much been confined to Tokyo, where there are several groups, each hosting tango parties several times a month. The groups usually rent a dance studio or small hall for the dance. There are reports that it is becoming visible in other parts of the country such as in Kyoto, where a tango couple from Argentina (the female half is Japanese) recently settled there and are working with the only tango band in that city. Although Argentine Tango dancers are outnumbered by ballroom dancers in Japan, their numbers are growing, and many attend some of the festivals held around the world throughout the year. Groups of Japanese are always visible at the previously annual CITA – Congresso International de Tango Argentina - in Buenos Aires. In 2006, six Japanese couples were among whose who made the cut of sixteen semi-finalists in the Buenos Aires Tango World Championship. In 2007 the Japanese were the only non-Argentines to make it to the finals in Buenos Aires. In 2009, a Japanese couple won the World Tango Championship and in 2010 a Japanese-Argentine couple won the top prize.

The tango in Japan still epitomizes the elite class. Advertisers of high-end products, such as expensive automobiles and luxury vacations, capitalize on this by use of the tango in their television and print advertising. The Argentines take particular pride that the tango is considered so 'chic' and popular in a country that is so far away, geographically and culturally, from Argentina.

Martial Arts, Zen Meditation and its Affinity with Tango

"Martial Arts and tango are similar in that they are both physical acts that require an enormous amount of time and training to master." (David Orly-Thompson, Internet)

Japan and tango have another connection in that both tango dancers and martial arts practitioners familiar with the two disciplines agree to a certain affinity between the activities.

Many cultures have had long relationships between martial arts and dance. Tribal dances of Africa - such as those of the Zulu warriors; the Arab and Jewish dances of the Middle East; North and South American Indians and Oriental countries, all have dances that depict a celebration of warrior skills that include battles, battle-like movements, and stances. Contemporary New Zealand Maori rugby players' ferocious exhibitions of traditional warrior's dances on the field before a rugby game begins are used to scare the wits out of the opposing players, or at least to unnerve them sufficiently to play badly. The popular Brazilian folk dance of today, the *caporeira*, originated as a cover-up for martial arts because practice of martial arts was illegal until the 1960s. The Hawaiian Hula dances were enactments of martial arts practiced only by men of the royal families. Later, missionaries and sailors arrived who were not the least bit interested in seeing men dance together and requested to see women dancing, and 'voila', the 'hula' was born.

In its earliest days, tango was patterned on fighting movements between two men, and some of the steps, such as the ocho are thought to have been derived from movements used in knife fighting. In any case tango is clearly a macho dance with powerful ground-taking steps menacing the partner. Practitioners of the martial arts and of Zen meditation are aware of many similarities to tango - much more than with other social dances. Although the Apache dance of France, from the first decades of the 20th century, had a physical confrontational aspect to it, it never became a regular social dance and was always performance or show tango.

Some dancers who have studied the martial arts, or yoga, or Zen meditation claim that tango has similarities to these disciplines in that they all require extreme body control, specific learned techniques, and a serious commitment of time and discipline. Many lessons, practice and workshops are essential to acquiring an adequate level of skill, and like tango, mental control plays an integral part of advancement. Ramiro Garcia wrote on the internet: "The level of mental focus required for tango or the martial arts is the same for me. I find them both to be equally demanding on my powers of concentration and learning. Tango is terribly difficult, terribly demanding, but very rewarding."

Except for a few classes in Tai Chi when living in Hanoi in 1988, I have no expertise in martial arts. Therefore, it is best that dancers speak for themselves about the various disciplines of martial arts in which they have experience.

Aikido

"I find tango and combat to be strongly related. Both involve two people in a very intimate form of physical communication.... Aikido often nearly becomes a dance in some styles; there's a lead, a follow, and the lead creates spaces for the follower to move into in a very gentle way. Of course, in aikido people play with the vertical dimension a lot more, and the follower usually lands upon the ground, and that's not very tango like. But, conceptually, abstractly, there are similarities." (Mike Hamilton, First Degree Black Belt in Karate)

Tai Chi

"Tai Chi is probably the most common form of martial arts which people find analogous with tango. The reason is that Tai Chi is very circular, relaxed and calm, and at the highest level of Tai Chi there is intent, energy and focus. When practicing tai chi with a partner often called pushing hands, one learns to listen very carefully to the partner through the body, as in Tango. One learns to move "sticky" with the partner, meaning to stay attached, and to not separate physically, mentally and even spiritually with your partner. In both arts, it is important first to master your self physically, i.e. balance, alignment, posture, flexibility, and fluidity, before moving onto higher levels of mental and spiritual mastery." (Leda Elliott, Tai Chi teacher.)

Karate

"One of the mental requirements of karate that struck me as having a reflection in tango was the necessity not to anticipate one's opponent, just as one would not anticipate a partner or the music. Karate movements are practiced over and over until they become literally incorporated and then, without focusing on any particular part of the opponent's body or thought of what he might do next, simply react naturally and immediately to his movement. This interplay between opponents or amongst partners and music, which is closer to the core of both martial arts and tango than its mere physicality, is what I find interesting." (D. Milne)

Meditation

"A man once asked a tango master, "How long will it take me to learn to dance tango well? The master replied, 'For most people, the answer is many years'. The man asked, 'What if I try even harder?' The master replied, 'Then it will take even longer." (Stephen Brown)

Diedre Guthrie wrote in the Yoga Journal – "The Tao of Tango": "Like an asana practice, tango requires simultaneous surrender and discipline. While dancing I am fully present, aware, as in yoga, of the most subtle movements of my inner anatomy."

GERMANY

"The Germans have stolen the tango from us." (Pupy Castello)

"I think there are more people dancing tango in Germany than there are in Argentina." (Tito Palumbo, Editor and Publisher, B. A. Tango)

Germany has a distinguished place in the contemporary world of Argentine Tango, due both to the acknowledged high quality of the dancing and the number of dancers, tango events and dance opportunities. Because the level of dance in Germany is so high, German dancers are enthusiastically welcomed wherever they travel - to workshops or festivals - visiting for business or pleasure. An indication of their skills occurred in 2006, when two German couples made it to the finals of the World Tango championships in Buenos Aires.

In Argentina the majority of dancers are still working class, but in Germany it is most popular among the professional classes. Recently an article appeared in the German academic exchange service on the internet stating that "tango has become a hobby typical for academics with master's degree or higher and computer scientists and medical doctors seem to flock to it." The article also mentioned "other types of dancers in Berlin are like aspiring existentialists who are attracted by the slightly decadent atmosphere. You know, the black turtle neck sweater type, like the ones who used to hang out with Sartre in Paris in the 1970s."

Berlin is the acknowledged capital of tango in Europe, with an estimated 2,000 to 3,000 active dancers and more than a dozen schools with twenty to thirty professional teachers. Every night there is a choice of places to dance and on weekends there are four to five venues, with as many as two-hundred or more dancers attending. Berlin also has an active gay tango club that is popular with dancers of all inclinations. There are fifty-eight tango organizations scattered throughout Germany (France has just over thirty). Dozens of multi-oriented dance studios that teach

Argentine Tango hold regular practicas and dances. So highly esteemed is German tango that Daniel Trenner, a U.S. tango entrepreneur, has been organizing dance tours to Berlin for over a decade, which include classes, practices, special events, and evenings in the milongas.

Some of the best dancers go to Berlin to take lessons from such skilled teachers as Brigitta Winkler and the doyen of German tango, Juan Dietrick Lange, a Uruguayan performer and teacher who has been teaching in Berlin since 1980. Tango teacher Sabine stated: "In the early 80s in Munich there were only four or five couples who danced the tango. One weekend a month we used to go all the way to Berlin for classes with Lange." In 1986, Antonio Todaro, the famous "teacher of today's teachers" went to Berlin to give teaching lessons to German instructors. After their stint in 'Tango Argentino,' Gloria and Eduardo Arquimbau traveled to Germany to teach. Both foreign and German dancers swarm to Buenos Aires to train with Argentine master teachers and to soak up the tango ambience of the city.

In Buenos Aires today, German visitors are encountered practically 'en masse' at classes, practices, and milongas, and in spite of their reputation for being good dancers, there is always astonishment that most of them really are good dancers. (If Germans show up at a milonga in Paris, everyone perks up in anticipation of being able to dance with one of them.)

An internet correspondent, Garrit Fleishmann, wrote: "In general, the tango addicts here in Germany are very mobile compared to those in other countries. Lots of people will go two-hundred to three-hundred kilometers for a milonga and more for a special weekend. I travel to

The Netherlands almost every month, where all the 'locos de Tango' from all over Europe meet on the first Saturday of the month for a weekend marathon of tango."

No one has satisfactorily explained the German affinity for tango. Many suggest that because of Germany's martial history and marching bands, the tango's walking beat is particularly appealing to the German psyche. The most famous tango of all time, The Cumparisita,' was written as a march and later turned into a tango by Roberto Firpo. Others think that a Germanic characteristic respect for order and discipline lends itself to learning and perfecting the tango, the most demanding of all social dances.

Although in the first decades of the 20th century tango was danced in Berlin as well in provincial areas, the Prussian emperor Wilhelm II forbade his officers to dance tango in uniform. He relaxed this prohibition during World War I on the theory that it increased the morale of his troops, permitted the tango to be danced again by all his troops.

Some believe that Germans developed a keener liking for the tango during World War II because the Axis countries did not permit the playing of any music from the U.S. and England. Thus deprived of the West's popular music, the tango remained in favor in both Germany and Japan during and after the war. There is reference to the close connection between Argentina and Germany during the two world wars, and it is proposed that some of the many Nazis who had fled to Argentina later returned to Germany with a love of the tango. In any case, the Nazis left a mark on tango because the term 'Tango Nazi' is popularly used to label those dancers who insist that there is only one correct style of dancing. These dancers, who consider there should be no wavering from what they consider to be the true tango tend to be authoritarian, highly critical, and demeaning of those dancers who do not dance 'their style' - generally the milonguero style. "Tango Nazis," are generally heartily disliked by other dancers and are all too prominent in some communities.

There is a macabre connection of tango with the German Holocaust. The tango has long been associated with both passion and death, through lyrics that talk about the death of one partner - or both. During the war, there were a few concentration camps designated as 'model' camps that allowed outside organizations such as the Red Cross to inspect them, where the Jews were permitted to form small musical groups that performed for visiting officials. Besides Wagner and certain prescribed German or Italian composers, the Argentine Tango was the only other music the orchestras were allowed to play. The Nazis supposedly approved of the tango because, unlike African-American jazz, it engendered no spirit of rebellion or incentive to disobedience.

Survivors of the Holocaust have spoken about the small orchestras of Jewish musicians who were obliged by the Nazis to play while groups of prisoners entered the gas chambers. Considering that some of the melancholic tangos resemble dirges, it doesn't seem outrageous. There was a particular tango with necrophilic lyrics that the Nazis liked, titled "Plegaria" ("Prayer"). It might have been a coincidence that the composer, Eduardo Bianco, was a long-time enthusiastic admirer of Argentina's right-wing governments. (A Jewish Romanian poet, Paul Celan, wrote a poem, *"Tangoul mortal,"* which translates as 'Tango of Death' about his experience in a concentration camp.)

THE NETHERLANDS

"Nijmegen is known around the world for its warm, communal atmosphere, and superb dancing." (Korey Ireland, Tango teacher, Kansas City)

Along with the Germans, Dutch dancers are recognized as being among the best in Europe. The El Corte School in Nijmegen, several hours north of Amsterdam, reputedly has over one thousand active tango dancers, and tango communities can also be found in small towns all over Holland.

The undisputed 'king' of Dutch tango - or possibly of all Europe — is Eric Jorissen, who runs the famous tango school, El Corte. When asked about the success of tango in Germany and The Netherlands, he replied: "There's no big secret. It's simply that the Germans and Dutch are so much better organized than the Italians, Spanish, and others. If we say something is going to start at a certain time, it will happen. If learning to dance tango well demands a lot of discipline and training, we are willing to invest the effort. Also, the Dutch are very open-minded, and the very nature of tango demands openness to new ideas.... At the beginning of this new wave of tango all the communities were small, so they had to network to be able to dance frequently. The Turkish, Russians, and Hungarians, are now growing steadily. The Irish have recently started. Even the Finns now have three Argentine Tango milongas a week in Helsinki."

El Corte's free monthly weekend tango marathon has been attracting an average of 300-350 "locos de Tango" dancers from all over Europe, many of them dance instructors, who meet on the first Saturday of each month and continue through Sunday afternoon. According to Jorissen, "There is always a large contingent from Germany and Switzerland, Italy, England, and sometimes from Hungary. Every month there are at least several dancers from the U.S., and there are frequent visitors from Argentina, South Africa, Australia, Russia, and Turkey - which is the latest "hot spot" for quality Argentine Tango."

I took the train to Nijmegen one weekend to meet friends coming from New York. We found the ambience super-casual and the international atmosphere friendly. When I danced with one man, I tried to find a language in which we could communicate; his response was, "I speak tango" and indeed, that was all that was needed to strike up a warm temporary friendship. The marathon idea has caught on in Istanbul, where one milonga holds a weekly weekend marathon. Based on the assumption that "there is no such thing as too much tango for tango addicts," Jorissen also hosts an annual New Year's marathon; a recent event had participants from eighteen countries, including the U.S., South America, South Africa, Turkey, and Europe.

Jorissen is interested in the cross-cultural aspects of tango and promotes it heartily, stating, "There are no cultural limits to the world of tango," and he seems particularly proud of his annual July International Week, which he initiated in 1992. The festival is held at El Corte and participants must sign up in advance. To assure a cultural mix, there is a limit of no more than four dancers from each country and forty visitors. Quotas for many of the countries fill up as much as six months ahead of time.

A marathon regular commented on the internet: "Eric takes the time to plan little mixer games - find the person of the opposite sex with a pin matching the one you got when you arrived; find the person who can answer a certain riddle, whatever. Maybe it seems silly, but it works." Guests purchase coupons at the refreshment bar - each one worth a different number of points. A small placard on the counter gives the number of points for each menu item. "One point will get you coffee, tea, or a candy bar"; "freshly squeezed orange juice goes for four points. For two points you can have "a soft drink, milk, or a foot bath." Across from the refreshment counter there are three chairs mounted on pedestals, each with a large stainless steel footbath bowls, hot water and salts!

The profit motive seems to be absent from Jorissen's monthly marathons as there is no charge for entrance nor for sleeping space; dancers bring their own sleeping bags, and prices for drinks and snacks are very reasonable. Sleeping arrangements are improvised and informal. Most dancers throw their sleeping bags by the side of one of the two dance floors; some sleep in easy chairs, and other go upstairs to an open sleeping loft. Two women friends and I slept at a nearby pension, and when we went to the studio Sunday morning, we saw about fifty to sixty prone bodies, either still sleeping or in the process of waking up. The music was mostly Piazzolla, slow and soft, and the only people on the dance floor were two girls dancing together. Shortly, in various conditions of disarray and with toothbrushes in hand, people began to wander towards the bathrooms. By noon the music grew louder and more danceable, and two by two, couples drifted to the floor to dance. An elaborate buffet (reasonably priced) was laid out on the counters in the main salon, and after eating, dancers went to the sinks to wash their dishes. In the afternoon, people began to say their good-byes, agreeing to meet again the next month.

Tango is danced throughout of The Netherlands. In the early 80s, the Rotterdam Conservatory of Music, with the aid of Osvaldo Pugliese, initiated a Tango Department that attracts students from all over Europe. A product of the school, the highly respected Sexteto Canyengue, constantly tours the world, playing frequently in Buenos Aires.

The Dutch not only take the dance seriously, but as with many in Europe, they have a passion for the music and lyrics, and regularly attend the frequent tango concerts. Their tango disc jockeys are well known and highly respected for their knowledge of the music. The noted DJ Rami, a well-known Amsterdam DJ has a collection of 33,000 recordings, with music from 137 orchestras. He says he hopes to go to Buenos Aires to meet with music historians there and to record the 11,000 songs his collection lacks.

TURKEY

Another country that probably would not be expected to have a thriving Argentine Tango community is Turkey. At the end of the 1920s, because of its extensive imports from Europe and interest in European life styles, the tango became popular via imported records and the gramophone. It was as faddish there in the highest social and political circles as it was in Europe and there are photographs of President Ataturk dancing tango with his adopted daughter at her wedding.

Turkish tango music is very different from Argentine Tango music because it has been deeply inspired by Turkish musical harmonies and tunes, and it has a decidedly oriental twist. Until recently there has been no bandoneon and sometimes a clarinet takes the place of a vocalist to accent the melody. Turkish tango music, with its oriental air, is certainly interesting; it is easily identified as tango

– but different. Sometimes called Tango Turk, Turkey like Finland developed a unique tango, with Arabic-influenced music, dance and lyrics.

As in Finland, the Turkish tango has had a straight run of popularity with no threat of a temporary disappearance. However, instead of being a rural dance, it has flourished in urban areas, and in recent years it has been giving way to the new Argentine Tango. Today it is popular all over Turkey, and in Istanbul it is possible to dance in up to half a dozen milongas every night of the week. Many workshops and festivals, some government sponsored, are held throughout the year with dancers from all over Europe, and because of Turkey's reputation as a serious tango community it attracts many well-known teachers, such as Imed Cheman, who travels from Paris to Turkey several times each year.

The first original Turkish tango music, an instrumental, was composed by a Turk ('Turk Tango') and published in 1928. By 1930 several soloists from the Operetta Sureyya had recorded European tango songs that had been translated into Turkish. In 1932 the first Turkish tango song, 'Mazi' (The Past), was recorded with lyrics in Turkish. The themes of Turkish lyrics are: love, disappointment, passion, nostalgia, separation, and the Argentine tradition of men confiding in their mothers. One popular Turkish song is about a man complaining to his mother about the lover who broke his heart.

Like the Finnish dance, the Turkish tango does not much resemble Argentine Tango steps and movements. Whereas the Argentine Tango is characterized by the complex and changing steps that make it so dynamic, the Turkish tango is calm, with simple, repetitious steps. The partners' frames are kept apart with a polite embrace and gentle touch.

Argentine Tango dancers generally deem it as uninteresting as the Finnish Tango.

In the past few years, the Turkish have taken to Argentine Tango, and they are drawing attention for their dancing excellence. A large annual international Argentine Tango festival draws dancers from all parts of the world, and regular, weekly tango marathons held in Istanbul are attended by many Europeans. Illustrating the burgeoning influence of tango in Turkey, a weekend festival in New York City was recently dedicated to "Tango a la Turca."

FRANCE

"The tango became a part of the musical landscape of Paris, like other music that goes and comes. But the difference was that for over one-hundred years, the tango never left Paris." (Jose Mosalini, Master Bandoneonist)

Considering the long-term close relationship of between Buenos Aires and Paris, it is not surprising that France has many strong Argentine Tango communities. In 2007, the government recognized this relationship when it issued two series of oversized stamps honoring the tango and the history of French-Argentine friendship.

In Paris, every day of the week there is a wide choice of venues for dancing tango. On weekends there are ten to twelve different 'Bals,' the French term for a milonga. One of the Bals is on a boat docked on the Seine, and sometimes there are dances on the large tour boats that glide up and down the river. The 'Balajo,' close to the Bastille, is a popular venue, appreciated for its original ambience, intact from the 1930s when it was a tango dance hall.

France has over fifty non-profit tango associations, of which Paris' le Temps du Tango is perhaps the most active, founded by Marc Pianko and Solange Bazely." It publishes a glossy, high quality bi-monthly magazine, "La Salida," which features articles on tango culture and lists regular and special tango classes, workshops, and other opportunities for dancing in Paris and all over France. In addition to running weekly milongas in Paris, it organizes a well-attended festival in Paris each spring with outstanding visiting teachers, a workshop in Brittany at New Year's, and two week-long summer workshops at an old chateau near the beach in Brittany. Other French Associations are also active in promoting classes, workshops, festivals, and tango-related vacations at ski resorts or cruising on a yacht around the Mediterranean Sea, stopping at exotic locales for evening milongas on the docks.

The special relationship between Paris and Argentines continued during Argentina's "dirty war" and tango's decline and near demise. After moving to Paris as an exile in 1976, bandoneonist Juan Jose Mosalini created an 'orquestra tipica' at a time when, according to Mosalini, "France was the only place in the world that recognized the teaching of the bandoneon on an official, university level and awarded a professional certificate from the Department of Education at the Ecole Nationale de Musique de Gennevilliers. This was at a time when Argentina did not have university level study for its national instrument. The French government paid me for five years to work out a teaching method for the bandoneon. When I spoke of this in Argentina they looked at me as if I was speaking Chinese. Finally we formed a typical tango orchestra of eleven musicians, of which there were three women among the seven French; the average age of the group was twenty-five years."

In the 1970s, the tango dance began a modest revival in France when teachers and performers such as Orlando

'Coco' Diaz and Victor Convalia and Carmen Aguiar began teaching tango classes in Paris. The "Trottoirs de Paris," a small Argentine nightclub in central Paris, became headquarters for Argentines living or visiting in Paris. It featured tango music but was too small for public dancing. It opened in 1981 and closed in 1994. The renaissance of tango dance following the enormous success of the show, Tango Argentino, led to widespread interest in all aspects of tango in France. Literary cafés sprang up on the Left Bank where tango became the subject of serious debates, tango music appeared on concert programs, and dance venues increased until there was a choice of milongas every day of the week. Classical musicians are paying attention to tango's appeal and are more and more often including tango music in their concerts. A recent concert at the Chatelet Theater by a chamber music group enthralled the audience with an encore tango especially arranged for quartet.

THE UNITED STATES

"Bozeman, Montana has the highest per capital rate of tango dancers in the world! We have a tango community of about thirty people, so with Bozeman's population of 30,000 that makes one tango dancer for each thousand inhabitants." (One of six dancers from Bozeman at the 2002 Congresso International de Tango Argentino in Buenos Aires.)

In the United States, tango is to be found from coast to coast. San Francisco and New York have the largest, most active communities, but many cities and towns hold annual festivals that have become so well known that they attract international participation such as Portland, Miami, Seattle, Denver, Las Vegas, New Orleans, Tucson, Los Angeles, Washington D.C., and others.

As discussed in an earlier chapter, in the winter of 1913-14, the tango was introduced to New York by the eminently respectable and fashionable American society ballroom dancers, Irene and Vernon Castle, who had learned it when they visited England. Subsequently, they sponsored the equally respected English dancers, the Waltons, to teach the tango in the U. S., where they were admired and very successful. The dance they taught was not the close embrace, sensual dance that first arrived in Paris nearly ten years earlier but the cleaned up version with "light between the bodies." From New York its popularity expanded to other large cities, such as New Orleans, whose racy French Quarter soon had a section called 'The Tango Belt.'

Hollywood played a part in popularizing the tango. At the beginning of the 1920s, Rudolph Valentino brought the tango to the attention of a vast audience of moviegoers when he danced a sultry tango in "The Four Horsemen of the Apocalypse." In the next two decades, Douglas Fairbanks and Carlos Gardel starred in films that featured the tango dance. In the early 1940s musical comedy extravaganza films featured couples in formal dress dancing a stylized tango in a cheek-to-cheek embrace with arms stretched straight in front of them, moving in a high stepping march.

In one movie, Charlie Chaplin did a slapstick tango with a well-dressed overweight aristocratic matron who indicated only mild surprise at finding her partner flopping around the floor, tripping over his feet, looking perplexed. Laurel and Hardy danced a tango together, relying on exaggerated steps and facial expressions for laughs. In a scene set in a luxury hotel, Groucho Marx, cigar in mouth, snaked alongside another aristocratic matron, eyebrows jumping up and down as he romped around the room, leaping on the furniture in an attempt to keep time to the tango music.

American films always presented the tango as a dance of the upper classes and made no attribution to its lower class origins. Always-elegant Fred Astaire, dressed in tuxedo tails, danced the tango with Dolores Del Rio in the film "Flying Down to Rio." In the movie, "The Scent of a Woman", Al Pacino played a retired blind Army officer who invited a young woman to dance tango in a fancy New York night club and told her not to worry about making mistakes because "Tango is like life, if you make a mistake you just tango on." In the film "True Lies," formally attired Arnold Schwarzenegger danced a passable tango with Jamie Lee Curtis.

By the 1990s large tango festivals with imported Argentine teachers and performers were being held annually in cities across the U.S. and Canada. From 1991 to 1996 Daniel Trenner and Rebecca Shulman, worked as tireless promoters of tango in the U.S. American dancers, as well as many around the world, are inveterate tango travelers and look forward to short or long business trips - in their own regions or in other countries - as opportunities to see and experiment with different dance styles. More and more dancers combine their vacations with tango to attend an increasing array of organized tango holidays in interesting locations. There is almost always some special event going on somewhere at any time of the year, and dancers around the world drive, take a train, or hop a plane to go to technical or stylistic workshops or festivals of classes and performances, dancing with the locals in the evening.

An event that brought tango into the mainstream of American dance, occurred in 1993 when Stanford

University's Department of Dance, headed by dance historian Richard Powers, introduced its first annual Tango Week featuring top Argentine dancers, teachers, and musicians. Its reputation grew so quickly that it soon attracted tango enthusiasts from all over the world. In 1998, an Argentine Tango teacher, Nora Dinzelbacher, living in San Francisco, took over and held the Tango Week at Berkeley; it has now become a premier U.S. tango festival, always sold out months in advance.

New York City's thriving tango community rivals San Francisco in quality and quantity of dancers. There are plenty of places to dance every night of the week, with numerous workshops and festivals held throughout the year. According to Rebecca Shulman, who along with Daniel Trenner, has been one of the earliest promoters of tango in the U. S. says: "New York has so many first class teachers it is not necessary to have many workshops with foreign teachers. But since most Argentines are happy to visit New York, there is a steady stream of important performers and teachers."

Tango Mujer – Rebecca Schulman and Brigitte Winkler

New York is home to the celebrated all-woman dance company, "Tango Mujer" (*mujer* in Spanish is woman), which performs around the world. Dance Review in 1999 called their show "visionary, courageous, ingenious, and marvelously entertaining"; on April 14, 1997, The New York Times pronounced it "witty and imaginative." According to Marc Shulgold in the Denver Rocky Mountain News, "the five women emerge immediately as distinct and distinctive personalities. They are tall, short, longhaired, shorthaired, American, South American, European, slender, and not so slender. They wear long dresses, short dresses, heels, bare feet, pants, powdered wigs, etc. Very little is repeated because there is simply too much to say.... The playfulness and the hot embraces never appear odd or uncomfortable. It all looks so natural, that, in fact, the presence of a man onstage would seem totally wrong."

New York's milongas are frequented not only by New Yorkers but also by the many people who go there for business or pleasure. Naomi Bennett of Austin wrote on the internet: "I was surprised to learn how many foreigners come to New York City to work and dance tango. New York City is like the United Nations; over half my dances were with people from other countries. I encountered some people of 'extreme character.' I had a very good tanda with a German man who wore a robe down to his ankles and a beautiful metal necklace. Last week I met a couple from Brussels; I danced with an Egyptian and a Puerto Rican and two Argentines."

Possibly because there are so many foreigners passing through New York City, it has a reputation for being friendly. Social tango dancing is not found in conventional dance clubs because the proportion of people dancing tango remains small and there are comparatively few places to dance. Therefore, tango events are held in offbeat venues such as: backrooms of cafes, bars or restaurants, old warehouses, church halls, gymnasiums, local cultural centers, or charmless dance studios with no place to sit. It is also known for organizing original tango events. Recently there was an intensive weekend of Turkish tango, with performers from Istanbul dancing to Turkish tango music. In the summers, there is outdoor tango in Central Park, and by the river at the South Street Sea Port.

Hit and Run Milongas

One of the most interesting ideas is the 'Hit-and Run Tango,' sometimes referred to as 'Guerilla Tango.' Lucille Krasne conceived the idea of spontaneous outdoor 'hit-and-run' milongas with no city permits. The changing locations are spread by word of mouth and the internet to arrange travel together to the dance sites. Ms. Krasne offered guidelines for successful hit-and-run milongas: "Free or cheap space, open to the public with little or no red tape and an interesting environment. And run or tango away quickly when chased by the cops." Other cities have taken up Krasne's idea and hold regular milongas in such places as the Charles River bridge in Cambridge; in Kansas City groups have tango-danced down center city streets and into and out of art galleries, to the delight of gallery visitors.

The two artists, Christo and Jeanne-Claude, held one of their worldwide art exhibitions in New York City in 2005, titled '*The Gates*' where they installed panels of deep saffron-colored nylon fabric along 23 miles (37 km) of pathways in Central Park (which actually has no 'gates'). To celebrate the exhibit, someone had the idea for tango dancers to meet for a 'hit and run' milonga at 1 p.m., at the Bethesda Fountain in Central Park, on the day before the 'Gates' were to be taken down: "Festooned in shiny blue scarves, the dancers performed to recorded tango music played on a boom box pulled through the Gates. The serpentine design of the walkways and the organic shape of the bare branches of the trees were mirrored in the continuously changing rounded and sensual movements of the free-flowing nylon panels moving in the wind." Jennifer Bratt of the Boston Globe reported: "Busted by a park ranger for playing amplified music without a permit, the milonga came to an end after about two hours, but not before everyone involved had a wonderful time."

Á MI ESTIMADO AMIGO J. CONRADO ESCOBAR.

SENDA DE ABROJOS

=TANGO MILONGA=

PARA PIANO POR

JUAN MAGLIO (PACHO)

PROPIEDAD RESERVADA

BREYER Hnos. — Florida 414

BUENOS AIRES

CHAPTER SIX

Roots: The Colonial Period - 16th to 19th Century

"The intermingling of its African and mestizo ancestors, together with other local and European strains, gave birth, in the space of a few decades, to one of the most distinctive cultural creations of the American continent."

(Luis Bocaz, Author, UNESCO Courier)

During the nineteenth century, when European and Middle Eastern immigrants were streaming into New York City, ethnic groups as a matter of course settled where compatriots who had arrived before them were living. The Irish, Italians, Eastern Europeans, and people from the Middle East largely segregated themselves into self-imposed ghettos where they kept their own languages, newspapers, music, and dances. Some, notably the Jews, brought with them rich literary traditions and soon established flourishing local newspapers, bookshops, and theaters. The ethnic groups strove to keep their own customs alive while integrating into the New World as quickly as possible.

In Buenos Aires, Italians outnumbered all the other immigrants, and to this day Argentina is dominated by Italian descendants. In Buenos Aires, and on a smaller scale across the mouth of the Rio de la Plata in Montevideo, Uruguay, a seminally different dynamic was at work. In North America entire families immigrated intending to spend their lives in the new land, whereas in Latin America the vast majority of arrivals were single men, and like the

Spanish conquistadores before them, they came seeking riches and planned to return to their European homes and families. But, for most, their expectations were dashed at not finding the streets lined with gold.

In the port cities of the Rio de la Plata, Montevideo, and Buenos Aires in contrast to the patterns emergent in North American cities, immigrants didn't necessarily seek out compatriots, but instead gravitated to cheap lodgings in the San Telmo and La Boca barrios by the docks and slaughterhouses where many obtained work as unskilled laborers. They lived in dark airless tenements called *conventillos,* virtually invisible to the middle and upper classes of the city's respectable center. They were housed cheek by jowl with nomadic gauchos who had been displaced from their beloved pampas by ranchers and barbed wire; with other rural emigrants from the impoverished countryside; former slaves who were unwelcome in the city's white society, and descendants of Spanish colonists who had not been economically successful in Argentina's New World.

The barrios with their bars and cafes also drew off-duty soldiers from nearby Army barracks and sailors on leave from docked ships. The area's few women worked as laundresses (washing clothes on the riverbanks), as waitresses, or in the thriving brothels. There was an underworld of pimps and petty crooks that created an unsavory reputation for these teeming *arrabales* (suburban fringes of the city) of Buenos Aires. With no common language or unifying culture, the only thing they had in common was their poverty and feelings of alienation. Yet from the turbulent human dynamics in this male-dominated urban frontier arose a uniquely spirited synthesis of music, dance, and language that would indelibly shape and color Argentine society and the world beyond with the culture of tango.

Although almost everywhere in the 21st century the word tango evokes the elegant dance which Argentines justly claim as their very own, "the tango is not really a national dance," as those who live in the Buenos Aires are quick to tell you for the tango was "born and raised" in Buenos Aires. In order to distance themselves from the rest of the vast (and unsophisticated) populace outside the capital, they still proudly refer to themselves not as Argentines, but as porteños, and conceive the city in relation to the rest of the country much as New Yorkers do: "There is The City, and then there is the rest of the country."

Tango: Out of Nothing

The degrading living conditions of the slum housing forced men onto the sidewalks where, because there was little money or entertainment, they drank in an agreeable climate, gambled, and fought when they were not working. Without a common language these men couldn't even amuse themselves with conversations or arguments. Some of them, however, had their musical instruments, even if only a piece of paper over a comb, on which they played music from their homelands and listened to each other's melodies. Eventually they invented a method of communicating through their music.

Historically, new forms of music and dance have originated in rural areas of a country, region, or even a continent. The tango, conversely, was born and grew within a few square miles of the port cities of Montevideo and Buenos Aires. However, as the music and dance began to enjoy expanded popularity, the tango became increasingly associated with Argentina rather than Uruguay. Buenos

Aires as the largest city in Latin America, was wealthier and more internationally influential than its sister city across the river. It also had the largest middle class in South America. Thus it came to dominate the expansion of the new music and dance through traveling musicians, recordings, radio, and eventually film.

Tango's Roots

Those immigrants and migrants who ended up in the *arrabales* didn't bring many material effects with them, but they did carry in their hearts the music from their homelands. Tango's roots are firmly embedded in a melange of musical cultures that clashed and eventually meshed in the city. One element, the rural milonga, with simple repetitive tunes played on the guitar, included both light-hearted melodies and the plaintive songs of the lonely countryside life of the Indians, the peasants, and the gauchos. The blacks' candombe drum music soared gaily and throbbed with complex rhythms. The music of early Spanish arrivals included the waltz and polka, both of which challenged prevailing mores because men and women touched hands and danced in front of one another. The mix would be steadily enriched by the addition of diverse musical traditions of subsequent European immigrants.

During this period when the *habañera*, a half-Spanish, half-black music with roots in the Antilles, was brought to Argentina by sailors from the Caribbean islands, social dancing took on a new look. The steps of folk dances mixed with the candombe and European immigrant salon dances. Among European influences on the emergent tango, Italy's was the strongest because of the high proportion of Italians who brought with them their homeland's pervasive tradition of opera, popular and classical music and, most important, musical literacy.

Other influences on the spirit and themes of the music that was evolving in the conventillos of the *arrabales* included the barrel organ and bandoneon of the Germans and the fiddle of Eastern European Jewish music. Unlike the earlier mostly upbeat rhythms, the new music reflected the sadness and melancholy refrains of later European immigrants who suspected they would never see their homeland again.

Because of its association with the seedy dock areas, the tango was confined to those barrios deemed unfit for upper and middle class society, so it was never danced outside those neighborhoods. However, by the last quarter of the 19th century, the tango had begun to make inroads into the city's center with its itinerant barrel organ players, the invention of the phonograph, and other technological advances. In 1870 the police raided a brothel where men were supposedly holding a meeting to plot the overthrow of the government, but when questioned by the police about their activities, the responses were, "We were just dancing tango." Thus the dance began its tentative incursion into the mainstream of Buenos Aires. Before long, it was becoming more and more popular among those living outside the city's slum areas. Wrote Luis Bocaz in the U.N. Chronicle, "One thing is undeniable: in the last ten years of the 19th century, tango music was held in high esteem in musical circles, and at the turn of the century, a whole galaxy of distinguished composers ushered it out of the suburbs and into the city center."

How did this change happen? Where did this new music come from? And why did it become so popular? The answers to these questions lie in mélange of Argentina's complicated history.

The Indians

Unlike other Latin American countries, Argentina has almost no visible evidence of its indigenous Indian cultures. It is possible to walk the streets of Buenos Aires for days without seeing an Indian or black face, unlike in Brazil, Uruguay, and other Latin countries, where the population is mostly *mestizos* - mixed Indian, African, and European blood.

Apart from vestiges of the Inca Road and a few remnants of Incan culture in the Northwest, there is little evidence of any important Indian civilizations in Argentina, such as the Aztecs and Mayans in Mexico, or the Incas in Peru. Instead, the indigenous people of Argentina were mostly nomadic, hunter-gatherer tribes, including the Quiches and the Querandi Indians who were scattered in small isolated villages from the north down through Patagonia. Northwest Argentina was originally home to nearly two-thirds of the native Indian population who survived with their hunter-gatherer culture. The Guarani, who lived in the northeast near Paraguay, were once 1,500,000 strong, but today they number almost 5,000. The 4,000 Indians on the island Mitre de la Isla were reduced by 1905 to 500; in 1980, there were only two direct descendants left. The Diaguita, the largest tribe, lived in the northernmost section of the country. The only material things of value in their territories were the herds of wild ostriches, cattle, and horses. As with other tribes, they were decimated by epidemics, hunger, malnutrition, professional assassins, military adventurers, and the owners of the large ranches.

Possessing no broadly based social mechanisms, the Argentine Indians at the beginning of the 19th century were essentially powerless before the accelerating incursion of European colonists into their universe. The Indians constituted an important part of the colonial economy by virtue of being used as forced labor, in which many were worked to death or sold into virtual slavery. The colonists as a rule were cruel overseers.

In 1810, soon after wresting independence from Spain, the new country's federal government set about ensuring that theirs would be a European-dominated population because they didn't admire the Latin American countries controlled by mestizos. Thus, the nation's leaders initiated a policy of extermination of the Indians as well as of Blacks who had escaped slavery and tried to lose themselves in the vastness of the pampas. They were hunted down like so many animals, with bounties paid on proof of death: ears, testicles, or heads. Those who were not systematically massacred were herded onto reservations and forced into slave labor in mines and agricultural fields, were used for building roads, railroads, and fortifications. Working and living conditions were so brutally inhuman that few survived. It was recorded that the Indians were gathered together a half an hour before sunrise and makde to work until a half an hour after sunset, with no rest and little food; for slight infractions they were given two-hundred lashes. They were literally worked to death. Women were taken as sex slaves for the clergy and soldiers, their mixed-blood offspring generally fated to live as homeless gauchos in the countryside. By 1879 scarcely five percent of the Indian population remained.

The pampas were inherited by the mestizo gauchos, whose parentage was a combination of either Indian and white or black and white. While little evidence remains of Indian culture, one of the fragments that has endured are the bolas (*boladores*) – small, hard leather balls attached to both ends of a short length of rope used to lasso cattle – which are still a staple of Argentine cowboys. They are also used in some folk dances performed with stunning skills. Buttons and clothing decorations made from ostrich skin and feathers are today's meager remnants of Indian handicrafts. Today's most conspicuous vestige of Indian culture is undoubtedly *maté*, the herbal tea drunk every day by the vast majority of all Argentines.

Musically, the Indians left nothing more than primitive flutes and drum rhythms adapted by the gauchos, who played them with early Spanish colonists' music to form the *crillola milonga* or rural milonga.

Colonial Period – 16th Century to 1870s

Prior to Argentine independence, the Spanish Vice-Royalty of Rio de la Plata included Argentina, Uruguay, Paraguay, and Bolivia; Argentina and Uruguay were the most similar in culture and history. The name Argentina derives from the Spanish word for the silver (*argent*) that the first European explorers hoped to find there, as had early Spanish explorers who became wealthy from the silver and gold plundered from the Aztecs, Mayans, and Incas in Mexico and Peru. But there were no similarly vast riches in Argentina, only the vast plains of the pampas with roaming bands of wild cattle and an occasional flock of ostriches.

In 1516 Don Juan Diaz de Solis, a Portuguese employed by the Spanish, attempted to establish a settlement at the estuary of the River de la Plata, but he and his crew were soon butchered by a band of Querandi Indians. Despite rumors of a rich interior empire, later explorers found little of interest other than small quantities of silver discovered in the northern state of Tucuman. Nevertheless, to be on the safe side, twenty years later the Spanish crown claimed all the northern land from the Atlantic to the Pacific to belong to Spain, and in 1536 (some sources say 1580), the Spanish King sent Pedro de Mendoza to found a second settlement at Buenos Aires ("Good Breezes") with sixty-six men, of whom ten were white and the rest mestizos. The Spanish invested in the second settlement ostensibly because military commanders wanted a garrison for protection against the many pirates then plundering colonial posts and interrupting trade.

Buenos Aires evolved into a typical colonial settlement with the white population in control of land, commerce, and trade and eventually all the herds of wild horses and cattle. The whites adopted the Spanish-American practice of intermarriage between daughters of leading creole Argentine-born children of colonists and the Spanish who had been sent to staff the garrison or to hold official posts.

By the late 1580s, systematic state-sponsored extermination had decimated the Indian population, leaving insufficient free labor for colonists' homes and small businesses. The Portuguese saw this need and began importing slaves from their African colony in Angola, and a flourishing slave trade was established with Buenos Aires as the central port for distribution of slaves over all of South America. (Because there were no large plantations in need of high-density labor, slavery was never as important in Argentina as it was in the United States; by 1813 slavery was abolished in Argentina, half a century before it was made illegal in the United States.)

The original Spanish colonists were joined by the British and Germans, who went there to take advantage of the possibilities for making money in the rapidly growing colony. Buenos Aires grew increasingly prosperous as it expanded into a military, administrative, and commercial center. By 1800 the British had established the city as a manufacturing center, and when the Germans began to take over the countryside, the hide trade grew increasingly important. By the mid-18th century, Buenos Aires had become the port through which those hides traveled for export to Europe.

The British soon dominated the nation's economy, and within a few years monopolized the import and retail sale of all textiles from Britain, took over shipping from the Americans and Portuguese, and launched and controlled the insurance industry. They built the port of Buenos Aires so that by 1900 arriving passengers no longer had to be rowed to land in small skiffs. They bought up government bonds, monopolized government contracts, built and maintained the railroads, and controlled the arms industry. By 1913 the British were responsible for over sixty percent of foreign investment.

With the British in effective control of the economy of Buenos Aires, the German and Spanish mercantile families were compelled to search out other financial opportunities, beginning with ranching and exporting beef. They soon realized that serious improvement in breeding was essential before the inferior local cattle could be seriously marketed as "tough hide is one thing, tough beef another." The beef was tough because the herds had to survive the sun, rain, and winds of the pampas; many were diseased or had deformed horns that twisted in towards their head, penetrating into the brains or eyes; their hooves also split and broke. They migrated at will in their continual search for water and pasture, feeding on thistle seeds and deep roots.

Realizing that serious money was to be made by shipping meat to beef-starved Europe, the English and Spanish began development of a breed of cattle suitable for consumption and grew the grains necessary to sustain them. The English and Spanish bought enormous tracts of land and moved into the countryside, keeping residences in Buenos Aires. The Argentine government was eager to help them establish ranches in the pampas, continuing its policy of a Europeanized Argentine populace.

By 1817 there were seventeen salt-packing plants in Buenos Aires, exporting to Brazil, Cuba, and parts of the American South. In 1826 the first refrigerated ship packed with ice and meat sailed to France and arrived ninety-seven days later with edible meat. By the end of the century, furnished refrigerated ships made regular voyages from Buenos Aires to England and France.

Based on the theory that empty geography is of no use to a nation, and concerned that neighboring countries coveted parts of northern Argentina, the government encouraged colonists to settle in the pampas by leasing public lands for periods of ten years with no limit to the amount of land any one person could hold. Hundreds and thousands of square miles were held by just a few ranchers, who created enormous *estancias* (ranches), many of which remain intact today.

Musical Heritage of the Early Colonists

A variety of music for social dancing in Europe and Argentina evolved in the 17th, 18th, and first half of the 19th centuries. Partners were positioned opposite one another, but at a distance, progressing in a line of dance around the dance floor. There were also round dances where couples danced in stationary circles with hands occasionally touching lightly. Such dances were usually called the contra dance and were derived from the English Country Dance.

The Viennese Waltz was the first popular dance performed outside aristocratic salons in which partners were connected in an open embrace with hands touching. Later the polka used the embrace. Both dances were considered low class until the mid-1850s, when the Paris Opera featured the waltz in some of its performances. The acceptance by Paris audiences assured the success of the waltz for the rest of Europe, which looked to Paris as the arbiter of refined culture.

A taste for dancing as a popular social activity was brought to Argentina by the Spanish who, as early as 1806, frequented French dance halls in Cadiz in southern Spain. In 1826 a Buenos Aires newspaper considered it newsworthy that an American, Guillermo Davie, had opened a dance hall in Buenos Aires. "Mr. Davie just opened his "academia" where all types of dance are taught. It is open from 7 p.m. until 12:30 three times a week," reported *El Tango*. Academias soon became common in Spanish and Latin American cities.

By the mid-1800s, in addition to the academias in Buenos Aires, salons opened that were not affiliated with dance schools but were simply places for the public to dance. Eventually the term *academia* came to identify both the private or public dance halls. In 1846 the municipal police department reported, "For the past three years there are public dance halls whose proprietors are Italians; the customers pay two pesos for each dance."

There were accounts of an *academia* in the San Telmo barrio where for purposes of practice men danced with each other. In 1841 a North American, William Debes, advertised a new dance hall: "Women who want to dance on Saturdays will have free entrance and men will pay two pesos." In the same year, another paper noted that the dance hall Del Tambor held dances exclusively for people of color.

Dance halls in San Telmo, La Boca, and other suburban barrios soon acquired bad reputations for attracting unsavory elements. In 1867 a police report noted: "This dance house of immoral corruption which jeopardizes the neighborhood has become so insupportable that cries for suspending their license are augmenting...Last night there were more than two hundred men of all nationalities together in a locale that could scarcely hold forty people. Some of them happy with drink shouted offensive and obscene words that make a scandal. Also, there were women who left the dance hall with cigars in their mouths and embraced the men who accompanied them.... Families in the immediate neighborhood are not able to feel calm without having to live with their doors closed in order to avoid having their children witness the immoral behavior of the people who frequent this dance hall."

There was also music played in places other than dance halls. By the second half of the 19th century, Spanish theater companies regularly toured Argentina. They introduced the slow, baleful habanera music, danced in 2/4 time (think Bizet's "Carmen") and the Andalusian tango, which was not truly a tango but a faster, more light-hearted version of the habanera. Both dances would play an important part in the development of the tango.

The Gauchos Emerge

Indians in the countryside were gradually replaced by mestizo gauchos, most of whom were of mixed Spanish and Indian or black blood. Their name probably comes from *gaucho*, which is Spanish for orphan. The 1869 census reported that four out of five gauchos were illiterate and their temporary housing was of mud and straw. They took the pampas for their own, roaming the countryside to follow the enormous herds of wild cattle; like the Indians they sometimes built rudimentary huts for temporary stays. They were proud of their independence and saw themselves as masters of the land. As long as the herds were plentiful and the population sparse, they were able to maintain their independence by selling beef, hides, and tallow to the domestic market.

Many gauchos had the dark skin of mestizos and married or lived with Indians or former slaves and raised children with them. By and large, however, the gauchos didn't like the Indians because they thought them too savage and cruel in their treatment of enemies and their own women. They did, however, hold great respect for the Indian's skill with horses and the bolas used for lassoing cattle.

When they occasionally visited European settlements or drove cattle to the slaughterhouses located in the suburbs of Buenos Aires, the gauchos were uncomfortable because the color of their skin and their unique style of dress set them apart. They were rejected by both the Spaniards and Indians; the general population was suspicious of them and considered them outcasts from Argentine society. They were perceived as lawless drunks, as lazy, and as underdeveloped intellectually, spending all their time in cantinas gambling and brawling. There was a saying: "Where there is a gaucho, trouble always follows." It was true that the gauchos had little respect for the niceties of urban society and of law and order, and when confronted with authority they became indignant at any violation or threat to their freedom. They were always eager to get back to their wilderness and the anarchic society of the pampas.

The gauchos possessed little: the clothes they wore, sometimes a guitar, their knives, their horses, preferably all of the same color, and saddles which they used as pillows. The gauchos delighted in the wildness of their horses, vaulting on and handling their mounts with the sureness and instinct borne of their way of life on horseback. They doted on their horses and spent most of what money they had on elaborate silver stirrups and silver-worked reins and headstalls. Hinged silver breast plates covered the horses' chests and clinked as the horses moved.

Every gaucho carried a knife which, besides being a weapon, was used for eating meat and slaughtering animals. It was a cross between sword and dagger, with a straight double-edged blade about eighteen inches long, a sharp point, and a handle of wood, metal, or bone. The sheath was often highly ornamented with chased silver and was thrust diagonally across the waist between the belt and the sash, with the handle pointed to the right. They also wore their bolas around their waist and felt hats with the wide brims turned up in front.

The gauchos did, however, enjoy a positive reputation for honesty and loyalty; they were fiercely protective of their fellow gauchos. They were thought of as being tough, able to ignore physical discomforts, and quick to settle arguments with a knife. No gaucho carried a gun because firearms were disdained as being unworthy of a gaucho.

The end of the gauchos' freedom came in the mid-1800s, when the whites began taking over the pampas for their enormous ranches. Ranchers rounded-up and fenced in the cattle with barbed wire as did the ranchers in the American West. Gauchos were valued for their expertise with cattle and horses, but they were not interested in the ordinary ranch work of clearing land, planting grain, and building fences, because they felt that any work not done on horseback was dishonorable. So the ranchers turned to the newly arrived European immigrants. The immigrants gladly accepted work on the estancias, and the landowners were happy to have them because, compared to the gauchos, they were docile employees. The halcyon days of the gaucho were over.

With their only means of making a living gone, the gauchos had little choice but to move to the suburbs of Buenos Aires with which they were familiar from driving their cattle to slaughter. But once there on a permanent basis, they were totally out of their element. They lived in the overcrowded conventillos, three- or four-story tenement buildings in the dockside slums of La Boca and San Telmo alongside European immigrants, whom they despised, calling them *gringo*, *turco*, or *moishe*, terms still in use today, but in non-pejorative ways. The gauchos desperately missed their life of freedom and were stifled at having to live in the sordid, unhygienic conventillos.

Some gauchos subsisted by peddling cheap items from pushcarts in the barrios while others carried their guitars and sang their gaucho songs for a few centavos. Some made a living by their knives and brawn, working as bodyguards to *compadrones* (barrio bosses). Most became depressed and discontented with their lives as despised outcasts in an urban society. However, the public's attitude toward them changed rapidly and forever in 1872, when Jose Hernandez published his epic poem, "Martin Fierro" which praised gauchos and made them into mythical heroes, portraying them as heroic figures and champions of an earlier, simpler life, who had become victims of society's modernization.

"Martin Fierro", soon a classic, romanticized gaucho life beyond all recognition. It extolled the gauchos for their independent spirit, their pride, loyalty, and honesty, their religious fervor, their prowess with horses, and even their musical artistry as payadores – itinerant singers who improvised poetry and stories to the accompaniment of a guitar. People began to appreciate the melancholy gaucho songs that depicted the sadness and nostalgia for their lost lands and way of life and of anger at the disruption of their world. The gaucho characteristics of fierce independence, masculine pride, and a strong inclination to settle affairs of honor with knives, won them the admiration of immigrant men, particularly Italians. Hernandez spoke about the gauchos as a fraternity of the condemned. Their reputation for loyalty and helpfulness is remembered today in the Argentine expression *"hacer una gauchada,"* which means to help someone in distress.

Like North American cowboys, the gauchos never moved into the mainstream of middle or upper class society. They were cautiously assimilated into the communities of the *arrabales* where they became accepted as part of that landscape. Today, gauchos are the object of admiration by a great part of Argentine society, looked upon as examples of the best of Argentine personal characteristics.

A Comparison: Gauchos and Cowboys

Gauchos are frequently referred to as Argentine cowboys because the gauchos' heyday coincided the same period as that of the cowboys of the American West. Other than their interest in working with cattle and horses, however, they shared little in common.

Before "Martin Fierro," the Argentines generally despised and had no respect for gauchos, wanting to have nothing to do with them, while at the same time in America cowboys were looked upon as likeable free spirits. Although they weren't in demand at dinner tables in middle or upper class homes, cowboys were not considered to be the dregs of society, as were the gauchos.

American cowboys didn't suffer the same discrimination as gauchos because when they went into town, their clothing and white skins allowed them to blend in with the ranchers and their families; they didn't look so obviously different. At the same time when "Martin Fierro" was romanticizing the gaucho's image, magazines and short novels in the U.S. began to romanticize the American cowboy. From the wildly popular novels of Zane Grey in the early 20th century and those of Louis L'Amour, to the endless trail of the Hollywood Western, both the cowboy and the gaucho are portrayed in their respective cultures as heroes in film and television today.

Unlike their American counterparts, gauchos were known to be very religious, and as a token of their religious devotion almost every gaucho wore a scapulary made of two small pieces of cloth joined by string passing over the shoulders, worn under their clothing.

The gaucho's life was also notably tougher, more isolated, and lonelier than that of the American cowboy. Rather than wander around the prairies on their own, sleeping in the open as the gauchos did, most American cowboys worked as ranch hands, receiving room and board, leaving the ranch only for cattle drives. Gauchos did not want to live on the estancias, preferring to sleep in the open with their saddles for pillows and their horse blankets for warmth.

The sheer vastness of the pampas insured that gauchos went for long periods of time without encountering civilization. They preferred the wilderness and isolation, and assiduously avoided townspeople, whom they did not trust. If legend is to be believed, American cowboys enjoyed and looked forward to going into town as frequently as possible, drinking, gambling, and mixing it up with the locals, particularly women.

Both cowboys and gauchos prized their horses, but horses took on far more importance to gauchos. Gauchos prided themselves on owning and riding the wildest horses they could find, and they built up herds of horses of the same color. Most of their money was spent on elaborate silver ornaments, silver stirrups, and silver-worked reins and headstalls. Silver decorations for horses continue to be important to today's gauchos, as well as to collectors.

Gaucho Musical Heritage

The loneliness of the gaucho was relieved with a modest form of music, mostly played on guitars and primitive handmade flutes easy to transport on horseback. Possibly because of their greater isolation, gauchos spent more time than American cowboys did inventing their own entertainment, and they prized music and poetry. Many acquired reputations as excellent musicians and singers and lyricists, so much so that their appearances in settlements were anticipated with enthusiasm. Gaucho music, called the rural milonga, combined Indian rhythms with music of the early Spanish colonists, and was the popular music of the pampas.

Payadores, most of whom were either mestizo or black, were itinerant gaucho musicians greatly admired for their ability to improvise poetry set to primitive music. With simple melodies and frequent repetition, the music echoed that of medieval minstrels in Europe. Their songs were performed in a half-sung, half-spoken form of poetry, with guitar or rudimentary flute accompaniment. The gauchos' poetic abilities shone in sharp contrast to their tough, macho image, but they were universally popular in the countryside and eventually in the cities.

There were impromptu or announced events, called *payadas,* which were competitions among *payadores* in rural areas with two gauchos singing and accompanying themselves on guitars. They had to improvise in verse on specified subjects, usually philosophic discussions about life, love, death, God, or nature. One singer posed a question and the other answered, always in verse, singing to the guitar music, with the winners chosen by audience applause. Some *payadores* were so good that when they traveled to Buenos Aires on cattle drives, they were in demand in cafés and restaurants. A few became so famous that they performed in respectable city center theaters. One of the most well known payadores was Jose Betineti, who gave concerts until 1915. Many of the most famous *payadores* were Black, including Gabino Ezeiza and Enrique Maciel, whose songs glorified the dictator General Rosas, a champion of gauchos and Blacks.

The payadore's custom of putting poetry to music influenced European dance music in Argentina, which at this time did not have structured lyrics. It is believed that because an interest developed in the gaucho songs in Buenos Aires, the custom of adding lyrics to dance music began to evolve. Thus the music of the pampas, the *milonga,* was one of the four basic elements in the formation of the tango.

Despite acceptance of the gaucho and black *payadores* in Buenos Aires, both groups continued to be considered outcasts from conventional society and were specific objects of discriminatory laws that criminalized vagrancy, gambling, idleness, carousing, and the carrying of firearms. Men and women caught breaking the laws were inducted into the national army for four years, but it was not unusual for the courts to sentence them to ten to fifteen years. Women received sentences of up to ten years and were forced to work as prostitutes or military seamstresses. Living and working conditions in the army were deplorable for both men and women, and extra time was arbitrarily added to sentences for little or no reason. Many were forced or lured into re-enlistment by promises that were never kept. By the 19th century, every Black man and most gauchos did non-voluntary military service in segregated units.

The Black Population

Unlike other Latin American cities, it is difficult to imagine that Indians or blacks were ever a significant part of Buenos Aires society. Yet in 1778, blacks comprised one-third of the population of Buenos Aires (7,256 out of 24,363). By 1810, census records show that Blacks accounted for twenty-five percent. But by 1887, that figure had fallen to two percent (8,005 out of 433,375.) What happened?

The startling disappearance of blacks from Buenos Aires – thirty percent in 1778 down to two percent in 1887 – can be traced to several events. First, they were unfairly drafted into the army and fought in the long-standing wars against the Indians and the neighboring governments of Paraguay and Brazil, where they served as front-line cannon fodder. From 1810 to 1870, Argentina was involved in a series of bloody civil wars over whether ultimate power would rest with a regional or a central government. Regional governments took advantage of the wars to decimate the Indian population by using gauchos and blacks in their armies.

The government purchased Black slaves for military service; some slave owners gave their slaves to the military as a patriotic gesture. Many slaves ran away from their owners and joined the army because new laws freed all slaves who volunteered, effectively from the day they enlisted to the end of their term of enlistment. In the mid-19th century the Argentine constitution was altered to declare that "all men are created equal and any slaves that stepped foot on Argentine soil would immediately become free."

Another factor that impacted the Black population was the yellow fever epidemic of 1871, which killed an estimated 14,000 to 26,000 people, with deaths reaching a rate of three hundred a day. Buenos Aires lost over a fifth of its population. Because they had long endured poor hygiene, poor nutrition, poor general health, and lack of medical care, Blacks were particularly vulnerable to the catastrophic epidemic. Cemeteries were ringed with sulfur fires and hundreds of tallow lamps were set on mounds of earth. It was reported that on some days coffins and corpses were piled up by the hundreds at Chacarita Cemetery.

A contributing factor to the high death rate among Blacks was the enforcement of the quarantine of infected parts of the city. Government troops prevented the inhabitants of the mosquito-infected neighborhoods of San Telmo, La Bocca, and Montserrat (all sites where incoming slaves were housed until sold) from leaving the infected areas. Black society was thus ravaged by the yellow fever epidemic.

Finally, the few Blacks remaining in the city were eventually assimilated into society through intermarriage. Because so many Black males had been killed in the front lines, many black women had little choice but to marry white men.

Candombe Music and Dance – Prelude to the Tango

In Argentina most slaves were imported to work for artisans or merchants, but the majority worked as house slaves. As a result, relations between slaves and owners were much more relaxed than in the U.S., and Argentine slaves generally had an easier time of it. One prominent family went so far as to bury one of their slaves next to the family plot in the exclusive Recoleta Cemetery. Slaves had Sunday afternoons free, during which time many congregated around Park Lezema in San Telmo and in Montserrat where they danced for hours to the candombe music of Africa. The candombe dance would become a vital element of the tango.

When the Blacks were first shipped from Africa, they brought with them nothing but "memories and fear of the future." Some attempted to bring consolation in the form of their candombe drums, which the ships' captains threw overboard because they felt the slaves became too agitated by the music, which sounded alien to the Europeans.

However, once they landed, slaves built the drums essential to their candombe music.

Candombe dances were integral parts of African rituals that consisted of chanting, prayers, and jerky dance movements imitating warriors or certain animals. They served as a basis for community identity as well as for entertainment and recreation. Today in Montevideo, candombe music often accompanies tango music.

Candombe music is entirely percussive, with three types of drums made out of gourds or wood and with the slapping of hands together or on the body. The smallest drum gives the beat, the middle one plays the improvisational melody, and the large one serves as the equivalent to a bass. The two largest drums are struck with padded sticks and the smallest one with a plain stick. The sticks are held in the right hand and strike the drums on the side and top, while the left hand slaps the drumhead. Most pieces begin slowly and softly, then rise and accelerate strikingly, often with a hypnotic effect. Early Argentine magazines and journals featured illustrations of Africans dancing in a primitive manner, some with eyes barely open, supposedly representing a languid frenzy.

The candombe dance was divided into three parts danced with separate lines of men and women who wore elaborate, colorful dresses, skirts and blouses, and large, brilliant headscarves. In the first part of the dance, the dancers swayed in place and chanted; then partners danced toward each other, rubbing their stomachs against their partners'. Next couples took turns dancing – without touching – inside a circle of couples. Finally, couples walked in a circular line until the drums broke into a frenetic beat and each dancer danced madly to improvised steps. Each piece lasted about half an hour or "until the dancers were exhausted." The dance ended suddenly when the lead drummer shouted out a command, causing the dancers to stop precisely on cue. This abrupt ending is probably the reason for the importance of today's final step in contemporary tango.

The candombe is today considered as a folk dance, performed in theaters or paraded in the streets of Montevideo or in Lezema Parc in Buenos Aires.

Black Society

During and after the colonial period, freed blacks settled in the barrios of San Telmo and Montserrat, which from the 1760s onward were known for candombe music and dancing in the streets, in private meeting places, and later in public dance halls. Whites were not amused by the wild-sounding music or with the organizations that were formed by runaway and freed slaves with a common heritage of the same area in Africa. Groups of black slaves with language and customs in common, became known as nations and presented a united front against abuse and exploitation. When needed, they provided mutual help with food and lodging, helped escapees to purchase freedom, and arranged payments to the Church for last rites. Such groups were kept under close police surveillance, but municipal and ecclesiastical authorities tolerated the groups so long as they kept a tight rein over the slaves during the brief sabbatical hours of freedom on Sunday afternoons.

Acutely aware of slave uprisings in the Caribbean, many whites felt that slave gatherings in Buenos Aires were potentially dangerous and a means for plotting against the authorities. Whites living in areas near San Telmo were not comforted at the sight of blacks having a seemingly uncontrolled good time. Many complained to the municipal officials, objecting to the lewd and lascivious movements and to the size of the gatherings, some of which were attended by as many as 2,000 individuals. A contemporary police report noted: "The slaves are so vice-ridden and irresponsible as a result of these dances that they became utterly useless to their owners: they shirk their duties and think of no other thing but of the time when they can go to dance." (Buenos Aires police report 1800s.)

Police responded when the occasional riot broke out, but for the most part the candombes were peaceful. In 1766 and again in 1770, however, the viceroy was persuaded to ban unofficial black dances, which were henceforward illegal except when held under the supervision of an appointed church authority. The viceroy thought the dances were a harmless way to release frustrations, so in 1796 blacks from the Congo were granted permission to dance on Sundays and holidays. Three years later, other black groups received the same rights. The viceroy, it must be said, did not live next door to the thirty percent of the city's population dancing to candombe drums. After Argentina became independent from Spain in 1822, the benevolent royal supervision came to an end, and citizens pressured officials to pass ordinances prohibiting blacks from dancing in the streets. In 1825 any kind of public dancing by blacks was forbidden. Blacks' fortunes changed again when Governor Juan Manuel de Rosas became dictator of Argentina and exhibited an interest in improving the situation of blacks and gauchos in exchange for their political support. He and his wife even occasionally attended candombe dances. After Rosas' fall in 1852, many whites remained suspicious of black music and dances, which they felt served to alienate the blacks from the white community. Municipal authorities were persuaded to impose curfews on dances sponsored by African organizations, causing blacks to dance clandestinely.

The Afro-Argentines valued their candombe as a small act of resistance to the absolute control of the whites. They held dances to raise money to pay for freedom of slaves and for cultural events and celebratory occasions, including Christian religious holidays, a practice which didn't sit well with Catholic Church authorities. Lent, celebrated as Carnival, was enthusiastically embraced. There were street parades of candombe dances and drum music with participants dressed in colorful costumes; these religious affairs often evolved into licentious, bawdy celebrations. During the mid-1800s, these celebrations were the only occasion on which social classes of Buenos Aires mixed freely.

Each candombe band consisted of twenty or more drummers, and it was not unusual to have three-hundred to four-hundred drums in one parade. At several times during the procession, there would be a drum battle among members of the drum corps, each trying to overwhelm the others with intricate drumming cadences. This is still played out in Buenos Aires on Sunday afternoons in Lezema Parc, when dozens of candombe school bands travel from Montevideo to parade and dance through the park.

Montevideo, with its large black population, is considered to be the capital of candombe music today, some of which is fused with jazz to create some remarkably interesting and beautiful contemporary music. It is not unusual for candombe bands with hundreds of drummers to march through the middle of the city, day or night, blocking traffic for hours.

At first the white youth in Buenos Aires poked fun at the black carnival bands by blacking their faces, mocking their posture, and mimicking their dance steps; drawings and photographs of that period show young men from the city's most prominent families participating in Carnival parades in blackface. However, the more the boys and young men were exposed to black music and dance, the more intrigued they became, and it wasn't long until whites began going to watch the dancing and listen to the music at Black's dances. Before long, the white youths became so intrigued with the exotic music and dance movements that instead of mocking the Blacks, white youths began to imitate their rhythmic steps and movements and to incorporate them into their own pre-tango dancing.

During this same era, Blacks were becoming disenchanted with their own candombe dance, which fell into disfavor because many young Blacks had become interested in integrating into white society. Partly as a result of integrated Carnival activities, they decided to learn the dances of the European immigrants, which had rhythms closest to their own, such as the mazurkas and polkas. Ironically, while the whites imitated the fluidity and vivacity of the Blacks' dancing, the blacks were trying to copy the courtesy and politeness of the whites' dances. Thus, the earliest tango steps were created when Blacks began using the European embrace. In the second half of the 1800s, when public dance halls were proliferating, many Blacks lost their jobs to the new European immigrants so a number of them opened small academias and dance halls, some of which became famous.

By the end of the 19th century, tango was the most important music of the Carnival, and was even played outside of the carnival period. The middle classes began to dance it, and tango even appeared in center city musical comedies and plays. The academias moved up to the center of town. Increasingly, young blacks began to look upon the candombe as old-fashioned and shameful, appreciated only by parents and grandparents. Documents show that the candombe was danced publicly until the early 1900s. One newspaper article reported in 1907 that a city ordinance was passed to prohibit the tangos of the Blacks.

During the last half of the 19th century as Buenos Aires was becoming prosperous, there was an influx of rural peasantry to the city in quest of work to settle in the poorest fringes of the city closest to the rural areas from which they came. Along with the newly arriving European immigrants, local men became enthusiastic patrons of academias as a good place to meet people and make contact with women. These academias provided improvised music played on guitars and candombe drums, most served alcohol, and many acted as discreet brothels. The improvised dancing in the academias merged with the African candombe. The *canyengue* and the milonga soon followed.

Later Waves of Immigrants

The nascent tango was dramatically altered by the wave of primarily poor, single proletarian males who left Europe during the last part of the 19th century. In 1854 when construction began on an extensive railroad system, Argentina experienced a labor shortage due to the decimation of the Indians and blacks, so the English sent representatives to Europe to enlist workers to immigrate to Argentina. The campaign was successful; the immigrant population leaped from under 5,000 in the 1850s to over 200,000 in 1889.

The Argentine government's desire to create a European country in Argentina led them to prefer immigrants from Western Europe and Catholic countries, but they were so desperate for labor the government also encouraged immigrants from Syria and Lebanon as well as Jews from Western and Eastern Europe. Officials were still convinced that a European-dominated Argentina would be more financially successful than the rest of Latin America with its large mestizo populations. Although rural Argentina was sparsely populated, Buenos Aires was enjoying the biggest boom in Latin America, thanks to the European market's need for cereals, beef and hides, with shipments from Buenos Aires via newly developed transportation with more efficient railways and steamships.

Besides the hoped-for improvement in their lives, immigrants were drawn to Buenos Aires because of the historic Paris/European connection which existed in the hearts and minds of many Europeans. They viewed Buenos Aires as the most civilized and European city in Latin America.

Immigrant Hotel

European Immigrants Warmly Welcomed

Immigrants were more warmly welcomed in Buenos Aires than they were in New York, where many were looked down upon and overwhelmed by the strangeness of the city. On arrival in New York, they were more or less tolerated, sometimes treated harshly, and left to their own devices to acclimate to the alien country. Buenos Aires, on the other hand, treated them as desirable guests and generously helped them to settle into their new lives.

Beginning in the early 1870s, until World War I, all immigrants to Argentina were invited to spend their first five days at the Immigrants Hotel, which was located by the docks, where they were given a clean place to sleep and three meals a day. New arrivals were given a numbered pass that permitted them to travel into the city and return at will.

The hotel could house up to 4,000 in halls for 250 people; men and women slept in different rooms, with a common room for socializing. In the mornings, guests were awakened by attendants and invited to a breakfast of tea or coffee and freshly baked bread in an immaculate white dining hall. There were no long waiting lines as the dining hall could accommodate up to 1,000. Three meals a day were served, plus an afternoon snack for the children; the meals were legendary for their abundance.

For many immigrants, it was the first hot meal they'd had in many weeks, a luxury for those who crossed the ocean in steerage. In the recently opened Museum of Immigration, there is a display of mementos from the immigrants' arrival, including a note saying, "In these first two weeks of my life *in Buenos Aires... I ate really well."* Glass cases in the museum contain some of the things that immigrants brought with them from home: a tiny, two-inch square French-Spanish dictionary, a tin box of cough drops, tins of medicinal cream, spools of thread and miniature sewing boxes, family photographs, trunks of all sizes and shapes, small handmade wooden toy cars, metal bunk beds, a treadle sewing machine, a marble-topped dining room table, etc.

The Immigrant Hotel had libraries with reading rooms, large maps of Argentina on the walls, shelves of books describing Argentina in many languages, as well as drawings of agricultural machines with explanations for how they worked. A central employment office made translations of the immigrants' documents and helped them find work. There were daily language classes and classes in various vocational skills, including those needed for agricultural work operating tractors and other farm equipment. There was even a stuffed horse so that immigrants could practice getting on and off without embarrassment.

When the Immigrant Hotel was recently turned into the Immigrant Museum, one of the most popular features was a bank of seven computers, with assistants available to help people research information on their ancestors' arrival in Buenos Aires. On opening day, armed with scraps of paper and dates, today's descendants of immigrants stood in lines numbering more than four-hundred to see what they could discover about their heritage. On the walls are original posters that had been distributed in Europe, advertising inexpensive steamboat crossings direct to Buenos Aires from Italy and Holland.

Immigrants Dominate

Argentine leadership had its wish granted to become a European style country. In 1880, when Buenos Aires became the federal capital of Argentina, it was by far the largest and grandest city in Latin America. Population figures from 1854 show 90,000, and by 1869 there were 670,000. Between 1880 and 1885, there were approximately 250,000 European and Middle Easterners in Buenos Aires. By 1895 three out of every four adult males were immigrants, and men outnumbered women ten to one. By 1914, sixty percent of the city's adult females and seventy percent of adult males were foreigners, with immigrant males outnumbering Argentine males by three to one. Small wonder that Argentines began to question their Argentine identity — a topic of continuing interest.

For many immigrants, however, once they had left the safety net of the Immigrant Hotel, life became extremely difficult. As in New York City, most available jobs were back breaking and paid miserable salaries; their living conditions were worse than dismal. Many soon lamented having left home but were unable to accumulate enough money to buy a return ticket. They looked back to where they came from as being more attractive than their present existence. Unlike immigrants in New York City who arrived with hopes of setting up a new, prosperous and vibrant life in the New World, many of the young, single, male immigrants had planned to return to their home countries as soon as possible with pockets full of money. Argentine immigrants didn't want to create a new life; they wanted their Old World, an attitude that still affects Argentine society today.

The Paris Connection

For its economic model, the colonial establishment of Buenos Aires chose Great Britain, but its heart, mind, and cultural life were relentlessly tied to Paris. Argentines felt inundated by an expanding immigrant population with which they had nothing in common. Those who had become wealthy isolated themselves from the rest of the country and made every effort to avoid the newcomers. Upper-class families set themselves apart by using French as their first language at home and at social gatherings. Established British, German, and French families had their own social clubs and guarded their cultures through language, entertainment, and separate medical and educational systems, a custom still common, though diminishing.

Turn-of-the century Buenos Aires was a magnificent European-style city that reflected the wealth and success of its downtown citizens, most of whom looked to Paris for cultural inspiration and even maintained second homes there. They subscribed to European newspapers and journals, wore clothing and hairstyles of European design, and European theatrical companies and musical stars regularly toured Argentina. Families who could afford it made an annual trip to France to purchase the latest clothing and furniture for their European-style homes, which sometimes were exact imitations of French mansions. Argentine architects who visited Paris returned with copies of original blueprints to reproduce private homes and public buildings in the city center.

Rich and pampered Argentine bachelors went to Paris on regular, extended visits and acquired reputations for throwing around enormous amounts of money on gambling, horseracing, polo, fine restaurants, women, and the theater, generally acting like children on a spree. They were well dressed, handsome, and personable and were enthusiastically welcomed into the salons of the aristocracy and upper classes. The French expression, *"Riche comme un argentine"* became a definition of enormous new wealth, an expression still in use.

In homage to Paris' Baron Haussmann's Grand Boulevards, the mayor of Buenos Aires ordered thousands of trees planted on the broad avenues. Replicas of Paris-style round, dark green metal kiosks stocked French magazines. Sarah Bernhardt and other prominent French actors, singers, and musicians regularly played Buenos Aires. The Teatro Colon, built at the end of the 19th century, still ranks among the world's great opera houses.

Elegant French-style cafés opened, including that owned by ice cream maker, Tortoni, which became one of the most famous literary cafés in the world and still prospers on Avenido Cinco de Mayo. As in Paris, on Sunday mornings, women promenaded in carriages through Palermo Parc, echoing Paris's Sundays in Bois de Boulogne.

The Dark Side of the Immigrant's Buenos Aires

However, few new European immigrants would have the opportunity to enjoy the elegance of the Paris of Latin America. As in other large cities of the Industrial Age, Buenos Aires spawned slums of unspeakable misery. The immigrants lived by the docks and slaughterhouses in the squalid San Telmo and La Bocca barrios, where the river regularly flooded, and sidewalks were elevated above stagnant pools of water where mosquitoes bred. Every bit as nasty as anything Charles Dickens ever described, the streets were muddy and filled with garbage. People lived in shacks or in conventillos where hundreds were packed into rows of narrow, sometime windowless rooms surrounding a central patio, with water and toilet facilities shared by up to one-hundred people. In 1880 there were 1,770 conventillos; by 1887 the number had exploded to 2,835.

In San Telmo, as many as thirty families lived in formerly single-family houses whose owners had moved to the North of the city during the yellow fever epidemic of 1871 and had not returned because of the river's periodic flooding. Some families even set up housekeeping in large sewer pipes stored on an empty lot belonging to a Frenchman named A. Touraint. They were called *"attorantes,"* meaning homeless bums, an expression that continues in use.

Countless petty criminals used the barrios as their headquarters, and toughs became feared and respected strongmen and influential leaders, *compadrones* and *compadres.* Many of them adopted the gaucho custom of carrying a knife, an essential part of their attire, as was the white scarf, slouch felt hat, raised heels, and tight jacket. These men considered themselves swells and dressed the part. With the arrival of the tango, some earned leadership of their barrios by the quality of their tango dancing.

Even though new immigrants to Buenos Aires received a more helpful welcome than did those who landed in New York City, many were soon desperately homesick. Working conditions were deplorable and salaries so low that it was impossible to live with any dignity. Everything was strange; nothing was the same as at home. Christmas came in the heat of the blistering summer: "even the water ran in the wrong direction. At first the gauchos and immigrants, living side by side, were hostile and suspicious of each other. The gauchos distrusted the "foreigners" and felt the immigrants were intruders, taking jobs away from them.

Although most of the new immigrants were ambitious and hardworking, there were some who preferred the easy life and brought petty crime with them.

Nevertheless, as they sat outside their tenements to escape the misery of their lodgings, they listened to each other's music played on instruments they'd brought with them: violins, flutes, guitars, accordions, and later, the bandoneons. Some expressed their feelings in a lonely whistling, which has become a popular icon of the tango - the image of a man leaning with hunched shoulders, whistling under a street lamp.

Unlikely as it would have seemed, the culture of tango's music, dance, and lyrics became the darling of Buenos Aires, Argentina, and eventually of the world.

Dedicado à mi amigo y colega David Roccatagliata (Tito)

LA DESPEDIDA

TANGO TRISTE

Para

Piano

Por

ROBERTO FIRPO

CHAPTER SEVEN

The Growth of Tango: 1870 to World War I

"People are always looking for the Mother and Father of tango. That's not possible to find because tango is a hybrid—no Mother and Father. Tango is made up of its ingredients." (Rodolfo Dinzel)

Exactly when and why the new music was called the 'tango' is shrouded in ambiguity. In the African countries of Angola and Mali, the word tango means a closed or reserved place to meet, but it is also close to the Portuguese word, "tangere," meaning to touch, which could have been picked up by Africans from Portuguese slave traders. "Tango" was a term for the place where slaves were held until shipped out of Africa, and where slave sales took place in the Americas. Some claim it comes from the two Spanish words tambor (drum) and tambo (a place for music and dancing.) A Cuban dance, the habanera was called the 'tango Americano', and the dances of blacks in Veracruz, Mexico, were known as "tangos." In Buenos Aires, the term was used to designate where newly arrived slaves and freed blacks gathered to dance to drums on Sunday afternoons. Adding to the confusion, there is a region in Japan called Tango.

Tango historians generally agree that the principle contributors to tango were blacks, gauchos, colonialists, and later European immigrants, but there is no agreement on the exact contributions made by each. Some contend that tango was essentially a black dance until the European wave of immigrants arrived in the mid-1800s. The tango's precursors, the "milonga," the "canyengue," and the "milonga candombada" (which features candombe drums), were folk dances, with no rules for music or specific dance steps. In any case, by 1875 the first hybrid tango music— good for listening or dancing—evolved with musicians playing music that sometimes sounded a lot like the "habanera" and sometimes like milongas, but all of it was influenced by the candombe.

Another important ingredient of tango was the dances of colonial Spanish Porteño society, including the "cheery," 2 x 4 upbeat contra dances such as the "tango andaluse," and the "habanera," which was introduced by French courtesans who had been brought to the Caribbean Islands in the late 18th century. After the Haitian slave revolt in 1825, many Europeans living in Haiti fled to Cuba taking the "tango andaluse" with them, as did Cuban seamen plying the trade routes between the Caribbean and the Rio de la Plata. In spite of the name, the "tango andaluse" had not the remotest connection to the tango. The "habanera" was danced in an embrace but maintained distance between the bodies. By the mid-19th century, popular dance in Buenos Aires was dominated by Western colonial dances with distanced embraces.

Myth has it that tango was not accepted by the middle and upper classes of Buenos Aires and Montevideo until World War I and after it had been to Paris and back, but this was not the case. It is true that the tango had to fight for acceptance in Buenos Aires because it broke the rules of social dancing by not keeping the bodies separated, but mostly considered to be unacceptable and disreputable because of its association with the underworld of brothels, poverty, crime, and easily available drugs. But by 1870 - 1880 it had become a recognizable dance with unique music and movements. In the last two decades of the 19th century, it was possible to dance tango in some parts of the center of the city, although it was not yet accepted by most of the middle and upper classes.

By the end of the 19th century, the population of Buenos Aires was overwhelmed by Italians who made up the vast majority of immigrants, and the immigrants' music - polkas, mazurkas, and waltzes - introduced a sophisticated lyricism to the spirit of the tango. Their lyrics were straight out of classical opera: jealousy, lost loves, betrayal, lives wrecked by alcohol and cocaine, joblessness, gambling, disappointed parents, and wretched children. Once tango music and lyrics ceased being improvised, the Italians' ability to read and write music overwhelmed the influence of the illiterate blacks and gauchos; the new lyrics began to emphasize the hardships of immigrants' lives in Buenos Aires.

The Old Guard – Guardia Vieja, 1875 – 1924

The first tangos were improvised on primitive flutes and guitars, but by the 1890s the groups increased to trios and quartets that added a clarinet or concertina, a violin or mandolin, a portable harp and later the bandoneon, these combinations made up what was called the "orquesta tipica." Once the music moved out of the streets, into the bars and cafés sometimes a double bass and a piano were added. The piano polished tango's image with a bit of class because it was a matter of considerable prestige to have a piano in middle and upper class homes.

An instrument that helped spread the tango throughout Buenos Aires, usually by itinerant Italians, was the barrel or street organ, a box with the mouths of pipes pointing forward. The player stood and balanced the instrument on two wheels while he played the keyboard. Then in 1886 the bandoneon, an accordion-like instrument, arrived from Germany, and before long became the quintessential instrument of tango. In spite of being very difficult to play, it continues to be the signature sound of tango music, producing the melancholy wailing that personifies tango music. The earliest recognized stars of tango music were all bandoneon players.

"One could not think of tango without the sound of a bandoneon. Could you think of a mass without faith? The bandoneon is the tango's faith." (Rodolfo Mederos, master bandoneon player)

The Bandoneon

The origins of the first bandoneon are like that of tango - unclear. Some give credit to Heinrich Band who at the age of twenty-two worked in his father's musical instruments' shop in Krefeld, Germany. In 1850 he ran a newspaper advertisement for his new bandoneon that read, "To friends of the accordion. By way of a new invention, we have once again remarkably perfected our accordions, and these new instruments, round or octagonal, with 88 to 144 voices are available at our store." In 1864 Alfred Arnold began to make bandoneons in Germany, classified as 'Double A' and claimed them to be" equal in musical excellence as Stradivarius is to the violin."

The original bandoneon had thirty buttons that produced sixty sounds, but around the turn of the century a 142-note version with seventy-two buttons became standard, and buttons were added to make 152 notes. The bandoneon is notorious for being difficult to learn because, while the accordion produces an entire chord at the press of a single button, the bandoneon buttons play only individual notes. It becomes very complex because each button produces two very different sounds, depending on whether the air is going in or out of the bellows. Towards the end of the first decade of the 1900s, after tango fever reached a pitch in Paris, French musicians asked for a bandoneon that was less difficult to play, so one was invented that made the same sound whether the bellows were opening or closing.

The bandoneon's range of sounds, from "delicate to ferocious," and "sentimental, dramatic and deep," is produced by two hand-filed reeds per note that sound simultaneously, one at a normal pitch, the other an octave higher. The air pressure of the bellows makes the metal reeds vibrate to create the unique sounds. The notes can be played with varying intensity, sometimes producing sounds close to human speech, or what is called a "cry." An expert player can make it evoke sad or melancholy feelings, giving special power to some of tango's depressing lyrics. The bandoneon has been called "an unhappy accordion."

The bandoneon is considered to be the essence of the tango. Although it was the last instrument to be integrated into the early tango orchestras, it's not possible to have 'real' tango without it. Some claim that the bandoneon was the single most important event in tango music and credit it with slowing down the original tango 2/4 beat to 4/8 and 4/4, because the 2/4 was too fast for the large, awkward bandoneons. It is credited with turning the tango from a lively, light-hearted dance into something slow, intimate, and meditative.

Like some concertinas, the bandoneon is octagonal or square with cut off corners. But, unlike concertinas, which are usually painted in gaudy colors, the bandoneon is nearly always black or mahogany, sometimes discreetly decorated with inlaid silver wire and mother-of-pearl. The bandoneon has buttons on both sides of the bellows; they are bulky and awkward to handle, and for this reason, they are held on the lap instead of in front of the chest while standing, as are accordions. In spite of the awkward size, there were a number of popular female bandoneon players in the early days. One of them was Paquita Bernado, who in 1925 was the first player to put her foot on a stool while playing.

During the early period of tango, the bandoneon was relegated to simple melody and did not play rhythm, but bandoneonistas were soon permitted to embellish arrangements with the left hand playing the heavy percussion of the candombe.

Jose Libertella Playing the Bandoneon

The Italians, who brought with them their rich musical heritage of opera and popular music, exerted the greatest influence on the tango, dominating the tango scene as musicians, composers, and later as arrangers for the large orchestras. Before long, more and more professional musicians arrived who began to write down tango melodies so that they could be played by musicians who had never heard the originals.

The composer Angel Villoldo (1864 – 1919), who was called the 'Father of Tango,' was extremely prolific and was the most prominent musician of the Old Guard, making extensive tours of Europe in 1907. He played the piano and the guitar, and he sang and wrote dozens of songs that became famous, including 'El Choclo' and 'La Cumparsita,' two of today's favorite tangos.

New Guard Tango Orchestras at the Turn of the Century

By 1900, the first tango orchestras, "orquestras tipicas," appeared in the center of town, making tango highly visible to all social classes. (But 'visibility' did not translate into 'acceptance' until later.) The earliest tango rhythms were akin to military marches, but by the end of the first two decades, the music had been influenced by rural and urban milongas. According to historian Oscar Himshoot, "the tango was never rejected as a musical composition—its rejection was solely because of the marginal ambience that gave birth to it."

Francisco Canaro and Roberto Firpo were the leaders of the most influential of the new orchestras. By the end of the first decade of the 1900s, the written tango had gained such importance that 30,000 copies of tango sheet music had been sold, with authors receiving the rights to their music. As tango musicians gained stature as professionals, they began to look the part by appearing in tuxedos or three-piece suits.

An "orquestra tipica" played at the new luxurious French-styled cabaret, 'El Armenonville,' in Buenos Aires with the pianist Roberto Firpo introducing the piano into his quartet of flute, bandoneon, guitar, and violin. The earliest instruments, the flute and the guitar, were mostly banished towards the end of the 19th century after the German bandoneon had arrived. From 1920, the orchestra was enlarged to ten or twelve musicians, plus one or two singers. In 1921, Roberto Firpo had an orchestra composed of four bandoneons, six violins, a contrabass, and piano. The mid-1920s ushered in the beginning of the end of the Guardia Vieja tango.

Lyrics

Improvised music and dance had evolved simultaneously and although early lyrics were ad-libbed, before long structured tango lyrics began to appear with the New Guard orchestras. The first, unwritten, lyrics were products of the bordellos and were usually aggressively obscene and sometimes fierce. Lunfardo, the slang of the *arrabales* was used so much in lyrics that without at least a rudimentary knowledge of Lunfardo, it wasn't possible to understand what the songs were about.

As more people living outside the *arrabales* became intrigued by the new music, lyrics began to be written by non-slum dwellers - middle and even upper class musicians and poets - and lyrics lost their unsavory flavor to become more romantic and more nostalgic. The new, written lyrics spoke about times past of an idyllic society that actually hadn't really existed.

When vocalists first began singing with the larger orchestras, about one-third of them ad-libbed the lyrics. As the tango made inroads into the city's center, it was recognized that the tango was about to turn into a form of popular song, so many serious musicians and poets turned to writing tango lyrics.

Middle and Upper Class Incursions

After gaining popularity in the *arrabales*, technological advances and inventions such as the horse-drawn tramway, the underground subway, the phonograph, the radio, and the movies, brought changes to Buenos Aires society that permitted the tango to leave the *arrabales* for the respectable center of the city. There it was taken up by the middle classes, and with perceptibly less enthusiasm, it crept into a (very) few upper class and aristocratic homes. Although some of the more adventurous among the upper classes hesitantly toyed with it, it made no significant inroads into Buenos Aires' upper class society until after its heady reception in Paris in 1907.

Tango teachers, a few with their wives, opened tango schools in Buenos Aires, many of them using the salons of high society figures. Magazine photographs from 1913 show tango classes and parties of elegantly dressed men and women. An August 1913 magazine article noted that the most constant clients of tango classes are those men and women planning to visit Paris and "knowing how admired the tango was there," wanted to be sure to be prepared for any social occasions where they might encounter the dance.

In the few upper class salons where tango was being introduced and tentatively accepted, live orchestras were hired. "The musicians' attire was strictly regulated: they had to wear black trousers and dress coats with cuello de palomita (butterfly collar), a solid black tie, and black patent leather shoes with a low heel. Their deportment was strictly regulated in that they were not allowed to drink nor were they permitted to have conversations with any of the women guests. They were instructed "to avoid the use of Lunfardo words, or worse."

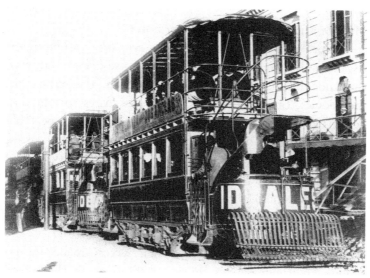

Tramway, Buenos Aires – 1891

Tramways

In 1875 new horse-drawn tramways ran from the river's dock areas in the southern suburbs to the center of the city, effectively breaking down the isolation of those living in the suburbs, thus permitting some communication between the social classes. This was the first time that people living on the fringes of Buenos Aires had easy access to the central and northern parts of the city, and it changed the nature of Buenos Aires (much as the RER - regional rail - in Paris changed the nature of central Paris in the latter part of the 20th century.)

Soon after their arrival in Buenos Aires, Italian organ grinders discovered the milonga and popularized it in their wanderings around the city; when the tango emerged it was added to their repertoires. With their portable barrel organs, they used the tramways to spread the new music to other parts of town, where it was played in circuses, theaters, bars, cafés, and dancing and dining places for the lower and middle classes. Coachmen and servants traveling by tram from the barrios brought tango to their work places in the center of town, and it was also popularized by tram conductors (mayorales) who played tangos on their coronets enroute. Later, the first underground subway in Latin America, the Subte, opened in 1913, making travel between districts of Buenos Aires even easier.

Phonograph

With the increase of middle class affluence, entertainment possibilities increased, including the invention of the player piano and the phonograph. Soon phonographs and records were being produced, and by 1901 the Columbia

Phonograph Company and the Victor Company were founded. By 1903 there were over a hundred phonograph companies in Germany alone, all producing records of good quality.

The metropolis of Buenos Aires, with its 1,300,000 inhabitants, was deemed the obvious place to establish a phonograph company; in 1910, Carl Lindstrom founded Parlophone, which was a boon to tango musicians. So great was the success of tango and the new recording industry that between 1903 and 1920 there were forty tango musical groups recording regularly in Buenos Aires and fifty other groups recording sporadically.

Between 1902 and 1910, one-third of the 1,000 records released in Buenos Aires were tangos. From 1910 to 1920 there were 5,500 records produced, one-half of which were tangos. The invention of the phonograph allowed people to listen to tango music in their homes rather than in the streets, bars, or bordellos, thus changing the nature of tango enthusiasts from those who only frequented the lower class *arrabales*. Although tango music had become popular throughout Buenos Aires, respectable women still were not able to go where tango was danced, so there was increasing interest in being able to have access to music in homes.

Player pianos became popular in families where there was money enough for a piano but whose families had not yet acquired skills enough to play. Making music by simply putting a perforated paper roll into a slot and pumping pedals was ever so much easier and faster than learning scales.

The popularizing of the tango was complemented by the proliferation of piano sheet music, usually consisting of two to four pages of written music with accompanying lyrics. In 1900, after written lyrics became part of the tango scene, as many as 20,000 – 30,000 copies of a single title were printed and sold. By this time, lyrics for tango had come to be considered serious poetry, and writers from all backgrounds began to compose lyrics for tango music. Once tango moved to the center of town and was no longer associated only with prostitutes, pimps, and brothels, so many counterfeit piano scores were being sold that to avoid being plagiarized, tango composers began to sign their compositions.

The Sainete and Classical Theaters

Between the 1860s and 1907 the popular *sainete* theaters held sway over theatergoers of Buenos Aires. Closely related to vaudeville, *sainete* theaters consisted of several one-act burlesque or comic farces with music, which was more and more frequently that of tango. The farces had large casts with lots of comedy and slapstick. The plots were based on life in the immigrant barrios with plots about the fear of being deported because of union activities or for criticizing the unfairness of their poverty. Circus performers who played in the *sainetes* were considered socially acceptable, but not actors and actresses.

The 'tango song' became more familiar when the tango invaded the classical theater. 'El Queco' was being sung around Buenos Aires and the tangos 'Bartolo' and 'Dama de la Lata' became popular. As early as 1889, the milonga was danced on a Buenos Aires stage in a play called "The Star."

Movies

The last of the technological advances to spread the influence of tango during this period was the silent film, which required musicians to provide background music. Many musicians had already become involved with tango music, and so it was natural for them to play it in the movie theaters. During World War I, the first films featuring the tango were made in Argentina. In 1916 Carlos Gardel starred in 'Flor de Durazno,' a silent film in which he appeared dressed as a sailor. In 1917, the first film devoted entirely to the tango was called El Tango de la Muerte (Tango of Death). After the war, in the 1920s Rudolph Valentino danced his famous Hollywood tango, which put him on the map as the most important male movie star in Hollywood, celebrated as "The Latin Lover."

Tango Orchestras

Once tango had begun its incursion from the suburbs into central Buenos Aires, the music changed from early military march rhythms and sprightly rural milongas to the more European lyrical romantic and melancholy style. After the last public appearances of the Old Guard composers of the twenties, many new musicians with formal classical training began to play tango. As a consequence, it soon began to take on some of the complex and intricate structures that would later characterize the music of the 1940s, ushering in what would become known as Buenos Aires' 'Golden Era' of tango. The bandoneonist Osvaldo Fresedo visited the United States and subsequently invaded the cabarets of Buenos Aires with his innovation of an orchestra that featured the influence of jazz and the refined sounds of harps and vibraphones. Both Fresedo and Julio de Caro were architects of the modern instrumental tango, which integrated the classic tango into the world of modern music.

Later orchestras were enlarged and featured two permanent vocalists. It's been reported that in Buenos Aires in the 1930s and 1940s, there were several-hundred tango orchestras. Tango had become so popular that for carnival it was necessary to book an orchestra a year ahead of time.

The Dance and the Men Who Danced It- Compadres, Compadritos, Malevos

By the 1880s the tango dance was dominated by the older strong men of the barrios, mostly Italians. Called compadres, they were a sort of urban gaucho, many of whom worked as bodyguards for barrio caudillos (bosses). Prestige in the barrios was based on their authority, their courage, and their word of honor - backed up by the knives they carried, a custom borrowed from the gauchos. Certain compadres emerged to become the effective rulers in the *arrabales*, looked upon as a sort of Mafia "godfather,' but unlike Mafia members, they were not serious criminals.

Compadres acquired the gaucho custom of helping others and gained prestige and power through using their influence in aiding newcomers and the disadvantaged in their neighborhoods, similar to political ward bosses in large U.S. cities at the time. In expectation of political loyalty, they helped new immigrants settle into housing, find jobs, and locate schools for their children; they also directed the needy or sick to government or private institutions that would assist them, sometimes even giving money out of their own pockets. They were popular, gregarious, proud, and independent, and looked up to, although some were feared more than they were liked. They assumed the gaucho characteristics of independence and pride combined with the Italian male desire to look good. They advertised their superior status through their style of dress and refined European manners. They considered themselves to be dandies. Their uniform was a black suit, slouched felt hat, trousers gathered at the waist with a black belt, spats over highly polished shoes, a white scarf around the neck, and a vicuna shawl on the shoulder. Their hair was carefully parted, and some wore a red geranium over one ear. Their appearance was close to that of the French *apache*, a radical dance style developed in Montmartre.

Compadres Dancing With Each Other

Contemporary illustrations and photographs show that at first the tango was danced by men dancing apart from each other. A popular form of entertainment was for two men to act out tales of men fighting over honor or a woman in a stylized combat performed as competition among neighborhood gangs. There was nothing effete about their dancing; the men danced together because of the drastic shortage of women in the barrios. The dance became so important to building a macho image in the barrios near the docks that men and boys spent countless hours practicing with each other, inventing new steps until it became an all-encompassing activity - many of them dancing every day, sometimes all day long. This obsession to dance well became a way for a poor man of the barrio to show his virility, a means of becoming 'someone,' even an influential political leader, and many tough neighborhood bosses built their reputations by challenging each other to 'dance duels' in the streets. Frequently the 'duels" led to serious fights, with the police called in to control riots that erupted over who was the best dancer. In search of new dance steps or simply to check out the competition, men would visit neighboring barrios; those forays were met with less friction if the men went with a friend who was known in the neighborhood.

Bar and café owners watched the men dancing in the streets and decided it might be good for business if the men danced inside their establishments and drank beverages when they became thirsty. They hired musicians to play tango music to lure the men inside. Waitresses were pressed into service as dance partners. Many of these waitresses became fascinated with the dance and turned into skilled partners.

Bordellos soon followed the lead of the bar and café owners, but not all the local men were able to afford the houses of prostitution. However, middle and upper class men from central Buenos Aires habitually visited the bordellos, and some became enamored of the dance and the music. A few even tried to introduce it into the homes of central Buenos Aires, but because of the taint of the brothels, these efforts were unsuccessful.

Compadritos

Compadritos were the next generation of young men in the *arrabales,* but unlike the compadres, they represented the worst element of society. Compadritos ("little compadres") were native-born street bullies trying to emulate compadres by flagrantly attempting to lord it over their neighborhoods. They swaggered through the barrios, but were not as popular as the compadres because they were neither responsible, nor helpful, nor as wise as the older men. They were flashier and sought attention. (Census records from this period show that in these barrios many men proudly registered their occupations as "rogue" or "scoundrel.")

Although many were affable enough, the compadritos didn't inspire the same admiration and respect as the compadres. Rather than being concerned with the welfare of their neighbors, many were considered "insolent braggarts and lay-abouts." Not exactly gangsters, they skirted the edges of the law as pimps, drug dealers, or petty criminals. They spent their nights drinking alcohol, imitating the candombe dancers of the blacks, and fighting with knives. Proud and arrogant, they were prone to fight for no other reason than to exhibit courage. They identified and hung out with other hoodlums in their neighborhoods, but there were no organized gangs. Instead of gang affiliations, they identified with neighborhood soccer and cultural clubs and with competency in dancing tango.

Though the compadritos were gregarious, they did not command respect or fear and weren't considered to be honorable. They were easily identified by their manner of dress, which was mandatory for men in search of admiration or trying to inspire fear. They wore a short, tightly fitted jacket with large shoulder pads and tight trousers frequently of a different material and color; their shirts were rose or wine colored. Their vests were unbuttoned in order to easily get to the knife they always had tucked into a belt. They emulated the compadres with a slouched felt hat, but it was worn cocked to one side with the brim over one eye and sometimes a red geranium tucked over one ear. Their highly polished boots had lightly raised heels, and they wore spats with buttons or elastic to keep them tight. The image of a compadrito lounging against a street lamp, hands in pockets, a cigarette dangling from his mouth, is still an iconic symbol of tango today.

Like contemporary blacks in urban areas of the U.S., the compadritos developed a particular style of walking. In Buenos Aires the special "walk" became known as the 'tango walk' and was used in the tango. Whereas in the US, and many developing countries, excelling in a sport was, and still is, a method of escaping from the slums, in Buenos Aires, outstanding dancing skill was, and remains today, a proven way to attract attention and admiration from both men and women.

Malevos

Other barrio types who danced the tango obsessively were the malevos ('bad boys'), who were at the bottom of the 'macho' social heap. They weren't popular because they acted as though they had chips on their shoulders. They were thought to be arrogant and antisocial, with reputations for cowardice and treachery. Unlike the compadres and compadritos who were congenial and gregarious, the malevos were known to be rude and insolent but they sought to be outstanding dancers as a way to gain respect in the underworld. They worked hard at becoming good dancers, but even though some became serious, even excellent dancers, they had difficulty shedding the malevo image. They never quite made it socially in the *arrabales* where they lived and were, in general, looked down upon as delinquents.

Where They Danced: Academias, Dance Halls, Cabarets, Sports and Cultural Clubs

The famous dancer, Cachafaz recalled: "The guys from our neighborhood met on the sidewalks and the streets to practice the tango. We never got tired of following the barrel organs across the city. Already at the age of eleven, while I was dancing, the men formed a circle around me and paid me with coins and refreshments." So many men were practicing dancing with each other in the streets that in 1917 a city ordinance was passed making it illegal.

When tango music left the barrios, the dance was initially introduced to the working and middle classes through circuses, vaudeville, and stage shows. For the first time, women outside the lower class neighborhoods could actually see the dance about which they'd heard so much. Women living in the barrios had already begun to dance a bit with men in the bars and cafés, but middle class women had to practice at home with uncles, aunts, cousins, brothers, sisters, or with brooms and chairs. Some families allowed their girls and women to take private classes with professional teachers, generally in their homes where they could easily be chaperoned. Teachers trained the girls until they could dance well enough to attend private parties or go to the public dance halls – chaperoned, of course - that had sprung up all over Buenos Aires.

Academias

Academias, where tango was practiced by men only, were modern forms of the traditional small dance halls in Buenos Aires where gauchos and *payadores* used to meet, trade, play music, dance, and recite poetry. By the last quarter of the 19th century there were academias frequented by the working class, in which men could practice together all year long, not only during Carnival. Soon there were academias that were not schools but simply places for the public to dance. Some academias were known as tango bars or tango clubs because they had drinking and gambling. In 1846 the Buenos Aires Police

Department reported: "For the past three years there are public dance halls whose proprietors are Italians." From this time on the term 'academia' was used to identify either a public or private dance hall.

Once the tango began to invade the city center of Buenos Aires, both cabarets and music halls began to proliferate, with brilliantly painted signs and French names: *Moulin Rouge, Royal Pigalle, L'Elysee, Maxim's, Montmartre, Le Petit Parisien, Les Folies Bergere, Trocadero, Les Ambassadeurs*, etc. They had luxurious, well-lit opulent vaulted salons decorated in an elegant European style with stages next to dance floors for the tango orchestras and for other entertainment.

Because it was an open secret that the cabarets were upscale bordellos, respectable women never frequented them. The clients were affluent men who followed the dress code of tuxedos or three-piece dark suits, patent leather shoes, spats, and silk top hats, who could easily afford the expensive food, drink, and entertainment. The "hostesses" or "cabaret girls" were almost all French, or at least European, fashionably dressed, attractive, more sophisticated "up-market" versions of the waitresses in the bars and cafés of the *arrabales*. Instead of the crude farmers from the countryside who acted as waiters in the barrios, the new cabaret waiters wore tuxedos and spoke French. Champagne replaced Pernod and red wine, and heroin and cocaine were sold cheaply in little packets.

By 1910, El Armenonville, the first cabaret opened in Buenos Aires and was frankly copied from a glamorous Paris cabaret of the same name located in the fashionable part of the Bois de Boulogne. Like the cabaret in Paris, Buenos Aires' El Armenonville was located in a large garden with rows of tables overlooking the park. The pavilion was large with elegant lines and bay windows and walls covered with red baroque material; tables, with sparkling white tablecloths and shining silver, circled the dance floor and stage. An enormous crystal chandelier lit the large room while the smaller rooms on the second floor were more discreetly lit. During the winter season, the El Armenonville closed, and its clientele moved into the city center to the Royal Pigalle, which was owned by the same proprietor.

In 1919, the number of cabarets in the center of Buenos Aires suddenly increased, precipitated by a city ordinance that prohibited women under the age of twenty-two from working as prostitutes and mandated that those twenty-three or older had to register for a special card. (The same law permitted brothel owners to have only one house of prostitution, with only one girl, and there could be no exterior signs indicating the sort of business being conducted in the house.) Brothel owners in the *arrabales* responded to this "preposterous new law" by opening 'tango cabarets' in the center of the city. Many of the women working in the bordellos were eager to move 'uptown' with the tango, but those who didn't have sufficient talent or prerequisites for success in the cabarets or music halls took to the streets in the center of town.

In Nardo Zalko's book, "A Century of Tango: Paris-Argentina," Tania Discepolo, a tango singer, recounted the atmosphere of the cabarets in Buenos Aires. "(Many of) the men who frequented them had never worked; idle men who drank champagne after champagne, generous but irresponsible. The atmosphere was languorous. Sometimes several days passed before relations were concretized with one of the dancing girls. Society men of wealth and their sons vied with each other to dance with the most beautiful and skilled women dancers. At times the women benefited from the largess of clients in the form of expensive clothing and sometimes they escaped from their tenements to be housed in beautiful apartments. It was not unknown for one of them to give a dancer a country house as a present."

Men who wanted to dance with the most desirable women had to be skilled dancers. They practiced among themselves at academias during the week with the younger men until they were considered good enough to dance with women, a process that normally took several years of concentrated effort.

Casas de Bailes

Although respectable women didn't go to the cabarets, they did get to dance in public when they went with their chaperones to the "Casas de Baile" (dance houses) that sprang up throughout Buenos Aires. Although they were neither as elegant nor as expensive as the cabarets, some of the houses, such as that of aristocrat Maria la Vasca's, were in old mansions with French furniture, mirrors and expensive paintings. The dance usually began with a polka with a special, early, dance session for younger dancers. There were also special days of the week reserved for the elderly. Women taxi dancers were paid three pesos per hour at a time when the monthly salary for an unskilled worker was 100-120 pesos. Musicians were paid five pesos for an evening.

Besides tango dancing, many of the more important dance houses provided nightly entertainment of the better music hall variety, such as the well-known Carlos Gardel-Razzano folk singer duo, hugely popular in Buenos Aires and the provinces. Some Casas de Baile, such as "Hansen's," "Hotel Victoria" and "Laura's," were so famous that they became legendary names in lyrics and literature.

Tango in Paris

During the first decade of the 20th century, the tango suddenly leaped across the ocean to a surprising, sudden successful acceptance in the salons of aristocratic society of Paris. Montmartre became the epicenter for tango. The historical affinity between Argentina and France helped tango get a foothold in the door in Paris, providing access for Parisian acceptance of tango music and dance. The center of Paris had changed after the late-19th century Commune Uprising when Baron Haussmann quite literally tore downtown Paris apart, a renovation project lasting nearly twenty years. The Butte (Hill) Montmartre in the northern part of the city escaped the renovations that remade downtown Paris, enabling it to retain its rural atmosphere with vineyards, quiet fields, and windmills. It became the center for artists, members of the city's underworld characters, and cabarets such as the Moulin Rouge (Red Windmill).

Tango musicians and performers who left Buenos Aires to take advantage of the tango's success in Paris no doubt felt comfortable in Montmartre because they found the same type of people living there as in the *arrabales* of Buenos Aires. It was the section of town inhabited by prostitutes, pimps, petty criminals and other marginal characters; alcohol and drugs flowed freely. The only 'respectable' outsiders were the same as those who went slumming in La Bocca and San Telmo. Montmartre gained notoriety for a dance called the 'apache,' which was frequently danced to tango music.

Apache Dance

In the late 1800s the Paris 'demimonde" had a dance called the "apache." The Argentines particularly liked the machismo aspect of Parisian 'apaches', a term that referred to gangs of minor criminals, both male and female. Usually female 'apaches' attached themselves to a particular male. They all carried knives and would use them at the drop of a hat." Rat Mort" (the "Dead Rat") was the name of a dance performed in cabaret shows outside Montmartre. Actually it was more drama than dance, with a squalid-looking prostitute dressed in rags (and sometimes with a red rose in her hair) who acted as though she was in a fight for her life at the mercy of a violent pimp/aggressor. The dance was highly structured: 1) the pimp asks the woman for money; 2) she refuses; 3) he threatens her and she tries to defend herself; 4) he throws her to the floor then takes her into his arms; 5) they walk together; 6) the man gets the money and the girl; and 7) the man returns to a card game as if nothing had happened, or he might pick up the woman's glass and break it over her head!

Sometimes at the end of the dance the man would throw his partner to the floor and attempt to kill her with his knife. (Once in a show the male dancer became so violent that he tossed the woman through a window.) At that very moment, the lights were turned down as actors dressed in police uniforms appeared and the spectacle came to an end.

At the 1899 Paris World Exposition, celebrating one-hundred years of the French Revolution, the Argentine Pavilion was one of the most popular attractions with its more than 3,000 exhibits, many featuring tango music. It astonished and fascinated the French population. Upper class French had already been exposed to the tango through the Argentine bachelors visiting or living in Paris who delighted in teaching the dance to distinguished Parisian society. During the "Belle Époque" (1890-1914), Paris was the undisputed center of high society, setting the standard for fashion, the arts and all culture in Europe and North and South America. Wealthy Buenos Aires families visited yearly and sent their "ninos bien" (attractive bachelor sons) for extended periods of time, some to stay in their own, second homes there. The handsome and affable bachelors were welcomed into Paris' aristocratic saloons. Many of them had learned the tango in the brothels of Buenos Aires and thought it a good idea to introduce the new music and dance into Parisian high society.

Its introduction to France was serendipitous; the first ten years of the 20th century was important for tango. In 1906, officers of the Argentine navy's training ship on a flag waving tour of European ports brought tango to France when the ship put into port at Marseilles. Among the baggage of some of the officers were printed sheet music of the tangos 'El Choclo' and 'La Morocha', which the sailors showed to local musicians to try to enlist their interest in playing it so that the sailors could teach the local women to dance the tango. Little is recorded of their efforts, but a year later in 1907, two of the biggest names in tango, Argentine composer Eduardo Arolas and Alfredo Gobbi, a Uruguayan tango musician and composer, arrived in Paris. Gobbi and Arolas had been sent to France to make recordings of tango music because Argentina's technology for making records was inferior to Europe's.

Oddly enough, the first tango recorded in Paris was to the accompaniment of the French Republican Guard orchestra, the most prestigious of all the French military bands; the song was "El Sargento Cabral." In the same year, the famous Argentine actor, singer, guitarist, and composer, Angel Villoldo, went to Paris to perform. In Argentina he was known as the 'father of tango,' and was famous for his tango compositions and his lyrics on the topics of social concerns and themes of working class life.

Also, in 1907 an important French industrialist visiting Buenos Aires was invited to a cabaret where he was captivated by the tango. On his return to France, he brought back a stack of tango sheet music. It was the first year that Argentine aero club members went to Paris with their hot air balloon and made a social success with their hot air antics. They charmed the upper classes by dancing tango in the best society salons. Finally, in 1907, the tango was danced for the first time at a reception held in a well-known aristocratic Paris hotel.

In 1908, one of the most famous French music hall artists of all time, Mistinguet, gave the first public demonstration of tango with her dance teacher in a musical review at the upscale Theatre Marigny on the Champs Elysees. In 1910, she danced the tango in a cabaret performance and created a sensation. After that, tango's future was assured.

French theaters also helped pave the way for tango's acceptance by providing new and exotic theatrical exhibitions that created an atmosphere of curiosity for things foreign and different. In 1909, Sergei Diaghilev introduced the Russian ballet, *Ballets Russes*, which rocked Parisian society with its explosion of talent, sensuality, vibrant music and exotic color; left its mark on almost every branch of fashion and the arts. In the book, "Tango!," Artemis Cooper wrote of the influence of the Ballets Russes. "It was an innovation to Paris society. Fashion colors became rich and vibrant and a whole range of exotic perfumes appeared, replacing the respectable floral scents. Previously only courtesans wore the sandalwood and patchouli that were now being used by high society. Women's clothing stressed sensuously draped fashions. Fancy balls were given in mansions decorated in fantasy replicas of Ballet Russes stage sets. Princess de Broglie gave a Bal des Pierreries in which costumes had to "evoke the magic of precious and semi-precious stones." Her dress was completely encrusted in pearls. Town houses were transformed into Persian palaces with fountains and rose-garlanded pillars."

During the same period, rich Argentine sons of wealthy families living in Paris introduced tango entertainers - singers and dancers-into private upper class homes, such as the Rothschild's. Paris' most famous host, the Comte Etienne de Beaumont, hosted tango dances in the white and gilt salons of his family's eighteenth-century palace on the Faubourg St. Honore, which in recent times held several tango dance evenings at the fancy sports club Cercle de l'Union Interalliée (of which I am a member). One of the most important advocates for tango in Paris was the Argentine playboy, writer and poet Ricardo Güiraldes, whose wealth originated from a family ranch in Argentina. He and his Argentine friends had learned to love the dance in Buenos Aires brothels; in 1910 he gave a "well received" impromptu performance of tango at a private mansion in Paris.

In the same year, 1910, at the Paris mansion of the Count and Countess of Rescek, two Argentines, Ricardo

Güiraldes and his friend Alberto Lopez Buchardo, led two young women in a tango. On another evening, when Pablo Picasso and Igor Stravinsky were conversing at a private dinner, they were surprised to see Güiraldes grab a guest and lead her through an excellent tango.

Several weeks after the exhibition at the lavish Rescek mansion, Lopez Buchardo, motivated by the interest shown in the tango, arranged to bring from Buenos Aires a tango musical group that he knew from one of *arrabales*. Cabarets featuring tango were frequented by celebrities, among them Isadora Duncan, Igor Stravinsky, Feodor Chaliapin, and Mistinguett.

Tango Goes to the Rest of Europe and the United States

Because Paris was the uncontested center of the cultural world for European aristocracy, the acceptance of tango there guaranteed attention throughout Europe. It quickly spread throughout Berlin, London, Vienna, and St. Petersburg, sometimes to mixed reactions.

By 1911 the tango craze, called 'tangomania,' had taken over fashionable Paris and had invaded Europe's aristocratic vacation spots and spas, such as France's Cote d'Azur, Germany's Baden-Baden, the Swiss Alps, and upper class Britain's (and Paris') summer getaway, the Normandy beaches of western France. Officials of European embassies in Paris took it to their home countries. In Germany, Kaiser Wilhelm II forbade his officers to dance the tango when in uniform, causing a devastating blow to high society matrons who considered no ball to be successful without a contingent of officers in their glittering uniforms. Nevertheless, the German Crown Prince was a well-known tango enthusiast. (Later, Hitler called the tango "a sissified dance.")

In 1912, articles on tango were published regularly in journals and newspapers, referring to tango dancers as "Les Possedees." One author denigrated tango and questioned if it was a ritual of a new cult that Parisians were becoming passionate about, turning heads, souls and bodies.

English writer, H. G. Wells, proclaimed 1913 the Year of the Tango, and in that same year it was reported that Great Britain's Queen Mary "found it charming." In Rome, the tango became as popular as it was in Paris. In Russia, Tsar Nicholas was perhaps the first monarch to see the tango danced when he watched a demonstration given by his two young nephews. Russian officials and military officers serving at the Russian Embassy in Paris took the tango with them when they conquered Finland. The Finnish embraced it with such enthusiasm that they took it as their own, making it their national dance so much so that today many Finns consider it to be a Finnish invention. The famous Russian poet, Maiakovsky, wrote a poem in praise of it, called "Tango con Vacas" (Tango with Cows). Some years later, a Japanese playboy living in Paris, Baron Megata, took the tango to Tokyo, where he established a free tango school for aristocratic Japanese.

In 1913, France's prominent "Le Figaro" newspaper wrote: "This winter we will be dancing the Argentine Tango, a dance that is gracious, undulating, and varied." Eduardo Bianco and his tango orchestra arrived in Paris, followed by Osvaldo Fresedo and others, whose orchestras played at Paris' exclusive Opera and at the even more exclusive Monte Carlo's Bal des Petit Lits Blancs annual charity ball.

In 1914 the well-known and distinguished American ballroom dance team, Irene and Vernon Castle, discovered the tango. In their book, "Modern Dancing," they wrote: "The only drawback in America to this lovely dance lies in the fact that nearly all teachers teach it differently." It was rumored that the tango was composed of 160 different steps, which was enough to terrify the most inveterate of dancers. The Castles said, "The Argentine Tango is unquestionably the most difficult of the new dances. Perhaps that is why some people maintain that they do not like it. Others, never having seen it, declare it "shocking."

Deauville

"Each summer, Deauville is unquestionably the most elegant place in the world." (Michel Georges-Michel, "L'Epoque du Tango", 1922)

Before World War I, a special train named *"The Tango Train,"* carried vacationers from Paris to fashionable Deauville, where the crème of European society met in the summers. The focus of social activity was a short street called Rue Gontaut-Biron, between the luxurious Normandy Hotel and the exclusive Casino. To the left of the casino's entrance was the Salon de Tango, where "the tango was danced incessantly by the *'gratin'* (big cheeses) of Paris international aristocracy." Tango contests were held in which all the contestants had to wear the tango color of orange. Tango was on everyone's minds, influencing society and fashion. By 1920 several serious books on the tango had been published, including Michel Georges-Michel's book about tango's impact on French society, titled "Three Époques: Before, During and After WW I."

When World War I broke out, public dances in Deauville were prohibited. However, orchestras and musicians continued playing tangos in restaurants and not long after there were at least twenty clandestine nightclubs where the tango was danced surreptitiously, with music by live musicians or to records. Before long, French tango dancers saw new faces from a military camp near Deauville, whose hospital cared for wounded British soldiers. In his book about tango, Georges-Michel wrote: "Following British custom, the soldiers would bathe in the sea early in the mornings and afterwards danced the tango on the beach with a pretty young Scots woman.... It is unforgettable to imagine the soldiers on the sandy beach dancing tango next to the English Channel before moving into the carnage of the Front to the east of Deauville where so many of them met their deaths." An unpleasant social comment was noted by French author Georges-Michel in 1919 when "objections were made" to the presence of some American Black soldiers who were dancing on the beaches, "a sad commentary on human intolerance."

Tango Teachers in Paris

In 1912, a reporter for the Buenos Aires newspaper, El Diario, wrote, "The tango, as it is danced in Paris, has little to do with ours except for the name and the music."

Because of its complexity, the tango was not easy to learn, so upper class hotels, dance schools, and society matrons from all over Europe sent to Buenos Aires for tango teachers and musicians. Suddenly dancers in Buenos Aires who had only danced for amusement became teachers. Tango performers who had been touring Europe's capital cities since early in the century began to teach and travel to Turkey, Russia, Germany, and Scandinavia. In 1913, a famous tango teacher, El Indio, came from Argentina to Paris, participated in a world championship tango contest, and stayed on to teach. At one-hundred francs for lessons, teaching tango became a lucrative profession; most teachers settled in Paris, creating the nucleus of what was to become a large tango exile community. By 1913 it was estimated that there were 100-150 dance teachers working in Paris. One of the first things teachers found they had to do was to change some of the tango's positions and movements to make it more acceptable to each country's mores. Europeans were fascinated with the music and the dance that provided an excuse for close contact with a partner, but many found the dance - cheek to cheek, chest-to-chest, with stomachs rubbing - much too lewd for polite society, so it was cleaned up. In 1917, in order to assure that dancers would not revert to the old, vulgar, improvised steps, Great Britain codified the dance, eliminating all movements that could be considered inappropriate. These codes, with few differences, are essentially still in effect for today's Ballroom Tango.

Tangomania

"By an unstoppable march, the tango is taking over all of Paris, to invade the salons, the theaters, the balls, the cabarets and night clubs, the grand hotels and the fashionable dance halls... The bodies undulate to an obsessive music in a feverish and vibrant atmosphere...elegant men and women enlaced torso to torso." (Sem, writer and cartoonist, La Ronde de nuit, 1923)

Within a few years, tango became the most famous dance in Paris and the Western world. Paris set the mode with tango danced in all the fashionable venues. In 1913 a prestigious tango contest held in Deauville was won by the Marquise de Semas and his niece, who had learned tango in Buenos Aires. In a French magazine, the writer Sem reported that "Paris had tango under the skin." Tango was soon used to sell almost anything: cocktails, desserts, high fashion clothing, perfume, post cards, medicines, etc.

There were tango matinee dances, champagne-tangos, charity tangos, dinner-tangos, tango conferences, and tango expositions. Afternoon tea dances sprang up all over Europe as in well as the U.S. They were held in important hotels, some of which had exclusive Tea Dance Clubs sponsored by society matrons with admission only by invitation. There were evening events, the "diner dansant," with dancing between multiple courses.

Champs-Élysées town houses were converted into dance halls, and tango dances were performed on ice at the famous Palais de Glace Theater on the Champs Elysees. Tango went from being an attraction to an unprecedented dance fad. Bright orange became the color of tango, and was featured in dresses, shawls, shirts, blouses, hats, shoes, and even on couches and chairs. Legend has it that the fashion originated with a Paris textile merchant who was stuck with a large number of bolts of an unattractive orange color which he was unable to sell. When he advertised it as "tango orange," it quickly sold out. At some point the color orange was supplanted by vivid red, which continues to be considered a "tango" color, along with the ever-present black. In 1913 a tango contest was held in Deauville for which contestants had to appear in the 'tango color' of bright orange.

Post cards were sold everywhere of couples demonstrating tango steps, and photographs of small children dancing tango were popular. A piano maker advertised a new model of Pianola that would play Beethoven, Chopin, Liszt, or 'tango a la mode.' Men continued to wear tuxedos for evening wear and dancing, but their jackets were lengthened to the long, Argentine style that permitted more shoulder and arm movement.

A new perfume was advertised for women who danced tango. "All the women who dance tango are familiar with a strange fascination; those who smell the perfume Tokalon-Tango find the same intense and unforgettable charm... The tango is an entirely different dance and this perfume is equally mysterious and unforgettable."

Tango also insinuated itself into the performing arts. Russian ballet star, Vaslav Njinski, danced a stylized tango on the stage, and Igor Stravinsky wrote a classical concert piece, "Tango pour Piano." A tango was danced at a theater performance of his "History of a Soldier" and a popular play's protagonist was a man who was unable to consummate his marriage until he danced the tango.

Tango Changed Women's Clothes and Lifestyles

In 1913, a French Countess wrote in the Chronicle of Parisian life: "The first preoccupation of elegant women who have recently moved to Paris is to take tango lessons."

There was the *"tango blouse"* of one piece that floated from the shoulders to wrists with billowing sleeves that accentuated tango's movements. Waists of dresses moved higher, to give more length and freedom of action for leg movements. Revolutionary *"coulottes"* - knee length, full cut trousers, were worn to facilitate long tango steps.

Women who had been enclosed in tight corsets were happy with the new special tango cut corset sold by Augustine Thomas in Paris. Named Le Tango, it permitted them to do the *'torqued'* movements with ease.

Shoes became pointed, supposedly to indicate direction of the dance steps. Ankle straps were added to keep shoes from slipping or sliding off when doing intricate foot movements.

Large hats then in style were not suitable for the close positions of tango, so they were made much smaller and tight to the head. The feathered aigrettes that were worn horizontally off the forehead were moved so that they pointed straight up, attached to a headband or very small hat.

In addition to clothing and the enjoyment of the dance, tango brought a bit of liberation to the lives of women by breaking with one of society's expectations, that of dancing with strangers: women went out unchaperoned and danced with men they didn't know. And there was much brouhaha about the mores broken when young women went to tango dances with men in automobiles – unchaperoned.

From the start, European women seemed more attracted to tango than were European men, possibly because the follower's role can be learned more quickly than that of the leader. In any case, it was recognized that many women had difficulty persuading men to accompany them to lessons. It was said that some women who needed partners enlisted their valets or hairdressers.

Boycott of Tangomania

Many Argentines living in Paris reluctantly joined the French in dancing tango, but not all were persuaded it was a good idea. In 1914, Enrique Larreta, the Argentine ambassador in France, exclaimed publicly: "No. Ah, no! Not in my house, no! There is in Paris at least one salon where the Argentine Tango will not be danced and that is in the Argentine legation."

Most of the prominent Argentines living in France were appalled at tango's acceptance there. They felt it was an undesirable blot on Argentina's image, but surprised at the success in French aristocratic circles, they were in a quandary. They felt that if they, too, embraced the tango as representative of Argentina, it reflected badly on their own identity; but rejecting the tango meant being out of step with current French fashion, music, and dancing. One Argentine tried with very strong words to convince Parisians that the tango should not be acceptable in their society. "When the ladies of the twentieth century dance tango, they know or they ought to know, that they are behaving like prostitutes.... Tango is not a national dance, nor is the prostitution that conceived it."

Ambassador Larreta, using his political influence to try to stop 'tangomania,' played a pivotal part in the 'anti-tango campaign.' Once, at a large reception he declared: "In Buenos Aires the tango is a primitive dance of ill repute and of dives – danced exclusively in houses of bad reputation and bars of the lowest category.... Never is it danced in the best salons nor by distinguished people of high society, nor of persons of breeding."

The anti-tango forces were able to gather some Parisian adherents against the "indecent dance." In his book 'Historia del Baile,' Sergio Pujol wrote: 'what the anti-tangoists did not realize was that in Paris, the best proof of 'vitality' and success of anything new was always scandal. Before the scandal - nothing, after the scandal - everything. The French don't get as excited about anything as they are about this moral campaign against the music of the barbaric South Americans."

Paris Obsession Criticized

"We are dancing on a volcano!" (Edouard Drumont, quoted by Argentine author Nardo Zalko)

The series of magazine articles which appeared in Paris in 1912 entitled, "Les Possedees" (today they are called "les

275

drogues" or "tango junkies") described how a vast number of people were obsessed with tango and how it affected them.

Besides Paris-based Argentines, some French people also questioned the acceptance of the tango and became quite angry about it. The poet Leopoldo Lugones called the tango "a reptile from the brothel to the salons of Paris." A contemporary magazine declared tango to be a menace to society, comparing it to a religious sect, "a sanctuary of a thousand chapels of this new cult about which Parisians were becoming so passionate, turning heads, souls, and bodies."

Cartoonists had a field day making fun of the obsession with tango. One cartoon showed a butler asking his (annoyed) employer for the night off. "I want to take my tango lesson." The city's kiosks were stocked with large supplies of tango cartoon post cards poking fun at adults or children dancing tango.

Anti-Tango Forces

In the United States, fundamentalist religions organized an anti-tango war against the dance, led by the famous gospel preacher, Billy Sunday, who demonized it because "the positions of the men and women were intolerable for a decent society." The tango was held responsible for the "degradation of women," criticized because of the immodest and immoral behavior of the women who danced it. Reverend Sunday insisted that women lost their sense of propriety when dancing the tango. But Vernon and Irene Castle, the most gifted and elegant of American ballroom performers carried the day by adding tango to their repertoire. In spite of it's difficulty, the public was attracted to the strange beauty of the tango.

The mere suggestion of people dancing in a close embrace was fuel to the anti-tango forces. Eager to see something demonic in the dance, they demanded that church authorities ban the dance, giving nightmares to Catholic Church authorities. The Archbishop of Paris banned it and the Roman Cardinal issued an interdiction against it being danced at any official occasion where the Queen might appear. However, many members of the Roman nobility who danced the tango were not happy about this interference in the dance halls. Some who had grown fond of the dance appealed to highly placed friends to talk to the more tolerant Cardinal Merry del Vale, who appealed to the Pope to ignore the pressure to have the Vatican ban it. But Pope Pius XI, one would imagine, was well aware of the popularity of the tango among Italians and the rest of Europe, so he decided he would not make up his mind until he had seen the dance for himself.

Consequently, in 1913, it was arranged for two young people of impeccable Italian nobility, a prince and princess, to give a demonstration of the tango for the Pope. The girl appeared in a modest dress with a black mantilla over her head, and they explained that the tango did not represent invitation to a path of degradation, but was a serious dance and that "the difficulties are great, so it is necessary to give total attention to it while dancing, in order not to make an undesirable step." The pope then invited them to give a demonstration while he watched from behind his desk. The couple danced in such a formal and passionless fashion that, according to the well-known teacher, Professor Picchetti, "the performance was more boring than indecorous."

The Pope commented that the dance seemed to emulate the contortions of Indians and Negroes, and asked tango dancers why they didn't prefer to dance "the more innocent Venetian Furlana," a sedate folk dance that was popular in Venetian salons, particularly during carnival. Some were afraid that the Pope's endorsement of the Furlana would be the *coup de grace* for the tango. However, thankfully, that proved not to be the case.

Not content with the Pope's reaction, the anti-tangoists mounted a last-ditch effort at changing people's minds, invoking Saint Augustine to their cause: "Dance is a circle at the center of which is the Devil." However, although the Archbishop of Paris banned it in Paris, the Central Catholic Church never did, leading one contempory commentator to remark: "Although the tango wasn't invited through Heaven's doors, at least it was admitted to Purgatory."

The French Lower Classes Were Anti-tango

Besides the moralists and religious fundamentalists, another important segment of French society did not take to the tango. Though it was a dance of the Argentine working class, the French working class abhorred it because in France the dance was associated with the aristocracy and upper class intellectuals. They felt it was the territory of the "grande and petite bourgeoisie," with which the French working class did not want to be associated.

Many of the conservative working class objected to the tango because they did not approve of the changes it brought about in women's attitudes and dress nor the inkling of women's independence that it foretold. They preferred the established dance favorites, primarily the classically vulgar polka, which was familiar and easy to dance. It wasn't until later when tango moved to Montmartre that some of the working class embraced it.

Some pro-tango French attempted to whitewash the tango to make it more acceptable, such as the prominent poet and music critic, Jean Richepin, who insisted that "the tango came in a direct line from the ancient Greeks." He raised the tango to intellectual heights never dreamed of when he presented the paper "Apropos du tango" to France's top intellectuals at the celebrated Academy Francaise and four other prestigious academic institutions. This opened the door for French and European intellectuals to consider the tango as a topic worth discussion. Others, such as Henri Bergson, tried to accentuate its importance: "The dance between sexes has the same importance as do words. One 'giro' (a woman turning around a man) tells more about the soul of a woman than ten volumes of Shakespeare."

Meanwhile Back in Buenos Aires

"Paris was the trampoline for the tango's final and complete conquest of Buenos Aires." (Oscar Himshoot)

"Tango entered Argentine society like intruders in unknown houses: without making noise and trying to pass unnoticed." (Nardo Zalko)

Because everything that happened in Paris was closely watched from across the Atlantic Ocean by upper class Argentines, it was inevitable that word about the obscene, forbidden tango being feted by Paris' high society would filter back there; the news was accompanied with much indignation and wringing of hands by respectable society. In 1913, the Buenos Aires newspaper, *La Nacion*, called the dance "ignoble, ugly, and inferior." An Argentine magazine, 'P.B.T.,' reported: "In Paris they are dancing the tango. Where? In the most aristocratic homes. Who is dancing it? The most distinguished and elegant women and men." The article went on to say that a dance such as the tango "could only give Argentina a bad reputation because in Paris there were "writers, artists and intellectuals, as well as politicians who would view Argentina as a nation in a bad light because of the obscene tango. Far from conquering the City of Lights, it seems as though we have put our wrong foot forward."

However, for Buenos Aires society, Paris could do no wrong as it continued to be the ultimate social arbiter for the middle and upper classes, who were at a loss as to how to stop tango's progress. One Argentine felt the tango was now vindicated with the prestigious laurels of foreigners.

In 1914, the "Guns of August" were the signal for Argentines living in Europe to return home although some waited until the actual German invasion of France. With World War I imminent, most of the Argentines left, indicating their intention to return as soon as possible. Paris was left bare of Argentines; the Spanish language journal ceased publishing for lack of readers. A few volunteered for the French Army and some went to New York, but most returned to Buenos Aires.

The tango that returned to Buenos Aires with the Argentine exiles was a very different dance from what it was when they had left. The lewd, rough edges acquired in Buenos Aires bordellos had been smoothed over, and it had been tamed into a form of dance acceptable to the sensitivities of European high society. It was called "tango a la francesa" and Argentines declared it "alien."

The returning exiles formed a new, exclusive social class of those who had been living in Paris. They found that in reaction to its success in Paris, tango had begun to penetrate a few high society salons of Buenos Aires. Nardo Zalko quoted aristocrat Elvira Aldao de Diaz, a pillar of porteño high society, who told about her encounters with tango while traveling to Paris on the luxury liner, La France: "L'aristocratie Francaise dansaint avec frenesie le tango." At first she was scandalized, but on arrival in Paris she saw more of it and claimed to be "enchanted." In 1912, Antonio De Marchi, an Italian baron who learned the tango in Paris, organized a well-received evening featuring Argentine dancers and singers at the ultra-respectable Palais de Glace in downtown Buenos Aires. The same Baron De Marchi had earlier decided to conduct his own test of tango's acceptance by organizing a soiree in a celebrated private mansion where by the end of the evening "the men and women had learned the dance." In 1913, he arranged for a large public ball and tango contest to be held at the Palace Theater in Buenos Aires, inviting important society women to judge the contest, which they did happily. A contemporary reporter in the journal Critica noted, "...the first night was formal, in keeping with attendance of the aristocracy, but the second night was quite the opposite. The atmosphere became 'populaire et democratique.' Even the Argentine dancers mixed with the public. On the second and third nights the entrance price was reduced from fifteen to five pesos, and it became much livelier."

After WW I was over, the Buenos Aires daily newspaper, *El Diario*, decided to investigate the extent of tango's acceptance in Buenos Aires. It found that there were one-hundred-seventy-five tango dances in just one week, "not counting private parties. Supposing there were one-hundred people at each dance, we would have 17,500 dancers."

At the end of the 1930s, when WW II loomed, Argentines living in Paris once more headed for Buenos

Aires. When the exiles arrived, the tango was beginning to be tolerated in some upper circles. High society balls had orchestras that played tangos, although they were not always publicized as such. In the thirties it was common for women to have dance cards that showed sets of the waltz that were actually tangos in disguise.

Although it continued to be frowned upon in theory, tango was actually danced in most upper class circles and at private parties and large balls—but only after midnight, once the dowagers had left. Tango enthusiasts were not overly concerned at these deceptions because once settled back into Buenos Aires, the exiles found that public opportunities to dance tango had increased dramatically after the passage of the universal suffrage law of 1912 tended to foster the legitimacy of tango in the working and middle class barrios. Tango had finally lost its bad reputation.

In spite of all the controversy, many Argentines were finally pleased and proud to have international recognition for something other than cattle and grain, although some would have preferred it to be in some area of achievement other than the tango. Nevertheless, it was true that tango had put Argentina on the map in a favorable light and it was absolutely *porteño*...unimaginable in any other place.

CHAPTER EIGHT

Tangomania: 1920s and 1930s

"Tango is the most hybrid musical product in existence; the elements of the tango are of such depth and complexity that it resembles classical music. A tango is like a Beethoven sonata...It can be understood as a symphony...in that it is not developed in forty minutes, but in three. But it contains the same elements. It is a music with an endless development capacity."

(Rodolfo Mederos, Master Bandoneonist, Buenos Aires)

At the beginning of World War I, Argentines living in Paris returned to Buenos Aires to find that tango, because of its unexpected success in Paris and Europe, had made inroads into the city's consciousness.

The tango the exiles brought back from Paris was not the one that had left Buenos Aires, but the sanitized version that had been adapted in Europe and North America. Argentines had difficulty recognizing it, but in order to secure acceptance with respectable Buenos Aires society, the unsanitized version of the tango made adjustments to its former style. The informal dance duels between men were transformed into a partnered dance, and men continued to practice with men throughout the next decade. Different styles emerged in the various barrios, leading to fierce competition among the men, who took the tango increasingly seriously and practiced assiduously in academias. Tango was still most important in the lower class barrios where it continued to be improvised and the goals of elegance and grace became universal.

Music Split into Two Paths

Tango music was experiencing fundamental changes that influenced the dance. Lyrics became more important, replacing the custom of throwing together words in a haphazard fashion. Traditionalist musicians, called the "Old Guard," were interested in preserving the essentials of tango's origins and the way tango was played up until the 1920s, with the beat as the central element and the melody of secondary importance. Traditionalist orchestras included the regular tango sextet, occasionally adding other instruments such as the clarinet, trumpet, or cornet. (Today the music from this period remains the most eminently danceable tango music and is played every day in milongas around the world.)

Evolutionists, or the "New Guard," were not content with what had already been played; they wanted to experiment with possibilities of melody, harmony and new techniques of interpretation and lyricism to create a more sophisticated music, different from the early traditional music that accented rhythm. When the piano was incorporated into tango orchestras, it so dominated the volume that other instruments were added, giving rise to what became the classic sextet of two bandoneons, two violins, a contrabass and a piano. When dance halls grew to accommodate thousands of dancers, typical tango orchestras increased to four bandoneons, four violins, a piano, and a contrabass.

Tango musicians were elevated to professional status and were in heavy demand for dance halls as well for accompanying the new silent films. For special performances, such as during Carnival when balls drew enormous audiences, orchestras were temporarily increased, and some of the larger orchestras had as many as thirty musicians. In 1917 and 1918, at joint performances, evolutionist Roberto Firpo and traditionalist Francisco Canaro's orchestras combined to feature twelve bandoneons. In 1920, evolutionist pianist and orchestra leader, Julio de Caro, began to codify the music for his sextet, replacing the unsophisticated style of the early tango bands to pursue a more disciplined and polished music. Contemporary tango historian Oscar Himshoot wrote that Italian composer De Caro was a creative genius who constantly introduced new musical concepts to the tango; the School of De Caro tango music so transformed the interpretation of tango that his influence is still felt today, and only Piazzolla has matched his influence.

In the twenties, a growing obsession with tango music and lyrics began to rival the already obsessive devotion to the tango dance. In Buenos Aires alone, there were more than one hundred tango orchestras of all sizes playing both styles. They played in any available venue: dance halls, social and sports clubs, cafés, confiterias (tearooms), and hotels. Some dance floors (or series of dance floors at one establishment) held thousands of dancers, making it difficult for dancers on the fringes to hear the music because microphones had yet to be invented, so the size of the orchestras grew even larger. There was also more demand for musical arrangers who could read music and who were familiar with harmony and counterpoint. By the end of the 1930s it was the musically literate Italians who dominated tango, and with the newly invented phonograph and radio, tango became more and more important.

In 1924, the Disco Nacional Odeon recording company began to sponsor contests for the composition of tango songs, and these became very popular because winners had their songs recorded and broadcast nationally; some musicians became famous after winning a contest. Originally tango musicians were male, but during the 1920s and 1930s, some women's orchestras were formed and were in demand, particularly for weddings, private parties and private dances, possibly because they might have been considered more suitable for events involving friends and family.

Because radio and records introduced tango music outside Argentina, tango musicians were soon in demand for live performances in Europe as well as in Argentina. In 1925 Carlos Gardel toured Spain playing to huge, enthusiastic audiences, and in the same year Canaro took his orchestra to Paris, where it was a tremendous success. In the 1930s other bands became prominent such as that of Osvaldo Pugliese and Anibal Troilo.

Each of the top orchestras had its followers who, night after night, followed them to whatever part of the city they were playing. Some orchestras played in as many as three places in one night. If the orchestras had played especially well, the dancers would chant slogans and the names of the orchestra as the musicians departed. In the mid-thirties, when Carlos Gardel began singing the tango song, lyrics became more important than the music, so much so that dancers began to stop dancing and stood still to listen to the vocalists. At this time, the traditionalist D'Arienzo inaugurated his 'new' style of a return to danceable tango music that favored rhythm over harmony and melody. His music had a recognizable lively strong, steady, danceable beat; it was said that "D'Arienzo returned the tango from the lips to the floor."

Osvaldo Pugliese

Pugliese influenced a change in the sound and feel of Tango in each of five decades beginning with his first hit, 'Recuerdo' (1921). His 'La Yumba' in 1943 was like a revelation from on high. You can hear his influence in almost every arranger's work since the start of the 20s." (Keith Elshaw, 'To Tango', Website)

"Pugliese's 'Souvenir" is so beautifully innovative it could be a 'tango for the year 3000." (Julio de Caro, 1924)

It is said that those who went to listen to Pugliese's music couldn't resist the desire to dance, and those who went to dance stopped dancing to listen. Some Argentines refer to him as "Saint Pugliese - Protector of Musicians." That's the way he is identified on the small paper cards printed and distributed in imitation of the popular paper icons of Catholic Saints. The cards are all over Buenos Aires: hanging on the rear-view mirror of taxis, taped onto school notebooks, stuck onto mirrors at home, or tucked into tango dancer's wallets. The idea of promoting him as a saint started out as a private joke of a Buenos Aires journalist, but almost a century later the cards are everywhere.

Not only was Pugliese revered for his extraordinary talent, he was also highly respected for his strong political ideologies that led him to participate in Argentina's left-wing politics. The black and white photograph on the card shows a red carnation on his dark suit, a reminder that whenever he was in prison for his political beliefs, his band would place a red carnation on top of his unmanned piano. He was jailed more than ten times in twenty years, and when he was anticipating an arrest, he wore his pajamas under his tuxedo because, he said, he "liked to be comfortable."

Pugliese was a Communist who practiced what he preached. He organized his orchestra as a cooperative, receiving the same salary as the members of his orchestra doing the same work. He also insisted that all his musicians participate in the decision-making regarding the orchestra's contracts and encouraged them to participate in the creative efforts of arranging and composing.

In 1936, he was so concerned that Argentina's musicians had no representation in matters regarding their working conditions that he helped form a musician's union. His band suffered consequences for their support of him, and from the mid-30s to the mid-50s there were times when members of his orchestra were barred from entering a club, or radio or television station to perform, even when they had contracts. Pugliese was blacklisted when Juan Peron came to power in the coup of 1955.

At one point, he was incarcerated along with others on the ship "Paris," docked on the river, which was used as a floating jail for political prisoners. Rumors circulated that the government had planned to sink the ship in order to rid themselves of "political pests," but the prisoners were finally released.

Through all his problems with authorities, the public never ceased to support him unequivocally. In "El Firulete" of July 1999, Albert Paz recounted an incident between Pugliese and the Buenos Aires police.

"While playing La Cumparisita (the song that traditionally ends tango dances), the police entered the club and ordered the dance to stop because Pugliese was not allowed to work. The organizers told the police that while the orchestra was playing and dancers dancing, nothing or

nobody would interrupt them. Word got to Pugliese about the imminent arrest, and he directed his musicians to continue playing the song over and over. The public caught onto the trick and kept dancing. The police grew impatient and uneasy and finally left. As the last beats of the tango concluded the longest Cumparisita ever, the thunderous applause and cheers brought a smile to Pugliese's face. Humbly, he stood up and pointed to his orchestra."

After Juan Peron had been ousted and then returned to power in 1973, realizing the power of Pugliese's popularity, he formally begged Pugliese to forgive him for his earlier mistreatment of him.

Pugliese was not only generous in sharing money with musicians; he was generous with his time and encouragement of young musicians. He was an exemplary and beloved teacher who accepted musicians from both Argentina and abroad and permitted them to serve apprenticeships in his orchestra. Many of them are still playing today, some with his daughter, Beba, who plays piano and leads one of today's most popular tango orchestras, Color Tango, which faithfully follows the style of Pugliese, including his trademark ending of each tango with the musical note 'sol', followed with an almost silent 'do.'

Pugliese's "La Yumba" is probably the most-played and beloved piece of tango dance music throughout the world, played someplace every day. It features the heavy accent on the first and third beat of the 4 x 4 rhythm, which is the most distinctive signature of the Pugliese. After La Yumba, tango was never the same. The culmination of his career was when he gave a concert at Buenos Aires' venerated Theatre Colon Opera House in 1995, the year of his death.

Lyrics

In the early days of tango, the lyrics were improvised and considered subservient to the music. Written lyrics didn't follow until after 1917, when the first tango song was written to fit particular music. The earliest lyrics, sung by payadores in the genre of folk music, were joyful and slightly comic with a melody frequently as background to a heavy African beat.

Early lyrics were simple in construction, and most had humor that depended on innuendo; many were just "self-descriptions of conceited compadritos telling the world of their virtues." Because the early lyrics were made up primarily by men of the *arrabales* who didn't spend much time contemplating the perplexities of life, these first refrains had a haphazard structure and no pretensions of seriousness or artistic value. This first music did not have the haunting sadness to the tunes that later became the signature of tango lyrics in depicting the depressing life of the *arrabales*. There was no attempt to set words to music in verses telling a story or describing a situation.

However, as early as 1874, tangos had begun to be sung around central Buenos Aires. Some of the improvised lyrics of the gauchos and blacks became popular and were passed along to other singers, but no two tangos were exactly the same. The subject matter was frequently that of the bordello and crude to the point of obscenity. Extemporaneous words were composed on the spot, and occasionally words were fitted to one or two early tangos, but this was not common. In any case, as a result of association with the brothels, lyrics were often pornographic, peppered with Lunfardo words and expressions. With the influx of European immigrants the nature of lyrics changed. Because the blacks and gauchos were almost all illiterate, the songs written by the literate

Italians came to represent the problems and cares of the immigrants, rather than those of the gauchos and blacks living amongst them. The changes they brought to lyrics were profound and changed the perception of tango forever

Lunfardo

"Lunfardo: Language of the Underworld and the Tango World" (Late 1800s)

Slang words and expressions are common to most urban areas, where sometimes as expressions of unity or out of necessity, the lower classes invent their own way of speaking to each other. It is almost impossible for outsiders to comprehend the meaning or the allusions in the songs.

Lunfardo, which became the language spoken in the conventillos of the slums, was a loose confection of the special vocabulary of gauchos, Italian immigrants, and peasants from the countryside which spread through the patios of the conventillo where the common bathrooms and cooking facilities were located. The jails were another source of Lunfardo vocabulary that emerged for a different reason. In the conventillos, words were invented in order to facilitate communication; in the jails, words were invented by prisoners to prevent guards from knowing what they were talking about among themselves. Lunfardo came to be known as the "language of thieves." By the end of the century, one-third of Italian speaking detainees in the prisons of Buenos Aires were young Italians. The use of Lunfardo also developed a strong association with prostitution because Argentines and immigrants used it when they met in the brothels; it was the language of the compadrones and compadritos.

Lunfardo was eventually used extensively in tango lyrics. It appeared occasionally in Argentine literature, but despite the fears of some at the time, it never caught on enough to become the dominant language of Argentina. The reasons were: 1) the primary schools of the marginal areas prohibited students from using Lunfardo 2) the relative mobility of Buenos Aires class structure permitted students of modest backgrounds to go to schools of better quality in other neighborhoods, and 3) the continued use of Spanish throughout Latin America (with the exception of Portuguese in Brazil.)

Interest in Lunfardo began to decline in 1943 when the military dictatorship outlawed the use of Lunfardo because it was thought that the vulgarity of the language was not good for Argentina's image. Consequently, hundreds of lyrics had to be revised in order to be permitted to be played on the radio or performed anywhere in Argentina. In 1949, President Peron repealed the law.

Lunfardo Today

"Lunfardo is not a dead language." (Marcelo Hector Oliveri, Academy of Lunfardo)

Although it used to be vulgar, today many Lunfardo words have become an acceptable part of contemporary Argentine language used by all levels of society and is considered 'chic' by some to use Lunfardo words and expressions in literature or when speaking.

Mr. Oliveri claims that new words and expressions are always being added to "The Dictionary of Lunfardo"; in 2004 there were 1710 new words added to the latest edition. The Academy of Lunfardo meets on the first Saturday of each month to discuss and analyze new words that might be added to the next dictionary. According to Mr. Oliveri, it is the youth of today that is inventing most of the new words, as was the case in the late 1800s when the young immigrants influenced Lunfardo.

The Tango Song - Tango Moved from the Feet to the Lips

In 1917 the first formally composed tango song with poetry carefully drafted to fit a currently popular tango was performed in a theater by Pascual Contursi in the cabaret Moulin Rouge in Montevideo. The song was an overnight success. 'Spicy' Lunfardo expressions told a depressing story of an abandoned lover's agonized thoughts while sitting in his room one night. Later in the same year, Carlos Gardel sang the same song, "Mi Noche Triste," (*My Sad Night*) at Esmeraldo Teatro de Buenos Aires, and it quickly sold thousands of copies of sheet music.

This tango song introduced the concept of set lyrics which until then had not been much more than words and phrases that were changed each time it was sung depending on the whim of each singer. The 'sung tango' poetry set to tango music telling a story or describing emotions and impressions, struck a note with the Buenos Aires public outside the 'sporting life' of the bordellos and tenements. The lyrics addressed a new audience with words that expressed the emotions of an underprivileged urban people. It was publicized as a "tango dedicated to anyone who had ever been disappointed in love, who would identify with the words and melancholy music." The new, written verses were called "the sung tango"—or "the tango song," to differentiate it from the previously improvised words that were usually gay and light-hearted. Many of the written verses were frequently about what emotions and ideas the writers wanted to convey, and although there were some comic lyrics, by and large they lost their joyfulness and began to reflect the hardships of ordinary people living in the barrios.

The sadness was due in part to the influx of Italian men with musical experience and Italian opera in their veins, and then tangos became overwhelmingly sad, melancholic and riddled with self-pity. Written from a man's viewpoint, the lyrics told of his pains, sufferings, dreams and desires. The men, at first always the main characters in the tango song, were embittered by loneliness, a lover's infidelity, girlfriends who lapsed into drugs or prostitution, or the indifference of a former friend. They were fatalistic about things ever getting better. They blamed fate for their failure. Only their mothers truly cared for them. (In 1960, research showed that one-third of tango songs from this period were about the protagonist's mother, with hundreds of lyrics written about how he had let her down, how she had always worked and suffered for him, and how she was the only person willing to forgive him and to offer uncritical and undemanding love.)

As tango made inroads into central parts of the city, it attracted the attention of experienced, serious musicians and poets. Upper class intellectuals began writing what they called "poems for the tango," and under their influence lyrics became romantic, nostalgic and much less threatening than those from the tough underworld neighborhoods. One of the most famous lyrists was the aristocratic Baroness Eloisa D. Silva, who wrote many popular tangos around the turn of the century even though tango was still prohibited in her social circle.

Besides switching content to the problems of ordinary individuals, many new tango songs began to take serious interest in the problems and unhappiness of people other then themselves by attacking unfair social conditions. They tried to raise people's social consciousness by exposing and criticizing a society that did not concern itself with unfortunates who were unable to help themselves. In melancholy fashion, the tango song commented on the burdens of a life of urban poverty, the fight for survival, the search for dignity in the conventillos, the disappointments in love, the loneliness and homesickness, the frustrations and anger; and misery, decadence and abandonment.

Other tangos were written for any occasion and to celebrate almost anything: a first or last love, a newfound or newly lost love, the disappointment of friends, the stunt tricks done on high-flying airplanes, the new fast trains, famous exotic cities and countries, the gauchos, new commercial airplanes, new automobiles, and the glory of certain foods and drink. There were even tangos written as commercial advertisements for furniture and clothing and homeopathic medicines, and a popular series of comic tangos poked fun at various professions with waiters, dentists and doctors as the brunt of many jokes. Name it and there was a tango written about it.

After the last two decades of the 1900s, anonymous lyrics began to be replaced by written, signed lyrics, most notably these of Angel Villoldo who between 1905 and 1920 wrote many songs that are still popular today. (He is credited with a sardonic song that became very popular about the Argentine law that fined a man fifty pesos if he insulted a woman.) Suddenly, instead of songs about pimps, prostitutes, drugs, and the killing of unfaithful lovers, tango lyrics told personal-type stories or expressed situations and emotions reminiscent of past times in an idyllic society. From 1917 through 1920, Pascual Contursi was a leading lyricist; during 1922 through 1935 Celedonio Flores and Enrique Cadicamo ruled supreme until the arrival of Enrique Discepolo on the tango scene. Homero Manzi and Catulo Castillo wrote many popular tangos between the 1930s and 1950s.

In the 1930s, the lyricist, composer, vocalist, Enrique Discepolo, became Argentina's foremost political and social philosopher, whose tangos are still widely appreciated and sung today. One of his most famous lines is from his tango, "The Junk Shop": "The 20th century is a trash heap. No one can deny it." He was cynical about the wealthy, as in his song, "What are You Going to Do?" - "What is needed is to collect a lot of money, sell your soul, raffle off your heart."

*"The tango is a sorrowful thought that can be danced." (***Enrique Santos Discepolo***)*

Enrique Santos Discepolo

From the 1930s through the 1950s Enrique Santos Discepolo outshone all other lyricists, and is considered to be the finest writer of tango lyrics of all time. He has gone down in tango history as an outstanding musician composer, vocalist, conductor, poet, actor, playwright, and filmmaker. Discepolo's earliest lyrics were bold and gay, but they soon turned serious when he began writing socially critical lyrics with themes of inequality and social injustice.

Discepolo was the son of an Argentine mother and Italian father orphaned as a child and raised in poverty. Through his talents as a writer and singer of tango songs, he became an intimate with leading Argentine intellectuals and was one of the tango's most important icons. Of all surviving tango lyrics, Discepolo's themes of social injustice and disillusionment continue to be particularly admired and popular throughout Argentina and much of the world.

As Fabrice Hatem, France's leading expert on tango lyrics explains: "Discepolo's descriptions of grotesque and unusual characters caused suspicion; his primary concern was the dearth of morality in human behavior and criticism of an unjust society was of secondary interest to him. He wrote of characters unlike those usually depicted in tango lyrics. In "Confession" he wrote of a poor man who wants the woman he loves to leave him so she could have a better life with someone else. She didn't want to leave because she was deeply in love with him but finally, after he beats her to within an inch of her life, she does. A year later he saw her out with an obviously affluent man and was so happy for her that he went home and "cried of happiness."

In "Malevage" a tough thug of the barrios falls so much in love that he begins to worry that his criminal behavior could result in his being locked up in jail and he would never be able to see his girlfriend again. He alters his behavior and becomes a coward. His friends think he has gone mad and he asks himself, "What has she done to me?" Then there was the satirical take on the theme of the abandoned husband when, instead of being desperate and ready to commit suicide, he is happy to be rid of the burden of marriage and is delighted to be able to spend time with his friends and mother.

In 1930 a military coup overthrew President Yrigoyen, a supporter of the poor who had only been in power for two years (following De Alvear who had been in power from 1922 to 1928.) The military dictator who followed him, General Uriburu, abolished the right to vote, causing the lower and middle classes to lose what small influence they had. Uriburu also did his best to stifle the voice of the tango, because he and the extreme right wing considered tango to be a source of cohesion among the people on the extreme left and right, thus making it dangerous.

In the late 1930s, when Argentines regained most of their political freedom the tango came out of the closet more popular than ever, invading the culture to become a symbol of the citizen's solidarity and pride.

> *The military regimes banned Discepolo's lyrics because they felt his songs about Argentina's "moral and material misery" did not match the rosy picture of Argentine society the dictators were attempting to portray.*
>
> *Discepolo's recordings of his own songs continuously increased his standing with both the ordinary people and the intellectuals and academics of Buenos Aires, where he was an honored member. As a vocalist he was most important for raising the status of the vocalists' vocation from the mundane to intellectual and social respectability.*

Some contemporary commentators on tango lyrics from this period lean heavily to socio-economic interpretations of lyrics. Alberto Paz, in his 'El Firulette' tango newsletter of February 1998 wrote: "Tango lyrics as a whole are a condemnation by the working class of the ethical, judicial, religious, cultural, and political norms and canons of a bourgeoisie society... that existed in the *arrabales*, which was an economic, social and political set of conditions established by a capitalistic society where the distribution of wealth was limited to a privileged few."

Discepolo dominated the ranks of vocalists from the thirties onward but he did not sing with an orchestra. However, his influence paved the way for the many vocalists who did sing with orchestras.

Orchestral Vocalists

Francisco Canaro was the first to integrate a full-time, permanent vocalist into his orchestra, and by the mid-1930s many orchestras had incorporated permanent singers in their groups. At first their contribution was minimal, and they had no more importance than any members of the band, but that soon changed.

One could hear on the radio the most important vocalists of the time when the most popular singers had thousands of fanatical followers. In 1934 this enthusiasm was revealed in an Argentine film titled, "Idols of the Radio," which featured singers Ada Falcón, Ignacio Corsini, Francisco Canaro, and others. At first vocalists singing with orchestras sang only portions of a song, but by the end of the 1930s as lyrics became more popular, they eventually began to sing entire songs. Visible evidence of their increased importance was that they were moved from performing at the side of the orchestra to the important position in front of it.

At first vocalists were male, but it wasn't long before female vocalists became as important as men. At first, in order to be accepted, women singers used men's names and dressed as men for their performances; one, Azucena Maizani, sometimes dressed as a gaucho. Later, some tango songs were written from a feminine point of view, and as women performers grew popular they no longer needed to dress as men. Outstanding women singers whose careers extended through the Golden Age of the 1940s and 1950s were Libertad Lamarque, Mercedes Simone, Azucena Maizani, and Tita Merello.

In the 1940s singers became so much a part of the orchestra that they became essential to an orchestra's success, as was the case in the U.S. during the same period. Many avid fans followed them wherever they sang. Not all tango singers performed with orchestras; the most notable was Carlos Gardel, acknowledged to be the greatest performer and tango singer of all time, who preferred to sing tangos with only his guitar as accompaniment.

Carlos Gardel

Carlos Gardel

"Carlos Gardel was, quite simply, the greatest singer of tangos who ever lived—and probably the finest individual talent ever to be associated with this particular form of popular music. I think he has the best voice of any popular singer in the 20th century." (Simon Collier)

"Carlitos" sings better every day." (Common 'saying' in Argentina)

More than seventy years after his death, Argentina continues its love affair with Carlos Gardel, affectionately called 'Carlitos' or "El Zonsal." (A bird of the pampas noted for its sweet song.) His is still the biggest name in tango, and it is impossible to over-emphasize his importance in legitimizing the tango during the 1920s and 1930s when he single-handedly took the vulgar dance and music of the brothels and tenements and metamorphosed it into the "tango song," giving it 'class' and respectability in Buenos Aires, New York, Paris, and the capital cities of Europe.

The tango song became even more popular after his death in 1935, assuming an importance equal to and frequently surpassing that of any of tango orchestras. The English-speaking world never became sufficiently familiar to appreciate his value as an artist and entertainer because he never recorded songs in English. But in the Spanish-speaking world and Europe, he established himself as the leading star of Spanish-language radio, recordings, and cinema. Just when he was making his mark in English-language American films, his life was cut short in the accident that prevented him from becoming the grand American movie star he might have been.

Carlos Gardel is recognized not only as a symbol of the tango, but also as the idolized image of the porteño. His face still dominates Argentine popular culture so much that even today it is impossible to escape his presence. One street in Buenos Aires was named after him in 1961; in 1973 a park square in Buenos Aires was dedicated to him and a Carlos Gardel subway station was established in 1985. Kiosks sell post cards and posters of him in a variety of different poses; billboards use his photograph to promote anything from toothpaste to automobiles, refrigerators, or holidays; school notebooks have his face on the covers; and small photographs of him hang next to Catholic saints on taxi drivers' rear view mirrors. His smile is used to sell anything from coffee mugs to cigarette lighters. There are large photographs of him on walls of private homes, cafés, restaurants, and bars, and one wouldn't be surprised to see his photograph in the churches! A Buenos Aires photo lab claims to have sold more than 350,000 pictures of him in the first twenty years after his death. Radio programs are still regularly devoted to him. Today there are active fan clubs all over the world whose members call themselves 'Gardelianos' who commemorate his birthday and death with special events and vow not to pass a single day without listening to at least one of his songs or watching one of his films.

In the Chacarita Cemetery where he is buried, there is a steady stream of pilgrims, both Argentine and foreigners who gather by his tomb. A bronze life-size statue of him stands on a pedestal covered with memorial plaques from tango clubs all over the world, and it is covered with flowers daily. Fingers of his right hand hold a perpetually lighted cigarette, as he used to do.

No other vocalist anywhere has come close to receiving the adulation given to Gardel. In the United States, the only comparisons are Elvis Presley and Frank Sinatra, but they fall far short of Gardel. One important difference is that Presley and Sinatra were the objects of frenzy primarily among girls and women. This was not the case with Gardel, who was, and continues to be, as popular among men and boys as with women and girls, in spite of recent hints about the direction of his sexuality.

For Argentine men he was and remains a role model for lower class males who were proud of his rise from the lower class arrabales to fame and success. They adored his acceptance into the very highest social circles. They loved the way he dressed in a classic distinguished manner, and he was always exceedingly well groomed. And they loved his common touch; his life of rags to riches represented life's possibilities. They all wanted to be like him, and many still do.

Although it was his voice that first drew people to him, it was his remarkable charisma and extraordinary presence — including his famous 'sweet smile'—that turned Argentines and the world into devoted friends and fans. Gardel was admired for his lack of pretense; in spite of his amazing fame and success, there was never anything of the prima donna about him. Throughout his dazzling career and the tumultuous tabloid-like attention his every move received, his head never turned. According to all reports, he remained natural, helpful to friends, colleagues, and acquaintances, he was and charmingly nonplussed about his success. He loved the adulation and the way of life it provided, but he never forgot or denied his humble roots in the Rio de la Plata— which he claimed was his spiritual birthplace.

"Carlos Gardel should have been born Argentine."
(Rodolfo Dinzel, 2006)

According to French records, Gardel was born in Toulouse in 1893. (Collier, one of his biographers, claims it was 1890.) He was the illegitimate son of a young woman "of modest means" and a married businessman, Paul Lasserre. In 1895, when Gardel was two years old, his mother, Berthe Gardel, took a boat for Buenos Aires in hopes of making a better life for her and her son. She worked as a laundress in Buenos Aires, and Carlos attended a local school where he supposedly sang in the school choir. In 1904 he left school to earn money, working odd jobs in the centrally located Abasto neighborhood where he lived.

It is not known exactly when he began singing for money in the local bars, cafés, and brothels, but within seven years after leaving school he had built a modest reputation. In 1911 he met and became friendly with a Uruguayan folk singer, Jose Razzano, who was also becoming known in Buenos Aires; the two formed a duo and became very popular singing Argentine folksongs. They began their partnership by touring small towns in Buenos Aires Province where their folk music repertoire consisted of country music, waltzes, and sambas. They did not sing tangos because the tango song did not yet exist.

In 1912 they made six gramophone recordings of Argentine folk songs, and between 1915 and 1917, the duo toured Brazil and Argentina. In 1917 they won an important contract to record their folk music. Later that year the 'tango song' was invented by a friend of Gardel's, and later that year he sang it at the Esmeralda Theater, in Buenos Aires. "Mi Noche Triste" became a milestone for tango—although not immediately.

It was not until 1923 that Gardel began singing exclusively tango songs. Although he wrote a few tango songs himself, he wanted to expand his repertoire and become active in encouraging writers to compose lyrics for tango music for him to sing. Later that year he made his first European tour, beginning with an enormous success in Madrid. Two years later, in 1925, when the Prince of Wales visited Argentina, Gardel and his partner were invited to perform for him; the Prince enthusiastically accompanied them on his "beloved ukulele" that he took with him everywhere.

Later that year, Gardel's partner developed a serious throat condition that required him to stop singing, so Gardel became a single act as a tango singer with guitar accompaniment. In 1927-1928 he was invited back to Spain, where he had a highly acclaimed tour before continuing on to Paris. His first performance there was at the nightclub, Florida, where he was received enthusiastically by an audience that included Josephine Baker, Maurice Chevalier, and the famous Japanese painter, Foujita, who lived in Paris.

The reviews were ecstatic. Le Figaro newspaper wrote about "the magnetic charm that he exercises on the public." The journal La Ramp described "...the astonishing star whose triumph each night at the Florida is indescribable. The enormous talent of this artist is incomparable. He is a true artist in the profound sense of the word." Gardel was surprised and moved. In a euphoric mood, he wrote to a Buenos Aires friend: "The sale of my records in Paris is fantastic. In the first three months, 70,000 were sold and the company is afraid they won't be able to meet the demand. A celebrated revue, La Rampe, in a luxurious end of the year presentation, has a color photo of me."

To another friend he wrote, "I debuted in the most difficult theater in Paris, The Empire, where the best artists in Europe appear. I am the 'star' that attracts the public, and I made a revolution because the audience asked me for ten encores. The journals say that even if I don't speak their language, the public understands what I'm singing only by the expression on my face." Another time he wrote: "I live like a millionaire in the best neighborhood of Paris, in one of the most comfortable apartments."

Gardel stayed on in Paris and in 1929 starred in a charity ball at the highly prestigious Opera. Gardel also sang ten successive nights at the Casino de Cannes in front of a public consisting of European nobility and international 'haute bourgeoisie.' In 1928 he was being paid 4000 francs a day, more money than France's top performer, Maurice Chevalier, was earning. He became the darling of the aristocracy as well as the idol of the common people. He was friendly with the Baron de Rothschild, the Aga Khan, Charles Chaplin, and 'everyone who was anyone' in Europe, including heads of State.

The 1920s and 1930s were exciting years for Gardel. He performed in Argentina, Uruguay, Brazil, Spain, and France, and beginning in 1933 he commuted between New York and Buenos Aires. Gardel's films were all immensely popular and made enormous amounts of money for their producers. He starred in nine American films for Paramount: four made in France and five in New York. All except one were in Spanish; the one not in Spanish was in English: "The Big Broadcast of 1935" starred, among others, Bing Crosby, George Burns and Gracie Allen. Gardel made more than 900 tango recordings, and at one time he had *two records of the same song competing with each other for sales—one with an orchestra and the other with only guitar accompaniment. Both versions broke sales records on the first two days.*

He never returned to Buenos Aires to live, and he explained his reasons on one of his only two visits to Buenos Aires between 1931 and 1935 in an interview for the Buenos Aires journal, "Sintonia,": "When one has known Paris, when one has been applauded by kings, one could never be satisfied to return to live in Buenos Aires...It isn't that Buenos Aires doesn't please me, far from that. But she is terribly monotonous, our city! And it is the fault of the Argentines themselves, full of haughtiness. Here, if people laugh, to their great shame, they apologize for it. In Europe they are more extroverted. They enjoy life. But I carry Buenos Aires in the deepest part of my heart, and if I ever hear anyone speak ill of it I will tell him that it is heresy."

Even if he was no longer living in Buenos Aires, Gardel continued to keep in touch with the porteños with whom he felt so much affinity. In 1932, Gardel made the first of many broadcasts to Buenos Aires from Paris, and in 1934 the Radio Broadcasting Company of New York broadcast him singing to Buenos Aires via telephone lines. He continued live broadcasting to Argentina until his plane crash in 1935.

Gardel's Persona

To the Argentines and many Spanish-speaking countries, Gardel has remained the shining example of escaping poverty because he made it out of the slums without giving up his honesty, dignity or honor. He is remembered with respect because of his loyalty to friends, his modesty, his friendliness, his humility and his generosity. Out of this respect, because legend has it that "Adios Muchachos" was the last song he sang before his death, in many countries it has become the custom not to be played for dancing in milongas.

Gardel was always an attentive son, and his Mother, 'Dona Berta,' was the only woman with whom he kept in close touch. While he was in Europe, she made fourteen transatlantic crossings between Buenos Aires and France to visit him.

Although women threw themselves at him, he seemed to have had only one rather serious but mysterious relationship, with Mrs. Sadie Baron Wakefield, an American socialite. His love affairs, if they ever existed, were not publicized. It was assumed that since Gardel was the epitome of the porteño man, the fact that he never spoke of his love life seemed to indicate to some that he was a man of honor and "did not speak about such things" to the public. He was referred to as a 'ladies' man' or "pinta" which is Lunfardo for good looking. He was handsome and very conscious of his image, but acquaintances insisted he was not proud. He had a sweetness about him that made it possible for him to talk his way out of anything. Women were integral to the tango audience, and the element of love was important. His songs projected the porteño ideal of love and the relations of a man to a woman. In a recent analysis of ninety-nine of Gardel's recorded tangos in terms of content and image, fifty-four percent had to do with suffering from love.

Gardel, however, did publicize his love for his racehorse, Lunatico. He was seriously interested in horseracing and spent a lot of time at racetracks. He was proud to be a good friend to many of the Palermo race track jockeys and trainers, posing frequently for photographs with them at the tracks It was no secret that he was a heavy better and lost a great deal of money gambling on the horses.

In April 1935, he was booked to do a publicity tour of the Caribbean for Paramount movies and RCA Victor records. It was to be his first tour by air, and when visiting family members in Toulouse in September 1934, he told them about it. His aunt asked him, "Aren't you afraid to fly in an airplane, Carlos?" Gardel answered, "No, not afraid, but apprehensive." On June 14, 1935, as his plane was taking off from Medellin, Colombia, it crashed into another plane on the airfield. Gardel and his friend and lyrist, Alfredo Le Pera, were both killed. The outpouring of grief was astounding. Throughout Argentina, and in some other countries, radio stations agreed not to play tangos for a week.

His body was flown to New York to be sent back to Buenos Aires and didn't arrive until the end of 1935. In February, 1936, a funeral and wake were held in the Luna Park Sports Center, the equivalent of New York's Madison Square Garden. The procession of the cortege was celebrated with "flowers cast from every balcony and every door" as it wound its way forty blocks from Luna Park to Chacarita Cemetery.

In 1985, in commemoration of fifty years since his death, there were scores of plays, exhibits, art contests, concerts at the Teatro Colon and other concert halls performed in his honor. In remembrance of his love for horseracing, the Palermo racetrack held a special Gran Premier Carlos Gardel race. In neighboring Chile they observed an entire week of homage to his memory.

Other Vocalists

Besides appearing with orchestras, vocalists in the 1920's and 1930's increased their popularity by making phonograph records and singing on the radio. In the early 1900s, the recording industry grew amazingly. Between 1902 and 1910 there were over 1,000 records released in Buenos Aires, one-third of which were tangos. From 1910 to 1920, one-half of the 5,500 records produced were tangos.

Radio

The radio was the most important phenomenon for the proliferation of music in the 20th century. In the 1920s, tango received the definitive seal of approval in Argentine society through the radio, first in Buenos Aires then throughout Argentina. While the tango had been around for several decades in theaters, cafés, bars and other places of entertainment, most families, especially the women, only heard about the tango from what men told them about it. Although records were popular, not everyone could afford a phonograph and the records. On the other hand, with the invention of the inexpensive radio, which just needed a flick of the knob to provide music all day and night, the tango became all encompassing. There were more than fifteen broadcasting stations in Buenos Aires alone and the tango penetrated into homes of all social classes.

The first vocalists to sing on the radio did it more as an adventure and as a means of promulgating tango than a means of earning money. In 1924, Rosita Quiroga, one of the first vocalists to sing on radio, said: "At first we didn't earn a penny; we were paid with coffee and cookies." In 1924-25 Carlos Gardel became an idol of the radio, making his appearance in front of a microphone for a 'café con leche and a package of biscuits,' but by 1928 he was earning "the important sum of five-hundred pesos for each performance."

By 1930, one could hear the most important vocalists of the time on the radio. The most popular singers had thousands of fanatical followers. In 1934, this enthusiasm was revealed in an Argentine film titled, "Idols of the Radio," which used singers such as Ada Falcon, Ignacio Corsini, Francisco Canaro, and others as stars. As the popularity of radio and tango grew, tango artists and their careers and private lives became the focus of intense public interest, and they began to be better paid, eventually receiving excellent remuneration.

Radio Advertising

Radio station owners soon realized there was an opportunity for making important money by charging for the advertising of consumer products. The recording companies began lending their tango musicians and vocalists to the radio stations, telling them they didn't need to be paid because they were receiving free publicity — which would help the sales of their records. Oscar Himshoot wrote in his "Club de Tango" magazine: "The performers would sometimes receive a package of cigarettes, a coffee or a drink and, if they were lucky, they might be given money for transportation to and from the radio station. Because the advertisers frequently paid the stations in products rather than cash, the artists found themselves going home with "boxes of soap, chandeliers, cans of oil or Victrolas."

The most famous of the tango orchestras and vocalists were not eager to work for peanuts, and the radio stations were not able to pay their high fees, so the stations had to invent new stars for their programs. They searched out and promoted artists who had not yet attained top ranking, but who were, nevertheless, good performers. Women artists were especially glad to perform on the radio because they could work during the daytime and avoid the risks of venturing out to theaters in the evening. Male singers, because of their trained voices, came to be in demand as radio announcers and some sang tangos in between their announcing duties.

In 1932, Carlos Gardel made the first of his series of three radio appearances from outside Argentina. The first one was for the radio station, Radio Colonial de Paris, and in 1934 he broadcast two programs via telephone for NBC in New York City. In 1935, Buenos Aires' Radio Callao broadcast a program devoted exclusively to his memory.

Later there were talk programs such as "The World and Tango," "Tango and its Stars," and "An Appointment with Tango" in which commentators discussed different aspects of tango music and song, announced news of performances, and held interviews with prominent stars. Radio stars became so important that many monthly magazines featured and documented the lives of vocalists. In 1924, the magazine Radio Cultura was one of the first Argentine magazines totally dedicated to radio and radio personalities. In 1940, one of the most important tango programs in memory, Glostora Tango Club, began broadcasting programs that continued to be popular for eighteen years.

Films

In 1921, Rudolph Valentino danced the first Hollywood tango in the film "The Four Horsemen of the Apocalypse." Although it propelled him to fame, his costume confounded the Argentines. He was dressed as a sort of bastardized Argentine gaucho in white wide, gathered pants, full-sleeved shirt, colored cloth waistband, high leather boots,

Mexican poncho, neckerchief, and black Spanish flat-brimmed hat. He would have been laughed off any Buenos Aires street corner. But the niceties of historical accuracy have seldom stopped Hollywood from doing what it thought would appeal to the paying public, and Valentino, with his Argentine Tango-dancer style pomaded hair, immediately became famous as the epitome of the cinema's 'Latin Lover.' The film was followed by other Hollywood movies of the same ilk in which they introduced popular tango music such as "El Chocolo," "Cumparsita," "Bolero," and "Kiss of Fire."

With the advent of sound during the thirties, many tango orchestras and vocalists were featured in films. In 1933 Carlos Gardel played in a movie called "The Melody of the Arrabale," and in the same year the film "Tango" - the first Argentine sound film - had an array of tango stars and orchestras. The end of the 1930s saw the beginning of a lessening of interest in tango in films with the appearance of the Black Bottom and other dances from the U.S. and Great Britain. However, at this point, Argentina was just gearing up for its most prolific and creative period of tango, referred to as The Golden Age. From 1940s to the advent of the dictatorship in the mid-1950s, tango invaded and occupied the heart and soul of Argentina.

Tango in Paris during the Twenties and Thirties

"After money, dance is today all that Paris loves...idolizes. Each class has its social dance...from poor to rich, small to grand, everything is dance. It is a fury, a universal taste." (Flaubert, Le Educational Sentimentale)

At the end of World War I, Paris once again beckoned to the Argentines who swarmed back across the Atlantic. Thanks to Argentina's mineral riches and the beef and grains consumed by the French and British armies, Argentina had profited enormously from the war. Rich Argentines were richer than ever, so as soon as the war was over, there was no hesitation about heading back to their beloved Paris. This time, crossing with them were tango musicians and dancers, many whom had become famous at home and hoped for even greater success in Paris. France welcomed them with open arms.

During the war, public balls had been banned in France but the tango managed to stay alive at private affairs and in clandestine dance halls. The prohibition on public dances wasn't yet lifted when Parisians began to seize on any occasion to organize big, important balls, such as the one given at the Opera for President Wilson on his visit to Paris to champion the League of Nations.

Paris had always had the reputation for being a city of pleasure and dance, and once the war was over, citizens enthusiastically turned to both. Author Andre Warnod wrote in 'Les Bals de Paris: "One could say that right after the war, Paris thought of nothing but the dance...tango was king. In other times it was dance for those watching, but at present one dances for one's own pleasure. With the tango, the dance has become essentially an egotistical pleasure."

Some, such as Louis Chevalier, professor of social history at College de France in Paris, noted that in Paris the 1920s and 1930s were called the "crazy years," referring to the obsessive interest in pleasure: "One of the reasons without doubt is the influx of strangers. They invaded the luxurious establishments close to Place Pigalle and Place Blanche where, during this Époque as in the past, were the essential parts of the 'grande machine du plaisir.' "

After landing in France, Argentine musicians, performers, and tango teachers headed straight to Montmartre which had changed little from when it was their center before the war. Artists such as Picasso, Matisse, Van Gogh, and Toulouse-Lautrec felt at home among the destitute poets, artists, prostitutes, petty crime, drugs, and dance halls that reminded them of the bar brawls of Buenos Aires. Artists such as Maurice Utrillo painted the small gardens and Toulouse-Lautrec built his reputation painting the insides of dance halls. Mostly, the Argentines installed themselves in Pigalle, the red light district at the bottom of the hill in Montmartre.

The second wave of tango from Buenos Aires to Paris followed the same route as the first, via Marseilles. Two famous tango bandoneon players, Manuel Pizarro and Genero Esposito, secured a contract to play tango in a Marseilles cabaret, 'Tobaris', but they dreamed of playing Paris. After their Marseilles contract ended, they went to Paris. Two months after arriving, Pizarro formed his own orchestra and sent for his three brothers and other musicians from Buenos Aires. Pizarro's orchestra played non-stop tango for eight straight years, alternating at prestigious cabarets and dance halls all over Paris, including Pavillion L'Armenonville in the Bois de Boulogne, Mimi Pinson on the Champs Elysees, the Perroquet, and L'Elegance. He came to be known as the 'ambassador of Tango' and was followed by a stream of other tango orchestras from Argentina.

The upper classes danced to Pizarro's music dressed, as before the war, in designer gowns and tuxedos, surrounded by the most luxurious settings. But the musicians, who were accustomed to perform only in tuxedos or black three-piece suits in Buenos Aires, were forced by law, to play the tango incongruously dressed as South American cowboy-gauchos, like so many misfits dressed incorrectly for a costume party. They must have felt silly and irritated to look like country bumpkins.

To have urban, sophisticated Argentine musicians and vocalists dressed as gauchos was a ludicrous concept because the gaucho was an illiterate and unsophisticated man of the countryside, at home with horses and cows. As with so much in French society, the basis for this anomaly was political. The powerful French musicians' labor union, angry over the perceived notion that foreign musicians would take work from French musicians, incited the government to pass legislation decreeing that all foreign musicians and entertainers had to appear in the traditional costume of their country. Thus, tango musicians and singers were forced to leave their tuxedos in their suitcases. They protested the humiliation but complaints landed on deaf ears, and the law remained in force until World War II.

On remarking the public's fascination with gaucho clothing, some entrepreneurs and managers wrote into their contracts that tango entertainers traveling to and from Europe had to wear their gaucho costumes, which explains the many period photographs of Argentine musicians posing in their gaucho outfits against the rails of luxury liners to and from Europe.

Argentine Musicians Dressed as Gauchos - Paris

Paris Cowboys

The tango lyricist, Enrique Santos Discepolo, visited Paris, and on his return to Buenos Aires gave a radio interview in which he spoke of his astonishment at what he had witnessed:

"I never saw so many gauchos as I did in Paris. Paris was infested with unbelievable and inexplicable gauchos.... There were gauchos in gold lamé with huge velvet flowers; there was an unforgettable gaucho who wore a suit entirely embroidered with semi-precious stones and whom young people dubbed, 'the gaucho with stones,'...another was seen in the Lapin Agile (nightclub) in a white suit embroidered with twenty small boats. The last one was named 'le gaucho marin.'"

A sign of the Argentine obsession with Montmartre was in tango lyrics. Baudelaire said, "To look for the soul of a poet you must look at his work to find the words that appear there the most frequently. That word will betray his obsession." In keeping with the idea of writing tango lyrics about anything and everything, Nardo Zalko noted: "The word recurring in Argentine Tangos about the French capital is Montmartre, even more than Paris. Some titles are: "Nuits de Montmartre" (Montmartre Nights), "A Montmartre" (To Montmartre), "Lune de Montmartre" (Montmartre Moon), "Montmartre Quartier Bien-Aime" (Montmartre, "My beloved Neighborhood), "Petites Rues de Montmartre" (Little Streets of Montmartre), Souvenirs de Montmartre" (Memories of Montmartre), "La Fleuriste de Montmartre" (The Florist of Montmartre), etc. No neighborhood in Montmartre was left out, as if the list of tango names was a resume of the streets and dramas of the human comedy of Montmartre."

The Princes of Montmartre

Many French people living in Montmartre identified themselves with Argentine music; some, particularly the men, even took on the manners and tastes of 'porteños' by wearing a light-colored felt slouch hat, a white scarf at the neck, and buttoned shoes, 'a la mode' of Buenos Aires. Such was the attire of the men who frequented one of Montmartre's most famous cafés, the Lapin Agile, where tango was played and danced almost non-stop.

The famous French singer and entertainer, Maurice Chevalier, said: "Le tango triomphait avec les princes de Montmartre. Il ne se passait pas de nuit sans que des batailles rangees eussent lieu entre Argentins et autres clients sous les pretexes les plus futiles. Un regard de femme, un mot mal compris a travers les bruits de l'orchestre de la danse." ("The tango is triumphant with the princes of Montmartre. Not a night passes without confrontations between the Argentines and other clients, under the most futile pretexts. A glance of a woman, a word misinterpreted over the noise of the dance orchestra.") A character in the novel, "Le Jouet" by Argentine writer, Alberto Arlt, 1926, declared, "They say that in Paris those who know how to dance the tango can marry millionaires...me, I'm going to leave... I'm going to go there."

In addition to Argentine playboys who flocked to Paris after the war, another kind of Argentine man arrived on the tango scene. Francis de Miomandre, in his "Le Greluchon Sentimental," wrote about "the worldly, dancing, gigolos" that peopled Montmarte after the war.

"They were all handsome. Moreover, they found themselves at the transitory moment where their beauty attained a sort of perfection. They dressed divinely. Traveling in all circles, having expensive tastes and modest resources, they had no professions and danced better than the professionals. They passed their time in the dance halls, where they preferred dancing with women of a certain age but also courted actresses and demimondaines who frequented fashionable dance halls, bars and restaurants in hope of having one of the foreigners fall in love with them." Miomandre went on to say: "Sometimes, if the gigolo was sentimental, he ended up returning to his homeland with one of these women he'd seduced for amusement but, tiring of her, he would then abandon her to some sort of brothel in Buenos Aires."

There were also the professionals who came to Montmartre looking for European 'merchandise' that was so prized in Argentina. The journal, *Detective*, reported a conversation with a professional gigolo. "Argentine men asked me to find them new women to take to Buenos Aires. I sold Juliette to the first buyer; she had only one blouse and a terrible dress. He dressed her like a queen and took her to Bordeaux, but she slipped out of his hands and returned to me. It was understood between us. I sold her five times.... The buyers were not able to complain to the police."

The popularization of the tango did not diminish its continuing brilliance in society salons. In 1922 the Argentine ambassador in Paris celebrated the Argentine election of 1922 with a reception in which Pizarro's orchestra played tango. Pizarro related his surprise to see French Princess Murat socializing with the musicians. "It's strange, because in Buenos Aires the tango is still 'mal vue' ("seen badly") even if in Paris it is played in the salons of the highest society."

Tango Musette and the French Working Class

Tango's popularity at last filtered down to the French lower classes, which had originally treated it with deep suspicion because of its association with the aristocracy. One event that helped to remove the aristocratic stigma took place on a 14 July, the Bastille Day celebration— Paris' annual blowout that celebrates the working class and its revolt against rule by the aristocracy. To commemorate tango's working class origins of 'musique populaire' or 'musique musette'), the city of Paris contracted with Pizarro's orchestra to play tango music for dancing in the streets. The musicians were put on a bus that traveled all over Paris, making stops to play at the usual places where Bastille Day is feted with music and dance. After this, the proletarian classes soon embraced the tango enthusiastically, and it became popular to take tango lessons somewhere other than with those teaching the upper classes. One teacher advertised 'very inexpensive tango lessons' on a small poster in the working class neighborhood of Montmarte. Another woman billed herself as 'the cheap tango teacher' at the local billiard hall.

The tango thus invaded the domain of the Bal Musette, the name for dance halls frequented by the middle and lower classes of French society. The tango retained some of the characteristics of the early tango and became known as the Tango Musette, still danced today.

Montmartre to Montparnasse: The Big Move

"By the 1920s, Montparnasse was so famous that one could, it was said, buy a direct ticket from Des Moines, Iowa to the Café du Dome." (International Herald Tribune, June 12, 1999)

"Montparnasse people are broadminded, where what would be a crime elsewhere is just a peccadillo." (Kiki, the "Queen of Montparnasse")

In 1910 a new Métro line, number 4, opened which enabled people to travel easily from the north of Paris to the south. Artists, and with them Paris night life, had begun to move south of the River Seine to the Montparnasse area on the Left Bank, from "one mountain to another," partly because Montmartre's seedy bordellos, with accompanying drugs and crime infecting the neighborhood of Pigalle and Montmartre, were controlled by underworld characters. Because it was less dangerous than Montmartre, Montparnasse became a gathering place for serious painters, writers, musicians, journalists, and artistic dilettantes, French as well as foreigners. It suddenly became the most important tango venue in Paris. Pizarro's orchestra inaugurated the dance floor of "La Couple" in Montparnasse on the other side of the River Seine, which became the new center for tango throughout the next decade.

The end of the thirties saw a diminishing interest in tango in Paris and other cities when the Charleston, the Fox Trot, and other new dances from the United States and Great Britain began to invade tango dance floors. This didn't happen in Argentina because the global revolution in communication had not yet taken place, so Argentines continued dancing tango with a fervor never seen before.

DEDICADO A BELGICA
BELGIQUE
BELGICA
TANGO
para PIANO
ENRIQUE DELFINO
$ 0.70

CHAPTER NINE

Tango's Golden Era in Argentina: World War II to 1955

"You could put on twenty stations on the radio and all you would ever hear were Tango.... Tango impregnated Argentine life... everyone sang or whistled tango.
Your Mother got up in the morning to do the laundry and she sang Tangos.
You sort of were born with the Tango inside you."
(Pupy Costello, Buenos Aires, teacher and performer)

At end of the 1930s with all Europe on the brink of war, Argentines living in Paris once again packed their bags and headed home to Buenos Aires. There they discovered that the tango had been enthusiastically taken up by the working and middle classes and even had a tentative foot in the door of upper class salons. The "déclassé" dance from the slums of Buenos Aires created by primarily non-Argentines had emerged into a national icon.

How was it that a dance invented by a few men living within an area of a few square city blocks in the seediest sections of Buenos Aires managed to create an dance for the entire, immense country of Argentina? Evidence suggests that throughout its history, tango's fortunes were greatly influenced by both domestic and international events, sometimes beneficial, sometimes not.

During and after World War II, Argentines were better off than ever before. Argentina remained neutral until the last days of the war, having benefited from a profitable relationship with Nazi Germany, which permitted them to ship beef, cereals, and mining products to Europe without U-boats attacking them. In August 1945, in the last gasps of the war, Argentina eventually declared war on Germany and Japan. Wealth in Argentina was more evenly distributed after World War II than it was after World War I. Employment was high, and people had plenty of money to spend on entertainment, which increasingly meant dancing tango.

Because of the great distances between Argentina and Europe and North America, the new dances and music of Rock and Roll and rhythm and blues that replaced the tango elsewhere had failed to reach Argentina, which meant that social dancing was pretty well confined to the tango.

Tango was Everywhere

Throughout the 1940s and early 1950s, Argentines were obsessed with tango. The radio played tango music every day, all day. Cafés, confiterias, bars, and restaurants played tango records, had tango on the radio, or had live orchestras. Ballrooms were open seven nights a week until five or six in the morning; during the day there were places to dance tango at lunchtime, matinees, and teatime - to recorded or live music. Argentine films began to feature tango singers and large tango orchestras.

Advertising in newspapers, magazines and radio sponsors unabashedly used the tango craze to sell everything imaginable. Many of the products had tenuous links to the tango: "If you want to have a good time dancing and not suffer a disaster, wear El Batacazo socks." Or, "Dance free at your favorite club during Carnival wearing a new suit from the Great Tailor Shop Paramount;" or "Keep dancing with Quilmes beer."

Cabarets flourished throughout Buenos Aires. The Luna Park sports arena held regular dances attended by masses of people. A schooner docked at La Boca on summer nights had tango dances on the decks with music flowing throughout the riverside barrios as hundreds danced on the wharves of San Telmo and La Bocca. Downtown theaters removed their seats to create huge dance floors with a festive ambience created by people in the balcony throwing confetti on the dancers below them.

Unprecedented numbers of dancers crowded into all sorts of venues. Neighborhood social, cultural, and sports clubs sponsored dances, and important soccer clubs with large stadiums rented them out for giant tango dances. Some clubs made enough money to build their own stadiums. The most important were in La Boca, San Telmo, Amagro, Palermo, and Villa Crespo—all still popular today. In 1941 the Boca Juniors soccer club announced the inauguration of their new covered dance floor with a capacity of 15,000 dancers. El Palacio Skating advertised that their dance hall was the largest in all of South America and claimed it could hold 30,000 dancers "in comfort." El Parque Japonés advertised a dance floor of 8,000 square meters, with 2,000 tables and 8,000 chairs and the best prices in town: entrance for women was .50 pesos; for men the price was 1.50 pesos and matinees were free for everyone.

In the center of town, dance floors became so crowded that dance styles changed when couples were forced to take shorter steps to keep from bumping into other dancers. This spawned a new, more subtle, close embrace style of dancing using mostly walking body movements, which is still the most popular style in Buenos Aires and other parts of the world. The more elaborate steps of the orillero style continued to be danced in the fringe *arrabales* where there was more floor space.

It was estimated that in any given week during the peak of the Golden Era in the 1940's, there were approximately 350 organized tango dances in Buenos Aires and the few large cities in Argentina; (some reports are as high as 600.)

Why was the tango so popular? During the forties, the tango had continued to evolve with dramatic changes in the music, lyrics, and the tango song; dancers were perpetually attracted by the challenges of improvisation. During this period, the musical tempo of the tango changed from the quick 2 x 4 to a slower 4 x 4, with dance styles altered to suit the new rhythm. The size and instrumental make-up of tango orchestras also changed and arrangers became pivotal to the larger orchestras. New themes for lyrics were introduced and the role of vocalists increased radically. Finally there were many new and different types of venues for dancing at public halls and neighborhood clubs which made tango more and more accessible.

Where They Danced

"C'est comme l'opium, ça intoxique." ("Le temps du tango" by Leo Ferre)

By the end of the 1930s Buenos Aires had hundreds of tango orchestras of all sizes and styles that played wherever there was a space to dance. Most evening milongas had two orchestras that alternated tango with swing and Fox Trot music, usually starting with the lively Paso Doble. The titles of the songs were not announced, but there was a short interval between each piece of the continuous music.

Many bars and confiterias had tango shows three times a day featuring popular singers. Performer Maria Nieves recalled: "The working class went to the matinee and early evening shows, and society people mostly went to the late night shows. If there were no live orchestras, there was a jukebox or just the radio."

Milonga (Tango Dance Hall) in Buenos Aires - 1936

Public Dance Halls and Neighborhood Clubs

Codes of the Forties

Earlier "free for all" behavior at dances became a thing of the past. Dance venues developed rigorous codes for dress, dance floor etiquette, and personal behavior, in addition to proficiency in the tango before being permitted to enter the dance hall. This was an era of strict moral codes regarding the sexes. A milonguero from this period explained: "Women were highly respected, and when they were growing up, men were indoctrinated to think about their own mothers and sisters when dealing with a lady. Men greeted women by removing their hats, offering their seats in public transportation, and opening doors for them, and polite language was always used in their presence." Men who did not observe the codes of the milongas found themselves without dancing partners.

Milongas in neighborhood clubs, at private parties, or public dances were decorous affairs frequented by dancers of all ages; single chaperoned women were all reputable and known in the barrio where the milonga was held. Dancing was considered to be the main reason for attendance at milongas, and there was very little overt socializing between the sexes. Off the dance floor the sexes stayed separate. The girls all had chaperones—older women, usually members or friends of the family who took their duties seriously, surveying the dance floor assiduously for fraternizing with the opposite sex. Occasionally boys and girls were permitted to walk as a group to or from the milonga, but they were closely monitored by the chaperones.

Juan Carlos Copes described milongas in his barrio in the 1940s and 1950s: "In my club, one side of the dance floor was called "the capital," the other side was called "the provinces." The girls from the provinces were on one side, the girls from the capital on the other. We, the milongueros, were in the centre of the floor. We observed the following ritual: as a beginning dance for example, I had to dance with girl number one, then girl number two, and so on. The girls from the provinces were ranked from one to fifty, and the girls from the capital were ranked from fifty to one-hundred. The girls from the capital were prettier; they all were accompanied by their mothers. The girls from the provinces came by themselves (they were somehow unprotected). But I had to dance with the number one first. The milongueros watched you and would either approve of you or not. This was an unwritten law. This was the university: I got my Ph.D. as a milonguero."

Maria Nieves says that women who danced were there for enjoyment of the dance, not to meet the opposite sex. She described her neighborhood club experience during the 1940s, which she claimed was similar to other barrios. She reports that the "tarty" women went to the bars and café to dance, not the neighborhood clubs: "I am a tango dancer who was brought up with the tango. It was the time when all the barrios had clubs. I used to go on both Saturdays and Sundays. On Thursdays and Fridays, we used to go every single time there was a dance, not downtown, always in the clubs in the barrios. A decent girl went to the club just to dance, and she would dance with a "ronoso" (meanie) and with a "groncho" (swarthy) and with a mummy's boy – mummy's boys were hardly ever good dancers. We would dance with everybody—with Negroes, too. We were swept away by our love for the tango. We just loved to go dancing. We didn't go out looking for sex, none of the girls in our barrio did; we didn't care what the man looked like. It was a nice, beautiful pure group of girls, interested only in the tango."

Both women and men dressed carefully and properly. Men wore impeccably starched white shirts, ties, and three-piece suits. Shoes had to be highly polished, shaving lotion slathered on profusely, and hair groomed with gomima (styling gel), and combed towards the back. Some men won approval when they placed a folded white handkerchief in the left hand, so as not to offend their partners with a sweaty hand.

During this period, there were still more men than women, and men and boys were not permitted in the dance halls unless they had proven that they were good enough to be worthy partners. In many dance halls and local clubs, boys and men were not allowed to enter unless they had passed a test given by older male dancers, and if they failed they had to continue practicing with men.

Learning to Dance

Long-time star of the traveling show "Forever Tango," Carlos Gavito, quoted on the internet, told of learning to dance during the 1940s: "I began my dancing career at seven at the local dance club where young boys were used as models for the older boys.... We would place ourselves in the position of girls so other older boys could learn the steps. When I became fifteen, the process was reversed and the younger boys did the same for me. In those days we didn't have teachers. We learned steps from each other on street corners. Someone would have a radio or play a guitar."

Well known milonguero, Pupy Castello, recalled, "When we learned to dance in the streets, we started off by learning as a woman which was very important. You can feel how people are leading you and that helps you to know how to lead. For example, you can learn where the woman puts her foot, and that will help when you are dancing with a woman because if she should make a mistake, you will be able to correct the situation.... At the academia they had me dancing six months as a woman and then another six months just doing the salida and the ocho. They didn't teach steps. We used to go to a practicas club run by Juan Carlos Copes. You would see something you liked, and you would be practicing, then practicing it out on the street or wherever."

During the 1940s, the code of dance etiquette was enforced everywhere, from central dance halls to neighborhood clubs. Carlos Gavito recalled: "The code of dance etiquette was very strict in the dance halls. For example, if a woman did a boleo or the man led his partner in a gancho, the couple would be asked to leave the hall. Likewise, if a couple bumped another couple or did not follow the line of dance, they would have to leave immediately."

From 1940 to the mid-1950s, a well-known practica was held every Tuesday and Thursday at the "Club Imperio Juniors," in Barrio Flores where between 200 and 300 men practiced the tango with each other. At the practicas, men who specialized in the followers' role were fought over because without a partner there was not the opportunity to prepare at a high level. According to renowned teacher Mingo Pugliese: "Men took their dancing very seriously as it could affect their standing in the community with both men and women."

Having to dance on cement basketball courts at neighborhood clubs didn't keep the clubs from being popular. One of today's most important milongas, Sunderland, dates from the 1940s and is still held weekly on the same basketball court. Far from the city's center, it continues to attract the Buenos Aires' best dancers, acting as a magnet for serious amateurs and professional dancers.

With the popularization of soccer during this period, suburban neighborhoods developed sports and cultural association clubs that held regular tango dances on the weekends. Families and friends met there to eat, to socialize, and to dance to a live band, records, or the radio. Paris-based teacher Orlando (Coco) Diaz remembered the 1940s in Argentina: "During this era, each barrio supported its own orchestra in the same manner it supported its soccer club. Each band of supporters often defended the colors of its favorite orchestra with its fists!"

Neighborhood clubs developed their own, distinctive dance style, of which they were proud. Men and boys frequently went into other barrios to watch the dancing to try to pick up new steps, but they could only watch because local girls wouldn't dance with them. These incursions were not always welcome, and to avoid trouble it was necessary to tread lightly, preferably going with a friend who lived in the neighborhood.

Neighborhood clubs were not as crowded as the clubs downtown. The extra space permitted them to dance with longer steps and modest figuras; some figures were intricate, but most clubs frowned on steps that involved feet leaving the floor. However, the suburban clubs did develop such styles as the *orillero*, which included steps with feet lifting off the floor.

Evolution of Music and Orchestras

The music and orchestras of the Golden Era were a far cry from tango's early groups. Besides the profusion of dance venues, tango music continued to increase its popularity among non-dancers through gramophone recordings, radio, and film. In 1940, one of the most important programs in tango radio history, "Glostora Tango Club" began to play tango music, and did so uninterrupted for eighteen consecutive years. Important orchestras and singers appeared on direct airtime, and some of the most prestigious orchestras broadcast from cabarets, such as Les Ambassadeurs, giving increased importance to the already popular dance.

Orchestras and Music Changed

Attend any tango dance today and people will be dancing almost exclusively to songs and orchestras from the late thirties, forties, and early fifties. The greatest tango orchestras and music of all time were created during this period, after improvised tango music had disappeared.

As more and more people were dancing tango, dance floors increased in size, making it difficult for those on the fringes to hear the orchestra. Loudspeakers had not yet been invented, so orchestras that had already increased the number of their musicians were forced to add even more. From the early "Orquesta Tipica" of four to six pieces, they tripled the size, with some having 20 to 30 musicians. In the 1940s, four bandoneons were considered to be the minimum, along with four violins, a piano, bass, and sometimes a clarinet or saxophone. During carnival, orchestras increased in size even more, particularly adding extra bandoneons.

When the orchestras got larger, there arose a need for arrangers familiar with harmony and counterpoint, and to help musicians adjust to written music. Improvisation and ad-libbing sometimes produced music of dubious quality so as more arrangers were used, the music became better and better.

Every orchestra developed its particular style, and many dancers developed a dance style appropriate to their favorite orchestra. At the beginning of the 1940s, Osvaldo Fresedo and Julio de Caro emerged as the top orchestra leaders, and each had its followers who, night after night, followed them to whatever part of the city they were playing. The most popular orchestras played multiple gigs per night, not finishing until five or six in the morning.

The tango song had begun in an era where the word 'tango' not only meant music and dance but also the poetic content of the written verses. With Gardel and other vocalists, so much emphasis had been given to lyrics and vocalists that the music and dance almost took a back seat. However during the 1940s, when the music became more sophisticated, all that changed and the music again became of primary interest.

Orchestras of this period varied in their approach to rhythms and accents on different instruments. The simple, direct, and emphatic style of D'Arienzo's orchestra, with Rodolfo Biagi on the piano, proved irresistible to dancers who loved the unvarying four by four beats. It was commonly said that "with D'Arienzo's orchestra the tango moved back to the feet."

D'Arienzo, who played the violin, made the piano the leading percussion instrument, and favored rhythm over harmony and melody. Called 'El Rey del Compas' (King of the Beats), he favored a strong, steady beat to restore tango to its original concept as dance music, rather than as background music for vocalizing. He said, "In my opinion, the tango, first and foremost is about rhythm, energy, vigor, strength and character."

Carlos Di Sarli's orchestra, featuring Di Sarli on the piano, created a new sound that emphasized melody without sacrificing rhythm to secondary importance, which contrasted with D'Arienzo's predilection for emphasizing rhythm over melody. Other bands, such as Francisco Canaro's, had strict beats but de-emphasized the beat in favor of more emphasis on melody and harmony. The music of the beloved Osvaldo Pugliese, is still played at every milonga throughout the world. Anibal Troilo was considered to be the finest bandoneon player ever, and his orchestra was popular both for listening and for dancing.

Other popular orchestras of the forties were led by Alfredo Gobbi, Alfredo de Angelis, Hector Varela, Angel D'Agostino, and Astor Piazzolla, who would later infuriate Argentines with his avant-garde version of the tango that first fused tango with jazz and classical music.

Anibal Troilo

"Tango chooses you. When it does, it gives you a glimpse, but as always, it was, it is and it will be surrounded by a halo of impregnable mystery." (Anibal Troilo)

"Troilo...truly creative, touched by God's wand." (Osvaldo Piro, bandoneonist, Conductor, Composer)

Anibal Troilo is a tango icon second only to Carlos Gardel in the affections and respect of Argentines. Although he only wrote a few tangos, he was not only a great bandoneonist but also one of tango's greatest arrangers and composers. Troilo's style and creativeness is legendary, and although he had much less musical training the other tango greats, his music is remembered for its solid beat, its sophisticated, complex rhythms, and its amazing melodic patterns.

He was born July 11, 1914; his father, a butcher, guitarist and singer, died in 1926. His mother wanted him to be a pharmacist, but he only had eyes for the bandoneon. When he was a small boy, he wanted so much to play the bandoneon that he constructed a bandoneon out of a pillow and practiced with it. When he was eight years old, his mother gave up on the idea of his becoming a pharmacist and bought him his first bandoneon on credit. Fortunately for the family, the store where they purchased it went out of business after they made four monthly payments so they didn't have to pay anything more. He took lessons and practiced so conscientiously that when he was only eleven years old he played in a benefit competition in a cinema and performed so well that he was hired to play with the permanent orchestra that accompanied silent movies.

His first lessons, in 1927, were with a neighbor, and later he was able to work with the great accordionist Pedro Maffia. When he was only thirteen, he was hired to play in a professional trio in a downtown café. In the same year, he played in the orchestra of the cinema Palace Medrano. Later that year, he was hired to be one of the two bandoneon players in a famous sextet of Osvaldo Pugliese.

Troilo was truly a prodigy. By the age of fifteen in 1930, he was playing in the very popular sextet of Alfredo Gobbi and gained a reputation as an excellent interpreter and composer. His reputation was constantly burnished with his many compositions and from that time on he never had trouble finding work as a bandoneonist, composer, or arranger. In 1932, when he was eighteen, he joined the orchestra of Julio De Caro and made his first appearance in a movie. In 1933 Troilo wrote his first tango, 'Midnight'. In the next two years he played in the important orchestras of Angel D'Agostino and Juan D'Arienzo. In 1936 he was part of a group 'Quartet of 1900,' and in 1937 he first directed an orchestra, one organized by Ciriaco Ortiz.

Troilo made his initial recording with Odeon in 1938. In 1940 he made his first appearance on the El Mundo radio station with his orchestra with four bandoneons, including Astor Piazzolla, who sometimes doubled as arranger and pianist. In 1942 his orchestra inaugurated the cabaret 'Tibidabo,' where he stayed for several years, during which time he made many radio appearances.

Troilo was a 'party man,' gregarious and well liked for his congenial personality. He was known for his proclivity for staying up after a night's work to drink and joke with dancers, musicians, and friends, usually picking up the tab.

Although Troilo approved of innovation, his music didn't stray far from its roots. He surrounded himself with the best musicians, poets, and singers and was known for the frequent use of his eraser to take out any part of an arrangement that didn't suit him. Once when Piazzolla gave Troilo an arrangement that Troilo felt was too sophisticated, he told Piazzolla: "No, little one. It's not like this.... We are playing tango to be danced to."

Once during a practice session of his orchestra rehearsing a new arrangement of Argentino Galvan, Troilo made three important changes, each time apologizing profusely. Galvan finally told him. "Troilo, you have already paid me for this arrangement; it is yours, do with it what you want." Later, he confided the conversation to a violinist in the orchestra, "This man has stolen my soul, but I would have loved to have composed the changes he made."

Troilo's most famous pieces are probably 'Danzarin', 'Los Mareados', and 'La Bordona,' but his favorite and signature piece is 'Quejas de Bandoneon.' He said that he would die while playing it. As fate would have it, in 1975 at age sixty, just after he finished playing it in a Juan Carlos Copes stage show, he collapsed off-stage and never recovered.

During his lifetime, Troilo gave away three of his bandoneons: to Aston Piazzolla, Rodolfo Mederos, and Raul Garello (Director of the Tango Orchestra of Buenos Aires). Garello said that "out of respect for Troilo" he never played his, but put it on display in a glass case in the Academia Nacional de Tango "so young musicians may have the opportunity to play the instrument of the greatest bandoneonista in the world. Troilo died on 18 May 1975, and is buried in Chacarita Cemetery not far from Carlos

Gardel. Like that of Gardel, Troilo's tomb has become an important pilgrimage site. In 2005 the Argentine government designated Troilo's birthday, 11 July, as National Bandoneon Day, to be celebrated annually, and there is a movement to have a subway station named after him.

Lyrics

By the 1940s, the subject matter of lyrics evolved from disappointed ambitions and family miseries to themes of social injustice and rebellion against a non-caring society. As lyrics became more interesting, there was greater demand for vocalists to sing them. Enrique Discepolo became Argentina's foremost political and social philosopher lyricist of the 1940s. From the 1930s through the 1950s, his popularity never waned, and he has gone down in tango history as an outstanding musician, composer, conductor, poet, actor, playwright, and filmmaker.

Vocalists

After Gardel's death in 1935, the tango song became even more popular, and in the 1940s it assumed an importance equal to and sometimes even surpassing that of the orchestras. The idea of integrating a vocalist into an orchestra was born in Paris in the mid-thirties when Manuel Pizarro's orchestra played at the cabaret 'El Garron'. Shortly afterward Francisco Canaro introduced a permanent singer, and other tango orchestras soon followed suit. At first vocalists didn't sing an entire tango song, but only portions of it, standing at the side of the orchestra. By the mid-1930s tango singers had become heroes, with many orchestras incorporating full-time singers.

In the 1940s, instead of only a portion of the song, vocalists began singing the entire song – standing in front of the orchestra. Vocalists became such an essential part of the tango orchestra that many orchestras' success depended on them. During the 1940's, featured vocalists were identified with an orchestra, and avid fans followed them wherever they played. According to Juan Carlos Copes, "There was one singer, Alberto Moan, similar to Elvis Presley; the women gathered about him in such crowds that it was very difficult to continue dancing."

Singers became so important during the 1940s that a tradition developed for dancers to stop dancing when vocalists sang, a custom that continued until recent times. Tango lyrics were treated as serious poetry, evoking passions about a wide range of personal problems and emotions. Most tango vocalists developed a style that was almost operatic, and most of today's vocalists still sing in the dramatic, histrionic fashion of the 1940s. They are prone to get very excited about the themes of the lyrics living each word with extravagant facial and body gestures, raising their arms theatrically, using their voices to denote great passions and pains. Tango singers and musicians became the objects of such great attention that there were dozens of fan magazines devoted exclusively to the tango stars of radio and the movies, which covered their private and public lives in detail, similar in content to movie fan magazines of today.

The earliest singers were men who sang lyrics written by men, expressing male sentiments and experiences. Some women singers used men's names and performed dressed as men, but most sang the lyrics as they were written - from a man's point of view. Mercedes Simone gained fame dressed as a man, and Azucena Maizani frequently performed dressed as a gaucho. Later tango songs were written from a feminine viewpoint of view, and as women performers gained acceptance, they no longer needed to dress as men or use men's names. Many women singers became very popular and were paid handsomely for radio appearances, making records, and appearing in movies.

Vocalists were much more famous than dancers because both male and female singers became popular through exposure on the radio and phonograph records, in the theater, and in tango-oriented movies. Paradoxically, there were very few tango dancers who ever became well known outside their barrio or neighborhood dance halls. There was no television and not that many movies featured tango, so dancers were only known outside their barrios through participation in dance competitions, where they could gain only a small bit of fames compared to that enjoyed by vocalists. Considering the vast audiences of a live radio show, the few hundred who might see a dance contest were miniscule.

The Dancers

The most talented dancers from the past never received the public recognition and adoration that singers enjoyed during the Golden Era, and since not much film footage of early dancers exists, they remain relatively unknown today. Some dancers of this period changed the way tango was danced at the end of the 1930s and influenced the way it is danced today. The ones who did attain some degree of fame were all male, because men choreographed the dance, with women taking a minor role. Until this time, women were only followers who were not much more than props for the men to look good while they performed, but beginning in the 1940s, good male dancers began to show off the women's skills and talents.

Dance in the 1940s

"Before the 40s, people were dancing 'all crumpled up,' as if they were boatman paddling upstream." (Internet)

In the 1940s, there were essentially four styles of dancing, although the oldest style, the canyengue from the days of the Vieja Guardia, was rarely seen after the 1930s. More common was the salon style danced in center city dance halls that featured walking steps. The *orillero* style with its intricate and sophisticated figures was danced in the suburban districts, where dance halls were less crowded. It was said that *orillero* dancers "wanted to dance without worrying about the fine points of elegance" and that "to be a good orillero dancer you had to justify it with good ganchos and speed." The 'Tango Fantasia' style, with its elaborate exaggerated steps, was not ordinarily danced in dance halls and was mainly danced on the stage.

Mingo Pugliese spoke about dancing in the 1940s and 1950s, claiming that there were really only two styles in the dance halls: "Those who danced in the old way and those who already were being part of the musical and dancing transformation. In the early days, only the salon tango, the plain and unadorned walking style, was allowed in downtown dance halls. Orillero style was danced in the fringes of the city."

Famous Dancers from the Golden Age

Cachafaz – (Jose "Benito" Bianquet)

"His upright upper body position revolutionized the Tango... he created the basics of the Tango de Salon style of the 40s." (Carlos Alberto Estevez)

Don "Benito" Cachafaz ("Benito the Insolent One"), referred to only as Cachafaz, started dancing to the sound of barrel organs in downtown Buenos Aires. In 1911 he won his first competition, which had lasted for an entire week. From the twenties through the forties he was Argentina's most famous dancer, recognized for revolutionizing tango by dancing upright with the body parallel and closer to the woman, holding his axis and upper body straight. Prior to this, partners leaned against each other like an arch. He was the first to insist on the goal of elegance, redefined by good technique, instead of the previously admired complicated step patterns.

With his pockmarked face, Cachafaz was not a particularly attractive man, but according to milonguero Juan Silbido, he was an impressive presence. "He had an elegant wardrobe, unusual for a milonguero. He chose his partners from the working class. While other performers wore tuxedos, Cacha did not reject refinements, but he had a way of dressing which did not deny his roots from the suburbs." Despite his lower class origins, Cachafaz was proud of the fact that he was in demand as a tango teacher to upper class Buenos Aires society: "Some people said that the distinguished people would not dance the tango. I was fortunate to bring the tango to the salons of the most distinguished people of the upper class. I have been the teacher of girls who are now grandmothers. My pupils have become Senators, deputies, ministers and ambassadors. I took fifty dollars per lesson. I made a lot of money and spent everything - that's what money is made for. I did not gamble. Money made it possible for me to live a high life. I danced in Paris with a big triumph. I got a contract for New York and danced at the Metropolitan. I stayed at the Astoria. Gran vida, gran vida!"

Carmencita Calderon, Cachafaz's partner until he died, continued dancing in milongas at least once a week until she was 102. Until her death in 2005, she regularly performed at tango festivals and special events in Buenos Aires. Admired for her spunk and saucy sense of humor on the dance floor, she recalled: "I started my teaching and performance career directly with Don "Benito" (Cachafaz). He taught the tango de salon—or other styles if people asked for it." In an interview in 2006, Calderon had little good to say about today's dancers: "In our day we didn't choreograph performances. Today it is a total bluff...It's all a lie, all those dancers, all those teachers are all swindlers; we call them greedy jumping jacks. We had to learn how to dance as a couple... Today's couples have sportive abilities, like the movability of their feet. But they are lacking the basic knowledge of the tango. Couples should never separate while dancing and they should never lift their feet, which should slide over the floor."

Petroleo – (Carlos Albert Estevez)

"Tango is a contained emotion that suddenly explodes. Nobody can say, "This is how the Tango is danced." You feel it; you dance how you feel it. It is a creation." (Petroleo)

Another of tango's outstanding dancers to come out of the barrios was Carlos Albert Estevel, known as Petroleo, supposedly because of his affinity for getting "oiled" with wine. Although he didn't perform on the stage, during the Golden Age he influenced Tango Salon by straightening the posture to a more severely erect position—even more than Cachafaz. He also developed a system of marking the lead by replacing the lurching, strong-arm embrace that had been the fashion with subtle hand and finger movements on the partner's back. Perhaps his most important contribution

347

was that he started dancing his steps to the 4/4 rhythm that the orchestras had begun playing in the 1920s. Until the 1940s dancers had refused to give up the original, faster 2/4 rhythm of steps and figures. As a result, Petroleo's style was perfectly in time to the music, and he danced in a more calm and poised manner, increasing the elegance of the dance.

Many of today's techniques are attributed to Petroleo, such as *the giro enroscada*, where the woman dances around the man, as well as *boleos, arastres, and passovers*. His invention of the woman's *cross* - when the woman steps back on her right foot and drags her left foot over in front of it - was revolutionary because this position enabled the couple to make any kind of change in direction by pivots or turn on their proper axis. It is still used in every tango danced today. His dancing was admired for its subtleties and nuances. Milonguero, Mingo Pugliese said of him: "Petroleo put ballet steps into the tango, giving it a different dynamic."

Petroleo was born in 1912 and began to dance when he was sixteen. He never toured because he worked at a bank and couldn't get away, but he did dance in over two thousand exhibitions. He had a permanent partner, Esperanza Diaz, and lived with her until she left him in 1949; after that he didn't have a permanent partner. Petroleo talked about his experiences during the Golden Age of tango: "In the salons, it was forbidden to dance with *cortes* (a break in the middle of a step in order to turn in the opposite direction). If we did, somebody would come up and ask us to stop by the office. There they'd yell at us and then kick us out. They called us 'compadritos.' In reality, those who danced Tango were all thieves, or at least they aspired to be robbers. At the dance halls there were pickpockets, knife-carrying thugs, horse cart drivers and milongueros. The dancers used to organize dances to raise funds for those released from jail. If somebody had spent a year in prison, each dancer would contribute ten or twenty pesos to raise about five hundred pesos to help him get back on his feet. When the police began to check out those parties we stopped doing them. There was a lot of competition among the dancers. We didn't give each other the time of day. The tango dancer is egotistical; he believes he is the best. I believed I was the best."

Juan Carlos Copes

"Juan Carlos Copes, the principal choreographer for the international stage hit 'Tango Argentino,' is the greatest living choreographer in any genre of ballroom dancing." (Mindy Aloff, Dance Critic)

Born in the Mataderos barrio in the northern suburbs of Buenos Aires, Juan Carlos Copes perfected his dancing in the local milongas. Soon after he started dancing at the neighborhood Club Atlanta he became known for his impeccable posture and cat-like walking steps. He and his long-term partner, Maria Nieves, were in demand for performances all over Buenos Aires and became famous for winning countless tango contests.

Inspired by Fred Astaire and Ginger Rogers, Copes developed a new style of tango that combined traditional dazzling tango footwork with longer steps and a polished elegance achieved by lacing it with classical ballet and modern dance movements. He literally invented the tango stage show and was the first to conduct tango workshops and festivals. His performances were revolutionary in introducing a "corps de ballet" of tango-dancers. He shocked many traditionalists by choreographing tango performances to the so-called "undanceable music" of Piazzolla and Troilo. He choreographed the original revue, "Tango Argentino" in 1983 as well as the reprise in 1989. He also choreographed and starred in Carlos Saura's film "Tango." Many consider him to be the greatest name in contemporary tango choreography.

Maria Nieves

Maria Nieves, arguably one of the most outstanding female dancers in the history of tango, recalled her earliest tango experiences: "I danced at home with a broom since I was three...tango was in my blood." Maria's older sister had been Copes' partner until he began dancing with Maria when she was fourteen; they married and their dancing relationship lasted thirty-six years. After their divorce, they continued to perform together. Nieves once said: "I was so angry with him that I danced better than I ever did before we were divorced."

Once, in 1952, Copes and Nieves entered a tango competition with over one-hundred couples in Buenos Aires at Luna Park. The judges gave the prize to an older couple dancing classic tango, but the five-thousand spectators protested so much, shouting "Copes and Nieves," that the judges were forced to retrieve the prize and give it to Copes and Nieves.

In 1997 Copes and Nieves stopped dancing together. "We'd go on stage swearing at each other, and we'd go off and carry on swearing. But in the middle – we felt the silence." In 2007, an internet contribution quoted Copes on the subject of Nieves: "I tell anyone and everyone that she is the best dancer of all time, not of the century like me who was given the Dancer of the Century Award. I've seen Nieves do things that I wouldn't dare to do. I always say it takes two to tango but one feeling between them...."

Copes now dances with his daughter, Johanna, and Nieves stars in her own traveling shows, such as the 2008 'Tanguera.' According to critics, she's performing as well as ever.

Antonio Todaro - Master Teacher

"In figures and in his school, he was the best." (Miguel Angel Zorro)

Antonio Todaro was one of the most renowned teachers of performance dancing in the Golden Age and is still revered for his teaching abilities. He specialized in dancing the follower's role and was one of the few teachers who taught both the man's and woman's steps. His was the most respected tango dance school in Buenos Aires, where he trained a whole generation of stage performers.

His preferred style was stage tango, or tango "fantasia," with the woman doing figures in the air to spectacular effects. His style was strong, masculine, fast, agile, and powerful, not the soft, romantic, slow tango that many dance today. He often practiced with other men like Raul Bravo, switching the lead and follow so that there was no masculine and no feminine. Both partners were equally strong. Because women did not go to practicas, the men went, invented figures, and then taught them to their female partners. Raul Bravo and Antonio Todara developed their own system and taught it together.

Competitions

During the 1940s and 1950s many social clubs and commercial dance halls regularly organized dance contests. The biggest and most important national dance competitions were held at Luna Park, with separate contests for folklore, tango, milonga and canyengue. According to tango lore, local or national contests were taken so seriously that not a few of them ended in violence. One musician reported on a contest between El Cachafaz and a dancer from a neighboring barrio whose followers started an argument. "Cacha won but the epilogue was a violent scuffle and a knife fight that left a lot of wounded men. Subsequently the salon was closed for some time."

Carlitos Albornoz, a contemporary milonguero, talks about competitions when he was a young dancer in the Golden Age: "There were lots of competitions in the 1940s, mostly with money as prizes. Earlier contests were judged by the clapping of the audience, but they began to be a bit more organized with some contests judged by a jury, but mostly the winners were determined by the public who, when they paid their entrance fees, had the right to vote. Contestants would bring all their family and friends. Petroleo won a lot...he would bring in three truckloads of people. Clubs liked competitions because they made a lot of money from the people who came to vote."

Pupy Costello recalled participating in numerous competitions during this period, "For the competitions we would dance two types of dances. First a tango Salon, which is elegant and danced very close together with your partner and very much to the music, and then there would be Tango "Fantasia" which would be doing all the flashy things you see on the stage. This is the same format used today for the Buenos Aires Annual International Tango Competition."

In recent years organizers of the International Ballroom Dance competitions have tried to persuade Argentine Tango dancers to take part in their competitions. But most Argentine tango dancers believe it is not appropriate since there is no way to compare an improvised dance with a choreographed dance. An Argentine teacher is Buenos

Aires declared "It's like comparing apples and oranges, and besides, who in their organization is capable of judging Argentine tango?"

Towards the end of the 1940s, events in the post-World War II period and new technology changed popular music and dance in Argentina. As in many parts of the world, with the availability of inexpensive transistor radios and television, Argentines were exposed to the new music of the Beatles, Rock and Roll, the Twist, and 'rhythm and blues' from the U. S. and Great Britain. The new generation fascinated with the unconnected freestyle of dancing with no need for taking lessons, lost interest in the dance of their parents and grandparents. Tango was considered a shameful reminder of their proletarian past.

Political Setting

The Great Depression of the 1930s had not left Argentina unscathed. Buenos Aires became the focus for a wave of newcomers. This time Argentine indigent migrant workers from the countryside, mostly mestizos, moved into the already overflowing underclass of the city. By the 1940s they constituted the largest constituency for Colonel Juan Peron, who was building a political base among Argentina's poorest workers.

In June 1943, the inefficient and corrupt government of President Hipólito Yrigoyen was overthrown by a military coup, which placed the government into the hands of a military "managed democracy." Because the resulting instability caused frequent changes of power, the era became known as "the waltz of the generals and the colonels." They didn't seem to know what they were doing, but they did come up with what they thought was a good idea to improve Argentina's image by banning the use of Lunfardo. When he became a general, Juan Peron's rhetoric and support of workers made him a popular figure; he traveled the country making speeches in favor of uniting and helping the poor of Argentina.

A bloodless coup in 1944 made Juan Peron Vice President, and in October 1945 an enormous demonstration in support of Peron's policies marked the beginning of his ascent to power. In September of 1945 widespread civil unrest caused the military leaders to feel that Peron's politics were far to the left, so on October 13, they arrested him and put him in jail. This was not a popular move, and four days later labor leaders organized a massive popular uprising in Buenos Aires, which secured Peron's release.

In 1945 Peron, age forty-eight, married Eva Duarte, age twenty-four, a pretty, blonde, minor actress from a poor family in the provinces. In February of 1946, Peron ran for President in the first election campaign in sixteen years, and Evita (her affectionate nickname) enthusiastically accompanied him on the campaign trail, becoming a popular speaker and advocate for Peron—something no Argentine politician's wife had ever done before. Peron said he would work for the poor and disadvantaged, promising to use Argentina's new affluence to create a "society of social justice" for the proletariat. He won fifty-six percent of the popular vote, and his party swept all fifteen provincial governorships, plus thirty seats in the Senate. After the election, the party name was changed to "Partido Peronista."

Evita and Juan Peron became a highly visible and valuable team working to fight poverty, and they tried to help the thousands of impoverished rural migrants who had moved into urban areas. The tango increasingly became the social glue that helped to assimilate the diverse ethnic groups of Argentina's melting pot of the lower and middle classes into a cohesive society. Recognizing this, the Perons referred to the tango as "the dance of the people," and as part of their policies of identifying with the "descamisadas" (the shirtless ones) they promoted tango by attending dances, tango festivals, and being photographed with tango musicians. To help Argentine musicians who had no protective organizations at this time, Peron created a law in 1949 that required at least half of all the music played on the radio to be Argentine.

In 1947, the year women got the vote in Argentina; France invited Evita Peron to visit Paris (some believed it was because France wanted Argentina's wheat and beef.) She decided to also visit other countries in Europe, where she was enthusiastically feted by General Franco in Spain and met with the Pope in Rome. One of the highlights of the trip for her was the renaming of a Métro station in the fashionable 16th Arrondissement to "Argentine," making it the only Métro station in Paris to be named after a country.

On her return to Argentina from her "Rainbow Tour of Europe," Evita threw herself into the work of her charitable organization, and in 1949 formed the Peronista Women's Party, which soon had 3,600 branches and 500,000 members. Their votes were a major factor in the 1951 re-election of Peron.

But the Peron administration became beset with disasters. Argentina's gold reserves were at an all-time low, and nationalization of the British-owned railways brought a wave of strikes. Inflation was rampant because the government printed money whenever it wanted more, and beef production was so low that it had to be rationed. As discontent led to growing opposition, Peron's government became more and more authoritarian.

In 1950 Evita was diagnosed with cancer, and when she died two years later at the age of thirty-three, the tango lost a loyal champion. Some claim that Evita's death contributed to the tango's fall from favor in Argentina. In 1955, the military junta deposed Peron and installed General Aramburu as head of the government. The junta had become suspicious of the uniting influence of the large gatherings of tango dancers, preferring to rule over a country that was fragmented. Tango had become an important part of nationalist feeling and identity to the Argentine people; so it was decided to weaken its influence. That decision marked the end of the Golden Era of tango in Argentina, which had been the pinnacle of success for musicians, singers, composers and dancers. While it lasted, it was euphoric.

After the military coup of 1955, tango competitions were prohibited, tango dancing was discouraged by the government; the tango went underground, into a decline so serious that it nearly disappeared from the public consciousness. However, although interest in the dance declined and disappeared from the public eye, tango music and song did not suffer the same fate.

CHAPTER TEN

Revival

*"The tango was our national music and was
a big part of nationalistic feeling.
By the 1960s there was no more tango. Orchestras, intimidated
by the new government no longer performed or recorded tangos.
Only one or two radio stations played tangos.
Only one television station featured tango performances."*
(Carlos Gavito)

From 1955 to 1984, an entire generation of
Argentines matured without the tango being an
important part of their public or private lives and national
identity. By the 1960s, the tango dance was routinely
shunned by Argentines except on special family occasions
when grandparents and parents insisted on dancing it.
It was the dance that suffered; tango music and lyrics
managed to survive, although much altered. Political,
social and economic forces greatly influenced the iconic
image of tango.

Political Reasons for the Decline of Tango

The military dictatorship following the coup of 1955
involved itself in all aspects of Argentine society: politics,
the economy, and daily life. When Juan Peron was president,
he had encouraged the concept of uniting the nation of
diverse ethnic and cultural roots by instilling a hitherto
unknown intense feeling of nationalism. He had hoped
that attention and loyalties would cease to concentrate on
countries of origin and instead look forward to a better
Argentina. But when a military junta deposed Peron, the

new government of 'the Revolucion Libertadora,' in the belief that it would be easier to control a divided country, struck at the country's strong feeling of nationalism, which had been ignited by the tango. The people were aware of tango's importance to their society and soon realized what the government was up to. An internet contributor wrote: "We would get together to have a barbecue, then to aid the digestion we would dance tango. The tango united us."

Before long, people became frightened. Curfews were established with stringent punishments for non-observance, and meetings of more than three people were prohibited. Police raided tango dance halls to check people's identity papers. Many were hauled to the local police headquarters where they were ill treated and forced to wait long hours or all night while their papers were verified. It didn't take long before dancers were discouraged from attending dance halls. By the 1970s, anyone suspected of not being supportive of the right-wing government was not just hassled. Worse, and more frightening, they began to disappear at an alarming rate. Fearful of displeasing the government, people dancing the tango danced only in marginal circles.

The Military Discouraged Tango

The new law prohibiting private meetings between more than three people was a death knoll for the tango dance. Although there was no actual ban, people involved in tango - musicians, dancers, and composers were systematically intimidated. Without any evidence, security police began arresting anyone whom they might suspect of conspiring against the government; they checked records of those involved in tango to see if they were pimps, prostitutes, or thieves. Because there were no individual human rights, only the rights of the State, whether those dancing were held by the police or arrested, depended on the whims of individual officers.

Like most other totalitarian governments, it was suspicious of intellectuals and anyone who thought too much, or talked about the government's activities. Anyone associated with unions, teachers, writers, journalists, and professionals of all sorts including engineers, lawyers, architects, artists, actors and actresses, and anyone to the left of Far Right came under attack. Authorities were capricious in deciding whom to arrest, and they took anyone off the streets whose appearance or actions displeased them. Many were never heard from again, referred to as "los desaparecidos" (the disappeared). There were assassinations, mass murders, and institutionalized torture. An international outcry went up when two French nuns were imprisoned, tortured, and disappeared, but nothing came of it.

Tango teacher, Cacho Dante, told his student, Julie Taylor, about his experience: "I had to give up dancing because the police would arrive and take everybody in for verification of their papers. It happened all the time. If they picked you up at the milonga, you had to spend all night at the Police Station. When this began to happen every time I went dancing, I couldn't work at my job. So I stopped dancing."

The repressive tactics stopped everyone from dancing in public places but tango was still danced in the privacy of people's homes. A few neighborhood clubs sometimes unobtrusively played tango records without fanfare. Mingo Pugliese remembered: "To give a party or to celebrate a wedding, you had to have a police permit, so eventually people stopped dancing everything: Tango, Rock and Roll, Boogie Woogie, etc."

In May 1969, a year after the Paris uprising of students and workers (which involved no deaths), there was an insurrection of workers and students in Buenos Aires. But Argentina was not Paris, and the Army intervened with trigger-happy soldiers who killed 114 people and wounded scores of others, further alienating the government from its citizens.

In 1973, the military government, feeling a need for a bit of popular support, permitted Juan Peron to return from sixteen years of exile in Spain. He received a hero's welcome. In 1973, in the first election in over ten years, Peron's candidate, Hector Campora, was elected, but the military forced him to resign after only four months in office. Bloody confrontations between Peronist extremists and far right extremists forced new elections, with Peron as candidate for President and his new wife, Maria Martinez (Isabelita) as Vice-President. Peron won the Presidency for the third time in his career with over sixty-one percent of the vote. His election was supposed to bring stability to Argentina, but Peron died in June 1974 shortly after his inauguration. (He is buried not far from Carlos Gardel.) His wife became President, but she was unable to control events. The economy was still a disaster, with inflation running over three-hundred percent. Armed Leftist guerillas resumed their threats, and another military junta seized power in March 1976. It was not until 1983 that Argentina held another election that resulted in a fragile democracy.

The period from 1976 to 1983 was the most violent and horrific period in Argentina's history. The government was hysterical over a perceived Communist threat, which they used as an excuse to increase repression, citing increasingly active leftist guerrillas throughout Argentina. Under the pretence of fighting Communism, the junta started an undeclared war against the population, which became known as the 'Dirty War.' The military became increasingly paranoid and announced that they would govern under the "doctrine of national security," insisting that the concept of rule by the people was too dangerous. In 1979, the State intensified its efforts to terrorize imagined "enemies of the state," and people disappeared by the thousands. No one felt safe from the idiosyncrasies of the ruling junta. To listen to or dance the tango became ever more dangerous. Many tango musicians and performers were so intimidated that they joined the exodus of exiles to Paris and the U.S.; those who stayed in Argentina went underground. With orchestras a thing of the past, musicians sought refuge in small instrumental groups.

The ruling junta did not recognize any rights of individuals, declaring that everything and everyone must act for the welfare of the State, with no limit on its power. According to their doctrine, the war was total, and its enemies had to be searched out wherever they had infiltrated Argentine society, including all political, economic, and cultural activities. According to the military, anyone suspected of not fully supporting the government was to be treated as an enemy, creating the necessity for "absolute warfare." It was Fascism in its purest sense. By the end of the Dirty War, there were at least 30,000 (some claim 40,000) dead and disappeared, never to be heard of again.

The Ministry of the Marine was the headquarters for the violent, repressive policies and was responsible for torture and other horrors. There has recently been publicity surrounding the hundreds of children who were taken from the families of the desaparecidos and given to favored officials for adoption. After the war, it was reported that when the military junta seized pregnant women, it made a practice of waiting to kill them until after their babies were born. The infants were then taken by childless military or police couples while the mothers disappeared. Today Argentines still shudder when the Ministry of the Marine is mentioned.

Today organizations have been founded to help adopted children try to discover the fate of their parents, and some are examining the amnesties of government officials who were responsible for the excesses of the 'dirty war.' In 2007 part of the building of the Ministry of the Marine, the "Escuela de Mecanica de la Armada," was turned into a museum as a "Space for the Memory and the Promotion and Defense of Human Rights." A plaque on the wall indicates that it is dedicated to "revealing realities of the 1976-1983 dictatorships."

Julie Taylor, author and tango dancer, who lived in Buenos Aires during this period, wrote in her book *Paper Tangos*: "At this same time the tango had been firmly marginalized by 'rock nacional' (which was also prohibited by the military) and rock international. So the middle classes were not dancing in Buenos Aires, although there was some tango dancing in the provinces, possibly because the military did not feel threatened by people living outside the large cities."

The only bright spot for Argentina in those years happened in 1978 when Argentina won the World Soccer cup, playing on their home territory. Astor Piazzolla wrote songs in celebration of the team's victory.

Social Reasons for Tango's Decline

Because the immigrant community had assimilated into Argentine society by the 1960s, tango was no longer needed as social glue. The Golden Era had fulfilled Juan and Evita Peron's dream of bringing the disparate nationalities together as one nation, or as close as it would probably ever be.

Although tango was discriminated against, with the blessings of succeeding military governments, Argentina entered a period of cultural protectionism that benefited folk musicians. Folk music was accorded more radio time than tango. There was still no official ban, but tango bands recorded less, and the tango market diminished because of the disfavor of the military rulers. It wasn't until after the end of the last dictatorship, in 1984, that the government began to recognize the tango as something of which Argentina could be proud.

Internationally, the beginning of the decline of the tango had been set in motion in the late 1930s in North America and Europe, when dancers began to be wooed away from the tango to other new dances such as the Black Bottom, the Charleston, the Cake Walk, the Two Step, the Fox Trot, and the Shimmy (described by Josephine Baker, the famous American dancer in Paris during this period: "The feet are kept tight to the floor without moving while the body shakes from ankles to the head."). This did not have much impact in Argentina because of its isolation during World War II. The tango was virtually the only music danced to, heartily encouraged by President Peron; it flowered in Buenos Aires and spread to the provincial cities.

During World War II in Argentina, the government forbade the playing of music from countries that were not part of the Axis powers, so tango was left as the only social dance of any significance. But in the post-war period the tango fell into disgrace and disuse when

Argentines, particularly young people, wanted to break out of their geographic isolation. After the end of World War II, Argentina's musical isolation diminished with the importation of transistor radios and television. By the 1950s, American and British music of rhythm and blues, the Twist, and Rock and Roll became ensconced in Argentina. Instead of couples dancing in an embrace with a follower and leader, needing skills in technique and movement, emphasis was placed on freestyle improvisation, with little or no relevance to any other dancer on the floor. No partners were required or wanted.

At this time, extracurricular activities in Argentine schools placed more emphasis on young women training in ballet or modern dance while young men and boys concentrated on sports. With female emphasis on dancing, male interest in dance dwindled so much that dancing became associated with homophobia, most particularly for dances where it was necessary to take classes in order to become proficient.

Argentine youth denounced the tango as 'old fashioned' and irrelevant, a dance 'for the old folks.' For the new generation, tango became a shameful reminder of their proletarian past. Oblivion was close. The tango, once the dance of outcasts of the disreputable levels of Buenos Aires society, became an outcast again in the era of social upheaval from 1968 to 1969. This time rebellious Argentine youth didn't like the fact that it was respectable and smacked of the despised, established, middle class of the old social order. As in Europe and other parts of the world, the young were rebelling against established order, and what better symbol to destroy than the favorite music and dance of their parents' generation?

Economic Reasons for the Decline

Besides the military's overt destruction of the tango, the military's involvement in politics ruined the economy so badly so that even if tango was not being discouraged, there was no longer money available for participation or promotion of the dance. Inflation made salaries impossible to live on with any dignity; people could no longer afford to pay admission to tango dance halls.

The military, which was economically clueless, recklessly squandered governmental resources, increasing decay and poverty throughout the entire country. There were expensive, ugly building projects, many of which were never finished. In an effort to appear to be doing something constructive, inexperienced and corrupt contractors created vast zones of depressing buildings that destroyed much of traditional Buenos Aires. One of the loveliest parks, Lezema, suffered an ugly, noisy, overhead highway built right over its prettiest locations. Autoroutes were begun but not completed. In Belgrano, one of the most beautiful areas of Buenos Aires with lovely villas surrounded by gardens and trees, architectural disasters of cinderblock skyscrapers created blights on the landscape and destroyed the fine architecture of the old College Francais. The neighborhood of Retiro was ruined by ugly buildings constructed with characterless concrete blocks, and an overhead autoroute to the airport ran right through the charming traditional barrio of San Telmo, obliterating views of its delightful colonial architecture.

By 1962 the Argentine economy was in dire straits, with salaries frozen, mass unemployment, and a cost of living that had risen astronomically. The formerly prosperous soccer and other neighborhood sports clubs were no longer able to afford to stage the huge tango dances from which they had profited so well during the Golden Age because they could no longer afford to pay the huge orchestras, thus throwing tango musicians out of work. Although clients of the chic, expensive cabarets could still afford to patronize them, even they closed their doors because of political pressure and fear. When the most famous tango dance venue of all, the Chanteclair, closed, it signaled the end of the era of the French-style cabarets.

Deprived of dance venues, tango was restricted to the tangueras, small, intimate bars where tango music was played but there was not enough space for the public to dance. Both tracks of tango music, traditional and evolutionary, sought refuge in small instrumental groups, but evolutionary tango became more and more poplar. Dancers were turned into listeners and eventually tango became oriented towards virtuoso musicians who composed and played the evolutionary style of music, while interest in the traditional style declined.

Tango Went Underground

The tango obsession was forced underground or out of the country. Many tango musicians and performers were so intimidated that they joined the exodus of tango dancers and musicians who left the country in hope of finding employment. Some musicians who stayed in Argentina were only able to find work in small ensembles of between three to eight or nine members, which could fit into the smaller cafés. It was possible to listen to tango but not to dance to it. Not much remained of the world of tango.

Being deprived of dance, people sought out tango music in small cafés and clubs. Traditional groups, such as the Sexteto Mayor with six musicians, played music the closest in style to the orquestra tipica, which more or less died out during this period, only to be revived in the

1980s. The evolutionists, with Piazzolla in the foreground, formed classical quintets whose evolutionary style became more and more avant-garde.

The new evolutionary style of music was not appreciated by many Argentines and actually despised in many quarters of the country; most dancers and traditionalists vilified it, declaring that it was not even 'tango'. Emotions ran high when Argentines discussed Astor Piazzolla, the uncontested 'guru' of the evolutionary tango style. Conversely, at the same time that Argentines vehemently reviled his music, it became more and more appreciated in Europe and the U.S., where it was being performed in prestigious clubs, theaters, and staid concert halls.

Strangely enough, in spite of the military government's disapproval of the tango, in 1977 the dictator Jorge Rafael Videla ordered an official recognition of the tango with an annual celebration on November 11, the birthday of Anibal Troilo and Julio de Caro. Who knows why this was done. Maybe he was just looking for friends. In any case, the Day of Tango is still celebrated nationally with government sponsored elaborate, weeklong tango activities.

Although the tango dance was, so to speak, on its last legs, the newly invigorated tango music was becoming more and more popular outside Argentina. Its greatest successes were in New York and Paris which, incidentally, were the two cities that received the greatest number of Argentine exiles fleeing political oppression of the dictatorships.

The Argentines Return to Paris

Because of the on-running love affair between Paris and Buenos Aires, Paris was the city that received the largest number of self-exiled intellectuals and tango artists. The Argentines felt particularly comfortable in Paris because many of them spoke French, a result of its being used in many homes, cafés, and literary circles of Buenos Aires. The special relationship between Paris and Argentina had never waned, especially among intellectuals, artists, and academics.

During this period, Anibal Oscar Claisse, an academy member, gave a paper at L'Académie française in Paris, titled "L'Obsession française" that examined the French influence on Argentine culture by analyzing 2,000 tango songs taken at random. He found that ninety-seven mentioned Paris or France; Pernod (the popular French drink) was mentioned only seven times, but champagne was cited seventy-three times; cabaret fifty-five; French personal names sixty-times. Montmartre was cited in thirteen different tangos; Pigalle in twenty, garçonnière eleven times; gigolo fourteen; cachet fifteen, and chic sixteen times. French poets and authors were also frequently mentioned.

In 1958 the Buenos Aires journal, "Ahora," reported that "in France, the public still appreciates tango for its songs and lyrics as well as for dancing," and went on to say that "Piazzolla was so popular that he had recorded forty-nine different tango pieces." Besides the composer-bandoneonista, Astor Piazzolla, other important tango artists moved to Paris, such as Susana Rinaldi, considered to be one of the greatest tango singers of the times. Osvaldo Pugliese, whose Communist sympathies were anathema to the Argentine junta, moved to Paris and gave concerts all over town, including at the Bataclan, where he played 'La Yumba,' his most famous tango. Tango orchestras played for dancing at the renowned café, "La Coupole," on the Left Bank, but because interest in the tango dance had begun to diminish at the end of the 1930s, they also began playing other types of dance music.

In the 1960s and 1970s, thanks to the expatriate Argentine musicians, interest in tango music was revitalized in Paris and, to a somewhat lesser degree, other countries around the world. It was being played not only in dance venues but in serious jazz cafés, theaters, and important concert halls. In 1981, Paris opened its first tanguera, a small club in the city center, called the "Trottoirs de Buenos Aires" named after a tango song. A small group played tango music with occasional dance performances by one or two couples. Until it closed in 1994, it was the focal point for Argentine exiles and lovers of the tango. (The revitalization, however, did not extend to the dance until after the production 'Tango Argentino' opened in Paris and New York in 1984, and then the rest of the world.)

In the period up to 1983, excellent tango music was available in Paris: Piazzolla's group performed at Quintette's Theatre Musical, and the tango trio of Juan Jose Mosalini, Gustavo Beytelmann, and Jean Paul Celea played to sold-out audiences. Leopoldo Federico had an orchestra with twenty bandoneons! Paris was where the first film on the drama of exiled Argentines was made: "Tangos: l'Exile de Gardel." The musical score was written by Piazzolla, for which he received a French Cesar, the equivalent of Hollywood's Oscar.

In Paris and Europe the brightest tango star was undoubtedly Astor Piazzolla, who gave well-received concerts. The Buenos Aires newspaper "Clarin" reported that Piazzolla was extremely popular with French youth. "For the French youth, the idol is Astor Piazzolla, of whose compositions there are forty-nine different recordings by French orchestras. Even though his records don't sell in enormous quantities, he is becoming famous."

Astor Piazolla (left) and Anibal Troilo

"I wrote all kinds of music, but never happy music." (Astor Piazzolla, (NY Times, Oct. 1998)

"Piazzolla forced us to study — all of us." (Osvaldo Pugliese)

"Seen in the classical tradition, Piazzolla looks a lot like Chopin, and like Chopin, his music goes to our hearts....He is certainly the Michelangelo of Tango music." (Bernard Holland, NY Times, March 3, 2004)

"Piazzolla wrested the tango from the dance hall and turned it into serious music, or what he called nuevo tango. Piazzolla became the single person responsible for moving tango into the concert hall. It was one of the century's most ingenious re-imaginings of a popular musical tradition, often compared to Gershwin's transformations of jazz." (Jeremy Eichler, The New Republic)

Piazzolla

Surrounded by more controversy than any other tango musician, Piazzolla was the one most responsible for taking tango music out of tango halls into the concert halls. His transformation of the tango surpasses what George Gershwin and Duke Ellington did with American jazz during the 1920s and 1930s.

Although he began his career in Argentina as a bandoneonist and composer for traditional tango dance music in the1940s and 1950s, by the 1960s he moved to the smaller sextet and single-handedly invented what he called "new tango," which was a fusion of tango, jazz, and classical music. Piazzolla's tango appealed to the comfortable middle classes rather than the workers and the middle lower *classes of the previous period. He was the first to merge traditional tango with jazz and classical music to create an 'avant-garde' style of tango - which he claimed was not to be danced or sung to, but only listened to. His music was not accepted by the public or by the tango establishment. In turn, he said he wanted nothing to do with singers, lyrics, or dancers, and once commented he would like to break the legs of anyone he saw dancing to this music. The traditionalist musical camp was outraged and vilified him for daring to tamper with their national icon. Piazzolla's answer was: "I still can't believe that some pseudo critics continue to accuse me of having murdered tango. They have it backward. They should look at me as the savior of tango. I performed plastic surgery on it."*

Piazzolla was born in 1921 in Mar del Plata, Argentina, but spent most of his first sixteen years in New York City, where his father had taken the family in search of the elusive American Dream. At the age of eight his father gave him a bandoneon which was not a pleasant surprise for Piazzolla: "My father brought it to me covered in a box and I got very happy because I thought it was the roller skates I had asked for so many times. It was a let down; instead of a pair of skates, I found an artifact I had never seen before in my life. Dad sat down, set it on my legs, and told me, 'Astor, this is the instrument of tango. I want you to learn it. My first reaction was anger. Tango was that music my father listened to almost every night after coming from work (as a barber). I didn't like it." The bandoneon stayed in the closet while he studied classical piano; at the same time he became fascinated with jazz. However, before long he taught himself to play it.

Through the Argentine community in New York, Piazzolla met and became friends with Carlos Gardel, who was impressed by his skill on the bandoneon and hired him to be his bandoneonist for a few months although he was only thirteen years old. When Gardel lived and worked in New York, he spent time with Piazzolla and arranged for him to work as an extra in his film 'El Dia que me Quieras.' In 1935, Gardel sent a telegram to Piazzolla inviting him to join him on his tour to the Caribbean and South America. Piazzolla once remarked to an audience: "In spite of the honor, my father wouldn't give me permission." Two weeks later Gardel and his orchestra were killed in a plane crash. Piazzolla once added: "If it weren't for my father, I wouldn't be playing the bandoneon today, but a harp."

When his family returned to Argentina in 1939, Piazzolla studied to become an accountant, but it had little appeal for him. Instead he got caught up in the tango craze and decided to play bandoneon in one of the traditional tango orchestras. While still a teenager, he was hired by Argentina's most famous bandoneonist and orchestra leader, Anibal Troilo. In spite of his involvement with tango, his interest in classical music did not fade. While working the orchestra's long, late hours, he would get up early to go listen to the Teatro Colon orchestra rehearsing, and several days a week after breakfast went to study formal composition with one of South America's most respected classical composers of the time, Alberto Ginastera. Before long he was arranging for Troilo, who complained that Piazzolla was turning his band into a symphony orchestra; they worked together for seven years until Piazzolla left to form his own orchestra. Piazzolla continued his studies and independent research into classical music and soon began writing his own classical chamber music. During the 1950s he was in demand to write tango arrangements for big bands, including Pugliese's.

In 1953 he entered a piano composition competition and his "Buenos Aires Symphony" won him a scholarship to study piano and composition in Paris with one of the most famous piano teachers of the day, Nadia Boulanger. Piazzolla recalled that one day Boulanger chastised him because his playing did not have enough feeling: "...some of which was very similar to classical composers." He was ashamed to admit that his primary instrument was the bandoneon and that he was a tango musician. When she pushed him for more information he was afraid to tell her he played in nightclubs. "She'll throw me from the fourth floor!" However, she insisted that he bring his bandoneon to class the next day. When she heard him play his tango music she said, "You idiot, that's Piazzolla!" She told him to forget the piano and academic European-oriented composition and spend his time composing tangos for the bandoneon. "I took all the music I composed over the last ten years of my life and sent it to hell in two seconds." The importance of having someone of Boulanger's stature approve of his tangos reinforced his inclination to combine his two musical worlds.

After the 1955 coup and the beginning of tango's decline, Piazzolla panicked and determined to preserve it from a final death. The only public places for tango at this time were small cafés, so Piazzolla formed his "Octeto Buenos Aires" but refused to play for dances. He also did away with the idea of a tango vocalist for his group. At that time most tango vocalists accompanied their singing with dramatic gestures, with much raising and waving of arms which annoyed Piazzolla: "*Habria que pegarselos con cemento.*" *(I'd like to stick them in cement.)* From this period on —in the 1950s and 1960s - Piazzolla's work included not only tangos but also classical forms such as concertos, suites, and one operetta—written with the famous Argentine poet and writer, Horacio Ferrer.

Piazzolla announced that his group would include percussion instruments and an improvised electric guitar, both of which had never before been used for tango. With all his reforms and strange ideas, Piazzolla made many enemies in the tango world; he was mocked and derided and not taken seriously. By saying that his music was for listening, not dancing, many tango enthusiasts claimed his music was not even tango, which resulted in "*Piazzolla's tango wars.*" Piazzolla said, "*In Argentina you can change hundreds of Presidents, you can change religions, but don't try to change the tango.*"

Emotions ran high. Argentines do not take their tango lightly, and the new tango music was argued about in all levels of society. There were "*Piazzollistas*" and "*Anti-Piazzollistas*" who with unrelenting fervor published endless articles advocating one side or the other. Lengthy conferences and debates in bars, cafés, or anywhere people gathered, were held to argue the validity of the 'new tango' and whether or not it could even be classified as a form of tango, and whether it could/should be danced to. Discussions sometimes broke into fistfights between the exponents of each ideology.

Piazzolla's musicians regularly received death threats, and once someone threw gasoline over the band members in an attempt to set them on fire. Disgusted, Piazzolla left for New York, where he hoped his music would receive a *better reception. He was confident of his ultimate success. "I never have and never will seek success among the majority. I introduced irreverence. People thought I was crazy. The tango critics said that my music was paranoiac. That's how they made me popular. The youth that had lost interest in tango began listening to me. Tango critics called me a clown. It was a war of one against all, but in ten years the war was won."*

In New York City, he worked with famed jazz musicians, including Gerry Mulligan and Dizzy Gillespie to incorporate tango with aspects of jazz. (That was as innovative then as is today's increasingly acceptable "techno-tango.") Jazz musician Gary Burton said: "As a jazz musician, I tend to compare Astor to a combination of Duke Ellington and Miles Davis." Jeremy Eichler, describing Piazzolla's fusion of jazz with tango in an article in The New Republic, said "Piazzolla distilled the tango's yearning and sublimated its aggression and preserved its anguished eroticism, and forged a highly accessible art music with cosmopolitan appeal. It is by turns ecstatically lyrical and harshly dissonant, and always tinged with a wistful awareness of quotidian sorrow."

In 1960, Piazzolla decided to return to Argentina, steadfast in his desire to transform the tango and win over a large portion of the public to his experiments. In 1961 he formed his first quintet, which had modest success in Buenos Aires. According to Azzi and Collier, "He had a need for domestic acceptance that he could deny but never escape." He was eager for the public to accept his music as tango music even if they were not dancing to it, which led him to invite the undisputed tango great, Osvaldo Pugliese, to rule on whether his quintet was performing real tango. Pugliese listened to it and pronounced that they were, and the "band was greatly relieved." In 1972, giving up on bucking those who insisted his music was not tango, Piazzolla named a new record "Popular Contemporary Music from the City of Buenos Aires."

Piazzolla decided to take his music to the world, where it was received as "highly original art music." During the dictatorship of 1976 to 1983, he lived in Italy where he picked up his fourth language, formed his second quintet, and met with acclaim when he toured Europe, North America, and the Far East. By the time he returned to Buenos Aires, Piazzolla was finally accepted in Argentina. In 1985, his music was featured prominently in the theater production "Tango Argentino" that toured the world for years and sparked the present worldwide Tango Renaissance. Nestor Marconi, master bandoneonist said: "Before Piazzolla, tango was a music in service to the dance; now it's a music in itself."

Piazzolla lived long enough to realize the extent of his impact on the musical world and to appreciate his acceptance in Argentina. His quintet remained in demand on three continents, deeply respected by both classical and jazz musicians. Before his death he performed in the most prestigious theaters around the world. His body of work includes approximately 750 short and long pieces, concertos, vocal works, film and theatrical scores, and an opera that is still performed regularly.

"Tango as Pure Melody Slinks in a Staid Concert Hall" was the headline for an article by Bernard Holland in the New York Times, in October 1997.

"The tango, whether as dance or pure music, remains public entertainment so long as we confine it to the smoky bars of Buenos Aires or a Broadway theater. Take it to the Brooklyn Academy of Music, make it a part of the Next Wave Festival, identify it with a known composer like Astor Piazzolla, and deliver it into the hands of conservatory-trained musicians, and suddenly the tango is seen as serious art worthy of Beethoven's company."

His classical works were received particularly well, including "Mozart's 40th Symphony as a Tango" and "Grand Tango" for piano and cello, written for Rostropovich; cellist Yo Yo Ma made CDs of his classical tangos. He composed "Four Seasons of Buenos Aires" which was performed by the violinist Gidon Kremer in Paris, alternating it with Vivaldi's "Four Seasons."

In 1990 Piazzolla suffered a serious stroke and died two years later. Each year, his music becomes more popular in concert halls, on the stage and, increasingly, on dance floors. Since his death, his reputation has risen in the classical musical world as musicians such as Yo Yo Ma, Gidon Kremer, Daniel Barenboim and many others record his works. In the late 1990s an internet contributor from Tokyo wrote that "Piazzolla is now the most popular composer in Japan."

Horacio Ferrer, considered the greatest living tango poet, defended Piazzolla's pronouncements that there is no 'true tango' and that tango must continue to change. "The grandeur of tango is that it is not the product of any one culture. Each person interprets it in its own fashion; each gives it its own truth, and the tango becomes more and more important. It can't exist as a unique truth, or it would already be dead."

Democracy Returns

The last Argentine dictatorship fell in 1983 due in great part to the courageous "Mothers of the Plaza de Mayo" who, with white kerchiefs on their heads and photographs of their missing loved ones, regularly and relentlessly demonstrated in central Buenos Aires against the disappearance of their family members. Their actions greatly embarrassed the government and ultimately led to its downfall. When the Socialist Raul Alfonsin became President, a bit of fresh air was introduced into Argentina's cultural life, and Argentina once again enjoyed democracy and freedom of expression, encouraging political exiles to return home.

They returned to a changed dance scene. The enormous dance halls that had held thousands of couples no longer existed. The large tango orchestras had long been disbanded. Rock and Roll music, with its non-contact dancing monopolized the dance floors, and it was difficult to find radio stations that played tangos. A generation had not wanted to learn the tango and had no inclination to do so. Tango was pretty much history. No one could have predicted or imagined the new wave of worldwide interest in tango that would eclipse the first tango craze of one hundred years ago.

As with the first international enthusiasm for the tango, the renaissance originated in Paris, this time it shows signs of becoming an even bigger success than the first wave at the turn of the last century.

Tango Argentino

The spark that ignited the present revival of the tango dance was the 1984 Paris theater production of 'Tango Argentino.' It was pure serendipity when the newly refurbished Chatelet Theater in Paris found itself with a week's unfilled slot. The manager mentioned this to Jorge Lavelli, an important Argentine theater director living in Paris, who just happened to have two friends from Argentina, Claudio Segovia and Hector Orezzoli, who had been thinking about producing a show which would tell the history of tango in dance and song. Until this time, dancers in Broadway-type musicals were considered a decoration for a dramatic production, but their idea was to have no story; only music and dance would illustrate the different styles that reflected the changes in Argentine society. The music would be traditional songs dating from the mid-1800s to Piazzolla's new tango.

The budget was small, so the producers proposed presenting the show in the least complicated way possible by simply having six dancing couples appear one after another on a plain stage with a tango orchestra and two vocalists. Although tango music had remained important in France, primarily due to Piazzolla's concert music, at this time the dance was all but dead, which made the venture very risky. An entire evening of only tango seemed a 'no starter'. Nevertheless, the excitement of the idea of returning tango to the spotlight won out. Segovia and Orezzoli eagerly returned to Buenos Aires to find tango's most important stars and put together a show. In keeping with the austerity of the production, the title of the show was to be simple, "Tango Argentino."

There was not sufficient money to purchase air tickets for the entire cast, so it was arranged to fly them to Paris in an Argentine military plane scheduled to go to Paris for maintenance. Performers and musicians huddled together in the cold, uncomfortable seats, worried about flying with one engine not functioning. To save money on hotels, members of the cast were housed with friends. Because of the shortage of funds for costumes, it necessitated imaginative solutions. There was not enough money for elaborate costumes, so to replicate the tango in the early 1900s, they were forced to scour second hand stores for original pieces of lingerie—they were perfect.

In contrast to contemporary musicals, the structure of the show could not have been simpler which involved a story, performers who could act, elaborate scenery and costumes, and a full orchestra in the pit. The proposed tango show had no story line, only six dancing couples, no actors, no elaborate costumes, and no scenery. Instead of a large orchestra, the six-piece 'Sexteto Mayor' was to be placed towards the back of the stage with a male and female singer standing in front of the musicians. The only styles of dance were fantasy, salon style and orillero. Friends of the producers believed it was destined for failure.

As opening night drew near, both producers and performers were worried about whether audiences would be satisfied with an evening featuring an outdated dance performed by six couples, some of whom were clearly middle-aged, overweight, and not especially attractive; the orchestra's six musicians were definitely aging. Audiences were accustomed to seeing musicals with young, lithe, smiling dancers flitting around the stage without a care in the world. What would they make of unsmiling dancers who were actually frowning? Would it be noticed that the lack of smiles on seemingly unhappy faces reflected serious intent and obvious passion for the electric and exciting music to which they were dancing?

One week before opening, only two-hundred tickets had been sold, which was not encouraging to the performers. The producers joked that the tickets were probably sold to expatriates and they worried about how many empty seats there would be. After consultations, the producers decided to give out free tickets so the theater would not be embarrassingly empty, but they did not know whom to invite other than journalists. Someone suggested that schoolteachers, generally known to be culturally open-minded, curious, and not well paid might appreciate a free night at the theater. The American School of Paris was contacted and told that anyone who would show up on the first night would be admitted free.

Long time Paris resident, Rosemary DuAime, a retired kindergarten teacher, remembered: "Previously when I had gone to performances at the Chatelet Theater, I could only afford tickets in the highest balcony, and was I thrilled when we were shown to the orchestra and told to sit where we wanted! Just before the show began, I looked around and was surprised to see what appeared to be no more than a hundred people in the audience. However, as soon as the lights went down and the music and dance began, I was breathless and knew I was watching something remarkable. The entire audience was enchanted."

The first night's reviews pronounced it a smashing success, and eventually more than 70,000 people saw the show before it left Paris. The original six-day run was extended to a month, and then the group went on to New York and other major cities in the U.S., Europe, and Japan. In 1985 the cast was expanded to eight couples, with the addition of Gloria and Rodolfo Dinzel and Gloria and Eduardo Arquimbau. It played a triumphal week at the

City Center in New York and moved to the Mark Hellinger Theater on Broadway for a five-week run, where it was such a hit that it played for the entire season of six and a half months. Everywhere it played it received glowing critical reviews, and in 1986 it won two Tony Award nominations. In 1989 it returned to New York and then to the Mogador Theater in Paris before disbanding.

In 1986, some of the dancers had abandoned salon style and began doing exaggerated dips and jumps—called Tango Fantasia or Stage Tango. The flashy steps, jumps and exaggerated leg movements received so much applause from North American audiences that others in the cast changed their choreography to include similar steps, and a few couples competed with each other to see who could do the most acrobatic movements. Tango traditionalists heartily disapproved of these stylistic changes and especially objected to the leader putting the head of his partner against the floor; something never, ever seen on the dance floors in Buenos Aires. A problem arose when the show was due to return to Paris where the Fantasy Style had not been seen in previous productions. The producers decided to stop the show for four months of rehearsals in order to have the dancers return to dancing the styles currently danced in the of Buenos Aires dance halls, with their feet on the floor. Argentina's most famous teacher, Antonio Todaro, was brought in to get them on the right track.

The show sold out in Paris and went on to play to full houses in the U.S. and Canada, and returned for a third visit to Paris, followed by tours to London, Switzerland, Holland, and Germany. The Japanese had never lost their enthusiasm for the tango with which it had been fascinated since the 1930's, and enthusiastically welcomed eight visits to Japan. In 1987, Emperor Hirohito and the Empress broke a thousand year old tradition of not being approachable by ordinary people at a distance closer than fifteen yards when they went backstage to greet the dancers in their dressing rooms. They even danced a few steps with them.

The worldwide demand for appearances of Tango Argentino was so great that the show could not fill all the booking requests. A number of other tango shows were spawned, many of which still travel the globe. In San Francisco, one of the most famous shows, "Forever Tango"; which was originally booked for four weeks, broke musical box office records by playing for ninety-two weeks. (It still returns to San Francisco for prolonged stays.) It was the longest-running musical production in show business history. After leaving San Francisco, it went to Italy where "wild and frenzied ovations" greeted its performances at the Spoleto Arts Festival, after which it toured cities in Europe and then went back to North America. In 1997 it opened at Broadway's Walter Kerr Theater, and a year later moved to the larger Marquis Theater on Broadway.

Other important shows, some of which still tour, included 'Tango Tango' with Juan Carlos Copes and Maria Nieves; 'Tango Para Dos', with Miguel Angel Zotto and Milena Plebs; 'Tango Passion', 'Todo Tango.' New shows are created every year. In 1991 the Paris Folies Bergeres got into the swing of things to produce a tango-based show entitled, "Fous des Folies." After more than twenty years of tango shows, superlatives continue to be heaped on them. On November 11, 2008, The New York Times gave a rave review to a performance of the tango-related New Generation Dance Company featuring a fusion of tango, ballet, and modern dance, calling it "insidiously seductive."

Why? What was the appeal of a low budget, simple performance of eight couples, some portly and bald, definitely not young, dancing an out-of-fashion dance on virtually a bare stage? For one thing, it was evident that the dancers were selected only for their skills, not for their appearance. Tango teacher, performer, and aficionado, Jef Anderson, said "What struck audiences so deeply was the visible relationships between the dancing partners, their way of playing with each other, their elegance and style, their daring abandon, their aura of raucous joy and seductiveness – this from men and women well past youth." The primarily middle-aged audiences were mesmerized by the intensity of the musicians, and fascinated by the dancers' complicated movements. It was riveting, like no tango they'd ever seen.

A New York Times review said, "The stage crackled with verve, spiced, sensuality, and humor. There were flashing feet and rapid scissors-like thrusts of legs between partner's legs; legs hooked to embrace or entrap a partner, and there were lightening-like turns and twists of legs and torsos." Instead of the Ballroom Tango familiar on television competitions or in the movies, with partners dancing steps that mirrored each other, each couple danced a different dance - usually with each partner doing different steps at the same time. There were as many as sixteen different dances being danced by eight couples, so when all the dancers were on stage at the same time members of the audience didn't know where to look. It was akin to watching a three-ring circus, appearing as if it could turn into total disaster at any minute.

Although there were some exceedingly attractive dancers normally seen in Broadway-type musicals, the dancers most applauded were middle-aged. These performances encouraged middle-aged members of the audience to believe that "if they can do it so can I." They thought that with a little practice, they too could dance the tango, and many left the theaters determined to take lessons as soon as possible. This was not easy, because the only tango then being taught in dance studios was the Ballroom Tango, which had virtually no relation to the dance they had seen on the stage. The other problem was that the prospective students had not the foggiest idea of how difficult it is to dance the tango well.

Since the style of tango on the stage was totally different from that being taught in dance studios, in some parts of the U. S. such as San Francisco and New York where the shows had long runs, those determined to take lessons convinced touring performers give them lessons outside their performances. Soon there were not enough performers to meet the demand for teachers, so tango teachers from Buenos Aires were recruited to al parts of the world teaching and setting up tango schools. There were still not enough teachers, so seeing that profitable work was to be had; many teachers of Argentine folk or other dances converted themselves into tango teachers. One of the young instructors who had not been around during the Golden Era remarked: "It was as if a totally new dance had just been born which we had to learn."

Audiences had not only been struck by the dancing but also by the unfamiliar music. Many claimed they were stunned by the beauty and complexity of the music they'd never heard before, most of which were dance tunes from the 1930s and 1940s. There were the melancholic, hauntingly beautiful tangos; the spirited and sometimes humorous milongas; and the achingly beautiful tango waltzes. The aging musicians, with sweat dripping from their faces, were clearly exhilarated by their efforts in performing the music they so obviously loved.

The stage performers who started to teach in the U.S. and Western Europe wanted to teach students how to dance the way it was danced in Buenos Aires dance halls at that time, but the students wanted to dance the showy steps they'd seen on the stage. So the teachers created a hybrid style of stage and classical tango and called it Argentine Tango.

During the first international wave of the tango at the beginning of the 20th century, the dance had been radically altered in different countries to accommodate local sensitivities and mores, but this time around there has been no attempt to change the original tango. Instead, dancers want to dance exactly the way it is currently danced in Buenos Aires. Because of today's easy travel, an increasingly large number of foreigners are going to 'the source' for the total immersion in tango that is unavailable any place else. And so tango traffic has reversed. No one has been more surprised than the non-tango involved Argentines, who constantly express amazement that people will travel across the world just to dance their tango.

Decline to Renaissance

Today's tango renaissance far exceeds all previous successes with a global reach that now has more people dancing tango than ever before. More than a hundred years after tango's first successful sortie into the outer world, Argentines have again begun to consider the tango in a different light. It now appears to be firmly entrenched in the social dance world. With their wide-reaching activities

in the propagating of tango, Rodolfo and Gloria Dinzel
have contributed exceptional force and energy in trying to
forestall any possibility of diminishing interest in tango
education and innovational scientific research.

Left to Right – Rodolpho Dinzel,
Gloria Dinzel, Mikhail Baryshnikov

The Dinzels: From Decline to Social Force

Certainly the Dinzels' two-pronged defense of
tango would not be possible today under the sort
of authoritarian governments that have plagued
Argentina in the past; they would have been jailed or
exiled or 'disappeared.'

Rodolpho Dinzel recently recalled: "In the
seventies there were only three professional couples
dancing regularly in small cabarets and cafés. Gloria

and I performed in the tiny Viejo Almacen 364 nights a year; in 1976 we were giving tango lessons in a basement in San Telmo to only three couples. We defied the government because we were afraid that if teachers didn't continue to teach, the tango would disappear completely. We began with four students, one of whom was French. We figure that since then, beginning with our programs in public and private schools, initiated in the 80s, we have personally taught tango to at least 20,000 students and by teaching the Dinzel method of tango to teachers, we have indirectly touched over 100,000."

Rodolfo Dinzel's "worst nightmare" is the possibility of another decline in tango - either for personal reasons or political reasons imposed by the whims of the government. He believes that a solution lies with the youth of Argentina. As a result, Gloria and Rodolfo Dinzel have been involved in pedagogical projects to expose young people to the tango in their studio and through programs in public and private schools. They are convinced, through their teaching efforts, that if enough young people become involved in tango, it will never again be at risk of extinction. In 1991, Gloria and Rodolfo created a structured curriculum for the Centro Educativo del Tango de la Ciudad de Buenos Aires, today known as the University of Tango, whose tuition-free diploma course consists of 29 thematic classes. Rodolfo and Gloria both teach there, and Gloria is the Director of the Artistic Department. They also work with the city of Buenos Aires, providing teams of volunteer teachers to produce educational tango programs in public and private primary and secondary schools.

They have also written books, collaborating closely on their first book, which has been printed in five languages. *Tango: An Anxious Quest for Freedom* analyzes the dynamics of the tango couple, their allotted space on the dance floor, and the role of esthetics. They are currently working on five other books on such topics as improvisation, theory and practice, technique and mechanics, writing about movement, and women and tango. Their textbook for a three-year teacher-training course is used at the University of Tango as well as in their studio; drawings accompanying the directions are so detailed and complicated that it cannot be used without the help of a Dinzel teacher. On first glance at the teaching manual, tango professional Jef Anderson said, "It looks like the scribbling of a mad nuclear scientist." However, when used with a competent teacher, the instructions are comprehensible and brilliant but demanding. Dinzel also developed a method of choreographic writing that has three-dimensional illustrations instead of two-dimensional. "In two-hundred years, there will be no problem in dancing exactly the way we dance today," Dinzel says proudly.

The Dinzel Dance Studio is Unique

Although Gloria and Rodolfo make regular teaching and performance tours to the U. S. and Europe, in order to devote sufficient time to their son and her teaching duties at the University, Gloria has essentially made the studio Rodolfo's 'territory.' She doesn't teach there and rarely visits, except to pick up Rodolfo to go to an appointment. But they are very much a team.

Mr. Dinzel runs his studio in a vastly different manner from other dance schools. "I don't think tango should be a commercial enterprise," and he practices what he preaches. The vast majority of his students are young Argentines who pay very little for lessons that are very inexpensive; if they can't afford them, he permits them to take classes in exchange for helping around the studio. He claims to have never paid for advertising or publicity and appears to be uninterested in turning a profit. There is no effort to attract affluent Argentines or tango tourists; the studio itself attests to this fact since it could possibly be the least attractive dance studio in the Western world.

Located in a lower middle-class neighborhood on a quiet tree-lined street, the dingy old building faces onto a seriously cracked sidewalk, with no sign or any other indication that it houses the dance studio of one of the most important names in the tango world. There is only a small house number on the wall, and the door, which is never locked, opens onto a forty to fifty feet long, high-walled passage with scattered broken floor tiles and is wide enough for only one person. The only suggestion that anything is going on inside is the faint sound of tango music that gets louder as you approach the end of the passage, which opens onto a small, nine by twelve foot patio. The studio is a rather scruffy ground floor, windowless apartment of about a hundred square feet, with bits and pieces of ceiling paint hanging loosely; the ceiling and walls all badly in need of a fresh coat of paint.

The patio walls are covered with potted plants, and there are small plastic stools scattered about. To the right is a small kitchen with a counter top burner for brewing the endless cups of mate tea which is consumed throughout the day. There is no air conditioning for the sweltering summer months; the toilet has no seat which could be further proof that foreigners are not encouraged nor sought out. A door that is only closed for an occasional private lesson separates the two small rooms; the wood floor is in lamentable condition, with missing pieces here and there.

The only evidence of the activity practiced there are two four-by-six foot mirrors and a small practice barre about which Dinzel, smiling rather mischievously, commented, "The mirror is of no use really, but people expect to see a mirror in a dance studio, so there it is." The walls are covered with casually framed photographs, certificates, articles, and programs from the Dinzels' long stage career. Mixed in with other photographs are ones with Rodolfo shaking hands with President Reagan, another with ballet star Mikhail Baryshnikov, and one with actor Anthony Quinn.

Music is supplied by a small, portable vintage CD-player in the corner of one room; each room can hold up to ten couples. Students dance with each other, with the teachers, and with professionals who are there practicing for performances. The atmosphere brims with informality as students or teachers break off to ask advice of one another or to give suggestions on technique or style.

The Dinzel studio is unique in that there are no regular formal group dance classes apart from two sessions a week in technique given by a Dinzel teacher supervised by Dinzel. He teaches only two weekly classes in theory that he describes as "the examination of the origins and evolution of the dance and the sociological and philosophical aspects of the tango." Students surround his desk, sitting on rickety stools or on the floor. When not teaching, he sits at his corner desk chain smoking, talking with teachers or students, visiting with foreigners, conversing with assistants working on his numerous research projects, or talking with out-of-town enthusiasts who have come to pay their respects. There are almost always at least four or five people waiting in line to see him and he is always gracious and generous with his time.

The atmosphere is friendly with much kissing of cheeks on coming or going, even among those who have never met before. Young mothers sometimes bring small children to play in the patio or sit in prams while they dance. For a daily or weekly low price, students are allowed to spend as much time there as they like, dancing with one or more of the available teachers, with other students, or just to discuss tango with one another. Many bring their food and eat in the patio while others go to one of the local restaurants. Some take breaks to run errands or they may stay around all day, taking breaks to drink mate and socialize. Occasionally tango tourists who have heard of the studio find it and are there for a day or a week or two.

Dinzel teaches using the Socratic Method, encouraging students' opinions. Their rapt expressions and serious contributions to the dialogue appear close to adoration, evident not only in class but in the way they talk about him. Besides being revered for his tango, his teaching skills, and his altruism, Rodolfo is also a true mentor, frequently seen huddled in serious discussion with a student who has come to him with a personal problem that will be seriously addressed. Once when I saw him in what seemed to be a riveting discussion with a young female student, I remarked to one of his teachers, Luis Lencioni, that it seemed as if many of the young women dancers were a little bit in love with Rodolfo. He replied, "Wrong, they are ALL in love with him."

Teaching Structure

When a new student comes to the studio, Dinzel has him or her dance with one of the teachers while he instructs the teacher to do particular movements or steps. After one or two dances he talks to the teacher and student and suggests what skills should be worked on. The teacher and student begin to dance; Dinzel retreats to his desk watching all the dancers, making occasional suggestions, and sometimes illustrating a few steps.

Dinzel is at the studio every day except Thursday when he leaves at four o'clock to teach at the University of Tango. His life revolves around teaching and his tango research. After daily stints at the studio and the University he returns home at 11 p.m. and studies philosophy until 2 a.m.: Kant, Hegel, and Nietzsche are among his favorites. For the past several years he has been seriously studying neurology "in order to better understand the significance and connection the brain and motor functions, to better comprehend Parkinson's disease." He says, "In all dance, training produces automatic responses for dance movements. But with tango, we negate this and create new nervous impulses to constantly make new responses."

Dinzel's egalitarianism is reflected in his teaching that in tango the woman is as important as the man, a concept that breaks with written and oral tradition. He insists that if the follower only does what the leader asks, it not a true tango partnership but merely a man's ego trip. "The woman who dares to converse, to try a dialogue, to express her own responses to the music, that woman is often suppressed by the man who performs his dancing in a monologue kind of attitude."

In recognition of his work promoting tango, Rodolfo was made a member of the prestigious La Academia Nacional del Tango de la República Argentina in 1942, whose forty seats in the Academia are bestowed for life and usually reserved for academics. Two years later, Gloria was invited to become one of the few female members. Although Rodolfo and

Gloria are hoping to ward off another decline in tango's fortunes through their educational efforts, it may be that innovative work on the role of tango in medical and psychological therapy will be equally, if not more, valuable to Argentine society.

Tango as Therapy

Rodolfo Dinzel doesn't come right out and say it, but he is convinced that most of the world's ills would disappear if only everyone would dance the Argentine Tango. He believes that the tango can improve the quality of life for anyone and is convinced that more than any other social dance it presents the greatest potential to normalize the lives of the physically and mentally disabled. He says, "In order to foster the trust and cooperation needed in order to master tango skills, and achieve its aesthetic goals, the disabled have to leave their isolation, to establish partnerships, however fleeting.

For the past ten years, Dinzel has been researching the theory of tango's therapeutic powers through careful, documented studies by teams of volunteer tango teachers qualified in psychiatry, psychology, and dance therapy. Apart from helping individuals, the Dinzels have been concerned with tango's place in Argentine society—the music, the dance, and the poetic literature.

In 1996, Dinzel and his team of teachers began teaching tango at a school for the blind. Some did so well that they were invited to take part in Dinzel's rigorous training program for teachers of the Dinzel System of dance. Thus, when visiting the Dinzel studio, it is not unusual to see visually impaired students dancing with sighted partners or to watch blind teachers help sighted students by kneeling on the floor to move a student's foot from one place to another. Blind dancers interact informally with sighted dancers both on and off the dance floor. Except for occasionally grabbing an arm to guide a blind dancer to avoid a collision or stumble, the sighted dancers treat the blind as they do any other dancer, joking, talking, drinking mate, or discussing tango. Dinzel does not charge blind dancers for practice sessions or for classes. His studio also welcomes Down's syndrome patients with free lessons and practice sessions. Many have become proficient dancers and are in demand as partners. It is touching to see this interaction in an atmosphere of such equality.

Volunteer tango-dancing psychiatrists, psychologists and other specialists travel weekly to give tango sessions at public hospitals, including the Hospital de Clínicas, which specializes in Parkinson's disease and the Alvear Hospital for psychotic adolescents. Many of the patients' family members and friends attend the dance lessons as well as hospital staff members, including doctors and nurses who have become interested in the experiments. Even patients confined to wheelchairs attend classes in order to enjoy the music and watch the dancers. All the spectators have expressed enthusiasm for tango's palliative effects on the patients.

Dinzel's volunteers work in teams meeting weekly to compare notes on individual patients and to share observations on the perceived progress of the project. They write papers and articles on their analyses in the hope that tango might become a regular part of suggested treatment. Although some doctors tend to be skeptical about the tango projects, many have taken to stopping by to observe the dance sessions and are visibly impressed to see seriously depressed patients smiling and laughing and interacting with other patients and staff.

Dinzel realizes that he has not yet completed enough research and evaluation to make a valid claim for the efficacy of tango's contribution to physical and mental health problems. "But," he says, "The doctors are waiting and watching. Until now, all has been based on faith. I am not yet able to tell someone that if he dances tango his pain will go away. Nor can I announce that dancing tango will delay the symptoms of a disease or that terminally ill patients will be less depressed or live longer than expected, because as of now, my theories are essentially based on faith. We must continue to observe and record and wait until we have the statistics to establish the legitimacy of tango's effects. Those of us who teach have seen what happens. The scientists do not yet know. But "I know."

Dinzel has been studying Parkinson's disease and working with patients, many of whom have problems with walking and balance and who often fall when attempting to turn. He was recently pleased to learn of an experiment conducted by Madeleine Hackney at the Washington University School of Medicine in St. Louis, Missouri. The February 12, 2008 issue of the *New York Times* ran an article titled: "When the band strikes up, people with Parkinson's disease may want to head for the dance floor," which reported the results that appeared in the The Journal of Neurological Physical Therapy. Parkinson's patients were divided into groups. One group was given tango lessons, and the other group was given exercise classes. The report stated: "Both groups demonstrated general improvement, but only the tango students appeared to do better when it came to balance."

One day I arranged with Dinzel to observe a tango class at the hospital for terminal cancer patients. On arrival it turned out that they were short a teacher, and I was asked to help out. I did and was delighted to see the enthusiasm of the patients, including those in wheelchairs. Later, when talking with Mr. Dinzel about the therapeutic benefits of tango, I told him about my former tango partner who had recently succumbed to breast cancer. He asked me to write about it for the book he is writing on the subject of tango's contribution to health of the mind and body. Thus, I wrote the following story of Anna:

Anna

Anna, *a beautiful Finnish woman in her 50's, became my steady tango partner when I was learning the man's steps in a group class in Paris. For over two years we practiced several times a week and took group and private lessons together. When we felt ready, we ventured onto the dance floors and received many compliments on our dancing. However, the breast cancer she'd had five years previously returned with a vengeance, and in spite of all sorts of terribly debilitating treatments, her condition deteriorated rapidly. At one point, after I had already made plans to go to Buenos Aires for tango, she said she had never been there and desperately wanted to go with me. Although we were still dancing regularly, her doctors said she was in no condition to make such a trip. She was so visibly disappointed that I suggested I bring her back a souvenir from Buenos Aires in the form of an impoverished young tango teacher I knew from Dinzel's studio. Anna perked up and insisted we make arrangements for him to give us daily lessons at my place, which had wood floors, for six weeks. Since he had never been to Paris, he was delighted to sleep in my small office in return for his air ticket and room and board.*

By the time I returned to Paris with our teacher in tow, Anna's pain had been getting out of control. She lived at home with her husband and didn't go out except to come to my apartment for our daily classes. Everyday she would arrive by taxi, and when I met her at the door her face was pinched with pain. I didn't have to ask how she felt. Within five minutes after we began to dance, she was smiling and laughing, and continued to do so until we'd finished the class. Once, when she was leaving and looked so happy and healthy, I asked her how long before the pain returned once we stopped dancing.

Unhesitatingly she replied, "About two to four hours." But as she got progressively weaker our classes became shorter, and eventually she was unable to come to my place, so I went to her. Though her carpeted floors were not good for pivots and turns, we danced until our sessions were reduced to half an hour, then twenty minutes. She continued to dance until the week she died. She requested her favorite tango, Hugo Diaz's "Cuesta Abajo," to be played at her funeral.

The Future of Tango

Because tango has increasingly become part of world culture, some tango enthusiasts worry about it losing its Argentine identity. While the Argentines will almost certainly remain the leaders for some time to come, the tango is clearly in a process of internationalization, a process of becoming global property. Like jazz, it is no longer exclusively identified with its country of origin.

For the moment, Argentine tangueras worry that the customs and codes of the milongas now under attack by some quarters will eventually erode the character of the milongas in Argentina. Dance styles have already changed from the open embraced salon style to the milonguero closed embrace, and there is evidence of interest in the flexibility and experimentation found in the "new tango." Foreign influence on the use of non-traditional music in milongas, such as Piazzolla and "techno tango" is a trend that has already begun in the alternative milongas. There undoubtedly will be more partners of the same sex dancing together, more women dancing as leaders, and men and women alternating roles within the same piece of music.

This is not a sexual matter but an exercise in exploring tango's inherent challenges, just one of many inevitable changes to come.

ABOUT THE AUTHOR

Virginia divides her time between Paris, France and Green Valley, Arizona, with frequent visits to Buenos Aires, Argentina. She has three sons and three grandchildren.

She studied Spanish and Pre-Columbian Archeology in Mexico City, and while there ran a modeling and performing actors agency. She then moved to Paris where she taught pottery and history at the American School of Paris and history at the Sorbonne University.

One of the courses she taught was the Vietnam War for which was she wrote a textbook. Intensive research on the subject led her to take a two-year sabbatical leave to volunteer as an English teacher in Hanoi, Vietnam, where she taught at the Vietnamese Ministry of Foreign Affairs. She then resumed teaching in Paris until retirement and later became involved in dancing the tango.

Virginia Gift

GLOSSARY

Vocabulary Used in the Tango World

ARRABALES – Outskirts of a city, suburb

APILADO – Close embrace

BANDONEON – Accordion-like instrument

BANDONEONISTA – Someone who plays the bandoneon

BARRIO – Neighborhood or district

CABECEO – Invitation to dance made by nod of the head and locking of eyes

CANYENGUE – Partnered dance that preceded the tango

CODIGO – Codes (rules) of behavior of the milongas

COMPADRE – Haughty, proud, generally respected and occasionally feared strongman of barrios

COMPADRITO – "Little compadre" – in barrios: a bully and braggart

CONFITERIA – A pastry shop that also serves snacks and light meals

CONVENTILLO – Tenement; large slum building with multiple rooms where workers lived

FANTASY/STAGE – Dance that utilizes exaggerated movements; sometimes ballet steps (because it takes up a lot of space, it is not normally danced in milongas)

GUAPO - One who practices the cult of courage; also means handsome or good-looking. (guapa; female)

LUNFARDO – Language of Buenos Aires underworld, used in tango lyrics

MILONGA – 1) Popular music from the countryside, 2) One of the three tango rhythms (tango, waltz, milonga),

2) A tango dance hall

MILONGUERO (A) – Someone with a great passion for the dance. An excellent dancer who has been going steadily to milongas since the 1940s and 1950s.

MURGA – A form of dancing to drum music in the streets that originated in early carnival parades.

ORILLERO – Suburb of a city

PAYADORES – Itinerant singers in the pampas, usually gauchos but frequently blacks

PORTENO – Resident of the port area of Buenos Aires

PRACTICA – A dance hall where regular milonga codes are relaxed

RUEDA – A new style of tango invented in the United States which is a form of Country and Western line dance with tango steps called out by a leader

SALON – Style of tango with partially open embrace

SWANGO – Dancing tango steps to non-tango swing or jazz music

TANGUERO (A) – Person who has a passion for the tango; however, the term does not necessarily indicate the quality of his or her dancing skills.

TECHNICAL DANCE TERMS

ABRAZO – The embrace between leader and follower

ADORNO – Unled adornment; a woman's improvisation

AMAGUE – A threat or feint. A kick by one foot across in front of the other; small kicks on the dance floor, but higher kicks used in show routines

ARRASTRE – Drag of a foot along the floor from one spot to another.

BARRIDA – A sweep. One partner's foot sweeps the other's foot along the floor.

BOLEO – From bolear, to throw - A high or low fast kick

made in the front or back of dancer; knees are kept together and the supporting leg swivels.

CAMINADA – A walking step. The body and leg moves as a unit with ball of the foot placed first.

CALESITA – Follower circles the leader who turns in place.

COLGADAS – A turn made with partners off their axis

CORRIDA – A run; series of fast, small steps

CORTINA – Spanish for 'curtain'. It is a minute or two of undanceable music played at the end of a tanda when all couples separate; leave the floor to return to their tables to change partners for the next tanda.

CRUZADA – The cross; the follower steps back right, then back left, crossing her left foot over her right foot before finishing the step

DISPLACEMENT – Displacing partner's leg or foot using one's leg or foot

ENGANCHE – To hook a dancer's calf against the partner's calf

ENROSQUE – A full body twist ending in crossed feet

FIGURA – A pattern of four – 8/10 steps

FIRULETE – An unled adornment; embellishment that doesn't interfere with steps

GANCHO – To hook a leg between partner's legs

GIRO – A turn around a partner when the follower does a molinette around the leader while he spins on one foot, hooking the other foot behind the spinning foot

LAPIZ – The pencil; uses the toe to trace a circular pattern on the floor

MILONGA – 1) Music of the countryside; frequently in 2/4 time 2) It is also a tango dance hall.

MOLINETE – To circle around a partner—as in "wind-mill," created by woman doing a series of forward and back ochos.

MORDIDA – "Sandwich" or "bite:" when one partner stops movement of a partner by using two feet to encase a partner's foot.

OCHO – Figure eight traced on floor with feet together on every pivot

PARADA – Stop

PASSOVER – When a leader's foot is stationary and the follower steps over it with her foot almost brushing his

RESOLUTION – The end of a figura

SACADA – To displace a partner's foot from the floor with foot or leg

SALIDA – Spanish for "to leave"; it marks the beginning of a dance

TANDA – A set of three or four dances linked by style of the same orchestra or by types of rhythm, i.e., waltzes, milongas, or tangos

VOLCADAS – Extreme leans, usually followed by an adorno; sometimes a drag of the woman across the floor

VUELTA – A turn made simultaneously by both dancers

BIBLIOGRAPHY

BOOKS

Aguiar, Carmen. *Le Candombe*. Paris: Association Dance Education Culture, 1998.

Andrews, George Reid. *The Afro-Argentines of Buenos Aires, 1800-1900*. Madison, Wisconsin: University of Wisconsin Press, 1980.

Azzi, Maria Susana. *Anthropologia del Tango:* Oxford, Oxford University Press, 2000

Azzi, Maria Susana and Simon Collier. *The Life and Music of Astor Piazzolla*. Oxford, Oxford University Press, 2000

Baim, Jo. *Tango: Creation of a Cultural Icon*. Bloomington and Indianapolis, Indiana University Press, 2007

Bernhardson, Wayne. *Buenos Aires*. Hawthorne, Australia: Lonely Planet Publications, 1992

Borges. *Historia del Tango*. Buenos Aires: Evaristo Carriego, 1955

Busaniche, Jose Louis. *Historia Argentina. Buenos Aires, Ediciones Solar*, Buenos Aires, 1965

Campbell, Joseph, *The Confrontation of East and West in Religion*, Highbridge Audio of 1970 Lecture, Published 2002

Castle, Irene and Vernon. *Modern Dancing*. New York, 1914

Castro, Donald S. *The Development and Politics of Argentine Immigration Policy 1852 – 1914: To Govern is to Populate*. San Francisco, Mellon Research University Press

Castro, Donald S. *The Argentine Tango As Social History 1880-1955: The Soul of the People*. Lewiston, NY: Latin American Studies, 1991

Chenault, Roger. *Tango Argentin Danse; Notions Fondamentales*. Courbevoie, France: Editions Roger Chenault, 2006

Collier, Simon, Cooper, Artemis; Azzi Maria Susanna; Martin Ricard. *Tango!*. London, Thames & Hudson, London 1995

Collier, Simon. *The Life, Music and Times of Carlos Gardel*. Pittsburg: university of Pittsburg Press, 1986

Dinzel, Gloria & Rodolpho. *Tango: An Anxious Quest for Freedom*. Germany, 2000

Di Giovanni, Norman Thomas. *Streetcorner Man, A Universal History of Infamy*. New York. P. Dutton, 1972, Translated to English from the 1935 publication by Jorge Luis Borges

Donna J. Guy. *Sex and Danger in Buenos Aires: Prostitution, Family and Nation in Argentina*. Lincoln Nebraska and London: University of Nebraska Press, 1991

Ehrenreich, Barbara. *Dancing in the Streets: A History of Collective Joy*. New York: 2007

Fernandez, Carlos Rivas. *Esclavismo y misiones jesuiticas en la colonia, 500 Anos de historia* Agentina. Buenos Aires: Editorial, 1988

Ferrer Horacio Arturo, "...El siglo de oro del tango," Buenos Aires, Manrique Zago Ediciones, 1996

Georges-Michel, Michel. *Life in Deauville: Three Epoques, Before, During, and After WWI*. Paris: 1922

Hatem, Fabrice. *Une anthologie bilingue du tango argentin*. Bagneux, France: Le Temps du Tango, 2006

Hernandez, Jose. (Translation by Walter Owen), *The Gaucho Martin Fierro*. Buenos Aires: Instituto Cultural, Walter Owen, 1967, 1989

Hess, Remi. *Le Moment Tango*. Paris: Anthropos Economica, 1997

Hess, Remi. *Le Siecle d'or du Tango.* Leon: France editions Manrique Zago, 1998

Hess, Remi. *Les Tangomaniaques.* Paris: Anthropos Economica, 1998

Jacobs, Deborah L, *From Bawdyhouse to Cabaret: The Evolution of the Tango as an Expression of Argentine Popular Culture.* Bowling Green: Bowling Green State University, 1984

Judkovski, Jose. *El Tango: Una Historia con Judios.* 1998 (ML 3465.J83, Lib. Congress)

Kinsey, Troy and Margaret. *The Dance, Its Place in Art & Life.* Great Britain: 1914

Labrana, Luis and Sebastian, Ana. *Tango: Una Historia.* Buenos Aires: Ediciones Corregidor, 1992

Lamas, Hugo and Binda, Enrique. *El Tango en la Sociedad Portenia, 1880-1920,* Buenos Aires: Ediciones Hector L. Lucci, 1998

Paez, Jorge. *El Conventillo. Buenos Aires: Talleres Graficos de Sebastian de Amdorrortu y Hijos,* S.A., 1970

Piazzolla, Astor. *Una Memoria.* West Yorkshire, England: Amadeus Press, 2003

Powers, Richard. *Tango in Paris.* San Francisco, Stanford University

Rock, David. *Argentina: 1516 – 1987.* Berkeley and Los Angeles, University of California Press, 1987

Rushdie, Salman. *The Ground Beneath Her Feet.* New York: Henry Holt and Company, 1999

Salas, Horaci0. *El Tango. Buenos Aires; Editorial Planeta Argentina,* 1995

Sarasola, Carlos Martinez. *Nuestros Paisanos Los Indios.* Buenos Aires: Editores Emece, 1992

Savigliano, Marta. *Tango and the Political Economy of Passion.* Boulder, Colorado: Westview Press, 199

Severgnini, Beppe. *La Bella Figura: A Field guide to the Italian Mind.* New York: Broadway Books, 2007

Sulc, Jorge Oscar. *Rosas y la problematica del indio.* Buenos Aires: 1996

Taylor, Julie. *Paper Tangos.* Durham and London: Duke University Press, 1998

Vidart, Daniel. *El Tango y sus Mundo, Buenos Aires*: 1996-7

Wilkinson, Susan. *Sebastian's Pride.* England: Sphere Books Ltd., 1991

Zalko, Nardo. *Un Siecle de Tango: Paris – Buenos Aires.* Paris: Editions du Felin, 1998

PERIODICALS

Aloff, Mindy, *"Dancing Cheek to Cheek, and That's Only the Beginning,"* The N Y Times, May 5, 1995

Aloff, Mindy, *"On Dance: After the Last Tango"*, The New Republic, August 2, 1999

B.A. Tango, Ano VI, No. 109, Alberto Zeldin, Buenos Aires, Argentina, Marzo 2000

Birnbaum, Larry, "Tango," Down Beat, November 1992

Club de Tango, No. 38, Parana 123, Buenos Aires, Sept, Oct. 1999

Coatalem, Jean-Luc, *"La Vie Est Un Tango,"* Le Figaro Magazine, 14 Nov. 1998

Cutler, Kim-Mai, *"The New Tango Trades Cheek to Cheek for Hot, Fast Moves,"* The Wall Street Journal, August 2005

Diliberto, Gioia, *"It Takes 15 to Tango on Broadway, Where Fancy Footwork and Sexy Moves Have Spawned a Smash,"* People, Dec. 2, 1985

Ehrenreich, Barbara. *"I Am, Therefore I Need to Dance"*, International Herald Tribune, Paris, June 5, 2007

Edelstein, Dr. Richard, *"Discovery News,"* Scheinfeld Center for Genetic Studies, 2007

Eichler, Jeremy. *"Tango and the Individual Talent,"* The New Republic, June 26, 2000, Oxford, England

El Tanguata, *"La Historia de Tango Argentino,"* Dec. 2006

Fulghum, Robert. *"Tango Memo,"* Robert Fulghum Official Website, July, 2007

Gallardo, Dr. Raul. *"Club de Tango,"* Sept. - Oct. 1999

Halperin, Jorge. *"Gardel no era un mujeriego,"* Capital Intelectual, S. A., Acuna de Figueroa 459, 24 febrero 2000

Harrison, Jim. Harvard Magazine, Sept. /Oct. 1998

Hatem, Fabrice, *"Le tango et le lunfardo: compagnons d'enfance,"* La Salida, No. 40

Hatem, Fabrice. Paris, France, *"La Salida,"* Dec. 2006

Holden, Stephen. *"Astor Piazzolla, Modern Master of Tango Music, Is Dead at 71"*, The New York Times, July 6, 1992

Holland, Bernard. *"Tango as Pure Melody Slinks Into a Staid Concert Hall"*. New York: The New York Times October 9, 1997

James, Barry. *"To Tango in the Midnight Sun: It's as Finnish as Baseball,"* International Herald Tribune-Paris, April 8, 1998

Kaufman, Sarah. *"Many Countries, One Whirl,"* The Washington Post, September 13, 1998

Kimmelman, Michael. The New York Times Magazine, January 3, 1999

Krauss, Clifford. *"So, Argentina, Start at the Beginning...,"* International Herald Tribune-Paris, May 30, 1998

Lechner, Ernesto. *"Taking Tango a Step Further,"* L. A. Times 5 January 1999 (Orange County Edition), Arts Section

Lee, Denny, *"Argentine Nights,"* The New York Times, March 16, 2008

Levitin, Daniel J., *"This is your Brain on Music: The Science of a Human Obsession,"* International Herald Tribune-Paris, Oct 27, 2007

McKinley, Patricia. *"Tango as therapy,"* McGill University, Montreal, USA Today, 17 February 2008

No author named, *"A Sense of Where You Were,"* The Economist, Dec. 22, 2001

Paz, Alberto. *"When the Tango Was in Jail,"* Sunnydale, CA, Firulete, July 1999

Palumbo, Tito. B. A. Tango, *"Guia Trimestral de Tango,"* Ano III, No. 10, Agosto, Septiembre, Octobre, 1999

Paris: International Herald Tribune, *"For Latin American Gays - 48 Rooms and 5 Stars,"* 1 Nov. 2007

Paris, La Salida, Association Le Temps du tango argentin, *"Les annees de jeunesse de Anibal Troilo,"* Bagneux, France, 2005

Rich, Alan, *"The Irresistibly Seductive Tango,"* House and Garden, August 1982

Rocchi Roxane, Sotelo, Ariel and Horvath, Ricardo, *"La Ciudad del Tango,"* Buenos Aires, Editado por Centro Cultural de la Cooperation, Cuadernos de Trabajo

Ross, Sonya, *"Argentine leader gets US-style state dinner,"* USA Today, 12 January 1999

Salmon, Russell O. *"The Tango: Its Origins and Meaning,"* Journal of Popular Culture, Vol. X, No. 4, Editor, Ray B. Browne, Bowling Green State University, Spring 1977

Saenz Lopez, Jorge. *"Una reflexion lirica sobre el tango,"* Club de Tango, Buenos Aires

Santiago, Chiori. *"The Tango is more than a dance—it's a moment of truth,"* Smithsonian, November 1993

Schwarz, Benjamin and Christina. *"Half a World Away,"* The Atlantic Monthly, September 1998

Scott, Janny. "Flirting With the Tango: It's Serious," New York Times, June 2, 1999

"Tango makes a comeback for tourists," Sydney: Sydney Morning Herald, February 5, 2008

UNESCO Courier, *"Tango Time,"* Paris, March 1998

TANGO MAGAZINES AND NEWSLETTERS

Buenos Aires Tango, Buenos Aires

Club de Tango, Buenos Aires

El Firulete, Paris, France

El Tanguata, Buenos Aires

La Cadena, Tangomaandblad voor, Netherlands

La Salida, L'Association le Temps du Tango, Paris, France

Les Editions Puro Guapo, Sainte-Therese (Quebec) Canada

Tango XXI, Buenos Aires

INTERNET

There were too many internet sources to list but they include:

Collier, Simon. "The Popular Roots of the Argentine Tango," History Workshop Journal, Vo. 34 (Autumn 1992)

Jacobs, Deborah L., *"From Bawdyhouse to Cabaret; The Evolution of the Tango as an Expression of Argentine ~Popular Culture"*, Journal of Popular Culture, Vo. 18, No. 1, 1984

Moerer, Keith. *"Sharps and Flats,* (online) salonmagazine. com/music/96 1122, Aug. 14, 1999

Chang, Sang Hyeon, Tango café in Korea, email to Tango-L, 11 August 1999

Chin-Bow, Stephen T. *Why do I dance the Argentine Tango?* From Stephen E. Chin-Bow's Argentine Tango Page; updated September 4, 1998

Pfeffer, Murray L., *A Brief History of the Tango,* 1994-1997

Paz, Alberto. *From Pacho to Piazzolla, Tales of Tango History –* Part 1, Planet Tango, 1996-97.

Tango-L, Cambridge, MA

Trenner, Daniel. *Milonguero Style/ What's in a name?* 1996

Trenner, Daniel. *Night Life in Buenos Aires,* Puente Al Tango 1998, March 1995

Trenner, Daniel. *Basic in Social Dancing Tango,* Puente Al Tango, 1998

PERSONAL INTERVIEWS

Naveira, Gustavo, The New Tango, etc. - 16 August 2006, 23 June 2007, 5 January 2008

Lucas, Linda, Numerous conversations, 2002-2008

Bianco, Marc, Tango in Paris, January 2002

Dinzel, Rodolfo, Numerous interviews, 2002 – 2008

Grelier, Robert, Finnish tango, 21 February 1999

Shulman, Rebecca, Tango in New York, July 2006

Iturbide, Horacio Mendez, Argentine Embassy, Cultural Office, Washington, D.C. July, 2006

Quintango, Joan Singer (Isaac) - Tango in the United States, 2003

Witter Dave, Tango Dancer and Behavioral Psychologist – Numerous Interviews- 2002-2006

Vadim, Congresso International of Tango Argentina – 4
    March 2005
Various Dancers at festivals and workshops – 2000-2008

*"O dancing Earth," says Goddess Ma. In our Indian Puranas
we learn that Lord Shiva danced you into being, He, the Lord of
the Dance.
Whereas the Greeks tell of Eurynome, the goddess of everything,
who loved dancing and created the sea and the land so that she
had someplace to groove.
I say that such also are we!, Men and Women!,
dancing our world into being.
I say, Dance!*
(Salman Rushdie, 1999)